LIGHTS OUT LUCY

A MUSIC CITY ROLLERS NOVEL

ELICIA HYDER

ACKNOWLEDGMENTS

Special Thanks to everyone who made this book possible:

First, to my Fresh Meat sisters who kept me alive through Derby 101: Chelsea, Amy, Cindy, Becci, Leigh, and Angela. I love you guys so much it *hurt* (past tense because we don't play anymore.)

To the Nashville Rollergirls. Without you and all you taught me, this book would not be possible. Thanks specifically to current and former skaters/staff for volunteering your names and likenesses for this book: Lady Fury, Electra Cal, Demoness, 5 Scar Jeneral, Bad News Baroness, Rocksee Rolls, Slugs Bunny, Susan, and Daddy Ho'maker!

To Chuck for introducing me to this crazy sport and for being the best surrogate brother (and fake husband) a girl could ask for.

To Taylor for being the inspiration behind Olivia. You are the most perfect model for a selfless best friend.

To author T. Torrest for allowing me to borrow Trip Wiley, the swoon-worthy movie star from her *Remember When* series. If you're into laugh-out-loud books, don't miss it!

To Susan Arrington—one of the most badass chicks to ever play the sport. Thank you for the wealth of wisdom you were in writing this. You'll always be my hero.

To Steve and everyone at Asphalt Beach in Nashville, TN— where I really did buy all my derby gear. Thanks for not laughing at me. You guys rock!

To Frogmouth Clothing for the Music City Rollers' awesome jerseys. They are a skater-owned and operated company that designs, cuts, dyes, and sews their jerseys. You guys were a pleasure to work with!

To Lady Fury for all your enthusiasm, energy, and hard work. Thanks for jumping in the trenches with me on this one.

To my kids who spent many nights with grandparents while I pursued this crazy sport, and many more nights while I wrote about it.

To grandparents. (See above.)

To Mom and Dad for everything. Always.

To Taffy for being the first to cheer for this book.

To Barbara Vey for constantly pushing me to be better.

To Nicole Ayers, my amazing editor. I dare not write a word without you.

To Chris. As always, thanks for being the inspiration for all my heroes. I love you and couldn't do this without your endless love and support.

TO MY AWESOME LAUNCH TEAM, THE BOOK SUMMONERS. I would be nowhere without you!

To my new Fan Club members, HYDERNATION, you guys are going to make this year SOOOO interesting!

And as always...thanks to all my readers who allow me to daydream and keep food on the table.

A NOTE FROM ELICIA

In 2008, my first husband was one of the first recorded deaths resulting from texting and driving in the state of Tennessee. He was 25 years old. At the time we had two children. Canaan was four. Will was two.

In the aftermath of that awful year, my good friend, Chuck, introduced me to the wild and wonderful sport of women's flat track roller derby. On a dare, I joined Fresh Meat (Roller Derby 101) with the Nashville Rollergirls, and "eL's Bells" (my derby name) was born.

Truth be told: I SUCKED AT ROLLER DERBY. I hung up my skates after my 2nd serious knee injury before I ever even skated in my first official bout...BUT new lifelong friendships were forged, my body became a formidable machine, and through the bruises, torn ligaments, and pulled muscles—my heart finally healed.

Fast forward to 2015 when I was diagnosed with cancer. My daughter—who was counting the days until she could play junior roller derby—was faced with the possibility of losing another parent. Unlike her brother, who only remembered their dad in pictures, Canaan knew the pain that seemed to lurk in our future.

As I planned my funeral (yes, that's dramatic, but I think every cancer patient considers it), I wondered if Canaan, too, would find her healing on a pair of quad skates.

And thus, the idea for this novel, Lights Out Lucy, was sparked.

I published my first book with chemotherapy burning through my veins. And while the doctors and nurses (hi, Rena) saved my life, I can honestly say that writing saved my sanity.

Three years later, I'm cancer free and Lights Out Lucy is my 9th published novel. It's also my favorite. In these pages, I hope you'll experience the power of friendship and determination. I hope you'll laugh, fall in love, and see the very best in yourself through our unwitting heroine.

There are thousands of roller derby teams worldwide. Just go to your favorite search engine and type: *roller derby *insert your city here** to find a team near you. A lot of them are non-profits that support local charities, so bring the whole family to a bout and have fun for a good cause!

And if you ever toy with the idea of joining Fresh Meat to FIND OUT WHAT YOU'RE MADE OF...

I dare you.

For Canaan.

You taught me what kind of woman I want to be.
I couldn't be more proud of you.

Love, Mom.
P.S. Please skip over the sexy parts while reading.

LIGHTS OUT LUCY

"IT'S NOT a matter of *if* you get hurt, but of how bad and when."

I can't say they didn't warn me.

Right now, I realize: *I probably should have listened.*

Because if there's anyone who has no business playing a sport that requires a helmet, pads, and a liability waiver, it's this girl. The *same* girl who once knocked herself out during a game of backyard baseball. I stepped up to the plate, pulled the bat back a little too far to swing, and clocked myself in the back of the skull. Boom. Lights Out Lucy.

That's how I got my roller derby name.

So yeah. Maybe I should have known better.

But what doesn't kill you makes you stronger, right? That's the whole reason I laced up a pair of skates to begin with. Well, *that* and this other little confession I need to make. Amidst all the estrogen and girl power that fuels the world of women's roller derby, this insanity may have started because of a guy.

Eyeroll, I know.

Sadly, today on the oval track, it's about to come to a very bloody end. And all this slow-motion introspection might be part of my life flashing before my eyes.

I'm going down hard and fast, with a set of Atomic Turquoise wheels aimed right at my face.

Lights Out Lucy, indeed.

ONE

ONLY I COULD PULL off a car accident sitting still at a red light.

For a second after the impact, I forgot about the wasp in my car. Then it descended slowly in front of my eyes again, a sinister buzz rippling the small space between my nose and its stinger. I slammed the gearshift into park and forced open the driver-side door with a loud *creak!* As I tumbled to the asphalt, the door caught sharply on its hinges, bounced back, and slammed against my leg. I landed hard on my hip, and my elbow almost unearthed the center line dividing the two westbound lanes of Old Hickory Boulevard.

But I was safe from the buzzing bringer of death, even if I was sprawled across the highway during rush-hour traffic. A few feet away, the driver of the large black truck—under which my coupe was wedged—slid out of his cab.

"Are you crazy?" he shouted as he rushed toward me, closing my car door as he ran.

All around us, car horns crescendoed in an urban symphony. Wasn't it a known fact that people *don't* honk in the South?

Weren't we supposed to be the land of "bless your hearts"s and deep-fried hospitality? I guess not.

The man grabbed my arm and hoisted me to my feet, spinning me around and pushing my back against the side of my car. Traffic in the lane next to us started rolling again, right over the spot where my head had landed on the road between the front grill of a garbage truck and the backside of a school bus.

The neck of my savior/victim was inches from my face as he yelled to cars honking behind mine, "Go around!" He smelled like cedar and sunshine.

Stars twinkled in my vision as I stared at the perfect angle of his jaw.

Maybe I hit my head.

"Are you OK?" He took a half step back and studied my face.

God, he was handsome. Tall. Thick, broad shoulders. Dirty blond hair that couldn't pick a single direction to grow. The turquoise in my dress reflected in his chocolate-brown eyes. His lips were full—and kissable.

Yes. I definitely hit my head.

Gingerly touching my fingers to my hairline, where I was fairly certain my forehead had smacked the steering wheel, I blinked to try and reset my thoughts. There wasn't any blood. Miraculously. "I—I'm so sorry."

"Are you all right?" He bent at the knees so he was eye level with me. "What happened?"

"There was a bee."

His head snapped back. "A bee?"

Oh hell. Kill me now. Heat bloomed in my cheeks, compounding my mortification. I hid my face behind my hands. "A wasp, actually. I freaked out, and my foot slipped off the brake."

He was silent.

Peeking through my fingers, I saw him biting down on the

insides of his lips. Probably to keep from laughing. I dropped my hands. "It's not funny!"

"You're right. It's not funny." He chuckled anyway. "Are you hurt?"

I shook my head despite the stars still twinkling in my vision. "I hit my head on the steering wheel, but I think I'm OK."

"Should we go to the hospital? Do I need to call an ambulance?"

"No, no. I'm all right." I hoped I was correct.

He examined my arm. "Your elbow is messed up."

"It hurts."

"Come on. I have a first-aid kit in the truck."

With his arm curled around my waist, he helped me to the sidewalk. Pain burned through my hip and down my leg as I stood by the back door of his truck. He pulled a small white box from the floorboard and balanced it on the rim of his truck bed.

"Let me see it," he said, gently taking hold of my wrist.

I winced as he pulled my arm up and across my body.

"There's a lot of gravel in the wound. I need to wash it out." He stepped to the front door, opened it, and leaned inside. A second later, he returned with a bottle of water. I tensed just looking at it.

He grimaced. "It's gonna sting."

I took a deep breath and held it. "Just do it."

Cool water splashed over my elbow.

"Sweet mother!" I twisted and arched my spine as the water burned my shredded skin.

The man studied me carefully, perhaps afraid I might scream or pass out. "You OK?"

I nodded, squeezing my eyes shut.

"Breathe," he said.

I inhaled. "I'm OK."

He tore open a packet of antibiotic ointment and smeared it

over the bloody hole, instantly dulling the blinding pain. I fully exhaled for the first time since the crash. Then he opened a large bandage and covered the area.

"Thank you." I gave him a thorough once over, checking him for injuries, of course. "I didn't even ask. Are you all right?"

He smiled. "Honestly, the truck didn't even lurch enough to make my seat belt catch. You sort of slid right under it." He nodded toward his truck. Its size made my car look like it could be remote controlled. "I think you owe me a new bumper."

The front end of my car was wearing his chrome bumper like a tiara. My head fell forward in shame. "I just paid off the car loan."

"That's the way it usually goes." He closed the first-aid kit and put it back in his truck. "Can you manage to stay out of oncoming traffic long enough for me to dislodge your car from my rear end?"

My eyes doubled in size.

So did his. "That came out all wrong!"

I burst out laughing and clapped my hand over my mouth. "Yes, it did."

He shook his head and jerked his thumb back over his shoulder. "I'm going to move my truck."

Still grinning behind my hand, I nodded. "OK."

The scraping metal against metal as he slowly pulled forward off my car made me cringe and plug my ears. My nose wrinkled as I stepped forward to inspect the damage. His bumper had settled at a slant below the tailgate, but other than that, his truck didn't have a scratch. I couldn't say as much for my car.

He pulled into the parking lot of the gas station next to the intersection, then parked and rejoined me in front of my car. "Well, unfortunately, I don't think it's drivable." He bent over my hood, which was stripped down to the base metal and crumpled like a sheet of discarded notebook paper. "Looks like my hitch tore a hole in the radiator."

Curse words drifted through my mind, but I would never say them out loud. Instead, I stepped toward the passenger's side. "I'll get my insurance information."

He grabbed my hand to stop me. "Is the bee still in there?"

I froze. "Oh! I don't know."

With a slight bow, he put his hand over his heart. "Let me."

This man. I wasn't aware guys like him existed in my generation. I stayed behind as he walked around the car. "Be careful. It's mean."

It took a few yanks, but he finally managed to wrench the door open with a labored creak from the mangled metal. "Whoa!" He ducked out of the wasp's way as it zinged past his head. "That sucker was huge!"

I tossed my hands up, then winced from the pain in my arm. "I know!"

He motioned me over. "Come on. The coast is clear."

In my glove box, all pertinent roadside necessities were neatly arranged. The paperwork was filed away in a black case behind a first-aid kit, a tire-pressure gauge, an ice scraper, and a flashlight. As I sat in the seat, carefully removing the items, he looked over my shoulder. "You're so well prepared, I'm surprised there's no bee spray in there."

I might have laughed had I not been trying so hard to fight back tears. I quickly found my insurance card and handed it to him. "Here. Take a picture of it with your phone."

"Good thinking. Have you done this a lot?" he asked.

I sighed as I got out of the car. "Don't ask."

With the camera on his smartphone, he snapped a picture of my insurance information. "Lucille Cooper?" He grinned and began humming the hit by Kenny Rogers, "You Picked a Fine Time to Leave Me, Lucille."

Rolling my eyes, I tucked the card back into the case and

stepped out beside him. "Boy, I've never heard that before. It's Lucy, actually."

He offered his hand. "I'm West Adler."

My brow crinkled. "West? As in north, south, east"—I pointed at him—"and you?"

He folded his arms over his chest, straining his short sleeves against his biceps. "That's a funny joke coming from a girl named Lucille."

I playfully shoved him in the shoulder, then noticed the embroidered logo on his chest. "Adler Construction. Family business?"

"You could say that."

The shrill wail of a police siren echoed through the jammed intersection. My heart sank.

"Uh-oh," West said with a grin. "Looks like someone called the fuzz."

My day kept getting better and better.

A white-and-blue Nashville Metro police cruiser, with red-and-blue lights flashing, inched its way across the busy road until it pulled to a stop behind my car. The officer, an older man with white hair and a matching mustache, angled out from behind the wheel and tugged his belt up over his belly as he sauntered toward us.

"It's your lucky day," West said quietly at my side.

"Right," I muttered.

The cop pulled off his mirrored aviator sunglasses. "West Adler, is that you?"

West met the cop halfway. I trailed behind him.

"How's it going, Danny?" West asked, stretching out his hand.

Officer Danny accepted West's hand with a hearty shake. "I'm having a better day than someone is having." He pointed to my mangled car. "What happened?"

"A killer wasp, I'm afraid." West grinned down at me. "Fortunately, there were no casualties other than the car."

God, his smile made my knees wobble.

"What'd it hit?" Danny asked.

West pointed toward his truck. "Tapped my bumper."

"Will it start?"

West sighed. "Haven't tried, but there's radiator fluid all over the pavement."

The cop grunted in response, then surveyed our surroundings. "Think we could push it into that parking lot?"

West looked at me. "Lucy, can you steer while we push?"

My mouth was gaping. I'd rear-ended him, and West Adler was saving the day. Who was this guy?

"Lucy?"

I snapped out of my daze. "Yeah. Of course. Sorry."

When my little blue car was safely off the highway and parked at the side of the gas station's lot, I got out and rejoined the men at my back bumper. West was dusting off his hands. I should've washed my car.

"I'll be right back," Danny said, wiping his hands on his pants as he walked back to his police cruiser.

I narrowed my eyes at West. "Are you famous?" It was a fair question in the music capital of the world.

He laughed. "No. Danny knows my father."

"Oh."

"He won't give you a ticket," he added, lowering his voice.

My shoulders relaxed, and I blew out a deep sigh. "Thank God."

The cop pulled into the lot beside us and rolled down his window. "Need me to call a tow truck for you, ma'am?"

West held up his hand. "I'll take care of it."

My head snapped up. "You will?"

"Of course, I will. I can't leave a beautiful young woman stranded on the side of the road."

I tapped my chest. "You know I ran into you, right?"

West ignored me. "I've got this under control, Danny."

Danny tipped an imaginary hat toward us. "Call me if you need anything, West. And give my regards to your family."

West waved. "Will do."

"Thank you!" I called out as the officer drove away.

True to his word, West Adler—knight in shining polo shirt—called a friend who owned a body shop. After a few moments on the phone, he covered the speaker with his hand. "My buddy says it's gonna be about an hour before he can get here. You can leave it, and he'll pick it up and call you about the damage, or we can call another company. It's up to you."

Between being rattled by the accident and feeling woozy from West Adler's cologne, I didn't know what to do. "If you trust him, I guess it would be OK to leave it."

He nodded, then pulled the phone back up to his ear. "Hey, man. We'll leave it here at the gas station. It's a dark blue GKS Sport with a front end currently shaped like an accordion. You can't miss it."

My mouth twisted into a frown.

West winked at me.

"I'll text you her phone number," he said before disconnecting the call.

I withered. "Thanks, West."

He tucked the phone into his pocket. "Don't mention it. My friend could use the business."

I knew he might be saying that to make me feel better. It worked.

He looked down at the shiny silver watch encircling his wrist. "I can give you a ride depending on where you're headed."

I crossed my arms. "Are you doing penance for some horrible past sin?"

"What?"

"Or maybe you're in the 'make amends' step of a recovery program and this is some part of a paying-your-grievances-forward plan?"

West scratched his head. "I have no idea what you're talking about."

"Nobody's this nice to someone who hit them at a traffic light. I know because I've done this before."

The corner of his perfect mouth tipped up. "Maybe you just haven't bumped into the right person." He pointed to his truck. "Do you want a lift or not? It's a pretty simple question."

"Umm..."

"Where are you going, Lucy?"

"Downtown," I answered.

Without giving me a chance to object, he walked to his truck and opened the passenger-side door. "Me too. Hop in."

Giddiness bubbled inside me. I felt a little dizzy. Maybe it was the concussion. "Are you sure?"

His eyes widened, and his sparkling smile was teasing. "Get in the damn truck, Lucille."

I laughed and got in the damn truck.

On the off chance he was a serial killer (such would be my luck), I texted my roommate Olivia Barker. *In case I go missing or wind up dead, a guy named West Adler is driving me to work. I wrecked my car, but I'm OK. Just wanted someone to know.*

She didn't respond.

West got in the driver's side and started the engine. It was so loud I wondered if I'd screwed up his muffler, but West didn't seem to notice. He put it into gear and rolled to the lot's exit. "So where were you headed this morning before all hell broke loose inside your car?" As he pulled onto the busy street, he waved his thanks to the driver who let him cut into the line of traffic.

"Work," I answered.

"What do you do?"

I tried to cross my legs, but the pain stopped me. "Marketing. I work for an artist-management company downtown."

"What kind of artists?"

"Country music mostly."

"Anyone I've heard of?"

I nodded. "Probably. Melvin Brooks, Jake Barrett, Lawson Young—"

"I love his new song," he said.

I rolled my eyes. "Most guys do."

Country crooner Lawson Young had recently released an entire album spawned by one of the worst, and most public, breakups in history. At least Nashville's history, anyway. And that was saying something in the home of country music. The first single—eloquently titled "Bitch, Please"—immediately blew up the charts, and the tabloids. The object of the breakup? My boss, his soon-to-be-former manager. Things at work were tense, to say the least.

"Do you like it?" West asked.

"The song?"

He chuckled. "Your job."

I nodded. "Most days." And it was true. Besides all the drama as of late, it was fun and exciting. And fortunately, it paid well enough to cover an increased car insurance premium and my hefty deductible.

My phone buzzed in my hand with a text message. *Are you dead?* It was Olivia.

Not dead. Call you later, I texted back.

"Where's your office?" he asked as we neared the on-ramp to I-65 North.

"Inside the Summit Tower. Do you know where it is? It's pretty new."

He checked his blind spot and merged with traffic. "I think I've seen it before."

"Probably. It's the biggest building downtown."

He shook his head. "The Batman Building is bigger."

"The *what*?"

"You're not from here, are you?"

"I've only lived here about six weeks," I said.

"Really? Where did you move from?"

"A teeny, tiny little town called Riverbend. Have you ever heard of it?"

He thought for a moment. "It doesn't ring any bells."

"It's between here and Memphis with a sixty-mile detour south off I-40. You're not alone. Most people haven't heard of the armpit of Tennessee."

"Armpit, huh?"

"It's a pretty place to visit, or maybe hide in the witness-protection program, but I don't recommend staying there."

He cut his eyes over at me with a grin that made my stomach tingle. "Are you in witness protection?"

I winked at him. "Not anymore."

"What brought you here?"

"The job brought me to Nashville, specifically, but I was considering any city with a population greater than three thousand." I looked out the window. "Lately, I really needed a change of scenery."

"How's that working out for you?" he asked.

I admired him from across the cab. *The scenery looks pretty great from here.* I didn't dare say that, however. I blushed and looked away. "I'll let you know, but so far so good."

"Look." He pointed toward the skyline in the distance ahead of us.

The tallest structure in the sky was a giant building with what looked to be two pointy ears. I laughed. "I get it. The Batman Building."

We arrived at my office way too soon. I wasn't ready for our meeting to end. He pulled up to the curb in front of the entrance and parked. "Here you are, m'lady."

I unbuckled my seatbelt. "Thanks again, West. You really didn't have to do all this for me."

He shifted sideways and pulled his phone from his pocket. "Let me get your number. I still need to send it to Randy at the shop." When he finished typing with his thumbs, he leaned toward me, tilting the phone enough for me to see the screen. He'd started a new contact file under the name *Hot Chick Who Wrecked My Truck.*

I almost melted into a puddle.

After exchanging numbers, I opened the door and groaned in pain as I slid out onto the sidewalk.

"Are you sure you shouldn't get checked out at the hospital?" he asked, his gorgeous eyes crinkled with concern. "I'm afraid you might be really hurt and not know it."

My heart, I knew, would surely never be the same. "I'm fine, I promise. And I'm really sorry about your bumper, West."

He shrugged. "It could happen to anybody." Quickly, he tapped his chest. "Not me, of course. But anybody else."

Laughing again, I closed the door.

He rolled down the window. "Let me know if you have any problems with the shop."

"I will. Thank you." I waved as I turned toward the building and started up the front steps.

"Hey!" I heard him call.

I looked back.

He pointed at me with a grin. "You owe me, Lucille. Don't you forget it."

Then he winked, and I slipped off the step.

———

Thankfully, West missed my blunder on the stairs as he drove away, leaving me and the butterflies in my stomach to duck, embarrassed, into my building. I limped to the elevator lobby and pressed the up button.

The Summit Tower was a spectacle in the center of the city, encased in glass from top to bottom. The elevator provided a spectacular view of downtown Nashville on my ride up to the sixteenth floor, but that morning I wasn't looking at the skyline. I was scanning the streets for a black pickup.

Maybe he got off the street. Maybe he parked and came inside. Maybe he sprinted up the stairs to be waiting when I step off the elevator. He'll take me into his strong arms and...

DING!

The doors slid open, and the building's geriatric gardener looked up from the fern he was pruning. He waved a handful of brown leaves at me in greeting. My shoulders drooped as I stepped into the hallway. *It's going to be a long day, Lucille.*

Claire Huggins looked up from the receptionist desk when I walked through the smoky glass double doors of Record Road Nashville. It was strange seeing her there. Normally, I arrived before everyone else and quietly slipped into my office to hide unnoticed all day. Claire glanced at the clock on the wall.

I held up my hand as I crossed the room, favoring my injured leg. "I know. I'm late."

She looked worried. "Is everything all right?"

I nodded. "I wrecked my car on the way in, but I'm OK. Anything I should be aware of?"

She shook her head, then her hand shot forward. "No, wait!"

Audrey is in the conference room doing a lot of yelling, so you might want to steer clear of there."

My eyes widened, even though our boss yelling at someone wasn't exactly a newsflash. "Thanks for the warning. Have a good day, Claire."

"You too, Lucy."

As quickly as my battered legs would carry me, I crept down the hallway lined with gold and platinum records toward my office. Audrey's muffled bark filtered through the walls, stirring my sympathy for whoever was on the receiving end of it. I assumed she was probably yelling at Ava, her sister and vice president of the company. The pair of them made me glad I only had a brother.

I relaxed when I reached my office undetected, but my relief was short lived. I heard the latch of the conference-room door tumble, followed by the familiar staccato click-clack of Audrey's heels against the tile. My spine went rigid, and I fumbled my keys before I could get the right one in the lock.

"Lily!"

I groaned and rolled my eyes up toward the ceiling, mouthing the question "Why?" to God or whoever might be watching. Before turning around to face her, I plastered a bright smile across my face. "Good morning, Audrey."

It was rumored in the break room that in another lifetime Audrey Scott had been a beauty queen. It was believable given her perfectly symmetrical face and long, silky dark hair. But that was before the pressure of running a powerful company in show business had etched a few extra years across her brow. I'd heard she was thirty-four, but she could easily pass as forty, or fifty, depending on how deep her stress lines went at any particular moment. Watching her stalk down the hallway toward my office, I could have been convinced she qualified for AARP.

She tugged up the sleeve of her tailored gray suit—which I

was sure cost more than my rent—to look at her sparkly watch. "Lily, I need your help."

I took a step to my right, out of the way of the name placard on the wall. "Of course. What do you need?"

She didn't notice my name. "I have a meeting with Lawson's lawyer and his business manager at nine. Can you get me the financial reports from all of last year's online advertising?"

Ahh...no wonder heads are rolling already this morning.

Lawson Young had been one of the agency's biggest clients until the younger of the Scott sisters, Ava, dumped him the night before their big Texas wedding. Now, four months later, Record Road was still working out the details of being forced to let Lawson out of his contract with the agency. Hence all the yelling in the conference room.

"You asked me for it yesterday, so I put it in your door pocket last night before I left the office. Did you see it?" I asked.

She blinked with surprise. "Oh! No, I didn't. I dumped all that paperwork on my desk this morning before my phone began ringing." She cocked her head, pressing her painted lips into a thin smile packed with fake endearment. "What did we ever do without you, Lily?"

She turned on her heel before I could say anything else. When she rounded the corner and disappeared from sight, I stamped my feet in frustration and jabbed my finger over and over at my name engraved in the gaudy brass plate on my door. *My name is Lucy!*

My head throbbed, only partly from the car accident.

It had been exactly forty-three days since I'd accepted the position of online marketing manager for the Scott sisters, and I was beginning to wonder if my senior boss had some kind of brain defect. Two weeks in, I'd given up on correcting her about my name. I was Lily. And there was no convincing her otherwise.

I walked into my office and flipped on the overhead light,

though the room hardly needed it. Before sitting down at my oak desk, I paused at the wall of windows to admire the view, and I inhaled a deep calming breath fragrant with citrus polish and glass cleaner.

As crazy as Audrey's tyrannical behavior threatened to make me, I truly loved my job. Which, in its simplest form, was to get whatever or *whoever* I was selling on as many computer and mobile screens as possible.

I spent my days creating email newsletters, building and tweaking social-media ads, and writing website and blog content. The writing was my favorite. Drafting articles that could make fans swoon *and* land a website on the front page of Google was truly a magical art form. My last job had been whoring out software for a no-name foreign company from a makeshift office in the basement of my parents' house. For the lighting upgrade alone at Record Road, I'd be willing to change the name on my birth certificate to Lily.

Thirteen new emails were waiting in my inbox, four of which were from Audrey. Two were from her assistant, Peter Jansen, following up on Audrey's four emails, and one was from my dad. The rest was junk. I clicked open the message from Dad first.

Hey, Lulabean. Just wanted you to know that Katherine and I are having a great time in Costa Rica. The internet is shoddy here, so I'm not sure if I'll be in touch again before we get home. Attached is a picture of a monkey. Hope you have a good weekend.

Love you, Dad

Wrinkling up my nose, I wondered if the picture was of Katherine, Dad's new bride. It wasn't. It was a picture of him with a capuchin monkey sitting on his shoulder. His face was tanned from the Caribbean sunshine, and he was laughing behind his salt-and-pepper goatee. I paused to remind myself for the millionth time that his happiness was what was important despite my feelings about the situation.

And he did look happy. I wasn't sure if that fact vexed me or not. It's not like I wanted him to be sad, but did he have to be *so* happy? So happy so soon?

I couldn't help but compare his smile to the one in our family photo that was framed on my desk. *Our* family. Before Katherine. Before cancer. Before everything had fallen so spectacularly apart.

Then I lightly smacked my own cheeks. "Stop it, Lucy."

Those kinds of thoughts would zap all my productivity for the next few hours, so I typed out a quick reply, saved Dad's picture to the appropriate folder designated for personal photos, then deleted his message. I returned to the inbox and promptly erased all the junk mail before tackling Audrey's requests. All of them had already been addressed and were sitting on her desk, except for one. I moved that email to my "To Do" folder, because it wasn't urgent, and deleted the rest.

Under the desk, my cell phone beeped inside my purse. My joints burned as I bent to retrieve it.

Just checking to make sure you made it inside OK...and without killing anyone. - West

Be still my heart.

I leaned back in my cushy office chair with a grin so wide it triggered a cramp in my jaw. I hit reply, bringing up a new chat window.

Me: *Safe and sound. I only allow myself one accident per trip.*

A second later, my phone beeped again.

West: *My lucky day. :) Of all the pickups in all the towns in all the world, she ran into mine.*

A gleeful squeal slipped out before I could stop it, and I spun around in my office chair, disregarding the pain that swirled in my head.

There was a knock at the door, and my feet slammed onto the floor so fast I almost toppled over. *Ow.* I brushed the hair that had whipped across my face out of my eyes and saw Ava, my other boss, smiling in the doorway.

She walked in and sat down on the edge of the seat across from my desk. "I *must* know what that was all about." She crossed her legs, resting her hands and the papers she was holding on her knee.

Ava was the carbon copy of Audrey, minus five years and all the wrinkles. She was softer and far less demanding, approachable but still firm. She was classy, but considering all the drama swirling around the office, she was also a bit of a rebel. I liked that.

However, she was still my boss, so I straightened in my seat and tried to look professional. It was no use. I couldn't stop smiling. "I'm sorry," I said, hiding my red cheeks behind my hand.

She waved her papers at me. "Don't be sorry. Just spill the beans. You're dying to tell somebody. I can see it all over your face. What's his name?"

I laughed and dropped my hands into my lap. "West Adler."

"Adler?" She turned her ear toward me like she wasn't sure she'd heard me correctly. "As in Adler Construction?"

I rested my elbows on my desk, then immediately jerked back upright, sucking a sharp, pained breath in through my clenched teeth.

"Are you OK?" she asked.

I looked down at the bandage on my arm. "I fell and scraped the skin off my elbow this morning, but yeah, I'm OK. You've heard of Adler Construction?"

She chuckled, then motioned around the room. "They built your office, honey."

I was confused.

She bent toward me. "The Summit Tower. They built it."

My mouth fell open. "Shut up."

"The Adlers are sort of like royalty in this town." She held up her hand, rubbing her fingers together. "Lots of money in that family."

Withering in my seat, I gripped my head in my hands. "Are you serious?"

"Girl, I never joke about men or money." She leaned on the armrest of her chair. "How did you meet him?"

I slid my hands down the sides of my face, pulling my lips into a distorted frown. "I ran into him at a stop light on my way into work this morning."

Her eyes narrowed. "What do you mean you 'ran into him'?"

I made two fists, then crashed them together with sound effects.

"Like *boom*?" she asked.

"Like *boom*. I literally slammed into the back of his truck."

She laughed, covering her mouth with her hand. "Uh-oh." She nodded toward my phone laying on the desk. "Well, he must not have been too mad about it if you're in here spinning around in your chair."

I bit down on the tip of my index fingernail. "He drove me to work, and now he's quoting *Casablanca*."

Obviously impressed, she slowly clapped her hands. "Congratulations. You must have left quite the impression."

I nodded. "Yeah, on his bumper."

We both burst out laughing.

Finally, she pointed at me. "Oh, Lucy. You and I are going to be great friends."

My heart swelled. *She knows my name.*

"Did you need something from me, Ava?"

She turned in her chair and craned her neck to look down the hall. "No. I was looking for a place to hide when I heard you squeal." She jerked her thumb toward the door. "Almost everyone else is in the conference room, and I'm afraid my ex is going to show up with his lawyer."

I grimaced. "You can hide in here as long as you need to."

"Thanks." She laughed. "I promise, things are normally more professional around here than they have been since you came on board."

I leaned back in my chair. "I believe that. You don't get where you are in this business by pure luck."

"Do you like it so far? The music business," she asked.

Tilting my head from side to side, I gave a noncommittal shrug. "I'm still getting used to it. It's a little surreal doing promos for people you hear on the radio all the time."

She cut her eyes over at me with a cheeky smile. "Try sleeping with them."

We laughed again.

My phone buzzed on the desk. I picked it up.

West: *Have a great day, Lucy. Maybe we'll "run into each other" again soon.* :-) :-)

———

The Scott sisters were so lucky to have me. My productivity level was astounding. By lunchtime, I'd found West Adler's Facebook page, his Instagram account, and every newspaper article written about him or his family since the birth of the internet. What else was a single girl to do in the digital age besides use the company Wi-Fi to cyberstalk the fourth-ranked most eligible bachelor in all of Music City according to *The Nashville Scene?*

West Adler was thirty-three.

Never married.

A graduate of Belmont with a master's degree in business.

He was a philanthropist. A benefactor of not one, but two children's hospitals, the performing arts, a rehab center for girls, the local women's roller derby team...

A roller derby team?

When I read the words again, a black-and-white movie reel flickered on in my brain. Women in short shorts and knee-high socks skated around a wooden bowl the size of my apartment, shoving and knocking each other out of the way. They all had tattoos. They all had Bettie Paige bangs adorned with Rosie the Riveter bandanas.

I searched the internet for the Nashville roller derby.

Employee of the Year, right here.

Founded in 2008, the Music City Rollers is an all-female, non-profit, skater-governed roller derby league in Nashville, Tennessee. We are dedicated to training up strong, independent female athletes who value character over appearance and integrity over winning. We are an inclusive league comprised of women with diverse backgrounds and skill sets who are committed to excellence on and off the roller derby track. The final home game of the season is Saturday, August 22 at the Municipal Auditorium...

I looked at the calendar beside my phone. The twenty-second was tomorrow. When I turned back to the screen again, my eyes fell on the logo for Adler Construction. They were the first listed sponsor. Maybe it was a sign.

I nibbled on my fingernail, then picked up my phone and texted Olivia again.

Do you have plans tomorrow?

When she didn't answer right away, I turned back to my screen and clicked the link for Adler Construction. The company website popped open in a new browser window, and vivid photos of high-rise buildings filled my screen. They were set against a stark white background, and the "heart and mission" of the company was described in a crisp sans font. God knows this love affair might have ended before it began had I stumbled onto animated GIFs and Comic Sans.

But there were zero pictures of West on the entire site. I checked. Every page.

My phone buzzed.

Olivia: *I'm having a threesome with a bag of Cheetos, a carton of rocky road, and the final season of Sons of Anarchy.*

Me: *Did you know Nashville has a women's roller derby team?*

Olivia: *Yeah. A girl I went to college with plays.*

Me: *I want to go.*

Olivia: *Have fun.*

Me: *Go with me!*

Olivia: *I'm busy.*

Me: *You just said you're staying home to watch TV.*

Olivia: *That's important business.*

Me: :-(

Olivia: *Don't sad-emoticon me. It's my only Saturday off this month.*

Me: *Please go with me.*

Olivia: *Fine. But you're buying.*

Me: *Deal.*

Olivia: *Why the sudden interest?*

Me: *It might be about a guy...*

Olivia: *Ugh. I changed my mind. I'm staying home.*

Me: :-(

Olivia: *You know it's an all-girl sport, right? If you're trying to get a date there, it'll have to be with a woman.*

Me: *That's your department...hey, maybe we can find YOU a date.*

Olivia: *Good point. I'm back in.*

Me: *I'll see you tonight.*

Olivia: *I'm closing. I'll see you in the morning.*

I put my phone down and turned back toward the computer. It was time to put cute bachelors out of my mind and get back to work. But the Music City Rollers still lit up my screen. And they were almost as distracting as West Adler.

TWO

ON SATURDAY, I slept in till after eight, which was quite a feat for the girl who had inherited the Morning Person Gene from her former military father and was usually out of bed with the birds each day. Perhaps it was the Advil PM I'd downed at bedtime the night before to combat the pain and stiffness that had settled into my joints since the accident. My first conscious thought was: Don't move. Because as soon as I did...

"Sweet, holy mother!"

Tears sprang to my eyes as I forced my legs toward the side of the bed. I groaned and prayed for death. For a moment, I considered pulling the comforter up over my head and hiding there all day, but my sore arms couldn't bear the weight of the blanket. Ultimately, thoughts of roller skates and West Adler slipped past the suffocating clouds of agony and coaxed me from my fluffy cocoon.

My body almost audibly creaked as I wrenched myself out of bed and stumbled to the bathroom for a few more caplets of ibuprofen. I winced as I pulled the bandage off my bloody elbow.

Then I poured hydrogen peroxide over the wound and swore as it bubbled on the raw flesh. I recovered it with a thick piece of gauze, a strip of plastic wrap, and enough athletic tape to bind the hull of the *Titanic*. The waterproofing was necessary because braving the shower was next.

And the shower was a mistake, no matter what Most Eligible Bachelor might have been looming in the future of my day. The hot water seared into scrapes and cuts too small for the naked eye to see. And if I thought washing and conditioning my hair was painful, it didn't even compare to the pain of blow drying.

"The things we do for men," I whined to my reflection in the mirror over the roar of the dryer.

Before finally leaving the bathroom, I gathered my dirty laundry from the basket and carried it to the washer in the hallway.

Olivia didn't emerge from her bedroom until almost time for lunch. I was folding my load of whites on the couch when she stumbled out of her room like she'd awoken from the dead. Her wavy brown hair was matted across her face, and her eyes were bloodshot and swollen. I had honestly never seen her look worse, and considering we'd known each other longer than I could remember, that was saying something.

I dropped the pair of cotton shorts I was folding onto my lap. "Whoa. Rough night?"

She rubbed her nose, then shuffled behind me toward the kitchen. "Some days, I really think I mortgaged my soul to buy this restaurant, only to put myself into an early grave."

"What happened this time?"

Olivia was the owner of a trendy hotspot in East Nashville called *Lettuce Eat*. Her restaurant specialized in farm-to-table cuisine and bad jokes. Each menu item was a silly pun rather than an appetizing description that actually made sense.

Case in point? Their newest side dish—Bitch, Peas—based on the current hottest song on the country charts.

Fortunately, the food was delicious and worthy of all the hype the names generated.

She pulled a mug from the cabinet and put it under the spout of the Keurig before pressing the start button. "I had a waitress poison her ex-boyfriend's dinner last night."

My mouth fell open. "No."

"Yes." She got my carton of milk out of the refrigerator. "The girl came in all red faced and snot nosed last week because, apparently, he cheated on her."

I sighed. "You're such a sympathetic boss."

When the coffee maker hissed to a stop, Olivia poured in the milk and carried her mug to the opposite end of the sectional sofa. "You have no idea the crap I deal with. Anyway, he came in last night to talk to her and had dinner at the bar." She propped her feet up on the coffee table. "Well, I guess he has a severe peanut allergy and she holds a bit of a grudge."

I pinched my lips together.

She nodded. "The girl poured about a half a cup of our Thai peanut sauce all over his grilled Marco Pollo chicken before slamming it down in front of him. We got the whole thing on the security camera."

"What happened to him?" I asked.

"Anaphylactic shock. Stopped breathing and everything. We had to call an ambulance." She slurped as she drank. "The cops came and arrested her right before closing. I was at the police station until about four this morning."

I cut my eyes over at her. "Are you sure you didn't poison someone? That totally sounds like something you would do."

She grinned. "I know, right? But it really wasn't me."

I laughed and shook my head.

"My job is never boring. What happened to you yesterday? Why were you getting into cars with strangers? Didn't your daddy warn you about that shit?"

I balled a pair of ankle socks together and added them to the stack on the coffee table. "Yes. My dad would have a stroke if he knew. Don't you dare tell him."

"I won't. What happened?"

"I got in a wreck."

She frowned. "Who did you hit?"

My mouth fell open. "Hey! How do you know someone didn't hit me?"

She raised an eyebrow. "You backed into the building manager's golf cart the day you moved in, and you took out the security arm at the front gate of the complex just two weeks ago."

"I didn't know it came down between every car!"

"There's a sign, Lucy."

I opened my mouth for a rebuttal, but I didn't have one.

"Nobody was hurt, right?" she asked.

I shook my head. "I'm really sore, but it's nothing serious. My car, on the other hand..." My bottom lip poked out. "The guy at the body shop said to prepare for a total loss. The adjuster is supposed to be there on Monday."

"That sucks."

"I know. The truck I rear-ended barely had a scratch. It messed up his bumper," I said.

She made a sour face. "I'd hate to see your insurance payments." She nudged me with her socked foot. "I just had a position open up on my wait staff if you need some extra income."

I laughed. "No thanks, but I appreciate the offer."

"How did you get home from work yesterday if you don't have a car?" she asked.

"Had to call an Uber," I said. "On the upside—"

"There's an upside to a traffic accident?"

"I met someone."

"Who?"

"The guy I rear-ended."

She snickered behind her cup like a twelve-year-old boy who'd heard his first dirty joke.

"Really mature, Olivia."

"Is this guy the reason you want to go see roller derby today?"

I put the laundry basket on the floor and tucked my legs underneath me. "Yes. He's a sponsor of the team."

"What's his name?"

"Have you heard of Adler Construction?"

She shrugged. "Sure. I've seen their signs."

"His name is West Adler," I said.

Her face scrunched up. "That's not a guy's name. It's a street name." She made the shape of a phone with her hand and pressed it to the side of her face. "Hey, Lucy. I'll meet you this afternoon at the corner of Main and West Adler."

I threw a couch cushion at her, then winced from the pain.

Laughing, she shielded her coffee from my attack.

"If he asked you to come, why do I have to go?" she asked.

"Well, he didn't ask me."

She blinked with surprise. "So we're stalking him."

"No!" Yes, I was totally stalking him. "I'm just hoping to run into him again."

She got up and walked toward the kitchen, glancing back over her shoulder as she went. "Not that I'm an expert on guys or anything, but I don't think the way to a man's heart is by crashing into his car multiple times."

"You know what I mean."

"Well, whatever the reason, I'm glad you're getting out of the house to go somewhere other than work." She opened the refrigerator door. "Have you done anything fun since you moved here?"

I folded a white camisole into a perfect square. "Does visiting you at work count?"

"No."

My nose wrinkled. "Then no." I tried to remember the last time I'd been out, period, even before I moved to Nashville. Nothing easily came to mind.

"And, of all things to do in this great city, you want to go watch roller derby," she said.

"I spent a lot of time on their website yesterday. It looks like fun. Have you ever been?" I asked.

"No." She returned a second later carrying one of the yogurts I'd bought. "But I've seen their flyers up all over East Nashville."

I pointed at her. "Are you going to eat all my food?"

She spoke around the spoon in her mouth. "I'll pay you back."

I pushed myself off the couch, then bent gingerly to pick up my laundry basket. "What should I wear tonight?"

"Clothes."

"I don't know why I waste my breath talking to you," I said, shaking my head as I crossed the room.

"Hey! What time are we leaving?" she called out as I walked down the hall.

"Doors open at six!"

The lobby of the Municipal Auditorium downtown was packed with an eclectic sampling of social diversity. In front of us in the ticket line was a young, suburban-type couple with a toddler. Behind us? A grown man in a teal tutu. There were nurses wearing scrubs and old people wearing clown wigs. A group of frat boys was chugging beers near the entrance, and I may have spotted a vampire in the corner.

Olivia gripped my good elbow with eyes as wide as mine felt.

"Well, this is interesting," I whispered.

She leaned close. "*Interesting* doesn't cut it. I feel like we've wandered into a Tim Burton film."

When we finally reached the ticket window, a small girl with a jet-black bob, bright green eyes, and cherry-red lips looked up at us. She had a colorful butterfly tattoo covering her chest from her clavicle to her cleavage, and she had a ring through her nose like a bull. She was chomping on a piece of bubble gum. "How many?"

I spoke through the hole in the glass. "Two, please."

"Twenty dollars." She blew a pink bubble half the size of her face as she traded my crisp twenty for two tickets. "Enjoy the bout."

"The bout?" Olivia asked as we walked toward the entry doors.

I just shrugged.

A large man wearing a Music City Rollers T-shirt tore our tickets and handed us two program booklets as we walked into the outer hall around the arena. It was loud with the sounds of the crowd bouncing off the concrete block walls and windows. The busy room smelled like fresh paint and popcorn. Olivia pointed toward a concession stand. "They serve beer."

As we waited in line, I flipped through the program. In the middle was a two-page spread of headshots—or maybe mugshots—of the players. I nudged Olivia with my elbow. "Listen to some of these names. Lady Fury, Black-Eye Candy, Bad News Baroness, Princess Die, eL's Bells, Medusa..."

She peeked over my shoulder. "Look for a girl named Haley Jones."

"There is nothing close to a normal name on this list," I said, shaking my head. "Never mind. There's a girl named Susan."

Olivia ordered a beer. "Lucy, what do you want?"

"Diet Coke," I answered.

A few minutes later, we carried our drinks and hot dogs (that

I bought) inside the arena and slowly made our way up the grand-stands, one painful step at a time. We found seats just a few rows up from the team benches. I looked around the large room. "Where's the big bowl?"

"The what?" Olivia asked.

I made a circular motion in the air with my hot dog. "In the movies, they skate around a big bowl thing."

A man who reminded me a lot of my dad turned around in front of us. "Most teams don't play on those anymore. See the big circles on the floor? This is flat track roller derby."

I scrunched up my nose. "Well, that's a little disappointing."

He chuckled. "I thought so too when I came to my first bout. When I was your age, it was still the bowl."

"You come to these a lot?" Olivia asked with a mouthful of hot dog.

He nodded. "My daughter is one of the blockers. She goes by Riveter Styx." He held up his program. "There are rules inside to help you understand the game."

"Thanks for the tip," I said.

He turned back around. "Anytime."

After finishing my hot dog, I spread the program across my knees and flipped to the rules of the game. "All right, are you ready for some Roller Derby Fast Facts?" I asked Olivia.

She took a deep swig of beer. "Educate me."

I began to read. "Roller derby is played on a flat, oval track with five players from each team, one jammer (denoted by a star on her helmet) and four blockers. Blockers play defense and offense. They try to stop the opposing jammer while trying to help their own jammer. Jammers score one point for each opposing player they pass. The team with the most points at the end of the bout wins."

"That doesn't sound too complicated," she said.

I sipped my soda and shook my head. "No, but there are about a bazillion rules."

She looked at me and crumpled the paper from her hot dog. "Only a bazillion?"

"No tripping, no elbows—"

"Aww...they cut out all the fun stuff," she whined.

I surveyed the room. It was a big arena with probably ten thousand seats. Not that there were ten thousand people there. Almost all the upper seating was empty, except for a couple of teenagers making out on the top row. The lower bowl of seats was almost full. And in front of us, near the oval track, people were sitting on the floor. Even though I'd never seen the game, somehow that seemed like a bad idea.

I didn't see West anywhere.

"Is that a penalty box?" Olivia asked, drawing my attention toward the direction of her finger.

On the left side of the track were two high-back white benches with the words BAD GIRLS painted across the back. I laughed and looked down at my program. "Yes. Players who have received a major penalty will be sent to the penalty box for thirty seconds."

A loud ruckus caught our attention near the doorway we'd come in. A very, uh, *spirited* group of individuals were running into the room with pom-poms, megaphones, wigs, and face paint. A few were wearing bright teal tutus. One of them was the guy who'd been behind us in the lobby.

Olivia and I exchanged amused glances. "What the hell is going on?" she asked.

The crowd went wild. People jumped up and cheered, clapping and waving Music City banners. The lights flickered a few times, and then the music blared as the tutu group ran around the bottom of the stands whooping and yelling, riling up the crowd.

A man in a full tuxedo and bright purple top hat walked out

to the center of the track. He put the microphone to his mouth and held up his free arm. "Give it up, Nashville, for your Music City Jeerleaders!"

We put our drinks down and stood, clapping along with the rest of the fans. I looked over at Olivia. "Jeerleaders." I laughed. "That's pretty funny."

Across the room, the Jeerleaders formed two lines out from a wide gap in the center of the bleachers.

The announcer raised the microphone again. "My name is Daddy Ho'maker, and allow me to welcome you to beautiful downtown Nashville, Tennessee! Everyone put your hands together for your favorite roller derby dolls, the Music City Rollers!"

The room actually rumbled around us from the commotion. The bleachers vibrated under my feet as the team skated out of the tunnel, making a wide loop around the room and slapping hands with the surrounding fans.

They were women of all shapes and sizes, all wearing the same uniform: fitted black-and-teal tank top jerseys with black booty shorts. They wore helmets, knee and elbow pads, and wrist guards, and they all had numbers scrawled in black on their upper arms. In a synchronized pattern, all the skaters huddled together in a slow-moving pack drifting around the track like a swarm of black-and-teal bumblebees.

Daddy Ho'maker pointed toward the pack. "Introducing lucky number seven, Shamrocker!"

A thin skater with a short lime-green pixie cut and the number seven written on her bicep pumped her fist in the air as she broke away from the front of the group. She circled the track, passing her teammates, and the audience cheered until she caught up with the back of the group.

A heavyset brunette followed after Shamrocker. "Number 9MM, Full Metal Jackie!"

When Full Metal Jackie rejoined at the back of the group, Daddy Ho'maker pointed toward the girl in the front. "Number 1111, Riveter Styx!"

I nudged the shoulder of the man in front of us, and he flashed a proud smile back at me. Riveter Styx appeared to have short hair hidden under her helmet, and her tiny shorts showed off a huge skull tattoo on the outside of her left thigh.

We clapped and cheered for each player as they skated around. Toward the end of the introductions, the crowd began a drumroll with their feet, making the floor shake like an earthquake. My eyes widened as I wondered what could be happening.

"And now"—Daddy Ho'maker's voice was deeper and more dramatic—"your All-Star team captain and 2014 National Championship MVP, number ten—Medusa!"

Caught up in the excitement, Olivia cupped her hands around her mouth and yelled next to me when Medusa skated into the center of the track, gliding effortlessly around the loop like a gazelle on wheels.

Slowly, the fans around us stopped stomping, and the tremors underneath me ceased as Medusa skated past her team, leading them off the track and into a crisp line of which she formed the head. She was a few inches taller than almost everyone else, and even from our distance, I could see the cut of the taut thigh muscles exposed by her tiny shorts. From underneath her helmet, her dark hair fell in two loose ponytails over her shoulders, an ombre dye job that ended with the tips in flaming fuchsia.

All eyes in the arena were still glued to her. And rightfully so. She owned the room.

"Finally, Nashville," Daddy Ho'maker said, "your matriarch of the league and fearless head coach—The Duchess!"

A stout woman in a gray business suit walked out from the tunnel. She had ashy brown-and-gray hair cut straight across her shoulders. She waved to the crowd as she crossed the room. The members of her team were clapping over their heads.

Styx's father looked back at me. "The Duchess has been skating since they still skated on banked tracks."

I nodded, impressed as The Duchess stood near the bench closest to us.

The Richmond Vixens, dressed in bright magenta-and-green jerseys, were introduced next and welcomed with half-hearted applause from the home-team crowd. The referees skated in behind them, followed by non-skating officials wearing pastel-pink shirts. The Charity of the Night, The Hope Haven of Nashville, was announced last. After the singing of "The Star-Spangled Banner" and then a series of warm-up exercises for both teams, the bout looked ready to begin.

Eight girls, the four blockers from each team, huddled together on the track. About five feet behind them, Medusa and Richmond's jammer, both of whom had stars on their helmets, were toeing the line, ready to charge. I scooted forward on the edge of my seat.

"Our jammers to start," Daddy Ho'maker said. "No surprise here, wearing the star for the Music City Makers, number ten Medusa! She is opposed by number 6VI6, Demoness."

Demoness looked mean. A solid black band was painted all the way across her eyes.

A whistle blasted and the two jammers took off. Like a hot knife cutting through butter, Medusa sliced her way through the pack. A referee inside the track pointed at her as she skated around the oval. But her opponent wasn't far behind. Medusa cut through the pack a second time, then made wild gestures with her arms, hitting her hands against her hips. The whistle blew again and everyone slowed to a stop.

I looked at Olivia. "What happened?" she asked.

Picking up the brochure, I flipped through the pages back to the rules.

The man in front of us turned around again. "Medusa was the lead jammer because she made it through the pack first, so she can call off the jam any time by flapping her arms around like that."

Olivia was obviously no less confused.

Daddy Ho'maker came over the loudspeaker. "That is the first four points of the bout, ladies and gentlemen. Music City four, Richmond zero!"

"But she passed them all twice," I pointed out.

The man shook his head. "She doesn't start collecting points till her second pass through. The first pass through the pack of blockers just decides who is the lead jammer." He held up four fingers. "So the score is right."

"Thank you," I said.

He nodded.

A new group of girls skated onto the track. The jammer for Music City this time was much smaller than Medusa.

Daddy Ho'maker's voice boomed. "That is Shamrocker, lucky number seven out there with star panty for the Rollers, opposite number 007, the Grim Creeper for Richmond!"

The whistle blasted and they took off. Shamrocker ducked under the linked arms of two Richmond blockers, then busted through the middle of two more behind them, taking the position of lead jammer. But the Grim Creeper was right on her wheels as they raced around the oval, and just before they reentered the back of the pack, Shamrocker called off the jam.

Olivia threw up a hand. "What happened."

"Defense," I said. "Now the other girl can't score."

Riveter Styx's dad turned and flashed me an impressed smile.

Medusa lined up again with Demoness for the third jam. Immediately after the whistle, #6VI6 blasted through the Music

City blockers with Medusa right behind her. As they rounded the turn, approaching the pack again, Medusa took the inside and cut to the right, slamming her shoulder into her opponent's torso. Demoness went sailing through the air, landing hard on her back. Even from our distance, we could hear her helmet smack the concrete.

My mouth dropped open.

There were collective "Ooos" and "Ohhs" from the crowd.

Medusa made her way through the pack before the slain Vixen had enough wits to end the jam.

Olivia straightened. "Whoa."

My mouth was still gaping as the team formed up again. "I'm beginning to see why she was the MVP."

Olivia smirked. "You think?"

The whistled sounded, whipping our attention back to the track.

Medusa quickly won lead jammer again, this time effortlessly slipping through the pack, knocking skaters out of her way as she went. She made one pass through. Then another!

"That's a grand slam for Medusa!" Daddy Ho'maker shouted.

The crowd was on their feet again.

I held the program up, so I could still see the action on the track in the backfield of my vision. "A Grand Slam is when a jammer passes all four blockers and the jammer from the opposing team!" I shouted over the noise of the crowd. "She collects five points, the maximum points for a single pass!"

My phone in my pocket buzzed. I gripped the program between my teeth and pulled it out. It was a text message.

Fancy meeting you here, Lucille.

My eyes searched the arena like it was the world's largest game of Where's Waldo—if Waldo was a life-sized, wealthy Ken doll hidden on the set of *Beetlejuice.*

I texted him back—and lied, lied, lied. *What are you talking about? You'll never believe where I am right now.*

Because this was the way the dating game was played, right?

Just then, commotion on the track caught everyone's attention. The Vixen's jammer, 6VI6, spun and clotheslined Medusa. There was a series of sharp whistle blasts from the referees accompanied by condemning boos from the crowd.

The pack parted, and Medusa lay at their skates visibly heaving in pain. Medical personnel standing just off the track jogged over, but before they reached her, she pushed herself up.

Everyone cheered.

Then Medusa sprinted on her skates across the track toward the offending Vixen. It took four other skaters to hold her back.

Even in my seat, all the way across the room, I drew back in alarm.

So did Olivia.

And everyone else in the arena.

But the tension quickly settled when the crowd began to clap again. Medusa skated around the oval, stretching her arms and her neck, and successfully ignored 6VI6 as she skated to the penalty box.

"That was insane!" Olivia said in awe. "Look at her shake it off like nothing happened. I'd kill a bitch for less."

I laughed. "I'm sure you would."

There was less violence for the rest of the first half. The bout was so intense, I almost forgot the whole reason we were there. But five minutes into the second half, I saw an arm waving in the stands across the arena.

An arm that belonged to West Adler.

I looked at Olivia. "It's him."

Her mouth gaped. "Huh?"

"West Adler," I said, pointing.

She followed my finger and strained her eyes. "The guy waving, I assume?"

"Yes."

"Are you going to go talk to him?"

I pressed my lips together and shook my head.

"No?"

"No. He can come here. I'm a lady."

She laughed and almost spit out her beer. "We're only here because you're an online creeper. You lost your lady card yesterday."

When I looked again, West was gone. My eyes scanned the crowd till I saw him walking down the stairs to the floor of the arena. He slapped hands with a few people as he walked the perimeter of the room.

I dug my nails into Olivia's arm. "Oh gosh, I think he's on his way over here."

"You need Xanax," she said, draining the last of her beer.

"What do I do?" My voice jumped up an octave.

She laughed. "I would say 'be cool' but that ain't happening."

West walked up to the team bench in front of our bleachers and shook hands with a few of the players. He paused to say something to The Duchess before patting the woman on the back and turning toward the bleacher steps. Our steps. I worried I might lose my hot dog.

He took the steps two at a time until he stopped at the row behind ours and sidestepped his way across the spectators to the empty seats directly behind us. "What are the odds, Lucy?" he asked, sitting down.

"Better than you think," Olivia mumbled beside me.

I elbowed her in the ribs as I turned toward him. "Hey there, West. What are you doing here?"

He motioned to the track. "I come to all the bouts. I love this sport."

"Me too!" I said with a little too much enthusiasm.

He blinked with surprise. "Really?"

"Sure! Well, it's my first time, but so far, I love it."

"How'd you hear about it?" he asked.

My mouth was open, but no words came out. Olivia caught my eye and glared as she turned in her seat, stretching her hand toward West. "It was my idea. I'm Lucy's roommate, Olivia."

He shook her hand. "Nice to meet you, Olivia. West Adler."

"I've heard a lot about you," she said, causing me to die a little inside. "Thanks for taking care of her yesterday."

"It was my pleasure." He looked at me. "How are you feeling?"

"So sore," I said, grimacing.

The corners of his eyes crinkled with sympathy. "I was worried about that. The next day is usually the worst. What did they say about your car?"

My nose wrinkled. "Nothing good. The car is probably totaled. I should find out for sure on Monday."

He put his hand on my shoulder. "That sucks. I'm sorry to hear it. Are you able to get around without it?"

I nodded. "My insurance company got me a rental car. How's your bumper?"

"Replaceable." He glanced at the empty plastic cup in Olivia's hand. "I'm going to get another drink. Can I buy you ladies a round?"

"Thank you," she said.

"What are you drinking?" he asked.

"Three Leprechauns Red Ale."

"Diet Coke," I answered.

He winked as he stood. "Coming right up."

When he was gone, Olivia nodded her head. "I admire a man who buys the booze. He's a keeper."

"He's cute, too, huh?"

"Yeah, he's cute. Is he single?"

I shrugged. "He doesn't wear a wedding band, and I found him on a list of most eligible bachelors, so I hope so."

Just then, one of Nashville's blockers cut sideways toward Richmond's jammer, 6VI6. The same skater who'd leveled Medusa. With a loud grunt that echoed around the room, the blocker plowed into 6VI6's rib cage with her shoulder. The jammer lost control and careened into the crowd sitting on the floor at about a thousand miles per hour.

Whistles blew, the horn from the scoreboard blasted, and emergency workers ran across the gym. I realized I was on my feet with the rest of the crowd and didn't even remember standing.

"And that's why we call them the suicide seats, folks! They're not for the faint of heart!" Daddy Ho'maker said into the microphone.

The jammer stood back up on her skates, aided by the fans she'd just mowed down. When she turned in our direction, I saw blood pouring from her nose into her mouth. She pulled her jersey over her head and pressed it to her face before slapping high fives with the fans around her legs. Everyone cheered, including Medusa and the rest of Nashville's players, as she skated back to her team's bench in her sports bra.

I exhaled, gripping my chest. "Thank God no one was hurt."

Olivia held her fists up. "That was awesome. I want more blood!"

I laughed and smacked her on the back of the head. Out on the track, 6VI6 was escorted back to the locker room by two men in khakis and polo shirts.

West returned a few minutes later balancing three drinks between his two hands. He sidled his way across the row again and reclaimed his seat at our backs. "Three Leprechauns," he said, handing a beer to Olivia.

She held it up like a toast. "Thanks."

"And a Diet Coke," he said, passing me the only cup with a lid and straw.

"Thank you, West."

He leaned toward me. "Now you owe me a bumper, a ride, *and* a drink, Lucille."

I silently cursed myself for not having a witty comeback.

He gestured toward my cup. "You know, if you're going to hang out on the derby scene, you're going to have to learn how to drink."

"I'm trying to be kind to my liver since I'm taking a lot of pain meds. And I've got to drive home later," I said.

He cringed. "Is you driving sober supposed to make us feel safer?"

My mouth dropped open. Olivia burst out laughing and showered the row in front of us with a light spray of beer from her lips. Thankfully, no one noticed. She slapped my knee. "Oh, I like him."

I turned my eyes back to the track, shaking my head, trying not to laugh.

He nudged my shoulder with his leg. "I'm only teasing."

"You're not funny," I said with forced indignation.

He held up his index finger and thumb with a millimeter of space between them. "I'm a little funny."

I laughed and sipped my drink.

"Power jam!" Daddy Ho'maker yelled over the speakers.

The whole crowd cheered.

Out on the track, Medusa was flying past every member of her team and Richmond's. Two of Richmond's players were in the penalty box, including their jammer who'd replaced 6VI6 in the game. After a fourth pass, everyone was on their feet, including us, and West was cheering loud over our heads. She passed everyone again.

"That's twenty-five!" West yelled.

She passed again.

"Thirty! She's going to run out of time," someone said.

"Run out of time for what?" I asked.

The man in front of us looked back at me. "To break the world record."

"Thirty-five!"

Medusa's knees were bent as she stepped, right skate over left, pushing her legs out hard around the corners. The Nashville blockers kept Richmond's blockers out of her way as she sailed past them again. The crowd began counting down.

"Ten! Nine! Eight! Seven! Six! Five! Four!"

"That's forty-five!" West shouted.

"Three! Two! One!"

EARRRRRRNGGGGG! The buzzer and the crowd were so loud I covered my ears. West made up half the decibels all by himself.

Out on the track, Medusa's entire upper body was heaving with heavy breaths as she slowed and her team ran on their skates out from the bench to catch her in their arms.

Someone turned up the volume on Daddy Ho'maker's mic so he could be heard over the fans. "Forty-five points in that power jam, and our captain reminds us all why she wears that star! Give it up for Medusa!"

Even the Richmond team was standing and clapping as Medusa skated a wide circle around the track, waving to everyone. She slid to a stop near the home team's bench, and the coach walked over and hugged her. Someone handed her a bottle of water.

"That was intense," Olivia said as we sat back down.

"What's the world record?" I asked.

"Fifty points," the man in front of us said.

West leaned down. "Medusa held the record at forty-five points for two years, but she lost it to a skater in Colorado who got fifty. The fifty-point jam even made it into the *Guinness Book of World Records.*"

"Ouch," I said.

"And to make matters worse," Styx's dad added, "they've changed the rules since then."

West nodded. "A power jam is when the opposing jammer is in the penalty box. It used to be that penalties lasted a full minute. Now they're only thirty seconds."

"So it's even harder to collect that many points," I said.

"Impossible, if you ask me," the old man said.

West laughed. "Tell that to Medusa."

Styx's dad pointed at West. "She's the only one who's come close. I gotta give her that." He looked at me and Olivia. "Only a handful of skaters in the whole world can break forty."

Olivia sipped her beer. "The whole world? I had no idea this was that big of a sport."

"They're talking about adding it to the Olympics," West said.

"Really?" I asked, watching Medusa, who was shouting at her players from the bench.

"Yep." He pointed to the track. "And when it does, Nashville will have a local on the team."

Just then, the buzzer blared through the arena again. The bout was over.

Music City had won.

———

I'd hoped West would invite us out for drinks or a late-night dinner after the bout. He didn't. He did, however, give me a hug that lasted a total of two Mississippis, and he promised we'd talk more soon. I swear I felt the literal tear of my heart from my chest as he walked away.

Olivia looped her arm through mine as we followed the

crowd into the hall. "That was more fun than I thought it would be. Thanks for bringing me," she said, leaning with the weight of three beers on my arm.

It hurt to be her crutch, but I patted her hand. "Thanks for coming with me. I haven't had that much fun in a really long time." And it was true, right up until the end.

She looked at me sideways, then reached over and stuck her finger in the dimple on my cheek, pushing it up. "No frowning. No being sad."

I hadn't even realized I was sulking. I wrinkled my nose. "I'm just a little disappointed."

"Because he didn't ask you out?" she asked.

"Yeah."

She sighed. "Give it time. It's clear he likes you."

"You think so?" I asked, my face brightening with a slight smile.

She turned her palm up. "Did you see how much beer he bought me?"

"Maybe he likes you instead."

"Not a chance."

In the hall, a girl shouting to my right caught my attention. I looked over as she thrust a flyer in my face. "Fresh Meat, Derby 101! Newbies welcome! Next Saturday at the Rollers' Sweatshop!"

I grabbed the slip of paper as the crowd pushed us through the door to the lobby. On the front was a cartoon logo with a raw T-bone steak and a meat cleaver. The title said, NOW RECRUITING FRESH MEAT. I read the page as we walked.

Tired of watching life from the sidelines? Want to see what you're made of? The Music City Rollers WANT YOU! Join us for the next informational meeting and orientation to learn more about the final Fresh Meat session of the season.

When? Saturday, August 29. 10 a.m.

Where? The Rollers' Sweatshop, the official practice space of Rollers. 19954 Nolensville Pike, Nashville.

No experience needed.

My first thought was "this is a bad idea," and I should have thrown the flyer in the trash on our way out the door.

I didn't.

THREE

I DROVE Olivia and myself home to the apartment we shared in a small sliver of South Nashville that was sandwiched between the suburb of Antioch and the city of Brentwood. The locals called our little piece of the map "Brentioch," the metaphorical tracks that separated the white collars from the blue.

"Do you have to work tomorrow?" I asked Olivia as I pulled into a parking space.

She nodded. "Lunch to close."

We got out, and I clicked the lock button on the key fob. "At least you don't have to open."

She rubbed her head. "It's a good thing. I may be hurting in the morning."

"Lightweight," I teased as we started up the steps to the second floor.

"You're one to talk."

When we neared our apartment, I stopped when I saw a pair of legs wearing jeans and men's Adidas sneakers poking out from behind the wall that formed an alcove around our door. I stuck my arm out in front of Olivia to stop her. She blinked and looked down at the legs.

"Who is that?" she whispered.

With wide eyes, I shrugged my shoulders. I inched past her and tiptoed through the breezeway. When I got close enough to see around the corner, I immediately recognized the messy mop of brown hair that was reclined against our door. I exhaled.

"It's my brother." I kicked his shoe. "Ethan, wake up."

Ethan jolted from his sleep, looking up with alarm. "Hey, Lucy. Thank God you're finally home."

I looked at my watch. It was after ten. "What are you doing here?"

"Came down to see a chick I met online."

"I'm guessing it didn't go well," Olivia said.

He shook his head. "She 'forgot' to tell me she was on house arrest." He used air quotes for effect.

I pinched the bridge of my nose. "What?"

"Can I crash on your couch tonight?" he asked through a yawn. "I don't want to drive back to Riverbend this late."

"Why didn't you call me?" I reached over him to put my key in the lock.

"Something's wrong with my phone again," he said, rolling to his knees to get up.

I stepped over him. "Did you pay the bill?"

He groaned. "You sound just like Dad and the phone company."

I flipped on the light, and they followed me into the apartment. I hung my keys on the hook by the door and carried my purse to my bedroom. Ethan flopped down on the sectional sofa with a groan.

"I'm going to bed, Lucy," Olivia called as I took off my shoes.

I put my sandals in the closet and walked back to the living room, catching Olivia at her door. "Thanks again for going with me tonight."

She winked at me. "Anytime."

When she was gone, I looked at my kid brother. Ethan was wearing a wrinkled chocolate-brown polo shirt tucked in (only in the front), a decent pair of dark jeans, and (shockingly) a belt. His face was soft and sleepy as he nestled into the corner of the sofa.

I wondered if his motives for showing up on my doorstep were completely centered around his failed date, or if he'd gotten lonely at our parents' house. His light brown eyes sparkled just like Mom's when he smiled up at me.

The magic vanished in an instant as he put his sneakers up on my coffee table. I swatted his legs. "Have some manners, Ethan." Wincing with pain, I sat down beside him.

His feet landed with a heavy thud on the floor, and he slouched against the back, folding his hands on his flat stomach. "Why are you moving like an old lady?"

"I was in a car wreck yesterday. I'm pretty stiff and sore."

"What the hell, Lucy? Why didn't you call me?"

I laughed. "Maybe I did. You don't have a phone."

"Did you call me?"

"No, of course not."

He frowned. "Why? I'm your brother."

"What would you have done? Besides, I wasn't hurt. I had the situation under control." I reached over and patted his head. "I do appreciate your concern."

"Where've you been all night? You never go out."

"That's not true," I said.

He lifted a doubtful eyebrow.

I ignored him. "Did you know Nashville has a roller derby team?"

"What's roller derby?"

My eyes narrowed. "Are you sure you went to college?"

"Pretty sure," he said, slipping off his shoes. "But those days were kinda fuzzy."

I leaned against his shoulder. "I feel like these days are kinda fuzzy too. Are you OK?"

He looked at me seriously. "I'm fine. I promise."

I studied his face for a moment before finally nodding. "Well, you're twenty-three. Not a frat boy anymore. Someday you're going to have to start acting like a grown-up."

He grinned and touched his finger to the tip of my nose. "Tomorrow. I'm going to start tomorrow. What's roller derby?"

"It's a women's sport—"

He cocked an eyebrow. "So it's boring."

"Quite the opposite, actually. Full-contact, on roller skates."

His head snapped back. "Really?"

"Yeah. A girl broke her nose tonight when she mowed down a group of fans by the track."

"Whoa!"

"I know. It was a lot of fun. You should go sometime. Maybe once your new girlfriend gets off parole."

He groaned and flopped against the back of the sofa again.

"Tell me about her."

He rolled his head to face me. "Her name's Daphne. She's twenty-two and studied nursing at MTSU. Beautiful girl. Blond hair, blue eyes, and..." His eyes bulged as he cupped two ginormous imaginary breasts in front of his chest.

I crossed my arms. "I can see where this story started to go wrong."

"We've been talking for a few weeks—"

"On the computer, because you don't pay your phone bill."

He nodded. "I told her I'd drive down this weekend if she wanted to hang out. She wanted to meet at her house in Murfreesboro. I assumed we would go somewhere."

"And you were wrong?"

He grimaced. "So very wrong." He covered his face with both hands. "She had an ankle bracelet and everything."

I dropped my head to stifle my giggles. "What did she do?"

"Too many DUIs or something, I think. I honestly didn't hang around long enough to find out."

I slapped his leg. "Good for you. See? You can make good decisions occasionally."

He groaned.

I got up and walked to the kitchen. "Are you hungry? Did you eat dinner?"

"I'm good. I got a burger from a drive-through on the way here." I returned with two bottles of water and handed one to him. "Thanks," he said as he unscrewed the lid.

"And what have we learned from all this?" I asked, tucking my leg underneath me as I sat back down.

He paused with the bottle halfway to his lips. "I have shitty taste in women?"

"Besides that."

"I need to stop meeting chicks on the internet?" he asked.

"It wouldn't hurt. You're a cute guy. You *could* meet girls in person—outside the house to ensure they're not on lockdown, but that's not what I was going to say either."

He shrugged. "I give up."

I pushed his shoulder, and he dribbled water down his chin. "Stop making decisions with Ethan Jr., and try getting to know someone before you drive two hours to pop up on their doorstep."

"His name is not Ethan Jr." He pointed to his crotch. "We call him the Kraken."

My face melted into a disgusted frown, and I covered my ears. "Eww."

He laughed. "That way, I can drop my pants and say, 'Release the Kraken!' Chicks dig that shit."

I furiously shook my head. "No, they don't."

He lifted his fist into the air and used a dramatic tone. "He rises from the depths!"

"Ethan, stop talking about your penis!"

Still chuckling, he dropped his hand. "You brought it up."

"And I'm sorry about that." I put the water bottle to my cheek to cool my hot and embarrassed face. "Different subject. Have you talked to Dad?"

He looked at me. "About the Kraken?"

I smacked him with a throw pillow.

"No. I haven't talked to Dad. When are they coming home?" he asked.

"You live there. You don't know?"

He pointed at his own face. "Do I look like a guy who knows things?"

I settled back against the couch. "They're supposed to be home next weekend."

"That's so long," he whined.

"It's two weeks. Stop being dramatic."

"I might starve by then, Lucy."

I laughed.

"He's going to want to see you when he gets back. Are you coming home?"

I hugged the throw pillow. "I think I used up all my fake smiles at the wedding. It's going to be a while before I can force another one onto my face."

He leaned his elbow on the armrest and cradled his head in his hand to look at me. "Is it just how soon it happened, or do you really hate her?"

I considered the question. "I don't hate her. I don't even know her. That's the problem. She's like the stranger in the white van who lured Dad away with casseroles."

Ethan chuckled. "She's nothing like Mom."

No truer words had ever been spoken. Katherine was, in a

word, *domestic*. Our mother had been anything but. Dad had plucked Mom right off the beach in Virginia, where he'd found her dancing in a bikini to The Beach Boys. "It was love at first sight," he liked to tell us before she died. "I saw her and I just knew—someday she'd be mine."

Someday turned out to be *that* day, and a few weeks later, Mom found out she was pregnant with me. They got married in a courthouse ceremony without even telling her parents. Dad had worn his Navy uniform. Mom hadn't worn any shoes.

It was hard to believe she'd been gone almost a year. And harder to believe how much everything had changed.

"He still refuses to talk about her." Ethan's voice snapped me back to our conversation.

All Dad's stories had stopped when Mom died, and since he'd married Katherine, Dad dared not even bring Mom up in conversation. At all. Ever.

Logically, I knew it was too painful for him, and probably by focusing on the future rather than the past, he could more easily put one foot in front of the other each day. But man, it was hard for me and, obviously, Ethan to just pretend she never existed when Dad was around. Thank God we had each other.

"You can't put him off forever."

I sighed. "I know. I *am* trying."

He grimaced. "You kinda suck at it, Lucy."

I sank into my corner. "I know. That's why I'm staying away."

"Well, hurry up and get over it, OK?" He reached over and nudged my shoulder. "I kinda miss you."

"I miss you too, Butter."

He made a vomiting noise. "I hate it when you call me that."

I grabbed his sleeve and pulled him to me, cradling his head in my arms and kissing the top of his head over and over. "No, you don't, Baby Butter. You love it. You do!"

Laughing, he pushed me off him. "You're so weird."

I stood and brushed my hair out of my face. "You share my DNA, you know."

"Oh, I know."

I jerked my thumb toward my room. "I'll get your stuff."

"Need help?" he asked.

"No."

In my closet, on the bottom right of the nine-cube organizer shelf, was a fabric storage bin with Ethan's name stitched on the front. I retrieved it, then grabbed an extra sheet, blanket, and pillow off the shelf above my shoe rack. I carried the stack back to the living room.

Ethan jumped up to help me with the load. I handed him the box. "There are pajamas in there and a toothbrush. You go change in my bathroom, and I'll make up the couch for you."

He looked in the box. "You bought me pajamas?"

"I've only lived here a few weeks, and this is the third time you've shown up unannounced to sleep on my couch. And don't forget the toothbrush. I can't handle your morning breath at breakfast."

He tucked the box under his arm and kissed my cheek. "Best sister ever."

When Ethan was settled on the sectional, I returned to my room to get ready for bed. I stopped first at my purse to find my phone and plug it into its charger. I checked the screen for any notifications. Perhaps a missed message from West.

There wasn't one.

———

In the morning, Ethan showered in my bathroom while I made pancakes for breakfast. Olivia was still asleep. My phone buzzed on the counter, and I grabbed it immediately.

West: *Did you make it home OK?*

My stomach tingled. I tapped out a response. *Safe and sound. You?*

West: *Nope. Texting you from "the other side." Heaven's 4G sucks.*

I sat down at the table, smiling so wide I feared he might sense it through the phone. *Heaven, huh? Now I know you're lying.*

West: *LOL. Did you have fun last night?*

Me: *I had a great time. Thanks again for the drinks.*

West: *Don't mention it. Let me know what you hear about your car this week.*

Me: *I will.*

Ethan walked out of my room, rubbing his head with a towel in one hand and reading a piece of paper he was holding in the other. I got up to flip the pancakes on the griddle pan.

My phone buzzed again as I crossed the kitchen. *How about we run into each other on purpose sometime soon? Have lunch, maybe?*

A quiet squeal slipped out before I could stop it. I bit my lower lip and leaned against the counter.

Ethan sat down behind me. "You OK?"

"I'm fine," I said, suppressing the urge to stamp my feet with joy.

I re-read West's message a few times before working up the nerve to reply. "Be cool, Lucy."

Me: *Lunch would be great. Let me know when.*

West: *I'm working downtown a few days this week. Once I know what my schedule will be, I'll text you.*

Me: *Awesome. Can't wait.*

I groaned, wishing I hadn't typed "*Awesome.*"

"Sis?"

When I looked up from my phone, I smelled the smoke rising off the griddle before I saw it. "Crap!" I grabbed the spatula and flipped the pancakes. They were charred. With a heavy sigh, I turned the pan over above the trashcan, letting our blackened breakfast slide into the garbage.

I turned to look at my brother. "Sorry."

He smiled and draped the towel around his neck. "Distracted this morning?"

"A little." I noticed the roller derby flyer on the table in front of him. "Ethan! What were you doing in my purse?"

He squished his mouth over to one side. "Looking for gas money."

I snatched the flyer off the table.

"I didn't take anything," he said, holding his hands up in defense.

"Because there wasn't any money in there to take," I said.

"Are you seriously thinking about playing roller derby?" he asked, pointing to the flyer in my hand.

I looked down at it. "I don't know. Maybe." I put it on the counter and retrieved the box of pancake mix from the pantry.

"You're the most accident-prone person I know." He got up and pulled a banana off the bunch from the fruit basket on the counter. "Now you want to play a full-contact sport on roller skates?"

I put my hands on my hips. "I'm not accident prone."

He peeled his banana. "You knocked out your two front teeth playing musical chairs in the first grade."

I frowned as I measured out another cup of the dry mix and dumped it in the glass bowl. "That game is dangerous. Erin Tucker dove headfirst into me. Not my fault." I mixed in three-quarters of a cup of water and stirred.

"In high school, you dislocated your arm trying to tighten your bra strap."

Fighting a smile, I poured four evenly spaced puddles of batter onto the hot griddle. "That was a long time ago."

"Last Christmas Eve at Uncle Matt's house, you broke two ribs coughing."

"I was choking!"

He pointed at me. "On your own spit!"

We both burst out laughing.

He picked up the flyer again and dangled it in front of my face. "This may be the dumbest idea you've ever had."

I flipped the pancakes over. They were golden brown. "I didn't say it was a sure thing. I'm just thinking about it."

"Well, don't think about it too seriously. I kinda need you around," he said, taking another huge bite of his banana.

I glared at him. "You kinda need my money and my couch."

He grinned. "You love me."

I scooped up the four perfect pancakes and dropped them on a plate for him. "You'd better be glad."

Ethan drove back home to Riverbend, but not before I filled up his gas tank at the station down the street, bought him lunch from McDonald's to eat on the drive, and gave him a wad of cash to have his phone reconnected. Little brothers: do they ever stop being exhausting?

Olivia was in the kitchen pouring a to-go cup of coffee when I walked back in. There were dark circles under her half-mast eyes and the bun on her head was a smidge lopsided.

I grimaced. "I'm afraid it's going to be a long day."

She yawned as she screwed the plastic lid on her mug. "I'll perk up when I get there. We're trying out a new appetizer today."

"Oh god. What's it called?"

"It's a cheddar fondue." She grinned behind her cup. "It's called That's What Cheese Said."

I burst out laughing. "That's terrible."

"I know. It's gonna be great." She slurped some coffee. "What are you going to do today?"

Probably sit at home and stare at my phone while I wait to hear from West Adler. I didn't say that out loud, of course. No need to draw attention to the depths of my patheticness and incite the taunts of my roommate. "Probably just stay home and watch TV. You know, Netflix and Chill."

Her eyes narrowed. "You know that means to go to someone's house for a booty call, right?"

"What?"

She laughed and rolled her eyes. "Oh, Lucy."

"I've said that to my dad." I gasped and covered my mouth with my hand. "I've posted that on Facebook."

She doubled over, nearly spilling her coffee. "Shit, that's funny."

I slumped against the counter, burying my red face in my hands.

She nudged my arm as she walked past. "As much as I'd love to stay here and give you hell about this, I've got to go to work. I'll see you tonight."

Still whimpering, I waved. "Bye."

"Don't wait up!" she called, walking out our front door.

When she was gone, and I'd somewhat recovered from my humiliation, I retired to the living room with my laptop and spent a ridiculous portion of the rest of the day researching roller derby online...and, yes, checking and rechecking my phone for lunch plans from West.

Roller derby was, surprisingly, a worldwide sport with thousands of teams in more than fifty countries. Some sites estimated that over a hundred thousand female skaters played across the globe, as well as a growing number of men in men's roller derby.

I wonder if West owns roller skates.

I checked my phone again.

Nothing.

I tossed it across the couch.

Apparently, junior roller derby was also a thing, allowing kids as young as six to lace up and play. It made me feel better about the prospect of surviving should I attempt to give it a whirl. Because if a six-year-old could do it, surely I could too. Right?

I typed the words "roller derby injuries" into the search bar of my internet browser, then clicked on "See All Images."

Oh. My. God.

The first image in the grid was of a woman's black-and-purple foot bent right at a forty-five-degree angle with her ankle bone protruding like a second misplaced heel.

Another image looked normal at first glance; then I realized the woman's skate was twisted around backward like a demon-possessed limb.

Farther down the page, a woman's collarbone was jutting through her blood-soaked shirt. Through her shirt!

With a shudder, I slammed my laptop screen closed.

Thankfully, my phone chirped just in time with a text message, and my stomach flip-flopped from nauseous to nervous with the beep. I moved the laptop to the floor and dove across the couch to snatch the phone off the far cushion.

It was Ethan.

Back n Riverbend. Stopped @ store 2 pay my bill. Phones back on. IOU $62. Thx.

FOUR

BY MONDAY MORNING, I still hadn't heard back from West about lunch, so I packed a turkey and cheese on honey wheat into my insulated lunch bag and went to work early, as usual. Thankfully, there was no yelling in the conference room that day, and I was able to slip quietly into my office and get right to work.

I started by printing the weekly online-activity report I'd created for our accounts. It displayed all the week prior's email and social-media statistics, showcasing what elements were working and which ones needed improvement. I also highlighted two different photos I'd taken screenshots of on the Music City Rollers' fan page over the weekend. Both were of Medusa. One was a professional picture from a photoshoot; the other was a selfie of a black puppy licking her face.

The professional picture with appropriate lighting and airbrushing had 113 likes.

The selfie with all her tattoos and puppy slobber? 1,872.

I printed both on the same page and wrote in the margin. *"Casual is better. Can we get a line item in the budget for puppies?"* I decorated the question with a sloppy doodle of a paw print.

Then I opened my inbox to find an email from Peter Jansen, Audrey's assistant.

Lucy,

>*Audrey received the file with the photos for Jake's new ad campaigns. She doesn't understand why we're paying a graphic designer to recreate the same photo four different ways. If you're asking for her to choose one, she says—and I quote: "Tell her to use the photo with the blue truck and move on to more pressing projects."*
>
>*Please advise.*
>
>*P.B.J.*

Peter, literally, signed all of his communications with "P.B.J." and I still didn't know him well enough to know whether or not he realized it was funny. Passing in the halls and across the table at staff meetings, Peter didn't seem to have much of a sense of humor, but who could, working directly with Audrey every day? Poor peanut-butter-and-jelly guy.

I typed out an explanation, not that I should've had to. It *was* my specialty, after all. One of the main reasons she hired me.

Peter,

>*Please tell Audrey I will be using all four graphics for the new social-media campaigns. I realize they are all very similar. It's called "split testing." Each image will be tested against the others to see which one delivers the best results: i.e. the most ticket sales. Promoting Jake's new tour still is the most pressing project, correct?*
>
>*Please advise.*
>
>*L.L.C.*

Yes, my initials are ridiculous as well, therefore throwing stones was allowed.

Peter's one-line response came quickly.

Will deliver the explanation. My money is on #3, the Atomic Turquoise truck, for the win. - P.B.J.

I smiled. Perhaps P.B.J. had a hidden sense of humor after all. I wrote back.

Glad you like them, but 'Atomic Turquoise' is not a color. #3 is RGB (0, 170, 204) - L.L.C.

A moment later, I clicked open another email from him.

Manic Panic says it's a color. I dyed my hair Atomic Turquoise once in high school. - P.B.J.

In the stillness of my office, I burst out laughing. It was hard to picture Peter with blue hair—or *any* hair, for that matter. He was bald and shiny up top now, a style forced upon him, as evidenced by the shadowy stubble that encircled the crown of his head on casual Fridays.

Another email popped into my inbox.

Our doors are open. I can hear you laughing. - P.B.J.

I hit reply, and my fingers flew across the keyboard.

I'm sorry. I'm not laughing at you. I'm laughing WITH you. Unless you're not laughing. In such case, I'm watching funny cat videos online. - Lucy

If you're watching funny cat videos, I'm telling Audrey. Just
kidding. Gotta get back to work before heads—namely, mine—
start rolling - P.B.J.

I laughed again, quieter this time. Apparently, Audrey hadn't
sucked all the life out of the office after all.

The four new ads were completed by lunchtime, and I ate my
sad little sandwich all alone in my office. Not completely
deterred by the injuries I'd seen the day before, while I ate, I read
an article I'd bookmarked called "22 Things Every Roller Derby
Fresh Meat Newbie Should Know." Number seven on the list
was "Don't Date Your Teammates." I was wondering if the advice
would apply to sponsors as well when my cell phone rang. The
call was from an unknown number.

Surely, it had to be West calling from his office or something
to make those lunch plans he'd mentioned over the weekend.

"Hello?" I answered, my voice a little too bright and cheerful.

"May I speak with Lucy Cooper?" the man—who was definitely *not* West Adler—asked.

"This is Lucy Cooper."

"Hi, Miss Cooper. My name is Ward Taylor. I'm your auto-
damage adjuster from Fieldsouth Insurance."

I slumped in my chair. "Oh, hi."

"I just finished estimating the damage on your 2009 GKS
Sport."

Putting down my sandwich, I leaned forward with my elbows
on the desk, cradling my forehead in my hand as I braced for the
news. "How bad is it?"

"It's a total loss, I'm afraid," he said.

My heart sank.

"I do have a check for you in the amount of $6,013. You can
either meet me here at the shop, or I can mail it to you."

I looked at the clock. It was just after noon. "How long will you be at the shop?"

"I'll be around this area until about two today," he said.

"Can we meet there in about half an hour?"

"That's perfect. I'll see you soon."

After hanging up the phone, I rested my head against the back of my chair. It had been so nice not having a car payment, for the two months that I didn't, anyway. I sighed, not looking forward to buying a new car by myself. Dad had always gone with me before, and now he was jaunting around Costa Rica with Katherine. Ugh. Waiting till he got back wasn't an option, either.

No longer hungry, I dropped the rest of my sandwich in the trash can under my desk. I set my office phone to "Gone to Lunch" and hit the sleep button on my computer monitor. On my way down the hall, I paused at Audrey's door to drop off the weekly online report.

Across the hall, Peter's door was still open. He caught my eye and mouthed something, but I was so distracted by the thought of him with blue hair, my brain processed it a second too slowly.

"Lily?"

Crap.

Peter had been trying to tell me to "run."

Audrey was behind her massive mahogany desk, holding the phone to her ear with her shoulder. As I put the papers in the pocket on her door, she motioned me forward.

I quietly shuffled across the room, her personal shrine to the company's role in shaping the landscape of country music. The two walls not made of solid glass were plastered with matching vinyl appliqués of the Record Road logo in an eighteen-inch font. Surrounding them were expensively framed album covers, record-sales awards, and autographed photos of country stars.

It was impressive. And gaudy. Nashville, to the core.

"I'll have to call you back later," she said into the phone and hung up without giving whoever was on the other end of the line a moment to protest. She looked up at me and took off her black-rimmed reading glasses. "Good afternoon, Lily."

I gritted my teeth and handed her the papers. "Here are the click-through reports on Jake's new ad campaign."

"Thank you. Please have a seat." She motioned to the chairs in front of her desk.

I looked at the clock on my phone. "I'm sorry, Audrey, but can it wait? I'm on my way to—"

Her glare cut me off, and I obediently sank into a chair.

"Thank you. I'll be brief."

I doubted it.

"I want this." She turned her monitor on its swivel around to face me. Dwayne "The Rock" Johnson stared back at me from a video window.

My lips pressed together, and I scratched my head. I thought about asking her, "You want what The Rock is cooking?" but I thought better of it.

"It's a live video stream from a movie premier's red carpet. Jana Carter did a brilliant live Q and A with her fans last week, and it's had over a half a million views. I want to use live video as part of Jake's launch strategy next month."

I blinked. "You want to do a live video instead of a pre-recorded one?" Visions of wardrobe malfunctions danced through my head.

"Yes. I think he should broadcast live from his launch party the Saturday after the album comes out. You know, make all the fans feel like they can be part of it."

I swallowed hard, forcing away images of my career going up in digital flames. There was a reason television networks added a delay on all live video. We wouldn't have that.

She sat back in her seat. "Can you work out the details? Make sure he has access, figure out how to use it, come up with a plan to advertise, et cetera?"

I nodded and forced a smile through my terror. "I'll do my best. When is the launch party?"

"Saturday, October eighth. You'll need to be there."

Had I not been sitting down, I would've fallen on the floor. "Me? You want me to come to Jake Barrett's launch party?"

"Of course I do. You're our online marketing manager. This will be your responsibility."

I swallowed hard, and with shaky hands, I pulled up the calendar on my phone to add the date. "Sure. I'll be there. Where is it?"

"At Jake's house."

I took a deep breath as I used my thumbs to enter the information into my phone.

"I'll have Peter send you the address and the time."

My pulse beat through my skull. "Sounds good," I forced out. "I'll get to work on it this afternoon."

"Fantastic." She shooed me away with her hand. "You can go now."

"Thank you, Audrey."

As I got up, she reached for her phone. "Close my door on your way out, please."

When I was out in the hallway, I closed her door, then leaned against it for support in case my legs gave out. *Breathe, Lucy. It's just a party. At Jake Barrett's house. Jake Barrett, number sixteen on People Magazine's current list of Most Beautiful People. No biggie.*

I fanned my face. Thankfully, Peter's office door was now closed, so no one witnessed my fangirlish meltdown. I couldn't wait to tell Olivia. I called her on my walk out of the building but got her voicemail, so I left a message. "Call me the second you get this. I have huge news to tell you. Bye."

The phone rang through the car's speaker system as I pulled out of the parking garage and onto Third Avenue. I clicked the answer button on the steering wheel without taking my eyes off the road. "You are not going to believe this!" I said by way of a greeting.

"Try me." It was West Adler's voice, not my roommate's.

I slammed on my brakes. Thankfully, no one was behind me. "Oh...hi, West."

He laughed. "Expecting someone else?"

"I thought you were Olivia. I just called her."

"Oh, well, just because I'm not her doesn't mean you can deprive me of my not believing," he said. "What are you so excited about?"

My cheeks were hot with embarrassment. I laughed and turned the air-conditioning vent toward my face. "My boss just invited me to a big party at the home of one of our artists."

"Really? Anyone I know?"

"Jake Barrett."

"Sweet! Can you bring a guest?"

I swerved a little getting on the ramp to the interstate and caught the edge of the curb with my right front tire. "Uh..."

"No pressure," he said with a laugh. "But if you need a plus-one, I'd be happy to help you out."

"You have to get past lunch first," I said, proud of my quick wit.

"Touché." He was quiet for a beat. "I was actually calling about lunch."

I smiled.

"I'm going to have to take a raincheck this week, if that's OK."

I frowned.

"I've had some stuff come up, and I won't be able to make it happen."

My wit failed me. "Yeah. OK."

He was quiet for a beat. "I hope you'll take me up on it again soon."

"Maybe if you ask nicely."

He laughed on the other end of the line. "Oh, I talked to my buddy at the shop earlier. He said your car's a goner."

I sighed. "Yep. Such is my luck."

"Well, if you're in the market for another car, try out CarMart in Cool Springs. Tell them you know me and they'll hook you up with a good deal. We just finished their remodel job a few weeks ago."

I took the Brentwood exit off the interstate. "Are you serious?"

"Girl, I know everyone in this town."

"You don't know Jake Barrett."

"Not yet," he said with a laugh. "Let me know how it goes."

"I will. Thank you."

I reached for the "End Call" button on the console.

"Hey, Lucy?"

My hand froze in the air. "Yeah?"

"I really am sorry about lunch. I'll make it up to you, I promise."

———

By the end of the next day, I had a new-to-me, year-old, bright blue SUV. Thankfully, the car payment was manageable, courtesy of a bit of name-dropping to my new friends at CarMart Motors. I hadn't heard another peep from West Adler, not even when I texted him a picture of my new ride.

So much for making it up to me.

Crushing on someone is exhausting work, and after three days of feverishly checking my phone, only to be devastated over and over again, I decided to lay down my torch and put West

Adler out of my mind. It was easier in thought than in practice, but I had a lot to keep me busy.

All day Wednesday was spent watching every live video I could find in our industry and cataloging them by their number of views, likes, and comments. Then I studied them to figure out why some had more traffic than others. What I found was surprising.

The videos with the poorest quality by industry standards performed the best. Jana Carter's Q and A session had been filmed on a cell-phone camera at the star's kitchen table. She was wearing polka-dot pajamas and slurping coffee from a mug that said "World's Okayest Singer" in big, black letters. She posted a link in the comments section to buy the mug online, but the store was sold out and was showing it had 412 backorders. There was a disclaimer in the description: *Thank you, Jana Carter, for loving our mugs. We are fulfilling orders as quickly as possible. We appreciate your patience.*

By Friday, I had completely rewritten Jake's release marketing plan to include live-streaming video, and I was a little excited about it. I was also equally terrified, so I drafted a list of every possible thing that might go wrong and how to head each thing off. Like, record early in the party before everyone's had too much to drink and have only Jake on camera to limit the number of possible liabilities.

I also needed to practice my video skills. So on Friday afternoon, when most of the office had cleared out of the building, I decided to post my first live video to the internet.

I propped the phone up against my laptop monitor and clicked on the live-streaming app that would post to all my social-media accounts. My face on the screen was shrouded in shadows thanks to the wall of windows behind me, so I moved around the other side of my desk to face the light. Better, except the phone was too low, causing a ridiculous case of double(or triple)-chin. I scribbled a note on my sticky pad: *Get a tripod.*

I held the phone up in the air and clicked the "Broadcast Live!" button with my thumb.

I cheerfully waved at myself on the screen. "Hey, everybody! It's Lucy. I hope you don't mind, but I'm using you all as guinea pigs to test out this live video feature for my new job here in Nashville. So let me know in the comments if you can see and hear me all right!"

A couple of stars exploded in the corner of the screen, signaling someone had starred my video. There was an eyeball icon in the corner of the screen showing one...no, two viewers!

"I guess I could give you all a tour of my new office," I said, standing up slowly and balancing the phone carefully in my hand. "I've got a gorgeous corner office at the Summit Tower, and this spectacular view of downtown Nashville!"

It took a second for me to figure out how to flip the camera's view around. While panning the room, someone left a comment that scrolled across my screen.

Hi, Lucy! - Elly Cooper

Elly was my cousin on my dad's side of the family.

"Hey, Elly!" I said, turning the camera back around.

Six viewers. Another comment scrolled by.

Looking good, Lucy. - Matt Owen

Matt was my mother's brother.

I turned the camera back around to face me. "Hi, Uncle Matt!"

Eleven viewers. Another yellow star dinged in the corner.

We love you, Lulabean. It's your old man here in the islands. I'm using Katherine's account. This is neat. - Katherine Woodville Cooper

A bowling ball landed in my stomach. "Love you too, Dad," I said, struggling to keep my voice chipper as I waved at the screen. "I have to get back to work! Thanks for watching my video!"

I clicked the "End Video" button so hard my phone almost slipped from my grip. Another button flashed on the screen. *Do you want to post your video?* Nope. It really wasn't necessary.

I sighed and put the phone down.

"Katherine Woodville Cooper," I said aloud, letting each syllable slide slowly off my tongue. That was going to take some getting used to.

Not everyone in my office was gone for the day. Ava's door was still open on my way out, so I stopped to share my progress with her—not Audrey.

I knocked lightly on her doorframe. The back of her black office chair was facing me, and she spun around with her cell phone pressed to her ear. She held up a finger to ask me to wait, then pointed to a chair opposite her desk.

I quietly walked in and took a seat.

"You can't do this to me," she was saying to whoever was on the other line. "Even for you, it's cruel."

My eyes darted to the floor.

She was quiet for a moment. Finally, she huffed. "I'll call you later."

I looked up with the sound of her slamming the phone down onto her desk. I cringed and jerked my thumb over my shoulder toward the door. "I can come back if this is a bad time."

Ava swiped her fingers under her eyes as she looked up, leaving her mascara a little smudged. "It's fine. Sorry you had to hear that."

"You all right?"

She forced a smile. "Yeah. What's up?"

"Audrey wanted me to add live video to Jake's marketing plan for the new album's release. She wants to broadcast from the launch party."

Her eyes were fixed on the wall behind my head. She was obviously still rattled by the phone conversation. "Sorry, Lucy. Live video from the launch party...yes, Audrey mentioned that to me. What do you think about it?"

My head tilted from side to side. "I'm torn. I think it could be huge, but it's also a huge liability."

She nodded. "Live video out to millions of people from one of Jake's parties? You have no idea how high of a liability. I can just imagine the headlines."

Nausea churned in my stomach. "Think we should try and talk her out of it? We can always record and upload it after we've checked the video. That's what most people do."

She shook her head. "No. This is the new big thing, and once Audrey has her mind set on something, there's no changing it."

"OK. I've done a lot of research to figure out how to best make it work." I handed her a printed copy of the marketing plan. "Since the launch party is on a Saturday night, we need to start mentioning it now. I'd like to send a formal email invitation out to the fan club first, then to his email list, and follow it up with invitations on all his social-media accounts. The week before, we should shoot some informal video invitations with Jake, if possible, and really hype the event."

Her eyes drifted away from the papers toward her window, lost in thought again.

"Ava, are you all right?" I asked, genuinely concerned.

She raked her nails back through her long dark hair. "Oh, I will be. Don't worry about me. This all looks really good, Lucy. You've done a great job."

"Thank you."

"I'll pass the word along to Jake, so he can plan on being on his best behavior."

"I've seen the tabloids. Is that possible?"

"Don't place any bets on it." Ava leaned forward, balancing

her elbows on her desk. "How are things going with the Adler guy? Are you seeing him now?"

I squished my mouth over to the side and shook my head.

Her shoulders dropped. "I'm sorry."

I turned my palms up. "At least it was nice to find out that there are some good guys here in Nashville."

She smiled, for real this time. "True. I mean, I don't know any but..."

We both laughed.

I stood. "Have a good weekend, Ava. Go do something fun to take your mind off this place."

"You too, Lucy."

A tiny surge of happiness rippled through me. "I plan on it."

And I did.

The first part of that plan was to stop at a shop in East Nashville called Asphalt Beach. I drove straight there after leaving the office, and I parked in front of the brick building with a blue roof and bright yellow window frames. I put my car in park and sat there, letting the engine idle. "This is a bad idea, Lucy," I said aloud to myself.

I turned off the car before I could talk myself out of going inside. Bells on the front door chimed as I walked inside the colorful room. The walls were yellow and lined with rows of roller skates and wheel displays. A black, red, and yellow oval was painted on the sleek tile floor.

"Can I help you?" a man asked, walking through a doorway to my right in front of the cash register. He was tall and fit, with a bright red ball cap pulled down low over his eyes.

I swallowed my nerves. "Um..." I yanked open my purse and fumbled through the main compartment until I found the roller derby flyer. I pulled it out and handed it to him. "I'm thinking about doing this, but I don't have any skates."

His lips spread into a thin smile. "Fresh Meat, huh?"

I gulped and took another shaky breath. "Maybe. The flyer says you give a discount for members of the team. Does that extend to possible members of the team if they don't die before they make it?"

He laughed. "Absolutely. Can you skate?"

I shrugged. "Haven't tried since I was probably ten."

He nodded confidently. "They'll teach you." Using the flyer, he beckoned me to follow him. "Come on. I'll hook you up. My name's Steve."

"Lucy."

"Nice to meet you, Lucy."

"You too." My eyes were on everywhere but where we were walking, and my foot caught the leg of a small metal stool. I stumbled forward and the man spun and grabbed my arm before I crashed to the ground. His wide eyes reflected my own doubts.

"You OK?" he asked, lifting an eyebrow.

Nervous laughter bubbled out. "I was distracted by your store! So much to look at. So many bright colors!"

He grinned. "Try not to break your neck before we get you into some skates." His grin faded. "And don't break your neck then either."

My giggles were laced with terror.

We continued past a stack of boxes topped with zebra and cheetah print helmets to a wall display of roller skates. He grabbed a pair off a knee-high shelf. "These are the quads I recommend for newbies. They're quality skates that will hold up for a long time, but I do recommend getting an upgraded set of wheels for the track."

I took the skate from him. It was heavier than I expected and solid black with black laces and Velcro across the top. The black and red wheels were mounted on steel plates.

"What size shoe do you wear?"

"Seven and a half," I answered.

He knelt down and looked through a stack of boxes before retrieving one near the bottom. Taking the skate from me, he handed me the box. "Try these."

I carried the box over to the stool that had tried to kill me and sat down. "How much are these?"

"They're on sale for one-nineteen, plus the ten-percent team discount."

I choked on the air as I pulled off my shoe.

He noticed. "They sometimes have skates you can borrow for the first class to see if you'll like it."

I'd already considered that. "No. If I'm going to do this, I need to commit. I'll buy my own."

I shoved my socked foot into the skate and set it down on the floor to tie the laces. The skate rolled forward as I bent to reach for it. I picked it up and placed it back on the space in front of me. I didn't look up because I knew I'd catch Steve trying to not laugh at me.

I successfully tied the boot, then put on the other.

"How do they feel?" he asked.

I nodded and rolled the skates forward and back on the floor. "Good. They fit well, I think."

"Think you can stand up?"

I gulped and nodded.

"Wait," he said as I started to move. He stepped back toward the helmets and grabbed a black one. "First, this."

I laughed. "Smart man."

When the helmet was secured with the strap under my chin, he offered me his hand. "Now, put your toe stop down on the floor to keep from rolling as you stand."

Taking his hand, I angled my right toe toward the ground and pushed myself up on the rubber stopper. I put all four wheels on my left foot down on the ground, still standing on my right toes. "I haven't done this since I was a kid."

He winked at me. "It's just like riding a bike. Gently push off with your toe."

Pushing with my right toes, I leaned onto my left foot as it eased forward. Immediately, my arms flailed.

Steve stepped to my side and grabbed my elbow. "Bend your knees and use your thigh muscles. Don't rely on your joints to keep you steady."

Like a toddler on ice, I skate-wobbled to the red ring painted on the center of the floor.

"You're doing well," he lied, still holding my arm. "To glide forward, push your skates back and out to the sides using the inside wheels."

My confirmation nod was more like a vertical nervous shudder. I pushed with my right leg and glided forward on my left. Then I pushed with my left and glided on my right.

Somehow, I didn't die.

"Good!" Steve cheered, releasing my arm.

As I scuttled around the ring, my arms did an erratic gypsy wave out to the sides of their own accord.

"Very good!" He grabbed my arm to stop me when I reached him again. "How do they feel?"

I looked down at my feet. "Like I need to increase my life insurance."

He laughed. "Still interested in getting them?"

"Yes." *Nope.*

"Great." He turned back to the wall. "I recommend getting toe guards to protect them from getting scuffed."

"OK."

"Have a color preference?" he asked.

I looked the wall. "Their colors are black and teal, right?"

He nodded.

"Let's do teal then."

"Got it. Do you want to upgrade the wheels?"

"Should I?" I bent and unlaced the boots.

"The upgraded wheels are softer, which will give you more grip on the slick floor," he said.

"Then absolutely," I said, pulling the right skate off.

"How's that helmet feel?" he asked.

"It's good." I returned both skates to the box and slipped my shoes back on.

"You'll need wrist guards, knee pads, and elbow pads." He held up a package of each. "I recommend these basic ones when you're getting started. You can upgrade them later."

I gave him a thumbs-up.

"You'll also need a mouth guard." He pointed to a rack by the wheels. "I've got white, black, pink, teal, and clear."

"Clear," I said.

"Good choice." He grabbed the clear mouthguard and added it to the stack in his arms.

I held up two fingers. "Go ahead and give me the teal one also."

He grabbed it and looked down at his arms, obviously taking a quick inventory of all he was holding. "I think that's everything you need. If you'll carry those skates over to the register, I'll switch out the wheels for you."

I stood, and my legs still felt a little unsteady underneath me. "Thank you."

Ten minutes later, Steve had changed the wheels and relaced my new skates with the teal toe guards. They looked pretty sharp. When he rang everything up, I felt queasy as I realized I was paying good money to put my life in danger.

I forced a smile, handing him my credit card. "Any last advice?"

"Don't die."

"Ha. Thanks."

He swiped the card through the card reader. "Just have fun.

We've got one of the best teams in the world, and they'll teach you if you're willing to learn and work hard."

"I am." And I meant it, although I wasn't exactly sure why. The whole roller derby thing had originally been birthed out of desperation to gain a cute boy's attention, but even with West Adler firmly out of the picture—and out of my mind—my determination to survive 101 was greater than ever. Maybe it was my brother's teasing. Maybe it was all my pent-up frustration with Dad and my boss. Maybe it was some unspoken need to be someone other than boring, caretaker, zip-lipped, small-town Lucy. Maybe it was the taunt on the front of the flyer: "*Find out what you're made of.*"

In a week, Fresh Meat had become my Everest.

I lifted my bags off the counter. "Thanks for all your help, Steve."

He handed my receipt. "You're welcome, Lucy. Maybe I'll see you on the track next season."

I flashed him a wide-eyed, hopeful, yet uneasy smile. "Fingers crossed."

And on my way out of his shop, I tripped over the door's threshold.

———

Since I was already in East Nashville, and because I'd spent my whole month's food budget on roller skates and gear, I stopped by *Lettuce Eat* to see Olivia and scam a free meal. It was only a few blocks away. By some miracle, I found a parking spot on the street less than a block up from the restaurant. The short walk was ample time for people watching at its finest.

East Nashville, also known as "East Nasty" among the locals, was a bizarre nook of the city. A true melting pot of culture, the east side had no defined social climate—unlike other popular Music City hotspots like Green Hills, Hillsboro, or West End. The majority of the houses were old fifties-style cottages with a few elegant Victorians sprinkled among them. The few newer structures were built to look vintage, and the houses that had been renovated and modernized still maintained their throwback appeal. Despite the retro, cozy vibe of the neighborhood, nothing in the area sold for less than a quarter-million—or so Olivia said—and its inhabitants were the grass-fed type, the granola twenty- and thirty-somethings that sported man buns and shoes made of wheat.

Lettuce Eat was sandwiched between a hookah bar and a heavily graffitied tattoo shop that all occupied the same brick building. The restaurant's section was painted lavender, and green steps led up to the blue front door. Inside was just as random and eclectic with local art and license plates hung on the colorful walls. Old wooden tables were scattered around the room with mismatched, secondhand chairs surrounding them. Fortunately for Olivia, who had opened the restaurant on a start-up's budget, frugality was all the rage in East Nasty.

In the corner, a man with a guitar (and a man bun) played an emotional acoustic rendition of "All Along the Watchtower."

"How many?" a bubbly redhead with a lip ring asked, stepping toward me with an armful of menus printed on shabby recycled paper and fixed to wooden clipboards.

I looked around the dining room. "Is Olivia busy?"

She blinked with surprise. "I'm not sure. She's in the office."

"Can you tell her Lucy is here?"

She nodded. "Sure. Do you want to wait at the bar?"

"Yeah. Thank you."

"You bet."

As she scampered away in her bright pink Converse sneakers, I walked to the long wooden bar near the small stage. Man Bun had shifted into a spirited cover of "D'yer Maker" by Led Zeppelin.

"Hello." The bartender stepped over in front of me. He was tall and skinny with a beard and a bald head. He wore jeans and a faded "D.A.R.E. to Keep Kids Off Drugs" T-shirt. "Can I interest you in our happy-hour special, *God Save the Cream?*"

I laughed. "What's in that?"

He shrugged. "It's a White Russian."

"I'm good. Just waiting for Olivia," I said.

He nodded and slung a white bar towel over his shoulder. "Let me know if you change your mind."

While I waited, I tried to call Ethan, but it went straight to voicemail. I hung up, then made the mistake of checking the balance of my bank account using an app on my phone.

I gulped.

Maybe this roller derby thing was a really bad idea.

Olivia walked through the door behind the bar that led to the kitchen. "Hey! What are you doing here?" She came over and leaned her elbows on the bar opposite of me. Her long dark hair was pulled up in a tidy bun on the top of her head like Cinderella.

"I was in the neighborhood."

"Why?"

I bit down on the insides of my lips for a second.

Her eyes narrowed. "What did you do?"

"Can you keep a secret?" I asked, lowering my voice.

She leaned closer. "Oh boy. This should be good."

"I was buying roller skates."

Her head dropped to the side. "Please tell me they are for a needy child."

I pulled the derby flyer from my purse and slid it across the bar toward her. She picked it up, read it, then peered over the top at me.

"Well?" I asked.

She laughed. "It was nice knowing you, my friend. Can you make sure to leave me a check for next month's rent?"

I scowled.

She looked at the flyer again. "You're doing this tomorrow morning?"

"Yes."

"And you went and bought skates?"

I nodded. "And a bunch of other gear. So I'm broke, and you need to feed me dinner."

"It says here you can borrow skates and gear," she pointed out.

"I know, but I really want to make a go of it. If I borrowed gear, it wouldn't be much of an incentive to stick with it."

Laughing, she handed the flyer back to me. "You've got balls, my friend. I'm impressed. Even if it does get you killed."

"I'm not going to die the first day," I said, putting the flyer away.

"I'm pretty sure they call it 'Fresh Meat' for a reason," she teased. "What do you want to eat?"

"The barbecue pizza, please."

She glared and shook her head. "That's not what it's called. Order it correctly."

I groaned. "May I have please have the barbecue You Want a Pizza Me?"

Chuckling with satisfaction, she looked back at the bartender over her shoulder. "Jimmy, can you put in an order for the barbecue pizza and pour her a Diet Coke?"

He nodded and walked to the kitchen.

My shoulders slumped. "You're so mean."

Olivia nudged my arm. "Sounds to me like you'd better toughen up. Why roller derby, Lucy? Is it the guy?"

"I don't think so. I mean, it started off as the guy, but I want to do it. It looks like so much fun."

Her brow pinched together. "It seems *so* unlike you though."

"I know. I think that's exactly what I need in my life right now. Anything that is *unlike* me. I moved here to start a different life, right? There isn't much further you can get from Riverbend than roller derby. I feel like I need to prove to myself that I can do this. Otherwise, what am I doing here?"

"You just squeezed a whole lot of life meaning into roller skating, Lucy."

"I know. It's all very metaphorical. But I *really* want this."

She squeezed my hand. "Then do it. I support you a thousand percent."

"Really?"

"Absolutely."

"Please don't tell anybody."

She smirked. "Who am I going to tell? Besides, why the secret?"

My eyes fell to the bar. "Because if I don't make it, I'd rather people didn't know."

She slammed her hand down on the bar, making me jump. "That's not the attitude of a survivor, Lucy!"

I felt all the eyes in the restaurant on me, and heat rushed to my cheeks.

Olivia pulled two shot glasses from under the counter and put them on the bar. She reached for a bottle of peach schnapps (because she knew I couldn't handle anything stronger, bless her) and poured the glasses full. She handed one to me and raised hers in the air. I did the same.

"I have all the confidence in the world that you can do anything you set your mind to, Lucy. So here's to impossible dreams and roller derby!"

She clinked her glass with mine, and with a few patrons around us clapping, I laughed as we drank.

FIVE

THE ROLLERS' Sweatshop was a conspicuous charcoal building with the team's teal, white, and black logo painted five feet high on the front. When I pulled into the gravel parking lot at nine thirty the next morning, I was already hyperventilating. And sweating. I'd spent hours the night before skating around the parking lot of our apartment building, but that hardly qualified me to show up, skates in hand, at roller derby practice. I was far out of my league, and I knew it. My clammy hands were wringing the steering wheel as I sat and watched the other women enter the building.

Two girls walked in side by side, toting big black duffle bags similar to the one laying on my back seat. One of them was a golden brunette, shortish and plump, wearing fitted yoga capris and a gray racerback tank top. Her friend was insanely tall, like Jolly Green Giant tall. She wore a pink cropped sleeveless tee that exposed her midriff and had two blond braids down her back.

Behind them, a slender girl with a familiar face was getting out of an old bright orange Volkswagen Beetle. I realized who she was when she turned toward the door and I saw the skull tattoo on her thigh—Riveter Styx.

Crossing in front of my hood was a group of three. They appeared to all be in their twenties, like me, but they were smiling and confident—*not* like me. My hand was on the gear shift ready to put my SUV in reverse.

A fist banged against my driver's side window. I shrieked.

It was Olivia.

I rolled my window down, panting as I tried to catch my breath. "Oh my god!"

She smiled. "Jumpy this morning, are we?"

"You scared the crap out of me. What are you doing here?"

She leaned against my door. "I came for moral support."

I pointed at her. "You came to laugh at me."

She shook her head. "That is not true. Since I can borrow skates, I thought I'd try it out with you. You're my best friend. Can't let you die alone."

I smiled. "I'm your best friend?"

She rolled her eyes and groaned. "Don't get all mushy on me. I haven't had enough coffee this morning for that shit." She pulled open my door. "Now, get your ass out of the car."

I turned off the engine and got out, retrieving my bag before locking the doors. She fell in step beside me as we walked toward the door. "What time did you get home last night?" I asked, remembering I didn't hear her come in.

"Around two," she answered.

"And when did you decide you were coming here this morning?"

She grinned as she opened the thick metal door for me. "When I heard you leave and come back in three times this morning."

"I kept forgetting things," I said and walked past her.

"Sure you did."

It was loud inside the building. Chatter and rock music echoed off the concrete floor and walls. Collapsible wooden bleachers lined the left and right sides of the room, and they were all pushed in except one set where girls were sitting and chatting. On the front wall and the back, stairs led up to rows of permanent bleachers on the second level. They were empty.

"Hello!" The bright and cheerful voice caused Olivia and me to spin around. A short, thin girl with a lime-green pixie cut was walking toward us wearing sneakers with high tops that stretched halfway up her toned shins. The girl stuck out her hand. "I'm Shamrocker."

Olivia's eyes were plastered to the girl's hair. "Of course you are. Hi, I'm Olivia. This is my friend Lucy."

Shamrocker shook my hand too. "Hi! Nice to meet you. Are you here for Fresh Meat?"

We both nodded.

"Great!" She licked her index finger and counted out two sheets of paper. "These are your liability forms and details about skater's insurance. I need you to fill out the forms and give them back to me."

"Seriously?" Olivia asked.

"Seriously," Shamrocker said, handing them to us. "Also, here's a packet of team information and the rules of the game for you to keep. If you decide roller derby is for you, there will be a test before tryouts. All the answers are in these pages, so keep them somewhere safe."

"How long is the test?" I asked.

"Fifty questions."

Olivia's mouth fell open.

"We're going to have an orientation meeting first, then do some really basic skate training. If you need to borrow gear, it's in the big black trunk in the cage." Shamrocker pointed to a makeshift room in the back made of chain-link fencing. "You will need your own mouth guard though. We don't provide those, and they are mandatory."

Olivia looked at me and raised her hands. "I guess no tests and skating for me. I don't have a mouth guard."

"Oh!" I dropped my bag on the floor and knelt to unzip it. I retrieved my two mouth guards. "I bought two!"

Her face fell. "Excellent," she murmured.

"Fantastic," Shamrocker said. She gestured toward the bleachers. "Find a seat. We'll get started at ten, sharp."

"She reminds me of Tinkerbell," Olivia said when Shamrocker was gone.

We climbed the steps of the bleachers and sat midway to the top. I estimated a headcount. There were about twenty prospects, Olivia and myself included. In the middle of the room, a few skaters were circling an oval track.

Olivia nudged my arm. "Do you have a pen?"

I unzipped my gym bag. Arranged neatly inside were my pads, my skates, a fresh change of clothes, the two mouth guards, and my purse which I'd tucked into the corner. I pulled two pens from its front pocket and handed one to her.

We'd both just finished with our forms when a sharp whistle blasted. Everyone in the bleachers stopped chatting and looked up.

Shamrocker, now wearing skates, skated over from the cage carrying a clipboard. "Listen up, bitches!" she yelled with a singsong tone. "My name is Shamrocker, lucky number seven!"

Several people applauded. A few girls cheered.

"Welcome to Roller Derby 101," she said. "From this moment on, you are our Fresh Meat! I'd like to introduce your other coaches from the All-Star team!" Riveter Styx and another woman I recognized from the bout skated up beside her. "Number 1111, Riveter Styx," Shamrocker said, pointing to Styx. "And Number 69, Midnight Maven!"

There was more clapping and cheering.

Midnight Maven was a strikingly beautiful woman with taut dark skin stretched over defined muscles. She wore a short pink plaid schoolgirl's skirt and a cropped black tank that showed off her chiseled stomach.

Shamrocker continued. "There are several other team members here today and more will join us during the next few weeks to help out and practice with you. I encourage you to get to know them and listen to their advice. We all started our careers in this room, just like you. And we're all here to help you learn."

I looked around for Medusa but didn't see her anywhere.

Olivia leaned into me. "Careers? Do they get paid to play?"

I shook my head.

"In the next eight weeks, Styx, Maven, and I will teach you everything you need to pass your basic skills test and become a Music City Roller," Shamrocker said.

Riveter Styx stepped forward on her wheels. "You will work hard. You'll sweat. You'll be sore. You'll be bruised. But you will learn, and you will have fun."

Shamrocker held up three fingers. "We practice three days a week, and you are required to attend seventy-five percent of the time. Obviously, life happens and things come up, but being tired, sore, or even injured are not acceptable excuses to cut practice."

"If you get hurt, which you probably will," Maven said with an evil grin, "you come anyway and watch or volunteer."

"Your skills test will be held on Saturday, October twenty-second," Shamrocker said. "By then you'll need to pass all the basic derby skill requirements, meet the endurance standards, and pass the fifty-question written test. You'll find a copy of the test as well as a copy of the grading sheet for your physical assessment in the packet you were given this morning, so you should be well prepared."

"We suggest you study!" Styx called out.

"We also suggest that you train outside of practice on and off your skates," Shamrocker said. "This sport is very physically demanding. You'll want to do everything you can to increase your stamina."

"That includes cross-training," Styx said. "Pilates, yoga, kettlebell—"

"Kettle *what?*" I asked Olivia.

She shrugged.

"—they're all great forms of cross-training," Styx finished.

Maven pointed toward the door. "If you're not willing to commit to practice, to study, and to work really freaking hard, get out now."

My eyes widened. We all looked around, but no one moved.

Shamrocker continued. "If you pass your tests—"

"If you survive them," Maven interrupted with a mocking laugh.

"If you survive and pass your tests to become a Music City Roller, you'll be promoted from Fresh Meat to our secondary team, the Rising Rollers," Shamrocker said. "Your first bout will be the Monster's Brawl, our annual Halloween party scrimmage."

Maven took a step forward on her wheels. "If you don't make the cut or you don't have the balls to make it to tryouts"—*man, that chick didn't mince words*—"we do have a no-contact rec league that scrimmages the last Saturday of every month. They call themselves the Nashville Rec'ing Crew."

"If puns are mandatory in this sport, you're going to be dubbed their queen in no time," I whispered to Olivia.

She smiled but otherwise ignored me.

"There are also plenty of volunteer opportunities outside of playing," Styx said. "We're always looking for new referees, nonskating officials, help with sales and merchandise, and more."

"Does anyone have questions?" Shamrocker asked.

A girl in the front row raised her hand. "How do you make the All-Star team?"

Oh boy. I didn't even realize there was more than one team.

"The All-Star team is chosen by the athletic board prior to the start of the new season," Shamrocker said.

Olivia raised her hand. "What's the difference between the teams?"

God bless her.

"Good question," Styx said. "The All-Star team is our internationally ranked, chartered team within the worldwide roller derby association. The Rising Rollers is our B-team. It's a travel team like the All-Stars, but it is not eligible for international ranking. We consider the Rising Rollers our training team to prepare you to compete internationally."

Jolly Green Giant put her hand in the air. "Do we have to pay to play?"

Shamrocker hugged her clipboard. "Official team members pay forty dollars a month in dues. That covers things like practice space and admin costs. No one makes money on the team."

"Any more questions?" Maven asked.

No one responded.

Styx cupped her hands around her mouth and screamed, "Then who's ready to work?"

Thunderous replies ricocheted off the walls, piercing my eardrums. One thing was certain: this sport wasn't lacking in enthusiasm.

"If you need gear, check the cage," Maven said. "You've got twenty minutes to get your asses on the track and get warmed up!"

I stood and picked up my heavy bag. "Let's do this."

With a reluctant sigh, Olivia pointed toward the cage and started down the steps. "I'm going to get some skates. I'll be back."

"Don't sound so thrilled about it," I said.

"I'm doing this for you!" she called back over her shoulder.

I had my new black-and-teal skates laced up and tied before I remembered I needed to put my knee pads on first. I pulled the skates off and tugged on the pads, then laced up the skates again. By that time, Olivia had lugged over her borrowed gear. She held up a well-worn skate. "If I catch foot herpes, I'm giving you the medical bills."

"Those look too big for you," I said as she sat down.

"They are, but they're the closest to my size I could find."

I slipped on my elbow pads and tightened the Velcro straps around my arms. Then I strapped the metal wrist guards securely across my palms between my thumbs and fingers. They were stiff, which made opening the mouth guard package almost impossible.

"Give me that," Olivia said, snatching it out of my hand.

She ripped it open and let the clear mouth guard drop into my palm. I stuck it in my mouth and squished it around against my gums. It was uncomfortable, to say the least, fitting against my teeth like a floppy rubber sleeve. I moved my jaw and let the guard clap around in my mouth. "Shomshings naht wite," I said, looking at my friend.

She grabbed the packaging she'd tossed beside her on the floor. "Lucy, this says you're supposed to boil it in water for one minute, then press it against your teeth to mold it."

I hooked the mouth guard on my thumb and pulled it out of my mouth. A gooey string of saliva broke from it and dribbled down my chin. "I didn't do that."

"Obviously."

I wiped my chin on my arm. "I guess we'll have to make do with what we have."

She finished tying her skate. "You owe me, *big time.*"

I tucked the mouth guard in the pocket of my gym shorts and strapped on my helmet while Olivia finished putting on her gear.

She held one of the borrowed elbow pads to her nose. "This smells like a jock strap."

"Eww," I said, pushing myself up from the ground onto my teal toe stops.

"I like your skates." Olivia pointed at my feet with the elbow pad before slipping it over her hand and forearm. "Were they expensive?"

"About a hundred dollars."

She laughed. "God, I hope you can skate." She nodded toward the track. "Go on then. Let's see what you've got."

Taking a deep breath, I carefully turned around, teetering on my toe stops like a graceless ballerina. Just like I'd practiced the night before, I pushed off with my right toes and glided forward on my left wheels. I rolled slowly toward the track without even a wobble.

As I put in my mouth guard, I looked both ways before crossing the black line onto the track. Riveter Styx sailed past me, wafting my face with the sweaty, stale air of the arena. She was close enough for me to see the tattoo wasn't a skull after all. It was a sketch of black roses, the negative space creating the skull face.

I stared long enough for her to lap me. This time, her eyes met mine, quizzically studying me as she passed.

"I'm not a creeper," I wanted to say. "I know your dad. Please be my friend."

But I kept my mouth shut and skated onto the track.

Like Steve at the skate shop told me, I pushed my legs back and to the sides to move forward. Slowly at first, then building up speed. I bent my knees and pushed my way around the first turn. When I rounded the corner, I could see Olivia standing on her skates, smiling at me.

She clapped her wrist guards together, creating a muffled knocking sound.

I waved her forward.

She popped the teal mouth guard into her mouth and pushed off on her skates. Holy hell, she skated like the pros. I rolled off the track to stop and watch, mouth agape and mouth guard flopping against my lower teeth. Olivia eased into the curve, leaning heavily on her left leg before stepping completely over it with her right to gain speed coming out of the turn toward me.

I put my hands on my hips. "Jou'f gosch chew be kitting me!" I shouted through my obstructed teeth.

She laughed, going around the turn in front of me, then skating backward to talk to me. "Wha'cha jewing ober der? Chum on!"

Groaning loudly, I pushed off my toe stops as hard as I could without falling to catch up with her. She skated faster, still backward, and I finally jerked my mouth guard out so I could talk properly. "What the hell, Olivia!"

She bent at the waist, gripping her knees as she laughed. "Oh man. The look on your face right now! That was worth getting out of bed to see!"

"Why didn't you tell me you could skate?" I demanded.

She shrugged. "You didn't ask."

I crossed my arms and glared. "It's because you're a lesbian, isn't it?"

She cackled again. "Just because I'm a lesbian, I must be good at sports, right?"

"So, what then? Have you played roller derby before?"

"No." She slowed so I could catch up. "But I was the Skate-Off Champion three years in a row at the Waynesboro Skate Center back home. I beat all the boys."

I noticed Styx had stopped just off the track and was watching Olivia skate.

"I hate you a little right now," I said, holding up my index finger and thumb an inch apart.

Olivia was still laughing. "I know. Just think of it this way, I can tutor you outside of practice."

"You'd better! This was my idea!"

The whistle blew again. "Huddle up, bitches!" Shamrocker shouted, waving her arms.

Olivia and I stayed where we were.

Midnight Maven skated to the center of the track. "Today, we're going to cover the very basics of skating. Stance, crossovers, and how to stop."

Maven continued. "The first lesson of Derby 101 is your stance, because a solid stance is crucial whether you're picking up speed or bracing for a big hit. Your feet are apart. Knees are bent. Your ass is down and your tits are up." She demonstrated. "You guys try it. Skate a few laps."

I pushed forward on my wheels. Ass out. Tits up.

"You need to settle into your hips more," Olivia said, karate-chopping my hip bones. "You're too rigid, and it's throwing off your balance. Push your tailbone down, and move your feet a little farther apart."

I did as she said. While it felt awkward, like I was about to give birth on the track, I did feel more steady. "Like this?"

"Put your elbows down. You look like you're about to drop a turd."

"Olivia, that's gross!"

"It's also true. Put your elbows down." She grabbed my arm and pushed it down by my side. "When we get into the turn, lean on your inside leg and push toward the outside."

I leaned.

I wobbled.

I fell.

The cushioned plastic covering my knees smacked loudly against the track.

She spun to a stop next to me and offered her hand to help

me up. When I was on my skates again, she smiled. "It takes practice, but you're better than I thought you'd be."

I scowled at her. "Thanks for the vote of confidence."

She laughed.

Shamrocker blew the whistle. "Some of you are already doing this, but in the corners, you should be crossing your skates over to increase your speed. Styx will demonstrate, so make some room."

We all vacated to the sidelines.

Styx skated onto the track and Shamrocker kept talking. "Crossovers happen when you pick up your right skate and put it across your left. Watch how Styx's left foot actually crosses back behind and under the right one and pushes toward the outside of the track. This is how she's picking up most of her speed."

Watching her skates rise and fall, the right continually crisscrossing over the left, visions of roller girls toppled in my head. Me tripping over my own skates, taking out the rest of my teammates like bowling pins. My mouth dried up like the Sahara. My pulse thumped in my ears. Or maybe it was the sound of Styx's dizzying wheels striking the concrete floor. I couldn't tell because I was trying not to panic.

Olivia nudged me with her elbow and laughed. "Lucy? You OK?"

I swallowed and nearly choked on my fear.

She playfully shoved me sideways, but I stumbled into the girl standing beside me. We crashed to the ground in a pile of padded limbs and tangled skates.

Every head in the arena whipped toward us. Toward me.

Styx skidded to a stop.

"I'm glad to see someone is setting the tone for how this is going to go," Shamrocker teased.

Maven was grinning as she crossed her arms over her chest. "Should we call an ambulance to be on standby?"

I wanted to crawl under the bleachers. Or run outside. Or die.

"I'm really sorry," I said to my victim.

"It's all right." She pulled her legs out from under my ass. Olivia hooked her arm under my armpit and pulled me up onto my skates. "Geez, Lucy."

"I can't do this," I whispered.

She shook my arm. "Yes, you can. Breathe, before you pass out."

I sucked in a deep breath and held it for a second before blowing it out slowly.

"For those of you who are a little shaky, we're going to learn crossovers in steps," Shamrocker said. "Start by skating in long strides on one foot at a time. Begin on your left skate and really bend and lift your right knee."

Styx pushed off onto her left skate with her right leg lifted in the air. When she reached the turn, she switched skates.

"You guys try it!" Shamrocker called.

All the girls around me started moving, but I was glued to my spot. Olivia grasped the front of my T-shirt and pulled me forward.

I stumbled but didn't fall.

"Come on. Do it with me." Olivia was rolling slowly, and she picked up her right skate so she was gliding on her left.

I tried to pick up my right skate, but I wobbled and shook my head.

"You're psyching yourself out," she said. "Stop overthinking it." She was right. *Mind over matter, Lucy. Don't make this into more than it is.* Holding my breath, I pushed off on my left foot. I rolled half the length of the track on my left set of wheels.

"See?" Olivia called, catching up with me. "I knew you could do it. Now switch."

"High knees, girls! And really push off with the insides of your wheels!" Shamrocker shouted.

After a few shockingly successful laps around the track, Styx skated to the center and spoke directly to me and Olivia. "Good job. Now roll on your left skate down the straightaway, and when you reach the corner, cross your right leg over, and push into the curve with your left."

Fear tingled across the back of my neck as I rolled on my left skate. The corner was approaching. I lifted my right skate and slowly crossed it over the left. When I put it down, my back wheels nicked my left toe stop. My body pitched forward, my left knee buckling and coming down hard on the concrete. My elbows made it up under my chest before I face-planted, and thankfully, I slid off the track on my pads before anyone tripped over me.

Someone behind me was clapping. It was probably Olivia.

One of the veteran skaters appeared next to me like she'd teleported there. She was tall and thin with a blonde bob framing her angular face. "Hey, what's your name?"

"Lucy."

"Hi, Lucy. I'm Kraken."

I thought of my stupid brother and his penis. My face flooded with heat.

Kraken offered me a hand up. "Go back to balancing on one skate at a time. Balance on your left skate first," she said.

Not looking at her face, I lifted my right skate and rolled on my left. She stayed right beside me.

"Good job. Now switch to your right skate."

I put my weight on my right skate and lifted my left.

"Great!" she said. "Switch again."

I switched to my left skate.

"Switch."

I switched.

We continued this all the way around the track. Olivia lapped me twice with her perfect crossovers.

"Excellent," Kraken said. "Now, this time when you pick up your right skate, I want you to bring it all the way across far in front of your left skate. Really overexaggerate the move."

My eyes darted up to meet her.

She smiled gently. "You can do it."

That time it worked. I probably looked ridiculous, like I was doing drunken lunges around the corner, but I didn't fall. "Good," Kraken said. "Keep doing it and make those steps smaller and smaller till they feel more natural."

I swallowed hard again.

"Take your time, Lucy. There's no rush."

We rolled slowly, side by side, around the track, my Fresh Meat counterparts bobbing and weaving their way around us. Stretch. Step. Push. Stretch. Step. Push.

"Good. Start reining those steps in," Kraken said.

My right foot came down just a handful of inches in front of my left.

"Good. Again," she said.

Closer. Closer. Step. Push.

My legs found a rhythm, and I sailed out of the far turn, pushing faster and faster.

There was clapping somewhere across the track. I looked up to see Styx applauding, smiling at me—at *me!*—with approval. Excited, I straightened a little too much and flailed like a madwoman as my skates flew out from under me, sending me ass-first onto the track. Kraken stopped and offered me a hand up. Surprising no one more than me, I realized I was laughing as I got back up on my wheels.

"Come on," she said. "Do it again."

And do it again, I did. Again. And again. And again. And you know what? Between getting up and Shamrocker blowing the whistle at the end of the drill, I only fell one more time—and onto my knees and elbows, no less! I was still as steady as a giraffe on roller skates, but I didn't die either, so you know, silver linings.

Kraken smiled and patted my back. "I'm proud of you. You'll master it in no time."

I wiped the sweat off my face with the tail of my T-shirt. "Thanks so much for your help. I really appreciate it."

"That's what I'm here for. Stick with it. You'll get there, Lucy."

As she skated off to join the other vets, I almost believed her.

I dusted the dirt from the floor off my shorts and scanned the faces in the group Kraken was talking to.

"Are you looking for someone?" Olivia asked, stopping next to me.

"I was hoping to see Medusa today," I admitted, lowering my voice.

I obviously didn't lower my voice enough because, in front of us, the Jolly Green Giant looked back over her shoulder. "Medusa won't be here. She's taking some time off."

Her short friend looked up at her. "Do you know why?"

"I overheard she's got some family stuff going on," the giant replied.

The other girl looked back at me. "She's amazing, isn't she?"

"Totally," I agreed.

Our chitchat was cut short by Styx. "Next we're going to cover how to stop."

My eyes widened. "Oh, that's good."

Olivia laughed.

Styx and Maven demonstrated the different types of stopping techniques. The first was the T-stop, placing one skate sideways behind the other and dragging it to a stop. Next was the plow stop, widening the legs and pointing the toes inward to slow a quick speed to a grinding halt. Then hockey stops, turning slightly and pushing the outer skate out on its inside wheels. And last was the stop I knew would get me killed—the tomahawk stop, or the turnaround toe stop.

Maven skated around the track, then spun completely around and slid backward up on her toe stops. My mouth was hanging open. "Oh no. I see trips to the emergency room in my future right now."

The girls around me chuckled.

Fortunately, we only practiced the T-stops that day. I sucked at them, of course, while Olivia mastered them right away. The bitch. Each time, my back skate stuttered across the floor like it was tapping out Morse code against the concrete. Maybe it was a subconscious distress call. Maven encouraged me to put my weight on my back leg, but when I did, I fell on my ass. My most efficient stopping method proved to be catching the wall before slamming into it.

After that, they moved on to teaching us how to fall. I tried to not take it personally. But surprisingly, there was a right and wrong way to bust your ass on roller skates. The right way was to not bust your ass at all, but to fall forward, utilizing those trusty knee and elbow pads. We were supposed to be mindful of our surroundings and "fall small" to prevent as much collateral damage as we could, like tripping other skaters or crashing into anyone else. And finally, we were supposed to get back on our skates as fast as possible, because we were no use to our team if we were out of the game.

Not getting killed didn't seem to be the point of the endless falling drills, but a byproduct I was certainly thankful for. My knee pads and skates were thoroughly scuffed by the time Shamrocker blew her whistle at the end.

"That's all for today. Stretch out before you leave!" she shouted. "If you're coming back, our next practice is Monday night, right here at seven o'clock. Good job, ladies!"

I collapsed on the floor, panting up toward the ceiling. My T-shirt was drenched with sweat, and I could no longer feel my legs. Even Olivia sprawled out beside me. "That sucked ass," she said, her breath raspy with exhaustion.

I ripped off my wrist guards. They were damp, and my nose curled at the thought of what they'd smell like soon.

Olivia rolled onto her side to face me, propping her head up on her elbow. "Well, was it everything you hoped it'd be?"

Smiling wildly, I nodded. "Yes, but I'm going to be so sore tomorrow."

"For real," she said with a groan. "And I've got to close the restaurant tonight."

The girl beside me was in worse shape than we were. She was puffing on an inhaler and trying to slow her raspy breaths.

"You all right?" I finally asked, concerned I might need to call an ambulance.

She looked at me, her pale face red and blotchy. "Yeah. I will be. Some workout, huh?"

"I know."

She pulled off her helmet, displaying the short layer of dark hair beneath. "What's your name?"

"Lucy. And that's my roommate, Olivia."

Olivia waved as she stretched her right arm.

The girl tapped her breastbone and coughed. "I'm Zoey. You're really good at this." She was talking to Olivia, not me.

"Thanks," Olivia said. "You might not say that when we start knocking each other around. I've never done that before."

"You," a voice boomed behind me. "What's your name?" I turned and looked up, but Maven was talking to Olivia.

Olivia squinted against the halogens above. "Olivia Barker."

"You're solid on your wheels. Are you coming back next week?" Maven asked.

Olivia shrugged. "I don't know. My work schedule is pretty

nuts. I only came as moral support." She gestured toward me, and I was tempted to run hide in the bathroom.

Midnight Maven looked at me like she'd never seen me before. Maybe she didn't recognize me since I wasn't running into stuff or falling into anyone. I gave a little wave. "Hi, I'm Lucy."

Her eyes scanned me from helmet to sweaty socks. "Nice to meet you." Her flat tone said otherwise. "Try and talk your friend into providing moral support again next week."

My shoulders wilted. "Sure thing."

When she skated away, Olivia laughed, and I threw a knee pad at her head.

SIX

ON SUNDAY I'd intended to skate the paved trails at Shelby Park, but my legs were stiff and burning like someone had poured them full of molten concrete. So instead, I curled up on the couch, popped a bag of popcorn, and downloaded the movie *Whip It*. That counted for something, right?

Dad called halfway through the movie. I paused the movie. "Hello?"

"Is that my Lulabean?"

No matter how old I got, I was sure I'd always be Dad's "Lulabean."

"Hey, Dad. Are you back at home?"

"Yes, ma'am. We got in late last night." His gruff voice from a thirty-year, two-pack-a-day-habit had the gentle drawl of a vacation hangover. Like all of his stress was still floating on a wave somewhere in Costa Rica. "How are you, kiddo?"

"I'm good. How was your trip?"

Geez, I couldn't even bring myself to say the word "honeymoon." I thought of my brother, his tone extra impudent in my head. *You suck at it, indeed, Lucy.*

"It was wonderful. If you ever get the chance to go, I highly recommend it."

"What was your favorite part?" I asked.

He was quiet for a moment. "Eating breakfast every morning with Katherine. I swear the sunrise is prettier in Central America."

My mother had *not* been a morning person. At all. I doubted she and Dad ever saw the sunrise together unless they had never gone to bed the night before. Which was a real possibility. Up until she got sick, their date nights were mandatory, not to keep some dying spark of their marriage alive, but because even after two decades and two kids, they were still that in love. Or at least, so I'd thought. He sure had found her replacement awfully fast...

"I also enjoyed zip-lining."

My brain snapped back to the conversation. "You went zip-lining?"

Dad laughed. "I know. Me! At my age!"

"Dad, you're only fifty-six," I reminded him. "You don't exactly need man-diapers and a walker just yet."

"I guess," he said with a chuckle. "I hope you'll come over soon and see all the pictures Katherine took."

"I'd like that," I said, trying so very hard to mean it. "Did she have a good time too?"

"Why don't you ask yourself? She's right here..."

My heart leapt into my throat. Leave it to Dad to pounce on any effort where Katherine was concerned. Before I could politely decline, a syrupy-sweet voice floated through the speaker. "Hello, Lucy."

And that was the thing about Katherine. She *was* syrupy sweet, all the damn time. And genuinely so, which nullified every reason I wanted to have to hate her.

I had thought Dad was joking the day he told me he signed up for SilverLinings.com, a dating site for singles of a certain age.

Mom had only been gone four months. I hadn't even finished moving her clothes out of his closet. Oh, but he wasn't joking. He wasn't joking even a little bit. He went on two miserable dates, which I'd wrongly assumed would scare him off the premature dating scene, and then he met Katherine.

Katherine Woodville—57, non-smoker, from Waynesboro, TN—squelched any hope I had of slowing my father's freight-train speed through the grief process. Katherine was beautiful in a classic sort of way, with a smooth complexion and her hair cut in a frosted golden-gray bob. She was a volunteer at the senior activity center, and her hobbies included tennis, swimming, and playing with her new granddaughter.

The baby's name was something floral...*Daisy? Daffodil?* I couldn't remember. But pictures of her were splashed across Katherine's dating profile. It was the only fault I could find with the woman, putting pictures of her grandchild on a dating website. Didn't she know that sickos lurked online these days? But of course, she didn't.

Katherine was also a widow—another point firmly in the We Can't Hate Her column of their relationship. And she was an excellent cook, which my mother had never been. Dad was lost to us after tasting that first stupid casserole. Poppy Seed Chicken, I believe it was.

I straightened on the couch. "Uh...hi, Katherine. How was Costa Rica?" I tried to sound bright and inquisitive, but my emotions were toppling like dominos in my head.

"It was beautiful. Everything was so green and lush, and the flowers were still blooming, even well into August. It was like a postcard." She gave a melodic sigh. "But we're also glad to be home. We've both missed our kids. How have you been? I hope your new job hasn't been too stressful."

"Ask her if she's met any big country-music stars yet," Dad said, so close to the phone that Katherine needn't repeat his query. He honestly didn't need to ask it either. This question was a staple of every conversation with my father since I moved to the city. A true product of Small Town, USA, Dad was easily impressed by all things that glittered in Music City.

"Tell him I got invited to a party at Jake Barrett's house next month," I said.

Katherine parroted my answer back to Dad.

"Jake Barrett, no kidding?" he asked. "Ask her if she can get me his autograph."

"Tell him it's a work thing, but I'll try," I said.

I realized I was still talking to my dad *through* Katherine, but that counted for me making an effort, right?

"See if you can take a peek inside his garage. I saw on CMT that he's got one helluva hot rod collection." Dad's voice was no longer muffled by distance. He must have snatched the phone back from his new wife. "Take some pictures if you can."

"I'll do my best."

"When are you coming home, Lulabean?"

"Soon, I promise. Though I won't be able to come for a whole weekend for a while. My Saturdays are all booked up at the moment," I said.

"Yeah? Got'churself a boyfriend now?"

"Oh no. Nothing like that. Just a new hobby. I'll tell you all about it when I come visit."

"Sounds mysterious. Nothing illegal, I hope." I could hear the smile in his voice.

I grinned. "You know me, always teetering on a life of crime."

He chuckled. "I miss you, kiddo."

"I miss you too, Dad."

"See you next weekend?" he asked, hopefully. "We can fire up the grill. Maybe make s'mores and drag out the cornhole boards. It's been a long time since we've had a weekend cookout."

My heart twisted. It had been a year, almost exactly. Because family cookouts had been Mom's thing. She loved to be out back by the river so much she'd insisted Dad pour the concrete for the patio, and she'd laid the rocks for the fire pit. Before cornhole became the tradition, it was family baseball, but that ended the day I knocked myself unconscious with the bat. Ethan had started calling me Lights Out Lucy, which would make a hell of a derby name, come to think of it.

How would we ever do any of that without her?

My jaw clenched. "I'll see what I can do. I love you."

"I love you too."

———

Nashville traffic during rush hour could be ranked among the rings of hell on a good day, and Monday morning was *not* a good day. There was a collision at the I-65 and I-40 split bringing the entire city to a screeching halt. Thankfully, I heard about it on the radio as I pulled out of my apartment complex, so I took the backroads, carefully following the directions of my GPS navigator, Christopher Walken.

"In   three...quarters   of   a   mile.   Turn   left. Onto...Blackman Road."

Even digital Christopher Walken was a badass.

I wound my way through the neighborhoods of Crieve Hall, Berry Hill, and Wedgewood until I finally turned onto Fourth Avenue, which would carry me almost the rest of the way to my office. I stopped for a red light, and a chain-link fence covered in a white banner caught my attention, or the logo on it did, anyway.

Adler Construction.

My heart stuttered.

Behind the fence was the bare steel frame of a two-story building. No workers. No black trucks in sight.

A car behind me honked. The light was green.

When I got to the office, Claire was booting up her computer at the receptionist's desk. She frowned when she saw me, always a great sign first thing on a Monday morning. "Audrey's looking for you. Wondering why you're late. Peter was just verbally decapitated."

I glanced at the clock behind her desk. Despite the traffic, Christopher Walken's zigzaggy directions, and my lingering at traffic lights, I was still five minutes early. "It's twenty-five after eight. We don't open till eight thirty."

She shrugged and flashed me a pained don't-shoot-the-messenger smile.

I sighed and started down the hallway. Audrey's door was wide open. "Knock, knock," I said, stepping in the doorway.

My very own Devil in Prada swiveled around in her office chair. She had that *look* in her eye, the one that told me a lecture was imminent. There were file boxes stacked next to her labeled *Lawson Young*. Dark circles weighed heavy under her eyes.

Ass out. Tits up. The thought popped into my head so randomly I almost burst out laughing. Thank you, Roller Derby 101. This was certainly the time to brace for a big hit. Or better yet, come up with a solid defense maneuver. Fast.

I held up my wristwatch. "Wow, Audrey. The office isn't even open yet. You must have a lot on you. Burning the candle at both ends, and all."

She opened her mouth to say something harsh, no doubt, but then shot a confused look at her own watch. "Oh my," she stammered. "It is quite early."

I kept my voice low. Soothing. "Is there some way I can help you?"

She took off her glasses and pinched the bridge of her nose. Stress was etched in the deep lines on her forehead. "No rush, but when you get settled, can you please bring me a copy of Lawson's advertising expense report for this year to date? With receipts and invoices, if possible."

It was cute when she said things like "no rush" and "please."

"Sure. Is there a problem?" I asked.

"They're saying they never received it," she said.

"That's not true." I knew because I'd personally gone over some of the billing charges with his new webmaster.

She nodded. "I know. His new management is just being difficult. About everything."

I offered a smile. "Don't worry. I'll bring the file down when I bring last week's online-activity report. Or I can email it unless you're sure you want it in print. I've got it all in digital files."

"Print is perfect. I'm going to courier it over their office, sign on delivery."

I grinned. "That's one way to shut them up."

She laughed, well, almost. "Let's hope. Thank you, Lily."

I didn't correct her. Again. "You're welcome."

On my way out of her office, I pulled the door closed behind me. Peter was walking down the hall on his way back from the direction of the bathrooms. His step was brisk, and his bald head still flushed with anger.

"You OK?" I asked, stepping away from Audrey's door.

He blew out a sigh that puffed out his cheeks.

"Follow me," I said, jerking my head toward my office. "I'm offering safe harbor to refugees today."

Peter cracked a smile as he fell in step beside me, then he collapsed into one of my office chairs when we were safely inside. "Some days I don't know why I put up with her," he said with a groan.

I put my stuff down behind my desk and unbuttoned my coat. "I've only been here a couple of months, and I completely feel you."

He leaned on the armrest. "I swear, if it weren't for Ava, I'd have been gone years ago."

"She's always like this?" I asked, sitting down at my computer.

"Lately," he said. "Since the whole Ava-Lawson debacle."

"I almost hate I wasn't here when all that went down. What happened?" I asked quietly.

He wagged a finger at me. "Count your blessings you weren't here, honey. And no one really knows what happened, but whatever it was, was so severe that we now have a clause in our employee handbook stating we're not allowed to be romantically involved with clients."

"That's too bad," I said. "The only reason I took this job was to get close to Jake Barrett."

He laughed. "Didn't we all?"

My phone buzzed on my desk. It was an email from Audrey. I read it out loud. "When shall I expect those files? Please advise. Audrey."

Peter stood as he laughed. "You know what she means when she says, 'please advise,' don't you?"

"Please give her an update?" I asked, confused.

"Oh, Lucy."

"What then?"

He paused in my doorway and lowered his voice. "'Please advise' is bitch-speak for 'What the...'" Then he mouthed the F-word and left.

————

After work, I drove to practice, stopping on the way for a fast-food cheeseburger. The moment I lugged my bag inside the practice arena, I was swarmed by Shamrocker, Styx, and Maven, all asking different versions of the same question.

"Where's your friend?"

"Is she coming back to practice?"

"Where's Olivia?"

No, "Hello."

No, "We're so glad you're sticking with it!"

Just, "Where's your superstar friend?"

If I didn't know it before, I knew it then: in the world of Nashville roller derby, I would forever be Jar Jar Binks to Olivia's Obi-Wan Kenobi.

It stung a little, but I steeled my face, strapped on my skates, and stuck my correctly fitted mouthguard into place before skating onto the track for warm-ups. *Today will be better,* I thought as I rounded the oval. *Look how much better you've gotten in just the span of a few days. You've got this, Lucy. You can do it.*

Because talking to oneself is a true sign of confidence and good things to come.

A whistle blasted, and I executed a very staccato T-stop, narrowly stopping right before I plowed into the back of the Jolly Green Giant. She turned and cocked an eyebrow. I mouthed the word, "Sorry."

Midnight Maven skated to the center of the track. She was wearing black tights with white stars all over them. "Tonight we're doing our first team warm-up. We will do these before every practice. Most of the time we'll warm up on the track, but always bring a pair of tennis shoes in case we're working off skates. First, we're going to start with a free skate."

My brain flashed back to middle school at the Waynesboro Roller Rink, and *NSYNC flooded my thoughts. I wondered if we'd have a roller-skate limbo contest too.

After a few easy laps around the track—all of which I stayed on my skates for, thank you very much—we started doing squats. Up, down. Up, down. Up, down. After only one lap, my thighs revolted and sweat beaded across my forehead. Toe-touches and lunges came next. My thighs screamed, and I wanted to die, but I didn't fall. Then we did "Rocking Horses," rocking from one skate at a time to the next, and I fell four times. We ended the warm-up with an exercise called "Sticky Skates," where we skated laps without picking up our wheels at all.

Shamrocker blew her stupid whistle. "Take two minutes to get water!" she called out.

I collapsed on the floor.

"That was brutal," Jolly Green Giant said, plopping down onto her knee pads next to me.

"And it was only the warm-up," her friend said, joining us.

I glanced over at them. "This is only day two, girls. We're in trouble."

The giant gave me a pointed look. "We're *stupid* is what we are."

The three of us laughed. "I'm Lucy," I said, unscrewing the cap on my water bottle.

"Grace," the giant said, panting.

The other girl raised her hand. "I'm Monica. Where's your friend?"

"The Stephen Hawking of the skating world?" I asked. "She's at work."

"Is she going to come back?" Grace asked.

I shrugged. "It's a popular question."

Olivia wasn't the only skater missing. Not including the coaches and the few veteran skaters I recognized, I only counted nineteen newbies.

Across the room, Zoey was talking to Styx and Maven. She paused to use her inhaler, but she was laughing.

"Hey, do you guys know Zoey?" I asked, pointing her out.

Monica looked over. "Yeah, she's really sweet."

I nodded. "She is, but I kind of worry about her. Do you know what the deal is? Is she sick?"

Grace shrugged. "I'm not sure. She hasn't said."

The whistle sounded, evoking a collective groan from our group as we all struggled to our feet. I was glad I wasn't the only one. Shamrocker skated out in front of us. "Today, we're working on track movement. In order to block, execute hits, and maneuver around blockers if you're the jammer, you need to be able to quickly move across the track. This includes lateral movement, skating backward, and jumping over obstacles."

My hands flopped against my thighs. "Great. Today I'm going to die."

Beside me, Monica snickered.

"First, just try walking on your skates to the right," Styx said as she demonstrated.

The sound of wheels clacking against the concrete as we all stepped sideways echoed off the walls.

"Now back to the left," Styx said.

We all walked left.

"I feel like we should bust out the Electric Slide," I said.

Grace began humming the song and everyone in earshot laughed.

"Good job. Faster this time!" Styx called out.

We all hopped to the right. It was surprisingly easier than I expected. Then I shifted to come back left, and my skates got tangled and I tripped, taking Monica down with me. My left thigh came down hard on her wheels. "*Yeowch!*" I screeched.

Monica cringed, for me because she was fine. "You OK?"

"I'm alive," I forced through clenched teeth.

Grace offered me a hand up, then pulled up Monica as well. Everyone was staring, of course.

"All right, again!" Styx shouted.

I stayed on my skates for the rest of that drill and only fell twice during the weaving exercises we did around lines of cones on the floor. But skating backward was a nightmare. Once I finally got my skates moving at all, they flew out from under me each time, like I was part of a live-action Wile E. Coyote reboot. The last time, I stayed down. "I quit," I announced, dropping my hands onto my lap.

"What are you doing, Lucy?" Shamrocker asked, skating over.

"I'm just going to stay here and be one of the obstacles everyone has to skate around or jump over during the hopping drill that's probably coming next."

She smiled and offered me a hand. I stood and dusted off my ass as we skated off the track.

"What seems to be the problem?" she asked.

"I move. I bust my ass. That about sums it up."

"Show me what you're doing," she said.

I sighed and turned around, stepping carefully with my wheels. I pushed off my toe stop, and as soon as all my wheels were on the ground, they slipped forward.

Shamrocker reached out and grabbed my arm to steady me. "Easy fix, Lucy. All you have to do is point your toes in, keep both skates flat on the floor, and move your skates apart. Then bring them back in. Sort of like a figure eight. Watch me." Her skates pushed out and slowly came back together, propelling her backward away from me.

I pointed at her feet. "Oh. I wasn't doing that."

"Try it. Keep all your wheels down, then in and out. In and out."

I pushed my feet apart and magically rolled backward. "Hey! I did it."

She clapped her hands. "Congratulations. Eventually, you'll cross your skates as you go back and even pick up the rear skate for more reach and—Lucy, look out!"

I slammed ass-first into Midnight Maven.

She snarled at me before pushing me off her.

Shamrocker doubled over laughing.

"I—I'm sorry, Maven," I said before skating away.

"That was hilarious," Shamrocker said when I reached her. "But you did well. Keep practicing."

I smiled, my cheeks still hot with humiliation. "Thank you."

The rest of practice couldn't have gotten much worse, and thankfully, it didn't. I was terrible at jumping. No surprise there. But I was getting better at popping back up quickly. Styx said that was a good thing. I suspected she might be stretching for a compliment, but whatever the reason, I appreciated the encouragement.

"We'll see you Wednesday?" she asked, lifting her brow and pointing at me.

I smiled and pulled off my helmet. "I'll be here."

"Good. And tell your friend we want to see her too."

"I promise, I will."

SEVEN

THE BURNING and tightness in my muscles subsided by
Wednesday, but by the end of that practice, I had developed two
sets of sensational blisters on the insides and outsides of both my
ankles. When I showed them to Shamrocker, she suggested
blister bandages, corn pads, and ankle protector socks I could buy
at Asphalt Beach.

Then she asked *again* if Olivia would ever be returning to
practice.

Olivia did return on Saturday. We left early from our apartment that morning to stop by the skate shop and pick up some
skates for her and some blister protection for me. I was excited to
prove to Steve, the guy who'd helped me, that I was still alive and
hadn't dropped out. Unfortunately, it was Steve's day off, and a
portly hipster wearing a Bob Ross T-shirt helped us instead.

When we walked into the Rollers' Sweatshop an hour later, I
did a quick headcount of the diminished group of newbies. Less
than half the skaters who'd shown up the week before remained.
I'll admit, my chest puffed out a bit.

All the remaining eyes were on my roommate as we crossed

the room with Olivia carrying her new gear in the bright yellow bags scrawled with Asphalt Beach across the fronts. The coaches noticed and skated over to where we plopped down to put on our pads and skates.

"This is a good sign," Styx said with a wry smile as she pointed to the bags.

"Does this mean you're sticking around?" Midnight Maven asked Olivia.

Olivia smiled up at them as she pulled the skates from the new box. "Maybe. I stay pretty busy with my job though, so don't get your hopes up too high."

"Where do you work?" Shamrocker asked.

"*Lettuce Eat*," Olivia answered.

"She's the owner," I added.

Grace, the Jolly Green Giant, was sitting in front of us, tightening a lime green wheel on her skate. She spun around on the floor to join our conversation. "Oh my god, I love that place. You guys have the best salads in East Nashville."

"Thank you," Olivia said. "My name's Olivia."

"I'm Grace."

Shamrocker looked at the other coaches. "*Lettuce Eat*...is that where Medusa was a bartender?"

Styx shook her head. "Medusa worked at *The Drunken Nun*. It's a little further up Woodland."

"How's she doing?" Grace asked with a grimace.

Maven gave a noncommittal shrug. "We haven't really heard from her. I called a few days ago, and she says she's OK, but..."

"What happened?" I asked as I ripped open the paper around a blister bandage.

"Her mom was in a car accident a couple of weeks ago," Styx said.

Maven's face fell. "She didn't make it."

My hands dropped onto my lap. "Are you serious?"

Shamrocker nodded. "Yeah. Medusa's up in New York with her family."

A vice gripped my throat. As a card-carrying member of The Dead Mothers Club, my heart hurt for this girl I'd never actually met. "Is there anything we can do?" I asked.

"The team sent flowers to the funeral," Styx said. "I don't know what else would help, especially not till she gets back."

I stared at the sticky bandage in my hand.

"Well, you guys get geared up," Shamrocker said, pushing through the awkward silence that settled over us. "Start warming up on the track when you're done. We've got a lot of work to do today."

Styx looked at Olivia. "It's good to have you back."

I didn't miss the quirky grin on Olivia's face as our coaches skated away.

Monica and Zoey were already on the track warming up when the three of us joined them. Monica skated backward to look at us. "Zoey and I were talking about going to lunch after practice if anyone wants to join," she said.

Grace nodded. "You know I'm in."

I raised my hand. "Me too."

Olivia looked up at the ceiling. "I can come for a little while. I don't have to be at work until five."

Zoey clapped, a little ball of wheezy sunshine. "Great!"

Shamrocker blasted her whistle. "Bring it in, girls! We have a special treat for you today!"

"Somehow I doubt my idea of a treat and Shamrocker's idea is the same," Grace said.

"Today we're doing 27 in 5s," Shamrocker announced.

I looked at all the girls around me because everyone seemed to know more about roller derby than I did. This time, everyone seemed equally puzzled.

Shamrocker continued. "This is your first endurance test. In order to pass your skills test in October, you'll have to complete a minimum of twenty-seven laps in five minutes. Today's test will be your benchmark to set the baseline for measuring your improvement over the next few weeks."

"Twenty-seven laps?" I asked under my breath. "On our skates?"

Olivia scowled over at me. "Really?"

I did the math in my head. Five minutes wasn't long enough. I would have to complete almost five-and-a-half laps per minute. That was approaching warp speed. "Right," I said with a laugh.

"We're going to do this in groups of five at a time. If you're not skating, then you need to be counting or cheering on your team-mates," Styx said.

"Who wants to go first?" Shamrocker asked.

If I could have sat on my hands, I would have. Olivia raised hers, of course. So did Grace. Monica and Zoey stayed back with me, my sisters in lethargy. I thought about linking arms with them to show our solidarity. Then Monica raised her hand and skated forward. *Traitor.* I looked at Zoey. "Don't you leave me," I said.

She smiled and nodded her head.

Two other girls, pretty sure their names were Beth and Cassie, skated to the track and lined up beside our friends.

"I'm glad at least a few of you have balls!" Maven teased, holding a clipboard to her chest. "What's the matter with you other bitches?"

The question was rhetorical, but I felt like I should raise my hand to answer. *No balls, right here.*

"Girls on the track, pick a partner to count your laps for you!" Shamrocker said.

Olivia spun around and pointed at me. "Lucy!"

I gave her a thumbs-up. Counting I could do. Twenty-seven laps, however...perhaps I should've quit then.

"Remember to work your crossovers," Styx said. "Push as hard and as long as you can with that left skate to make your strides as long as possible. This will conserve your energy and make you faster."

Shamrocker held her whistle up to her lips and looked at those of us on the sidelines. "Counters ready?"

"Ready!" we echoed back.

"Skaters, on your mark!" she shouted. Then the sharp blast of the whistle bounced around the concrete room.

Olivia quickly blew past the other skaters and charged into the first turn a car length in front of Grace, the closest skater behind her. She sailed by me at the starting line. "One!" I screamed loud enough for her to hear.

By her third pass, she was already a full lap ahead of everyone else. The coaches were watching no one else. "Four!" I screamed.

"Five!"

"Six!"

"Seven!"

"Eight!"

"Nine!"

"Ten!"

"Eleven!"

"Twelve!"

"Thirteen!"

Just after she passed me the thirteenth time, Shamrocker held up her stopwatch. "That's halfway, girls. Pick up the pace!"

Olivia's face was blotchy and shining with sweat. Her cheeks were puffing in and out with labored breaths. Her determined eyes, however, were set straight ahead.

"Fourteen!" I yelled.

"Fifteen!"

"Sixteen!"

"Seventeen!"

"Eighteen!"

"Nineteen!"

Olivia looked like a stroke was looming. Still, head down. Eyes forward.

"Twenty!"

"Twenty-One!"

"Twenty-Two!

"Final minute!" Shamrocker shouted.

"Twenty-Three!"

Monica stumbled and fell. Olivia jumped over her leg and kept going.

"Twenty-Four!"

"Twenty-Five!"

"Twenty-Six!"

Everyone was screaming and stomping their skates.

"Twenty-Seven!" I almost jumped in the air, but thankfully remembered I was on wheels.

Olivia made it almost halfway back around to me before Shamrocker blew the whistle. Then she rolled off the track and collapsed, flat on her back, her chest heaving like her ribs might splinter right through her shirt.

I skated over to her, pumping my fists in the air. "You did it!"

She just nodded, draping her arm over her eyes as she panted. "Water," she choked out.

Styx appeared beside me, twisting off the cap of a bottled water that sweated with condensation. "Congratulations," she said, handing Olivia the water. "It's rare we see anyone make it on the first shot."

Behind us, the second group of skaters had begun their five minutes of agony.

Olivia propped up on her elbow pads and tipped the bottle up to her lips. She drained half of it before slamming it on the floor beside her and flopping back down again. Her helmet smacked against the concrete. "I...might...die," she huffed.

"We haven't lost anyone yet," Styx said, winking at her. She slapped me on the back. "You ready for this?"

I feverishly shook my head. "Nope."

She squeezed my shoulder. "You don't have to hit twenty-seven today. Just push out as many as you can. Each time it will get easier. Come on. I'll count for you."

If I could skate as fast as my heart could pound, I'd nail the twenty-seven laps in half the time. "OK," I said, forcing a nod.

Olivia sat back up. "Good luck, Lucy."

Grace and Monica were in similar states as Olivia, sprawled across the floor and soaked like they'd run through a water hose. "How'd you guys do?" I asked, stopping beside them.

"Twenty-four," Grace answered, splashing water on her face from the bottle she was holding.

Monica flashed two fingers twice. "Twenty-two," she said.

"That's good," Styx told them. "Some girls don't break twenty the first time."

I held up my hand, then pointed to my own face. "*Some girls,* right here."

Grace and Monica both smiled or tried to, anyway, through their open-mouth panting.

"Zoey, you and Lucy are up next," Styx said.

Olivia pushed herself up and slowly skated over to join us. "I'll count for Zoey," she offered.

Styx pointed at me. "Or you can count for Lucy, and I'll count for Zoey. I know you two are close." Her words had a bit of a fishing-for-information tone to them.

"I see enough of her at home," Olivia said, pushing against my shoulder.

Styx pointed at both of us. "You two live together?"

"Roommates," I clarified, in case Styx had any doubt regarding the nature of our relationship.

She nodded, and I saw the tiniest twinkle in her eye.

Shamrocker's whistle blasted and another group of skaters collapsed to the concrete. None of them hit twenty-seven laps, which, honestly, made me feel better. That was, until Styx pushed me toward the track. "You're up, kid."

I swallowed.

Zoey tugged on my sleeve. "Come on."

"You can do it, Lucy," Olivia said.

I looked back over my shoulder and laughed. "Yep. I'm gonna beat your record."

She winked at me. "That's the spirit. I'll pay your rent this month if you do."

Zoey and I lined up beside each other on the starting mark. She had an emergency inhaler in hand. *I'm such a wuss*, I thought, watching her tuck the inhaler into her sports bra. I could feel my pulse throbbing extra hard in my sore fingers and sweat under my helmet tickled my scalp.

The sound of creaky hinges caught everyone's attention across the room. My head whipped toward the door as it slammed behind the woman who'd just walked in. She was stocky with broad shoulders made even broader by the shoulder pads of her black blazer. Her long brownish-gray hair was parted down the middle with bangs cut straight across her forehead.

"Oh shit," the girl to my right said. "It's The Duchess."

"Coach!" Shamrocker cheered. "You made it!"

The Duchess threw up a hand as she walked over. "Sorry, I'm late. Long meeting at work."

"We're doing the third round of 27 in 5s," Shamrocker explained. "We've already had one newbie pass." Shamrocker pointed at Olivia.

The Duchess crossed her arms over her chest and nodded at Olivia. "Nicely done."

Olivia smiled.

"Carry on," The Duchess told Shamrocker. "Pretend I'm not even here."

"Yeah, right," I muttered.

Beside me, Zoey snickered.

Shamrocker's whistle of death sounded. Everyone cheered.

I pushed off a second after everyone else for fear of tangling my wheels with anyone and hitting the floor before ever leaving the line. I watched the other girls enter the first turn, their knees bent, and their skates braiding and weaving as they crossed over through the corner. My feet didn't cross. I tottered side to side as I rounded the turn.

"Bend your knees!" Styx shouted as I finally passed her. "Loosen up!"

With the whole section of the track completely to myself, I bent and pushed my feet wide to the sides. I sailed forward down the front straightaway, and as I entered the turn—*holy smokes!*—my right skate came over the top of my left. I pushed with my left wheels as long as I could.

Stretch. Step. Push. Stretch. Step. Push, I chanted in my mind.

I rounded the next turn so fast that I wobbled coming out of it. For a second, I looked like I'd rolled over a patch of black ice, but I quickly recovered and kept going.

"Seven!" Styx screamed.

Whoa! Seven already?

I could hardly hear my skates striking the floor over the sound of my ragged breathing.

"Eight!"

Just keep swimming. Just keep swimming. Thank you, Nemo. Or was it Dory?

"Nine!"

Stretch. Step. Push.

"Ten!"

BAM! My skates tangled midway through the far turn, and I came down hard on my knees. I jumped back up on my toe stops and scrambled back to the track.

"Eleven!"

Shamrocker's voice echoed around the room. "Two and half minutes left! You're halfway there!"

Halfway? I was wrong. Five minutes was *too freaking long.* I no longer gave a crap about having enough time to complete twenty-seven laps. Five minutes was a flipping eternity.

I couldn't breathe. Stars danced. Bile churned.

Sweat trickled from under my helmet right into my left eye, obscuring the left side of the track. I dried my face with the edge of my T-shirt as I flew down the straightaway.

"Fifteen!"

"Sixteen!"

Zoey skated off the track and used her inhaler. I looked back to make sure she was OK, but Maven had already gone to her.

"Seventeen!"

My lungs burned. My shins and calves twisted into knots. My lower back felt like someone had smacked me with a baseball bat.

"Eighteen!"

"Final minute!" Shamrocker screamed.

I fell again. This time coming down hard on my knees and on my wrist guard. My fingers smacked the floor, and I yelped with pain. But I got up. I got back-freaking-up.

"Nineteen!"

"Twenty!"

The whistle blasted, long and loud, rattling off the bleachers and metal ceiling. I skated off the rink and collapsed, my breath ripping violently through my chest. *Hehn-hehn-hehn-hehn.* I sounded like a goose with emphysema.

Olivia appeared over me. "You did it!"

No, I really didn't. But I couldn't answer over the fight for consciousness. The halogens above were casting a halo of light around her head. Either that or I was crossing over to the other side.

"Here." Styx handed me a water bottle.

Olivia pulled me up to sitting. I drank a few deep gulps, wishing it wasn't so very cold. My chest tightened with a cramp. "Is Zoey OK?" I asked when I could finally speak.

Styx nodded. "She's fine. She knew to not overdo it. You OK? You look like you might stroke out."

"I might." I was holding the twisted muscle in my side, just under my lungs.

She pointed to my hand. "Breathe in through your nose and out through your mouth to keep from getting a stitch in your side."

I forced a smile. "Thanks for the tip."

The Duchess, the head coach of this sport I had no business being a part of, walked over. My smile faded. *Forget the stroke. I'm dead. And this is my hell.*

"What's your name?" The Duchess asked, looking down at me on the floor.

"Lucy," I answered, my stomach churning in knots.

The corner of The Duchess's mouth tipped up into an almost smile. "You don't sound too sure about that."

I cleared my throat. "Yes, ma'am. My name is Lucy Cooper."

"Well, Lucy Cooper, that was good work out there."

What the—?

Maybe she hadn't counted my laps.

"I didn't even come close to twenty-seven," I admitted.

"Most girls don't the first time," she said. "I'm talking about you getting up and finishing. You're scrappy. I like that."

Maybe I did have a stroke and didn't realize it. "Thank you."

She pointed at my face. "I'd better see you in October."

I nodded. "You will."

And I knew right then, she certainly would.

———

Olivia parked in the lot behind her restaurant, and we walked the four blocks to The Mad Cow, rather than attempt to comb the busy street for an empty space we probably wouldn't find. "Wanna play count the hipsters?" she asked when we emerged from the alley and turned left down Woodland Avenue.

"I'm surprised at you making fun of your clientele," I said, slipping on my sunglasses.

"There's one!" She pointed to a guy with a handlebar mustache in a white T-shirt and cuffed jeans.

I laughed.

She pointed again. "There's another...no, never mind."

It was a guy walking two dogs down the sidewalk toward us. One was big and solid black, a Lab maybe, with a tongue dripping with slobber that dangled sideways out of its mouth. The other was a small beagle, mostly brown with big black-and-white spots.

"Lucy?" the man said.

My eyes jerked up, and I stopped walking so fast I nearly toppled forward. West Adler was holding the dogs' leashes. Olivia was right. Definitely not a hipster.

"Oh, hi," I said, trying to not sound as stunned as I felt.

"Hi." He looked around, obviously surprised as well.

Olivia didn't mask her shock. Her eyes whipped from me to West and back to me again.

"West, you remember my roommate, Olivia, right?"

He smiled. "Of course. Good to see you again."

Her brow pinched together with disapproval. "Sure. You too." She nudged my arm. "I'm going to go on and meet the girls. See you in a few?"

I nodded. "Sure. Be right there."

The black dog suddenly jumped up on me, planting his heavy paws against my chest, knocking me back a step. West yanked on his leash. "Cash, down! I'm sorry. He gets excited."

I knelt down and scratched behind the dog's ear. "Cash, huh? As in Johnny Cash?"

"Yeah. How original, right?"

"I hope he never gets lost. It would take an army to sort through all the black-dogs-named-Cash sightings in this city."

West laughed, and my double-crossing heart tugged in my chest. Cash slurped my cheek.

"Geez, I'm sorry, Lucy."

I wiped my face on my shoulder. "Don't worry about it. Who's this?" I let the curious beagle sniff my hand.

"His name's Puck."

I cupped the dog's tiny face in my hands and scratched his neck. "Hello, Puck."

"How've you been?" West asked.

My knees ached as I stood back up. "I'm good. Really good. How are you?"

"I've been really busy lately."

I wasn't sure if that was supposed to be an apology or an excuse, but I wasn't about to ask. Instead, I pointed down the street. "I'd better go. We're meeting friends for lunch."

"Oh." He nodded. "Well, it was really good to see you again."

I smiled and it was almost sincere. "You too, West." I waved as I passed him. "Bye."

"Hey, Lucy!"

I stopped and turned back to look at him. He was unfairly handsome, really, the kind of guy that could almost make a girl forget he'd promised to call and never did. Almost.

He stared for a moment, like he wanted to say something but didn't know what. Finally, he waved and pulled the dogs on down the street.

On my walk toward the restaurant, I counted the cracks in the concrete.

"That was crazy!" Olivia popped out from the doorway of a boutique.

I took a squealing breath and grabbed at my heart. "You scared the hell out of me!"

She grabbed my arm. "I'm sorry."

"I thought you left," I said as we started walking again.

"I couldn't miss out on that!"

"Could you hear what he said?" I asked.

"Yeah. He said a whole lotta nothin'. What's his deal?"

I shook my head. "I have no idea." My face fell back toward the sky. "Ugh. I like him so much, Olivia."

She looped her arm through mine. "I know you do."

"Why are all the good ones defective?" I asked, leaning my head against hers.

"I don't know."

My phone buzzed in my pocket. *West,* I thought.

Nope. It was my brother. "Hello?" I answered.

"Hey. Where are you?"

"Out with some friends," I said, confused. "Why? Where are you?"

"I'm at home. Dad thought you were coming today," he said.

"Crap." Nothing in me wanted to drive to Riverbend. "Tell him I'll come next weekend."

"You're not coming home on Wednesday?"

Wednesday?

"September fourteenth," he added.

I stopped walking. "Oh. No, I doubt it. I have to work."

It was true. I hadn't earned vacation time yet.

Ethan sighed on the other end of the line. "Maybe I'll come to your house instead."

"That's a great idea. You definitely should."

Olivia tugged me toward the restaurant, and my feet started moving again.

"All right. Gotta run. Since you're not coming home, maybe I can get laid tonight."

"Ethan!"

He chuckled. "Bye, Lucy." He hung up the phone as we reached the restaurant door.

———

Grace, Monica, and Zoey were gathered around a corner booth in the back of the small restaurant. Like a lot of other places popping up around the city, it was a very industriously chic space with painted black brick walls, a glossy concrete floor, and a ceiling that wasn't a ceiling. The air ducts and pipes were exposed all the way up to the roof. The girls waved.

We walked over and scooted onto the bench with Zoey.

Monica splayed her hands over her menu. "I'm going to go ahead and say this now. I think this should be a mandatory lunch date after every practice until our skills test."

"Here! Here!" Grace said, lifting the fruity concoction she was drinking into the air.

"When is the skills test again?" Olivia asked.

"October twenty-second," Zoey answered. "Unless they let you take it early. Wait, do you even have to take it at all?"

Olivia's head flinched back a little. "Why wouldn't I have to take it?"

The other three girls exchanged a confused glance.

"Aren't you a transfer from another team?" Monica asked.

Olivia laughed. "No."

Grace's eyes doubled. "Wow. You're really good."

"Yeah, you're a rock star out there," Zoey said with a hint of amazement in her voice.

"Thanks. I'm having more fun than I thought I would. I originally only came to help Lucy make it through the first practice," Olivia said.

Monica smiled. "That's so sweet."

I cut my eyes over at Olivia. "And she swept in and stole the show."

The waitress came over and took our order. When she was gone, I pointed across the table at Grace and Monica. "You two are obviously friends. How do you know each other?"

"Cherry slushy," Monica said.

Confused, I looked around for the waitress. Was Monica trying to order a cherry slushy? It wasn't until Grace burst out laughing that I realized I was on the outside of an inside joke.

Grace fanned her face with a napkin. "God, that's funny. I haven't thought about that day in a long time."

"What are you talking about?" Olivia asked.

"Grace is a kids' clothes designer," Monica explained. "She has the cutest shop in Hillsboro Village called Sparkled Pink."

Zoey perked in her seat. "I think I've seen it. Is it over by the Pancake Pantry?"

Grace nodded.

"It has a hot-pink, glittery sign?" Zoey asked.

"That's me," Grace said with a smile.

"It's an adorable little boutique," Monica said. "She hand makes almost everything."

I was impressed. Art and design was only my thing in the

digital realm. Making things with my hands, not so much. I'd struggled making popsicle-stick ornaments as a kid.

"A couple of years ago, my mother-in-law and I took my girls to the shop for a Black Friday sale. Grandma had bought them both slushies about a half hour before." Monica wilted across the table and covered her face with her hands. "My youngest, Ariana, vomited cherry slushy onto a rack of white christening gowns."

"A rack of handmade, intriquitely-beaded white christening gowns." Grace laughed, then made a puking noise with projectile hand motions. "All over them. Monica cried. Ariana cried. I've never seen such a mess."

Monica whimpered. "In my defense, I paid for them all!"

"And she helped me clean everything up," Grace added.

"My daughter was absolutely inconsolable though, so Grace gave her a beautiful new dress to wear home. It was so kind and much more generous than we deserved, especially after having trashed her store," Monica said.

Grace waved her off. "It was totally worth it. Monica took me out to lunch a few days later to apologize again, and we've been best friends ever since. Now she lets me pretend I'm 'the cool aunt' to the girls."

"They love you," Monica said.

"That's such a sweet story," Zoey said.

Olivia made a sour face. "It's a disgusting story."

I laughed. "How did you both get into roller derby?"

"The team skated in the Nashville Christmas Parade last year," Grace said. "Monica and I took the girls. The team was handing out flyers for their spring charity bout. We've attended almost all of their home bouts ever since."

"Joining Fresh Meat was all Grace's idea." Monica shot Grace a side-eye glance. "She needed to let go of some aggression."

We all looked at Grace.

Olivia crossed her arms on top of the table. "There's a story there, and I want to hear it."

Grace took a long pull on her straw. "It's not an exciting story. I'm in the middle of a nasty divorce because my husband can't keep it in his pants. He's a pharmaceutical-sales rep and was having an affair with one of his doctors."

Zoey reached over and squeezed her hand. "I'm so sorry, Grace."

"What a jerk," I said.

Olivia snickered. "Did he at least make the sale?"

Grace looked up from her drink, surprised. Then she laughed and offered Olivia a high five over the table. "I hope so because I'm taking him for everything I can get."

Olivia slapped her hand. "That a girl."

Monica pointed at her. "The money should be a lot, too, considering the shit he pulled with you."

"What shit?" Zoey asked.

"We'd been trying to get pregnant for about two years." Grace's eyes fell to the table. "I found out about the affair when he showed me a positive pregnancy test."

Zoey gasped.

Olivia dropped the f-bomb.

My mouth dropped open. "Hers?"

Grace was tapping her fingernails against her glass and blinking furiously, probably in an attempt to hold back tears. "Yep. She's due in January."

Zoey sighed. "What a jerk."

"Men suck," I said.

Grace held up her drink. "Amen to that." She tipped her glass toward Monica. "Well, all men besides Derek. Monica's husband. I really think he should be nominated for sainthood."

Monica's cheeks flushed. "He is pretty great."

"I really couldn't have gotten through the past couple of months without them. I'm really lucky to have a lot of support."

Zoey gestured around the table. "And now you have even more."

Grace smiled. "I certainly hope so."

I pointed at Zoey. "All right, since we're all getting acquainted here, I'm going out on a limb to ask the question we all want to know."

Zoey sipped her drink and put it down. "You want to know why I sound like I'm dying all the time?"

As I nodded, I silently prayed that she wasn't actually dying.

"Last year, I was diagnosed with Hodgkin's Lymphoma. I did radiation therapy and chemo, and one of the chemo drugs is really hard on your lungs. Mine haven't quite recovered," she said.

We all sat in stunned silence for a moment.

"How are you now?" Monica finally asked.

"So far, so good." She laughed, then coughed. "I just can't breathe."

Olivia leaned against my shoulder and lowered her voice to just above a whisper. "You OK?"

I smiled and nodded. Her concern for my feelings was sweet.

"Can we do anything to help?" Grace asked, her face drawn with concern.

Zoey smiled, but it was a little sad. "Don't judge me too hard if I fall back sometimes at practice."

"Never!" we all said almost in unison.

I sat back and put my hands in my lap. "Who would I be to judge? At least you have a good reason. I'm just clumsy and out of shape."

"You'll get better, Lucy." Zoey pointed at me. "Just don't quit."

"I won't."

The waitress delivered the sodas Olivia and I had ordered. "Is roller derby really such a good idea?" Olivia asked, peeling the paper off her straw.

"My doctors said it's OK, as long as I don't push it. I don't see myself making twenty-seven laps in five minutes anytime soon, but that's fine with me. I'm in no rush."

I smiled. "That's really awesome, Zoey."

"Yeah. Good for you," Grace agreed.

"If we can do anything for you, will you let us know?" Olivia asked.

"Anything at all," Monica added.

"I will. Thanks, guys," Zoey said. "I'm so glad to be able to finally be a part of Fresh Meat. Maven—well, I call her Noel at work— encouraged me to try out for the team once I got my all-clear from the doctors to skate. She and I work together at Hope Haven of Nashville."

"Why does that sound familiar?" I asked, looking at Olivia.

"It's a shelter for women and their children who are victims of domestic violence. We were the Charity of the Night at the last home bout a few weeks ago," Zoey said.

I nodded. "That's why."

"Noel? I didn't know that was her name," Grace said.

Zoey nodded. "Noel Sullivan."

Monica smiled, letting her head tilt to the side. "It sounds so *normal*."

"I know. It's hard to think of them as real people," Grace agreed.

I thought about Midnight Maven's tall, athletic frame, her sleek black hair, and her rock-hard abs. "She doesn't look like a Noel or a social worker."

"At all," Olivia said.

"You'd be shocked to learn some of the girls' professions on the team," Zoey said to us.

Grace looked at Zoey. "I heard Doc Carnage is actually a

neurologist at Vanderbilt. True?"

Zoey nodded. "I think so. And I know Madam Veruca is a senior investment banker at TennSouth."

"Wow," I said.

"Do you know what Styx does?" Olivia asked.

Zoey thought for a moment. "She does something for the Nashville Theater. Set design, maybe."

Grace looked at me. "What do you do, Lucy?"

"I work in marketing downtown for an artist-management group," I said.

Grace shook her head. "No clue what that is."

"She works for the company that manages Jake Barrett. She's going to a party at his house next month," Olivia said.

Monica sighed and got that dewy-eyed look that generally accompanied the mention of the name *Jake Barrett*. "He's beautiful."

"Smoking hot," Grace agreed.

"You get to go to his house?" Zoey asked, her eyes wide like a deer about to be struck by a semi.

I nodded. "Yes, but it's not what you think. I have to work. He's doing a live-streaming thing, and I have to...well, I'm not sure what I have to do other than supervise, but I will be there."

"That's so cool," Zoey said.

I narrowed my eyes. "I work in an office and stare at spread-sheets all day. I promise it's not as glamorous as it sounds."

Monica held up a finger. "Shush. I have to live vicariously through my friends, and you're killing it for me."

"Why?" Olivia asked her. "What do you do?"

"I teach the sixth grade at McNaught Elementary. Very exciting stuff."

"Mon, guess where Olivia works," Grace said.

Monica's brow lifted in question.

Grace put her hand on Monica's arm. "Lettuce Eat."

Monica looked around, confused. "Is our food here?"

"No. She runs the restaurant Lettuce Eat," Grace said.

Monica clasped her hands. "Oh, we love that place!"

"I don't think I've ever been," Zoey said over the rim of her glass.

"It's so good," Monica told her. "They have this strawberry-walnut salad with feta cheese that I would give up a kidney for. We love your restaurant."

I knew that salad. It was called the Berry White.

"Thank you," she said.

Zoey wagged her finger between me and Olivia. "How do you two know each other?"

I looked at Olivia. "Do you want to answer that?"

Olivia picked up her glass. "You go ahead."

"We've known each other almost all our lives," I said. "We grew up in a little town called Riverbend on the Tennessee River. It's really small, and everybody knows everybody. She was a couple of years ahead of me in school, and when she graduated, she moved to Nashville for college."

"College was an excuse. I moved to get away from that place." Olivia tapped her temple. "Small town. Small minds."

I'd been dreaming of leaving Riverbend since the first time I could remember Mom showing me pictures of her college years in Virginia. To my seven or eight-year-old ears, Virginia Beach sounded so exotic with its boardwalk festivals and beach clubs, far away from the smelly cow pastures of Riverbend. I decided at a very early age, that the small-town life of Nowhereville, USA wasn't the life for me. I wanted out.

I had succeeded once, going away to college in the eastern part of the state and then taking a job in Charleston, South Carolina. But that was before Mom's cancer. Her collapsing health became the black hole that sucked me back into the alternate universe that is Riverbend.

However, to be quite honest, I'd simply wanted to leave our hometown because it was boring; Olivia had actually needed to escape. Being gay in our small town was a social death sentence. The girls across from us nodded sympathetically.

"We kept in touch through Facebook," I said. "When I took the job downtown, I asked if she knew anyone looking for a roommate."

"I had a spare bedroom and wasn't about to turn down someone to help pay the rent, so she moved in." She smiled over at me. "I think it's turned out pretty great."

I clinked my glass with hers. "Very great, indeed."

"How'd you get into roller derby?" Monica asked.

Olivia looked at me. "Lucy dragged me along to be her wing-woman for the last bout. She was stalking a boy."

Their eyes snapped to me.

My cheeks immediately flushed. "I was not."

"Who was it?" Monica asked. "Anyone we would know?"

I held up a hand to stop Olivia when her mouth opened. "It was nothing. And it didn't work out, so I really don't want to talk about it."

They all deflated a little. Denying girls of juicy gossip often has that effect.

"So was the last bout your very first one?" Monica asked, shifting the conversation back to Olivia.

She nodded. "Yeah. I'd heard of it before, but I'd never seen it."

"Seriously. That's so amazing," Zoey said, dazzled again.

Grace rolled her eyes. "That's so disgusting."

The rest of us laughed.

"Well, you picked a good season to join in the madness," Zoey said. "The All-Stars are going into the Division-One Playoffs as second seed this year."

I held up my hands. "I really have no idea what that means,

but it sounds like a good thing."

"The teams are ranked according to how they played in the regular season. Then they play each other in the playoffs to see who goes to the World Championship," Zoey explained. "They play on Saturday, September seventeenth."

"Have they ever been before?" I asked.

Zoey nodded. "Almost every year. They won the championship back in 2014."

"Oh, I knew that. At the bout they said she was MVP," I said.

Monica lowered her voice like she was about to tell us a secret. "She's one of the best skaters in the world."

Grace plucked the skewered cherries from her tall glass. "I heard a bunch of the players from the B-team are driving up to Indianapolis to watch the playoffs. I really want to go. Are you guys going?"

"Are we allowed to?" Olivia asked.

"Of course. It's open to the public," Zoey answered.

"How far is Indianapolis?" I asked.

Zoey pulled out her cell phone. "Let me check."

Monica looked at Grace. "I'm sure Derek won't mind watching the girls. I'll go if you will."

Grace nodded. "We should all go."

I turned to Olivia. "Think you can get the whole day off?"

She leaned into me. "I do make the schedule, you know."

"It's four-and-a-half hours to Indianapolis from Nashville." Zoey looked up. "The bout isn't until six. If we leave right after practice at noon, we could totally make it."

"We could take my van," Monica offered.

My heart fluttered with excitement as I glanced around the table. "So we're all going?"

Heads bobbed in confirmation.

Grace held her drink in the air. "Road trip!"

We all clinked our glasses with hers.

EIGHT

ON SEPTEMBER 14, I broke the cardinal rule of Fresh Meat training. I skipped practice.

Ethan texted while I was still at work to let me know he was on his way to Nashville, and I left early to be home to meet him.

The year before, on the day Mom died, Dad had taken off work, Ethan had come home from college, and by then I was living in the basement of our two-story ranch on the Tennessee River. At least we'd all been together.

Mom's illness had been quick, relatively speaking. By the time she actually went to the doctor, the cancer had already spread from her lungs to almost every other organ in her body. There wasn't much they could do to help her, except make her comfortable for the time she had left. It wasn't much. Only seventy-eight days.

She'd slipped from this world with all of us beside her.

My doorbell rang.

"I brought the booze," Ethan announced when I opened the front door of my apartment. He handed me a brown paper bag as I closed the door behind him.

I peeked in the bag. Tequila. I shuddered. "Don't you have to work tomorrow?"

He shook his head as he flopped down across my sofa. "Nope. Took the day off. Figured I was going to need it."

"Well, I didn't take the day off, so you can partake of this poison all by yourself." I handed the bag back to him and walked to the kitchen.

He raised the bottle over the back of the couch. "Cheers."

I returned to the sofa with a water. "How's Dad?"

Ethan shrugged and rested the edge of the tequila bottle on his forehead. "Beats me. He's been at work all day, and tonight, Katherine is taking him out somewhere."

"They were going to leave you home alone?" My volume dialed up a few clicks.

"I told him I was coming here."

"Oh." I folded my leg underneath me. "Well, what do you want to do tonight?"

He took another swig of tequila. "Drink."

"Besides that. Get a movie and order pizza?" I asked.

"Sounds good." His eyes were fixed on the ceiling.

"Ethan, are you all right?"

He put the bottle down between his knees and rolled his head to look at me. "Katherine rolls my underwear."

"What?"

He swirled his two index fingers around each other. "She rolls my underwear up like a burrito when she does laundry. I like that. It helps me tell the dirty ones from the clean ones in my drawer."

I blinked. "Aren't they all clean in your drawer?"

He didn't respond. He didn't have to.

"I like that," he said again. "And it pisses me off that I like it."

Oddly, I knew what he meant. Things were different, and the

different is what bothered both of us. I had run away. Ethan was still living there with all the many changes.

"Do you want to come stay with me and Olivia for a while?"

"Thanks, but no."

"What about school? Why don't you go back and finish? You've only got a handful of credits left."

"I don't want to."

I decided not to press the issue. Ethan would move on when he was ready. Dad certainly had. I was trying my best to. "I'm sorry. I'll let it go."

He sighed and pushed my phone toward me. "Apologize with a pizza."

I ordered a large Hawaiian flatbread, Ethan's favorite, then called my dad to check on him. His voicemail picked up, and I didn't leave a message.

When the pizza arrived, I carried it to the sofa. I handed him a plate and opened the box. "How's the girl with the big boobs and ankle bracelet?"

"Haven't talked to her again." He chose the biggest slice in the pie and lowered it to his mouth.

"That's good to hear."

"I met another girl who lives in Waynesboro," he said around a mouthful of pizza. "She has no criminal record that I'm aware of."

"Congratulations, little brother."

"What about you? Dad thinks you have a boyfriend," he said.

I thought of West and shook my head. "I certainly don't have a boyfriend."

His brow wrinkled. "Then why are you always busy on the weekends?"

I didn't answer.

"Lucy?"

"Can you keep a secret?" I asked.

He pointed at me. "Holy shit. You have a *girlfriend*. You're becoming a lesbian like your roommate."

I frowned. "It's not contagious, Ethan. And no, I don't have a girlfriend either."

He grabbed another slice out of the box. "Then what is it?"

"I'm playing roller derby."

He paused with the slice suspended in the air midway to his open mouth. "You're what?"

"The roller-skating sport I told you about."

"Yeah, I got that. And you're not dead?"

I shook my head. "I do have some pretty gnarly bruises though." I pulled up my pants leg and showed off the ones on my shins. "I'll spare you the ones on my hips."

He put his whole plate down and turned toward me. "Have you lost your mind?"

"No. And I'm getting a lot better at it."

"It's dangerous."

"How would you know? You'd never even heard of it before I told you about it."

"I looked it up on YouTube when I got home. I watched a girl snap her leg in half!" He leaned toward me. "In *half*, Lucy."

All at once, I lost my appetite. "Well, I haven't snapped my leg in half. Or even come close to it. I'm really enjoying myself for the first time in..." I tried to do that math in my head and couldn't. "A really long time. Even Olivia's playing."

Ethan didn't look convinced.

"I've made new friends, and I'm getting out and experiencing the city. It's good for me."

"You got any hot teammates?" he asked, cutting his eyes over at me.

"A few." I should've started with that angle. "Once you experience it in person, you'll get it. I know you will."

"Have you told Dad?" he asked.

My eyes widened, and I shook my head.

"Good. Unless you want him to drive up here and wrap you in bubble wrap."

I shot him a smirk. "Dad doesn't worry that much about me."

"Oh yes he does," Ethan said.

I crossed my arms. "He hardly ever calls to see how I'm doing."

"He thinks you're mad at him."

I was a little mad at our father, but I'd never admit it out loud. Mom was gone, and in a way, so was Dad. As if dealing with the loss of a parent wasn't hard enough, he had abandoned us and gotten himself a brand-new family. One that wasn't freshly heart-broken and scarred. One complete with a grandbaby and endless home-cooked meals.

It was the first anniversary of Mom's death, and he couldn't be bothered to even answer the phone.

Ethan cracked a smile and waved a hand in front of my face. "Is that a therapy topic for another day?"

"Yes." I stood and gestured to his plate. "Are you done?"

He handed it to me.

"Want to hear something funny?" I asked as I walked to the kitchen.

"Please," he begged.

"There's a girl on the roller derby team who's helped me out a lot." I put the plates in the dishwasher. "Guess what her derby name is."

He turned around on the couch and held up his hands. "What?"

"Kraken."

Ethan flopped back on the couch, and the sound of his laughter gave me an idea. I looked at the clock. Derby practice had just started at the Rollers' Sweatshop. It was going to be a shortened Fresh Meat session because the All-Stars were scrimmaging that night to practice for the playoffs.

"Ethan, put on your shoes. We're going out for a while."

———

We walked into the Sweatshop as my red-faced Fresh Meat teammates were skating off the track toward the sidelines to take off their gear. The All-Stars were just warming up.

Ethan's eyes bulged.

I pointed to where I spotted Olivia talking to Riveter Styx. "There's Olivia. See the girl with the big skull on her leg?"

"Whoa, the chick with the tattoo is smoking hot. She single?" he asked.

"Not sure." I was watching Olivia. She was giggling. Styx's hand was on her shoulder. "Something tells me you may not be her type."

"Bummer."

"Olivia!" I shouted, waving my arm in the air.

Her face brightened when she saw me, and she skated over, doing a hockey stop in front of us. We hadn't even learned those yet. Styx was right behind her. I was pretty sure I heard Ethan's breath catch beside me.

"You made it!" Olivia cheered, hugging me. "I didn't think you'd come."

"No point in sitting around being sad, right?" I asked. "Styx, this is my brother Ethan."

She shook his hand. "Hi, Ethan." Styx glanced at Olivia. "She told me what was going on. I'm really sorry for your loss."

I forced an awkward smile. "Thanks. I hope I'm not in too much trouble for sitting out tonight."

"Not at all," she said. "You came. That's what's important."

I nudged Ethan. "I heard there's a scrimmage tonight, and I decided my brother needed to have his horizons broadened."

"Awesome." Styx smiled at him. "Hopefully we'll make a convert out of you."

By the look on his face, I was pretty sure she already had.

"Are you staying?" she asked Olivia.

Olivia nodded. "Of course."

"Great. I'll see you after."

They exchanged a curious smile before Styx skated off and Olivia turned back to us. My brow lifted. "What's all the grinning about?"

"I don't know what you're talking about," she lied.

"Lucy!" Grace called.

I looked over and waved.

"You staying to watch the scrimmage?" she asked. "I'm going to go buy beer!"

I nodded and pointed at Ethan. "We're both staying!"

She held up the OK sign with her fingers.

Olivia nudged my arm. "I told them why you weren't here. Hope that's all right."

"It's fine."

"I told them to not bring it up unless you do."

"I appreciate that."

By the time the All-Stars finished warm-ups, Olivia, Ethan, and I were on the front row of the second-floor bleachers along with the rest of the Fresh Meat skaters who'd stuck around to watch. Downstairs, The Duchess was dividing up the players into two teams, and Zoey was setting up the digital timer and scoreboard.

Olivia was explaining the rules of the game to Ethan when Grace and Monica finally ascended the stairs toting a cooler.

"Just in time," I said, looking up as they walked over.

Grace sat down and flipped open the lid of the cooler. "Derby's always better with beer," she said handing me a can. She handed one to Ethan. "Hi. Who are you?"

"This is my brother, Ethan. Ethan, these are my friends, Grace and Monica."

Monica waved, smiling at him.

"Nice to meet you," Grace said.

Suddenly, the loud smack of the heavy front door slamming shut caused everyone to look across the room. All the skaters on the track plowed to a stop.

Medusa.

I excitedly slapped Olivia's thigh. "She's here!" I squealed quietly under my breath.

Medusa's head was down as she lugged in a gym back twice the size of mine. "Am I too late to play?" she called out, dropping her bag onto the floor with a thud.

Everyone cheered.

The team captain's face broke into tears before anyone reached her. Maven was first, barely stopping before skating into Medusa's open arms. Medusa buried her face in her friend's shoulder before the rest of the players gathered around them for the largest group hug I'd ever seen.

In that moment, the word "team" took on a new meaning. This was more than a bunch of girls who liked to skate and knock each other around. This was a family, and even though I was still on the outside looking in, I was slowly becoming part of it.

"Who is that?" Ethan asked, leaning against my shoulder.

"Medusa. She's the team captain," I said.

Olivia lowered her voice. "Her mom died a few weeks ago. I think this is her first practice back with the team."

"That's so sad," Grace said with a sigh.

"We should do something for her." I looked at Olivia. "Maybe put together a gift basket of stuff to make her feel better or something."

"That's a great idea. Wanna go shopping on our way home?" she asked.

"Sure," I said.

"I'll talk to Styx and see if there's anything in particular she likes."

I cracked a smile. "I'm sure you will."

She elbowed me in the ribs. "Shut up, Lucy."

My eyes, and most likely everyone else's as well, were fixed on Medusa the rest of the night. She was spectacular. Fluid. Smooth. Fierce. She eructed guttural screams whenever she knocked a teammate off the track. Each time, everyone flinched.

It was clear, every skater in the room respected the team captain. Not because of her rank, but because with each powerful blow, she freaking earned it.

Ethan pointed at the track with his beer can. "You actually do this?"

The referee's whistle blasted when Shamrocker called off a jam.

I put my feet up on the railing in front of us. "Yeah. Believe it or not."

He laughed and shook his head. "I definitely don't believe it."

I shoved his shoulder. "Then I guess you'll have to come back and watch me play next season." *If I make the team,* I silently added.

He reclined against the bench and smiled at me. "I won't miss a single game, I swear."

Medusa's team beat Shamrocker's team by over forty points, and when the final jam whistle blew, I finally uncurled the death grip I had on the bleachers beneath me. "That was amazing," I said, looking over at Olivia.

"Amazing," she agreed. "Wanna go downstairs and say hello?"

My eyes doubled. "To Medusa?"

She shrugged as she stood. "Sure. Why not."

"Because she's..." I couldn't even think of a word.

Olivia grabbed my hand and pulled me up. "She puts her skates on one at a time just like we do. Ethan, you coming?"

He jumped up. "Hell yeah, I'm coming."

"Wait for us!" Grace said, laughing, and maybe a little drunk.

We walked down the steps to where the team was stretching out on the floor and taking off their gear. Grace and Monica went over to help Zoey pack up the scoreboard.

Styx got up and skated over. "Hey, girls." Her face was red and splotchy. Sweat glistened in her short dark hair.

"Good practice," I said.

She was still panting. "It was fun. We haven't worked that hard in weeks. It's good to have Medusa back. She keeps us on our toes."

"Lucy wants to meet her," Olivia said.

My stomach did a backflip.

"Got a little crush, do we?" Styx asked with a teasing wink.

"She's such a badass," I said.

Styx shook her head. "No argument here." She glanced back over her shoulder. "Medusa! You've got some newbies to meet!"

Behind her, Medusa looked over from where she was talking with Maven. She pulled off her helmet, then stood up on her skates. *Don't say anything dumb. Don't say anything dumb. Don't say anything dumb,* I chanted to myself as she skated over.

Medusa plowed to a stop next to Styx. Up close, she was shorter than I expected, only taller than me because of her wheels. Still, I felt small. And weak. And a little stupid for being so nervous. Blood rushed to my cheeks so fast it made me dizzy.

"Hey" was all she said, but I nearly fell over.

Styx jerked her thumb toward Olivia. "This is the newbie I was telling you about."

Medusa nodded, impressed. She stuck out her hand to my roommate. "You're the one they're calling The Prodigy?"

Olivia blinked with confusion. "The Prodigy?"

"Yes," Styx answered for her.

"They say you're really good," Medusa said.

Olivia tried to suppress an embarrassed smile and failed. "Thank you. I'm having a good time."

"I look forward to seeing what you've got," Medusa said.

Then she turned to look at me.

I swallowed.

"This is my roommate, Lucy," Olivia said.

My hand jutted out. "Hi! I'm Lucy."

Cocking an eyebrow, Medusa pointed at Olivia. "She just said that."

I grinned harder, my hand still suspended awkwardly in the air. She hesitated a moment longer before finally shaking it. "You're new to Fresh Meat?" she asked.

"Brand new," I said.

"I've seen you around. Do you come to a lot of bouts?"

"Almost zero." I giggled nervously.

The corner of her mouth twitched up like she was about to laugh at me.

Oh god, kill me now. My heart felt like it was about to beat out of my chest.

I waved and took a few steps back, still smiling like a madwoman. "Well...it was really great to meet you, Medusa! Good luck on Saturday!" My foot came down hard on something that moved. A skate. It zipped sideways, taking my leg with it. I fell, nearly doing a split before smacking my ass hard on the concrete.

Several people applauded. Medusa was one of them.

Ethan offered me a hand up. "What's the matter with you?"

Olivia was snickering behind her hand. I wanted to give her the finger.

"Oh god," I whispered as my brother pulled me to my feet.

Medusa's face was caught between amused and mocking. "It was nice to meet you, newbie. Good luck out there."

She turned, and I read the back of her black shirt: *Damsel NOT in Distress*. I was very much the opposite. Medusa skated back to her friends. Maven was rolling her eyes with her hands on her hips.

Styx squeezed my shoulder. "You're not the first person to lose their shit over Medusa. Shake it off."

"That was humiliating," I said.

Styx laughed. "It was pretty bad, but it could've been worse."

I cocked an eyebrow. "How?"

Ethan put his arm around my shoulders. "You could have *shat* yourself when you fell."

I elbowed him, and everyone laughed.

"So what'd you think?" Styx asked him.

His smile was really, really wide. "It was a lot of fun. And you're great at it."

"Thank you. You know, we're always looking for guys to help out. We could even train you to be a referee." She pointed to the refs who were taking off their skates.

He brightened. "Really?"

I nudged his arm. "But you don't want to move here, remember?"

"I can move." He grinned. "What I said was, I don't want to live with you."

I rolled my eyes.

"Check out our website. All the info is on there," Styx told him.

"Thanks, I will."

"It was nice to meet you, Ethan. Lucy, I'll see you in Indiana, right?"

"I'll be there."

Styx turned to Olivia. "Can you help me for a second?"

"Sure!" My best friend followed after her.

"Are they...?" Ethan's question trailed off as he pointed to Olivia and Styx.

I crossed my arms. "I have no idea."

———

Ethan and I followed Olivia to Target after practice. On the drive, my phone rang. Dad. I answered the call on the car's speaker. "Hey, Dad."

"Hi, honey." His voice didn't sound as mournful as it should have.

"You're on speaker. Ethan's here," I said.

"All right. Are you kids having fun?" Dad asked.

We *had* been smiling before the phone rang. To be honest, I'd completely forgotten about the woes of the day a few times during the scrimmage. I was pretty sure Ethan had too. "We're staying busy. How has your day been?"

He sighed. "I took the day off. Katherine and I painted the living room this morning, then we went out to dinner tonight."

I put a little too much pressure on the brake pedal as we neared the left turn into Target. The SUV stopped so suddenly, Ethan and I lurched forward. "You painted the living room?"

"Yep. It matches the kitchen now. A nice taupe color."

My hands twisted around the steering wheel. The kitchen had been lime green. The living room, lemon yellow. Mom had chosen colors that made her feel the most cheerful. Now taupe? The folding of his underwear bothered Ethan, yet he failed to mention Katherine redecorating Mom's house. He was staring out the passenger side window, unfazed.

"Um...I'm sure it's great. Hey, Dad, we've got to run. We're just pulling into the store." My fingers were twitching in the direction of the "End Call" button on the screen.

"All right. Do you have any plans to come home soon?" he asked.

To the taupe living room and kitchen? No thanks.

Ethan's face whipped toward me. "What about this weekend?"

"This weekend's no good," Dad said. "We're going up to see Bryan and Lindsley."

Bryan with a *y* was my new, super-successful stepbrother. Geez, *stepbrother*. I would never get used to that. He was an investment broker in St. Louis, and his wife, Lindsley (dubbed by my brother as "Little Miss Botox") was a stay-at-home mommy who held her neighborhood's record of getting back in her prebaby skinny jeans. She told me all about it at the wedding reception as I ate a second piece of cake.

They were the parents of the floral baby who'd been exploited all over her grandma's dating profile. *What's that kid's name? Begonia?* Whoever she was, Dad liked to send me pictures of her. I was beginning to wonder if he was dropping hints for grandchildren of his own.

"OK. Well, I hope you guys have a nice trip," I said, trying to sound as cheerful as possible.

"I'm sure we will. Dahlia is sitting up now and talking a little bit."

Dahlia! How could I forget a name so morbidly beautiful?

"That's great," I said, even though I couldn't possibly care less.

"How about the week after?" he asked.

The week after was the roller derby playoffs, and I'd be in Indianapolis with the girls. "I've got plans that weekend. We'll figure something out though. I'll let you know when I have a chance to look at my calendar."

"All right, Lucy." Now he sounded mournful. "I love you, honey."

It broke my bitter heart. "Dad, are you OK?"

"Yes, I'm all right. It's just a tough day, and I miss you," he said.

"I miss you too. I'll come home soon, I promise. I love you."

"I love you, Lucy. Bye, kids."

Ethan was quietly singing the lyrics to Cats in the Cradle when I ended the call. I backhanded him across the chest. "Oh, shut up, Ethan."

He cackled as I pulled into the parking lot. "What are we doing here?" he asked, looking up at the store.

"Buying a gift to cheer up Medusa," I said as I parked the car.

His head tilted to the side. "Kind of ironic given the day, isn't it?"

I'd thought the same thing while driving.

Obviously, Olivia had too, because her first question when she met us at the entrance was, "Are you sure you want to do this tonight?"

I nodded. "Absolutely."

"What do you buy someone to make them feel better, anyway?" Ethan asked, as the doors to the department store slid open.

Movies had been my thing right after Mom died. To be quite honest, I'm pretty sure I was personally responsible for any success *Magic Mike XXL* had at the box office. Her death coincided with the movie's addition to our local discount theater's lineup. So every Monday night for the six weeks it played, I caught the nine o'clock showing like I belonged to some weird one-woman Channing Tatum (or, really, Joe Manganiello) cult.

Yum.

I didn't even care about the plot. But it had been two hours of mind-numbing eye candy, an ab-infused salve to the soul. Cinematic therapy for a few dollars a ticket. Because grief is weird like that. Sometimes comfort is so elusive that it seems to be found in only the most unlikely of places.

I might watch it again before bed.

"I was thinking about getting her movies and booze," I announced.

"I was just thinking about booze," Olivia said with a laugh.

We stopped at the card section first. Ethan picked up one with bright red hearts all over it and turned it toward Olivia. "Maybe you can get this for Styx." He made kissy noises.

She looked around, then snatched the card out of his hand and put it back. "Knock it off."

"What's up with you? Why are you being all secretive?" I asked.

"She's an All-Star member and our coach." She pulled me down the aisle toward the sympathy cards. "I don't want people to think I'm sleeping my way onto the team."

My mouth dropped open. "You're sleeping with her?"

"Details, please," Ethan said, closing his eyes and folding his hands in prayer.

Olivia punched his arm. Hard. "That's not what I meant. We're just talking."

"You really think people would assume that? You're so good," I said.

She picked up a card with the words "THIS SUCKS" scrawled across the front. "I don't want to chance it. Neither does she."

"Then you two really need to work on your covert skills. It's so obvious," Ethan said.

"Really?" she asked, grimacing.

"Yes," he and I answered in harmony.

We moved on to the movie section next. Olivia picked out *The Birdcage*. Ethan picked out *Superbad*. I picked out *Magic Mike XXL* because who knows? Maybe Hollywood added subliminal messages of comfort and healing to the baseline of that

Nine Inch Nails scene. I almost fanned my face just thinking about it.

With my luck, Medusa was a lesbian.

We added a few bars of expensive chocolate to the cart along with a bottle of wine and a case of beer Styx had suggested. I found a pretty teal wicker basket on the home-goods aisle, and I picked up a twenty-five-dollar movie-theater gift card on our way to the check-out line.

"How are we going to get it to her?" I asked Olivia as we unloaded the cart.

She pulled out the case of beer. "Styx said she can give it to her before they leave for Indianapolis."

I reached for the "THIS SUCKS" sympathy card that had been hidden under the case. "Maybe we shouldn't sign our names, so she doesn't think we're brownnosing."

Olivia nodded. "That's a good idea."

Ethan shook his head and looked at me. "Or maybe not. God knows, you're going to need all the help you can get!"

NINE

"I THINK I SEE BONE." At practice on Saturday, the day of the
playoffs, I stuck my bare foot in Olivia's face. "Do you see bone?"

She shoved my foot away. "Gross, Lucy!"

It had been a month since we started Fresh Meat, and while I
hadn't yet died from a concussion or a broken neck, I was fairly
sure gangrene was growing on my ankles. Foot funk. What a
ridiculous way to die.

"Have you girls found any magical cures for blisters?" I asked
Grace and Monica as we put on our gear.

"Nope," Grace said with a frown.

Monica shook her head. "I wish."

"What's the problem?" Zoey asked as she dropped her heavy
gym bag on the ground beside me.

Frowning, I pointed to my bare feet. "Blisters."

She laughed and waved her hand. "That's nothing." She sat
down and yanked off her shoe and sock. "Try missing toenails."

Her big toe was missing its nail. I leaned back away from
her. "Eww!"

Grace looked over. "What the hell, Zoey?"

"It's all good. It doesn't hurt anymore," she said.

I eyed her suspiciously. "You're terribly chipper for a girl with mangled feet. What's up?"

Her smile widened. "It's been a really, really good week."

"Care to share?" I asked, covering a blister with a bandage.

Zoey pulled on a knee pad. "I got the results of my latest PET scan yesterday."

My breath caught in my chest. My mother had a PET scan after her initial biopsy surgery to see if her cancer had spread. It hadn't been good news.

"The doctors say there's less than a five percent chance the cancer will come back now."

Olivia clapped her hands.

"Congratulations!" Grace cheered.

"Yes, congratulations," Monica said, squeezing her shoulder.

I smiled. "That's excellent news, Zoey. I couldn't be happier." And I was truly happy for her. At least some people were able to beat that heinous disease.

Zoey blushed. "Thanks, guys. That means a lot to me."

Olivia discretely squeezed my hand.

I smiled gratefully and stuck my foot in my right skate, wincing quietly from the pain of my torn skin. I'd never dare whine to Zoey about it again.

Full Metal Jackie, one of the All-Star skaters, rolled up in front of our group. "Listen up, ladies! With all your coaches being away at playoffs, today we're running on a skeleton crew. If you haven't heard, they won the bout this morning over Chicago, one eighty-six to one fifty-two."

Our Fresh Meat gang erupted in applause.

"That means they're playing Richmond this evening!" she yelled.

I leaned toward Zoey, who was standing beside me. "Isn't Richmond the team we played at the last bout of the season?"

"Yep," Zoey whispered. "It's going to be a bloodbath.

"We're going to try and keep today's practice short for those who are planning to drive to Indianapolis," she said. "So we will not be doing 27-in-5 trials this week!"

There was more thunderous applause, but for a different reason.

Jackie laughed. "But I suggest you do them on your own time, especially those of you who still haven't reached twenty-seven laps!"

Especially me, in other words. The week before I'd clocked twenty-four laps. It was a significant improvement but still an eternity away from twenty-seven.

Jackie held up her hands to silence us. "We've got work to do in the short time we have, so let's get to it. In our sport, the jammers may get the spotlight and the stars on their helmets, but where the real action is—and what the fans really show up to see—happens in the pack. I'm talking about hits! Nasty, powerful, ball-busting hits!" She pounded her fist into her palm.

Our group pounded their skates against the floor and cheered.

Jackie's voice boomed over the group. "And there's no better skater to teach you the art of laying a bitch out, than our very own retired MVP Blocker and four-time season Whammy Award winner, Stone Cold Kelly!"

Olivia and I looked around the room as the cheers intensified. My eyes were searching for another She-Hulk on roller skates. Instead, they fell on a girl about Zoey's size with not much more meat on her bones. Waving to the crowd, she skated up next to Jackie. The number on her jersey was 1-in-a-million.

Stone Cold Kelly held both hands up over her head, almost

immediately silencing the room. "I know what you're all thinking. What beanstalk did this giant climb down?"

We all laughed. A few ripples of snarky commentary fluttered through our group.

Kelly reached for Jackie's arm and then motioned Grace forward from our group. Grace and Jackie flanked Kelly, the two of them looking like Samson and Goliath respectively next to the tiny MVP Blocker.

"I am living proof that size doesn't always matter, at least not out here on the track." Kelly smiled up at both of the tall girls. "Footwork, speed, and fearlessness are what make a blocker truly great." She reached up and patted Grace and Jackie on their shoulders. "Thanks, girls."

They rolled off to the side.

Kelly held up her index finger. "The first step to becoming a formidable blocker is to find your center. To knock someone off their skates, you must be balanced on yours. Can I get a volunteer?"

Olivia grabbed my elbow and pushed my arm up into the air. Before I could yank it back down, Kelly pointed right at me. "You, thank you! Come up here!"

Olivia snickered, and before I skated away, I elbowed her in the ribs.

"What's your name?" Kelly asked when I reached her.

"Lucy," I said, my voice squeaking.

"Hi, Lucy." She mimicked my squeak and winked at me. "Turn this way." She nudged my shoulder, and I turned so that my right side faced the crowd. "The correct skating stance is low and wide. Lucy, spread your feet apart and bend your knees."

I spread. I bent.

Kelly pulled me back up a few inches. "You only need to bend your knees to about a forty-five-degree angle." She put her hands on my waist. "Your head, arms, and torso should always be centered over your skates."

My butt was sticking up in the air behind me, and I felt like I would face-plant any second.

Kelly continued talking to the group. "If the majority of your body weight is ever shifted out of line with your center, you *will* become unstable." She smacked my protruding butt, and my body pitched forward, my face aimed at the concrete.

Two strong hands reached out and grabbed me. It was Full Metal Jackie. She smiled as she steadied me back on my wheels.

Kelly stepped over beside me and acted out what she was saying. "Don't let your center move over your toe stops, behind your heels, or to either side." She leaned side to side before turning her attention back to me. "Get centered again, Lucy. This time, keep your ass down."

When I bent again, I was much more stable on my skates.

Kelly leaned toward my ear. "Stay just like that."

She pushed me again from behind, but this time I rolled forward and didn't fall. The swarm of other newbies clapped their padded hands together.

"Good job, Lucy!" someone yelled, probably Zoey.

I dragged my right skate sideways behind me, pulling off a decent T-stop. Then I turned and skated back to Kelly. She was smiling. "Good work."

"Thanks for the heads-up that time," I said.

Kelly looked back at the group. "The best thing you can do to improve your stance and your balance is to strengthen your core." She pulled up her T-shirt, exposing a flat, toned stomach which she smacked her fist against. It didn't budge. Someone whistled. It sounded like Olivia. "Crunches and leg lifts need to become your new best friends. Anything you can do to strengthen your core will help you on the track."

Without being asked, I pulled up the front of my T-shirt and poked the smooth flesh above my belly button. The whole canvas quivered like gelatin. I laughed. So did everyone else. Jackie rolled up beside me and pulled her shirt up, letting a fat roll flop down over her waistband. She and I both burst out in giggles together.

I shook my head, pointing between her and Kelly. "I don't want to get hit by either one of you."

Jackie slapped me on the back.

Everyone was still laughing, including our teacher. Kelly held her hands up again to quiet us. "Mastering your footwork is equally important to maintaining a proper stance. After all, if you want to hit someone, you're both going to be moving. You'll need to be light on your feet to be able to line up and then execute a hit. That's going to come with practice, practice, and more practice. Jackie, would you like to take Lucy out to the track and show off a couple of basic blocks?"

My eyes doubled in size, and everyone laughed again as I stumbled backward on my skates away from Jackie.

Kelly laughed. "Is that a no, Lucy?"

I shook my head. "That's a *hell no.*"

"I'll take her," Grace said, raising her hand in the air.

Jackie's smile was devilish. "You're on."

The two of them skated to the track with impressive speed. We all turned to watch.

"You'll notice, that even though Jackie is our most sizable player, she's got quick feet and deadly aim," Kelly explained.

Grace skated a fast lap around the track, while Jackie skated slower, constantly watching over her shoulder. Grace moved like she was going to come around Jackie's inside but then darted right to come just outside of Jackie's right shoulder. Jackie sidestepped quickly on her wheels and plowed into Grace's side with her right upper arm. Grace was knocked sideways out of bounds like a cartoon character being pummeled by a giant red fist on a spring.

Everyone cheered.

Jackie skated over and helped Grace up off the floor. Laughing, they both looped arms across the other's neck.

"You'll notice that Jackie hit Grace using the upper part of her arm. That's a legal blocking zone." Kelly gestured toward me. "Come here, Lucy."

I hesitated and everyone snickered again.

"Come here, I'm not going to hit you," she promised.

I skated back over to her.

Kelly made a karate-chop motion against the side of my shoulder with one hand and against the side of my thigh with the other. "You can use any part of your body from your shoulder to above your knee to hit another player. It's called your legal blocking zone. You cannot use your elbows, forearms, or hands." She pretended like she was elbowing me in the face, and I ducked to dodge it.

"You can use any part of your legal blocking zone to hit any part of your opponent's legal *target* zone. The target zone is almost the same area on them, except you can hit all parts of the arm and hand, and you cannot hit the spine." Kelly used my body again to demonstrate. "Any questions?"

I raised my hand.

"Lucy?"

"Not to be insulting, or anything, Kelly, but how do you hit people legally? You're a lot smaller than a lot of those players like Jackie."

She smiled. "That's a good question." She looked back at Jackie. "Can you come here for a second?"

Jackie nodded and skated forward.

"The main blocking technique I use is called a J-block," Kelly said. She crouched down beside Jackie, then came up and over to bump her in the hip with her shoulder. "Now, come at me Jackie," she said.

Jackie crouched, but couldn't get low enough with her shoulder to hit Kelly with her upper arm. She turned and bumped her with her hip instead.

"See?" Kelly said. "I can hit her target zone, but she can't reach mine very effectively, at least not legally."

"That's what makes her so good!" a girl I didn't know shouted. "She puts everybody else in the penalty box!"

"Do you understand?" Kelly asked me.

I nodded.

She looked around at the group. "All right, I want everyone to pair up with someone of similar height. I want you to focus on maintaining a proper stance and your balance. I don't want you slamming each other around out there just yet!" She grabbed my arm and pulled me close beside her. "I want you to do some light shoulder bumps and hip checks with your partner." When she bumped me with her bony hip, I almost tumbled over.

"Any questions?" No one responded. "OK, find your partner!"

By the time I turned to look at Olivia, one of the B-team skaters had already pulled her onto the track. Grace teamed up with Full Metal Jackie, and Monica skated off with Zoey. I looked around, my shoulders sagging. The odd duck out.

"Come on, newbie," Kelly said, skating up beside me. "You can practice on me."

I was equal parts grateful and scared to death. My knees were quaking in my knee pads as we skated to the track.

"You take the outside, Lucy," Kelly directed when we crossed over the tape.

I lined up on her right side. A trickle of sweat slipped down my jawline.

"Now, don't let me knock you over," she said.

Oh hell.

She came at me slowly and bumped her shoulder against mine. I teetered but dug my right skate into the floor and didn't fall. "Good. Again." That time, she bumped me with her hip. I nearly lost it. "Bend your knees more," she said, grabbing my shoulder and pushing it down.

I bent just in time for her to hip check me again. I pressed on the inside wheels on my outer skate and bumped her back. "Nice!" she cheered. "Switch with me."

She grabbed my shirt and pulled me to her left side, my arms flailing as I rolled. She pretended not to notice. "You come at me this time."

I nodded and turned my toes toward her, gently bumping her with my side.

Her glare was disapproving. "You've got to commit to it, Lucy. Really hit me."

I sucked in a quick breath and skated at her again. This time she wavered but her skates didn't budge.

She dragged her rear skate to stop, pulling the tail of my T-shirt to stop me too. "Listen," she said. "This is as much of a mental game as it is a physical one. This is the perfect opportunity for some aggression therapy. Dig up some anger, channel its energy, and use it to destroy your opponent." She put her hands on her hips. "What pisses you off, Lucy?"

West Adler never asking me out pissed me off, but that would lead to daydreaming rather than aggression. Even though it had been weeks since I'd vowed to put him out of my mind, the thought of his grin still made my knees gooey.

My boss often made me nuts, but I was pretty sure we'd shared a moment over the whole Lawson Young ordeal, albeit a very small one. She'd basically left me alone since that morning, and I was feeling more sympathy for her these days than hostility.

Dad and Katherine's lightning-speed romance was up there on the frustration scale as well, but something that made my dad so happy could never give me enough fuel for physical brutality.

That left my mom. And, yep. There was a crap-ton of fury

still bottled up in that compartment. I was mad at the cancer. Mad at the universe. And even a little mad at her, though I tried to keep that one slathered with thick layers of sorrow and longing. When it comes to the dead, sadness is so much easier to stomach than anger.

Kelly pointed at my face, jarring me from my thoughts. "That. Whatever *that* is. Knock my ass out with it, Lucy."

As we took off down the track, snapshot memories clicked through my mind like slides on a View-Master wheel.

The time I'd begged her to stop smoking.

The day she'd laughed off going to the doctor because her cough was "just allergies."

The vision of her pale and tiny body, lifeless in that bed.

My pulse throbbed in my ears. I charged Kelly again, bending deep in my knees before exploding up and slamming my shoulder into her rib cage, just behind her arm. Her right skate came down hard on the floor to push back against me, and I bounced off her, falling sideways and backward onto the track...

...onto the track right in front of Grace's wheels.

Grace tried to stop in time.

But failed.

———

Just before impact, I rolled to my side and ducked my head into my arms. Grace's zebra-striped knee pad came down hard on the back of my left shoulder. I didn't exactly pass out, but the pain triggered stars that twinkled in my eyes and paralyzed me on the floor. The sound of the whistle was still ringing in my ears while I watched the remainder of practice from the bleachers, and held an ice pack to my shoulder.

"Let me see it," Olivia said with a twisted grimace when she skated over at the end of practice.

I turned my back to her and removed the ice pack. Kelly had helped me strip down to my sports bra when we applied the ice. I had worried she'd have to cut the shirt off me, it hurt so badly, but she didn't.

I heard Olivia suck in a sharp breath through her teeth. "Oh, Lucy."

"Is it bad?" I asked. I hadn't seen it since it first happened. Immediately, the spot had flashed a bright pink.

She leaned closer. "It's going to be a nasty bruise. Do you think you should go to the emergency room?"

Kelly had asked the same thing.

"No. I can move my shoulder. It just hurts like hell." I turned back to face her. "You were great out there today."

And she was. She'd spent the last twenty minutes of practice knocking around the coaches like she was Muhammad Ali on roller skates.

"Thanks. It was fun." She dropped down onto her knee pads in front of me and began unlacing my skates, a task I'd been unable to do myself.

I could have kissed her. "Thank you."

"You're welcome. I also have some ibuprofen in my purse if you want some," she said, glancing up at me with a sympathetic smile.

"That would be great."

Grace, Monica, and Zoey skated over. Grace looked like she might burst into tears. "Are you OK, Lucy?" She'd asked that question about a hundred times since I fell underneath her. "Can I do anything at all to help?"

I forced a smile and a nod. "I'll be fine. Nothing's broken. And it wasn't your fault, Grace. Stop beating yourself up about it."

Olivia freed my feet from the skates, then pulled off my knee pads. "I'm surprised you made it till now without serious injury. I'd had you pegged for a broken leg last week."

I winced as I stood. "Shut up."

"Do you still feel like riding all the way to Indianapolis?" Grace asked. "It's going to be a long time in the car."

"Yeah, I'd like to. If I can get a shirt on," I said.

Grace carried my skates and pads over to my gym bag, and we followed her. She flashed a smile as she put my skates in my bag. "I'm pretty sure shirts are optional at the playoffs."

I laughed, and it hurt.

"If it makes you feel any better, you were killing it out there with Kelly before you went down," Zoey said.

I smirked. "Thanks."

"Seriously. I even heard Kelly say so when she came back from the track," Monica agreed.

"Really?" I asked.

"It's true. I saw you hit her just before I..." Grace's voice faded away and her eyes fell to the floor.

With my good arm, I threw the ice pack at her. "Let it go. It was *my* fault."

She nodded, but her expression was unconvinced.

Full Metal Jackie skated over to us, carrying something in her hand. "How's the shoulder?"

"Kinda feels like fire and death are brewing under my shoulder blade, but not too bad," I answered.

She laughed and held out what she was holding. "Put this on a couple of times a day. It should help."

I looked at the white jar. "Arnica cream?"

"I use it all the time. It's great for bruises," she said.

"Thank you, Jackie."

"Don't mention it. Something tells me you're going to need a lot of it."

I laughed and dropped the jar into my bag. "You're a fast learner."

"You're doing good though. Keep it up."

I could've melted into a puddle on the floor.

"Are you going to watch the bout today?" she asked.

Nodding, I gestured around to my friends. "Yeah. We're driving up there as soon as we leave here."

She gave me a thumbs-up. "Great. Then I'll see you there."

I held up the jar. "I'll replace this for you."

She waved her hand. "Don't worry about it. I'm retiring, so I won't need it anymore."

"You're retiring?" Grace asked beside me.

Jackie touched her stomach. "Yep. Came down with the Nine-Month Injury. I'm due in the spring. My first kid with my husband."

"Congratulations. That's awesome," I said.

She beamed. "Thank you. I'll see you guys in Indiana."

———

The inside of Monica's minivan reeked of sweat and arnica cream by the time we reached Indianapolis five hours later after stopping for lunch and to refresh my shoulder's ice pack. We'd spent almost the whole drive studying for our roller derby written test. We arrived at the Indianapolis White River Fieldhouse just after five o'clock that evening. The arena was buzzing with activity. It was a similar scene to my very first derby bout in Nashville, except this time I knew a little bit about what was going on...and there would be no West Adler lurking in the crowd.

Or would there be?

It was possible he'd be there, I guess. He was a team sponsor after all, and the team was going for the championship.

No. No. No. You're over him. You will not spend the entire day out with your friends searching for the guy who blew you off.

I did spend the entire wait in the ticket line searching for him, however.

"This is so exciting!" Zoey squeaked, gripping my arm when we finally got our tickets.

"Come on," Grace said, pulling Monica forward. "They're selling Nashville merchandise."

We followed her to a table full of T-shirts, buttons, magnets, and posters. Kraken was working it. "Hey!" she cheered when she saw us. She came around the table to give us hugs.

"Hey!" I embraced her, carefully favoring my tender shoulder. "Are you not playing today?"

"Yeah, I am." Her eyes searched the crowd. "Just waiting on Jackie to get here and take over sales for me. You guys want some swag to support the team? You get twenty percent off."

"Definitely!" Grace said. "I'm buying shirts for everyone."

"You don't have to do that," I argued.

"I almost killed you today, Lucy. A T-shirt is the least I can do." She tossed me a white shirt off the stack.

"What happened today?" Kraken asked.

"I was doing hits with Kelly and wiped out in front of Grace." I turned and pulled down the stretched neckline of my shirt.

"Ouch. That's going to be pretty tomorrow."

"I know." I sighed and shook my head. "Sometimes I really wonder what I was thinking when I joined this sport."

"I think we all feel that way from time to time. When I started, I couldn't skate at all." She put her hand on my good shoulder and lowered her voice. "I was even worse than you."

I laughed.

"Hang in there, Lucy. Someday you'll be skating in the play-offs too."

Olivia and I found seats in the crowded arena while Grace, Monica, and Zoey went to get drinks. All three levels of the stands were filled with fans sporting an assortment of team colors. I looked at my brochure. Twelve different teams were playing that weekend, and if Nashville won again, they'd play on Sunday for the championship spot in November.

The girls finally crossed the arena. They were carrying beers and popcorn. I waved from our spot halfway up the bleachers.

They climbed the stairs and inched their way across the row to us. We slid down the bench to make room.

"One for The Prodigy," Grace said, handing a beer to Olivia.

"Oh geez." Olivia rolled her eyes as she accepted.

Monica leaned forward with a wild smile. She handed me a cup. "One for The Trip Hazard."

"Hey!" I whined.

Laughing, Olivia pointed at my face. "That's so you."

I couldn't really argue.

Grace raised her cup in the air. "This beer's for Zoey. Congratulations on kicking cancer's ass!"

"To Zoey!" we all cheered and awkwardly clinked our cups together over the heads of the people in front of us. I, of course, had the hardest time stretching toward them, but my teammates came the rest of the way to meet my cup.

"I'm so glad we did this," Olivia said, looking around the arena.

Zoey wiped her mouth on the back of her sleeve. "Me too."

Grace leaned forward. "How are you feeling, Lucy?"

"Or should we start calling you Trip Hazard?" Olivia interrupted. She pointed at Monica. "Because that's funny."

I slumped in my seat. "You guys are so mean to me."

"Have you thought about another roller derby name?" Monica asked.

"Maybe." My cheeks flushed with heat.

Olivia swiveled in her seat to punch me in the good shoulder. "You didn't tell me!"

I rubbed the spot she'd hit. "You didn't ask."

"Well, what is it?"

I grimaced. "It's not much better than Trip Hazard, actually."

"Tell us," Zoey insisted.

"Lights Out Lucy," I said, scrunching up my nose. "My brother used to call me that when we were younger."

Grace dropped her head back and howled with laughter. "Oh my god, I love it."

Monica's eyes widened and she pointed at me. "Your number could be LoL, like L-zero-L."

Olivia clapped. "That's awesome."

"What about you, Prodigy? Have you come up with a name?" Monica asked.

Olivia shook her head. "Haven't given it a single thought."

Both of Zoey's hands shot straight up in the air. "I know what mine is!"

We all turned to look at her. "What?" Olivia asked.

She put up her palms and wiggled her fingers for dramatic effect. "Chemosabe!"

I laughed and sipped my beer. "That's very appropriate."

"What about you?" Olivia asked Monica.

"Are you kidding? My name *is* a derby name." Monica reached down beside her and pulled something from her purse. It was a Lockwood Academy name badge on a lanyard.

"Dr. Monica Hooker," I read aloud. "You're a doctor?"

Olivia laughed. "You're a hooker?"

Nodding her head, Monica tucked the lanyard back into her bag. "Yes and yes. I have a PhD in music and teach high schoolers at Lockwood Academy. I also failed to keep my maiden name when I married Derek Hooker. Roller derby will be the only place I don't have to threaten detention over my name."

"Oh my god, your number could be how much you charge an hour," Grace said.

"How much are hookers?" Zoey asked.

We all exchanged confused glances. "You should Google it," I suggested.

"Heck no!" Zoey's face was bright red. "I use my work phone and don't need that showing up in the history."

Grace was looking up at the ceiling. "I'm pretty sure Julia Roberts charged a hundred dollars an hour in *Pretty Woman*."

"That's going to be so funny," Olivia said, her chuckles finally fading.

I looked down the line at Grace. "What about you, Grace? What's your derby name going to be?"

"Because I'm a seamstress—" Grace drummed her fingers on the table—"Britches Get Stitches."

We all laughed until the people in front of us turned to look.

"That's great." I was laughing so hard, my eyes were watery. As I dabbed the corners with my sleeve, I looked at Olivia. "Any ideas?"

"She's The Prodigy," Grace insisted.

She blew out a slow sigh that puffed out her cheeks. "I can't use The Prodigy. People will think I'm a snob."

Grace waved her hand. "Who gives a shit what people think? The vets say you're the best newbie the team has ever seen."

"They do?" Olivia straightened in her seat.

Monica nodded. "Everyone says it."

"Well, I'm not going to be the Trip Hazard." I frowned and shook my head.

"Why not?" Olivia leaned against me. "Everyone says that too."

I couldn't hit her, so I stuck out my tongue.

She started laughing. "I wonder if they can print one of those falling stick figures on the back of your jersey."

"A stick figure wearing skates," Zoey added.

Olivia pointed at her. "You're right. She doesn't even need a name. Just the symbol. Like Prince."

"I hate all of you," I said, staring out at the track.

"You really should win some kind of award for being the first major injury of our group," Monica said.

"I couldn't agree more," Grace said. "After all, that's what this sport is about, right? Big hits and big injuries."

Monica nodded. "It's not a matter of *if* you'll get hurt, but of how bad and *when*."

Alarm bells should have sounded in my head at this revelation. They didn't.

Zoey raised her cup in the air. "I'm changing the toast! This one's to Lucy. May you stay alive the rest of the season!"

Everyone in the arena started cheering. But, thankfully, it wasn't for me. We all looked out just as our team skated onto the track followed closely by the skaters from Richmond.

Unfortunately, the cheering wouldn't last.

The Music City Rollers lost the bout to the Richmond Vixens in a blowout.

87 to 176.

TEN

BY MONDAY, I was mobile again, but it still hurt to move my left arm. The back of my shoulder was sporting a black and deep purple bruise the size of a small cantaloupe. If the arnica cream was working at all, I would've hated to see the site without it.

When I got to work, on my walk down the hallway to my office, Audrey called my name. Well, she called out for Lily, anyway. It was the first time my metaphorical testicles didn't shrink at the sound of her voice. We'd bonded, I was almost sure of it, and the icy chill I seemed to feel whenever we crossed paths had officially faded.

"Good morning, Audrey."

She didn't look up from her laptop screen. "Jana Carter released another live video this past weekend. They showed a clip of it on Good Morning America today."

I blinked. "Um..."

"Where are we at with it in our marketing plans?" It was obvious she was struggling to maintain her volume and tone. The icy chill returned with a quickness.

Sure, Jana Carter was a trendsetter in Nashville. She was

bordering on legend status in country music and had sold something crazy like thirty million albums worldwide. I got that. But
why, oh why, was she ruining *my* Monday with her stupid live
videos?

"I talked with Ava about that last week," I said. "It's all set up
and ready to go. We just need to send out a couple of teaser clips
inviting fans to watch—"

"For Jake," she said, cutting me off.

I nodded. "Well, yeah." Wasn't that what we were talking
about?

She turned her palms up. "What about everyone else?"

I looked around the room like *everyone else* might be standing
behind me. "Huh?"

She finally looked at me. Nope, *glared* at me. "Have you
figured out how we can implement it to use with all of our other
clients?"

"Uhh..."

Sitting back in her chair, she folded her arms over her chest.
"You've been working here for a while now. I assumed you would
know that I expected to be able to implement this marketing
strategy for everyone we represent."

For a flash, I considered giving her the "when you assume,
you make an ASS out of U and ME" speech but I didn't. Instead,
I forced a smile. "I'll get started on it today as soon as I run last
week's online activity report."

"Thank you. I'd like updated marketing plans no later than
Friday. Before, if at all possible. Please keep me abreast of your
progress."

I stood from the chair.

"And Lily?" She stuck her finger out at me. "Keep this in mind
for the future. I'd like to avoid embarrassing mistakes like this for
the duration of your tenure at this firm."

Anger threatened to boil over inside me, but I bit down on

the inside of my lips and scurried out to the hallway. I stalked to my office, opened the door, then almost slammed it behind me. At the last second, I twisted around and caught it to prevent the bang that would echo back to Audrey, and smashed my fingers in the doorjamb instead.

I swore through clenched teeth, the worst of all cuss words, as blinding tears pooled in my eyes. Then I danced around my office, hugging my wounded hand to my chest and chanting profanities. My fingers were bright red, and a perfect line was etched across my knuckles.

"Lucy?"

I spun toward my door which had bounced open off my fingers.

West Adler was standing in my doorway.

———

Pain, confusion, anger—they all swirled around inside my head, rendering me catatonic in front of the flaky Adonis who'd invited himself into my office. At least I'd stopped hopping around the room like a drunken jackrabbit.

"Are you OK?" West asked *twice* before I finally shook my head.

Still unable to speak, I held up my throbbing fingers, my thoughts caught somewhere between "I need to go to the hospital" and "What the hell are you doing here?" It also crossed my mind that I should just be holding up my middle finger. Good thing for Mr. Says-He'll-Call-But-Doesn't, my fingers were frozen in a claw, maybe in the early stages of rigor mortis.

West gently held my palm. "What did you do?"

"Door," was all I could creak out.

"Is there ice in your break room?" he asked, carefully turning my hand over to look at both sides. The underside of the finger he deserved was streaked with purple at the middle bend.

I nodded.

"Come on." He took hold of my elbow and ushered me down the hall directly to the office break room. Of course he knew where it was. Then he searched all the cabinets around the sink until he found a glass bowl that he carried to the refrigerator.

My knees felt a little wobbly, so I sank down at the table while he filled a bowl, first with ice and then with water. Then he sat down beside me, gingerly took my hand, and eased it into the freezing water. Tears finally ruptured from the edges of my eyes and trickled down my cheeks.

West's free arm curled around my shoulders and pulled me close to him.

It was a moment of weakness, for sure. I should've turned the ice water over onto his lap. But he was so very kind. His touch was nerve tingling and gentle. And he was disarmingly beautiful. Like his face had been put together for the sole purpose of making women question their judgment.

My face rested at the bend of his neck, where fresh cologne and pheromones provided the ultimate analgesic. I sniffed and wiped my nose on the back of my good hand. "I'm sorry," I whispered, pulling back and drying my eyes with my sleeve.

He smiled that earth-shattering smile of his. "Are you kidding? I get to save my favorite damsel in distress a second time before breakfast."

My laugh bubbled out more like a whimper. "What are you doing here?"

"I came by to apologize in person for never calling you."

My head snapped back. "Really? It's been weeks."

"I know, I suck," he said.

Couldn't argue there. It was a good thing he was so pretty.

He tucked a sweaty strand of my hair behind my ear. "I've had a lot going on. I promise it's not you."

It's funny how that's the one statement in the English language that can truly make a person feel exactly the opposite. I hadn't realized my face fell until West ducked his head in front of me to meet my eyes. "Are you free right now though? Maybe for a set of X-rays?"

Damn that charm.

My face broke into a smile, and I nodded. "OK."

West bundled some ice in a wad of paper towels and gently laid it across my knuckles. Then he tore a few more sheets from the roll and folded them into makeshift bandages which he secured around my hand. He dumped the bowl in the sink.

"Where'd you learn to do that?" I asked, admiring his handiwork with the substitute first-aid supplies.

"I've seen lots of injuries on job sites. You learn to work with what you have."

We stopped at my office, and West picked up my purse and keys where I'd dropped them on the floor, then we walked down the hall toward the front. "Why are you limping?" he asked.

Shit.

"Uh, new shoes." It wasn't a complete lie. The shoes were pretty new. They just weren't the cause of the blisters.

"Girls," he said with a sigh.

I paused at Audrey's door which was still open. West knocked on it.

Audrey looked up from her desk and pulled off her glasses when she noticed the paper towel cast. "Lily, what's going on?"

West looked at me. "Lily?"

I ignored him. "I accidentally slammed my hand in my office door, and I may have broken some fingers."

"I'm going to drive her to the emergency room," West added.

Concern and fear flashed across her face, probably fear that I might sue for workman's comp. "Oh, OK. Let me know what they say."

"I will," I said.

West held the door to the receptionist area open for me. "I thought your name was Lucy? Your door even says Lucy Cooper."

I sighed. "It is. Don't get me started."

Claire signed me out on our way through the lobby, and West escorted me to his truck that was parked at the curb. "I see you got a new bumper," I said as he opened the passenger-side door for me.

"Yeah, but I kept the old one as a keepsake." He held the small of my back as I climbed inside and waited until I fastened my seat belt. "I'm thinking about mounting it over my fireplace."

"Very manly," I said.

Smiling, he closed my door and walked around to the driver's side. "You gonna be all right?" he asked, pulling out onto the street.

The first answer that sprang to mind with the memory of my shoulder was "I've recently been worse." I didn't say that, of course. I wasn't ready to tell the world about my adventures in roller derby, especially immediately after proving I couldn't enter a room without incurring serious bodily injury.

I managed a smile. "I think I'll live."

"That's good to hear."

God, he was gorgeous.

"How have you been?" he asked.

"Great, actually. Busy with work and hanging out with friends." I hadn't spent a lot of time with people my own age since before Mom got sick, and it felt good. Really good. "How about you?"

"The same. We've got a new residential high-rise going up in The Gulch. We'll actually get close enough to see it here in a minute. We're hoping to finish it before Thanksgiving, and then, hopefully, business will slow down some in the winter."

"Why didn't you tell me you built the Summit Tower?"

He grinned. "Been asking around about me, huh?"

Nope. Internet stalking.

"Would it have mattered?" he asked.

"Yes."

He shot me a questioning glance.

"I wouldn't have had to give you directions the day you took me to work."

He laughed.

We drove past the Johnny Cash Museum, which already had a line of tourists forming at the door. Then he turned left onto Broadway, the main drag of downtown's honky-tonk scene. Even before nine in the morning, the neon signs were glittery and glowing. Most everything was still closed, so the sidewalks were quiet, but the traffic—which was becoming legendary in Music City—was bumper to bumper as far as my eyes could see.

"You know what? I have a better idea," West said, looking over his shoulder to check his blind spot. He cut into the left lane, then into the turning lane, and turned down a side street. "There's an urgent care on the other side of the river. That would be going away from traffic and would probably have less of a wait time."

"They do X-rays?"

"Yep."

I nodded. "That's a good plan. I really don't want to waste any more of your morning than I already have."

"Don't worry about my morning, Lucy. There's no other way I'd rather spend today."

I frowned and raised my bandaged hand into the air. "Really? You can't think of *anything* better?"

He laughed as he stopped at a red light. "You know what I mean."

"Now that I think about it, half the times I've seen you, you've tried to take me to the hospital."

He shrugged. "Busted. I commissioned the wasp that attacked you in the car, and I filed the door edges in your office extra sharp. All so I could rush in and save the day."

"You did build the tower, after all."

"You've got me all figured out." He flashed a smile across the cab. "Maybe next time I'll try a tactic a little less hazardous to your health. Like dinner, perhaps."

"Dinner is preferable to the emergency room," I said, barely able to sit still in my seat.

"Are you free on Friday?"

Fireworks exploded in my mind. "As long as my injuries aren't fatal, I think I am."

The light turned green, and he grinned and stepped on the gas. "By all means then, let's waste no time getting you the best medical care possible."

——————

There was no wait at the urgent-care clinic since we walked in just as the receptionist unlocked the front door. She was eyeing him with a pinched expression, clearly trying to figure out why she recognized him. I had a feeling this would be a common thing if we ended up spending any amount of time together. And, oh, I hoped we did as I watched him sign me in at the check-in desk because my writing hand was out of commission. Our babies would be beautiful, certain to make Bryan with a *y* and Little Miss Botox jealous.

"Just fill these out, and we'll get you right in to see the doctor." The woman handed West a clipboard filled with papers.

West looked down at the top sheet, then smiled up at me. "Oh, this is going to be fun." We sat down in the waiting room, and he began to fill out the form. "First name, Lucille. Last name, Cooper. Middle name?"

"Louise."

His eyes widened. "Shut up. Your name is Lucy Lou?"

I snapped my good fingers in front of his face. "Focus, please."

"Birthdate?"

"April twenty-fourth, nineteen-none-of-your-beeswax."

He smirked. "You're what? Thirty-eight?"

Had one hand not already been potentially broken, I might have punched him.

"What's your address?"

"534 Echelon Way, Nashville 37211," I answered.

"Echelon Apartments?"

"Don't tell me you built them."

He chuckled and shook his head. "No, I didn't build them, but I do know where they are. Phone number?"

"You have my phone number," I reminded him.

"Not memorized. I'm not Rain Man."

I spouted off my phone number.

"Email address?"

I gave him my work one. Somehow my lulabean424 address felt too personal. Then I told him my insurance and work information.

He flipped to the second page. "Now we get to the good stuff. Reason for visit. *Accident prone.*" He cut his eyes over at me, daring me to argue. I didn't. "Do you smoke?"

"No."

"Does anyone in your home smoke?"

"No."

"Do you drink alcohol?"

"Occasionally."

"How many per week?"

"Two a month, maybe."

He looked up. "It's a fill-in-the-blank question. Think I should divide?"

I grinned. "Sure."

"OK. A half a drink per week. Do you have any of the following medical conditions?" He stopped and put his pen down. "Maybe this is too personal for a first date."

A FIRST DATE?!?!

He said it, not me.

I almost had to fan my face to keep from passing out. *Be cool, Lucy. Be cool.*

"It's fine. Go ahead," I said, trying to keep my voice even and not doing a very good job of it.

He read through a long list of medical conditions to which I answered no. Then he froze—and blushed. "Do you have any STDs?"

I wanted to crawl under my chair and die. "No."

He breathed a dramatic sigh of relief. "Well, I'm glad we've got that over with." He leaned closer and lowered his voice. "Me either, by the way."

I doubled over and buried my red face in my arms on my lap. "Oh my god."

He was laughing, and he nudged me with his elbow. "Come on, we've got to finish this. Do you have any family history of the following: heart disease?"

"No."

"Diabetes?"

"No."

"Stroke?"

"No."

"Cancer?"

Ugh.

"Yes."

He stared at me like he was waiting for me to elaborate. I

didn't. With a slight nod, he checked the "Yes" box. "Do you have any allergies?"

"Bees," I answered.

His face wilted into a mix of sympathy and endearment. "Really?"

"Yep."

"Aww, I almost feel bad for teasing you about the accident." He smiled. "Almost."

"Lucy Cooper?" a woman in purple scrubs said from the door.

I stood, and West looked up at me. "Want me to come or wait out here?"

It wasn't like I was getting a Pap smear. "You can come if you want to."

He got up and nodded toward the door. "After you, my lady."

The nurse took the clipboard and led us back to a small cubicle with half-walls. She took my blood pressure and temperature. Both were normal. "Step up on the scales so I can get your weight," she said.

My eyes shot to West.

He laughed and crossed his tanned and chiseled arms over his chest. "Seriously? I can hear about your sexual disease history but can't see how much you weigh?"

My heart was pounding in my chest. "No. Turn around."

His eye roll seemed to be the pivot on which his whole body turned. The nurse was trying not to smile. I kicked off my charcoal ankle boots—because every ounce helps—and stepped up on the scale. She wrote down the number, and I quickly stepped off. "You can turn around now," I said to West as I slipped on my shoes again.

He sighed and shook his head. "Girls are so weird."

"Follow me," the nurse said, walking down the hallway.

When we reached the tiny exam room, there weren't any

chairs. West helped me up onto the exam table, and then stood beside me.

"So what happened?" the nurse asked.

"Yeah," West echoed. "What exactly happened?"

I frowned. "Jana Carter."

They both exchanged a puzzled glance.

"I was a little mad at my boss, so I slammed the door in my office. Then I thought better of it and tried to catch it." I held up my bandaged hand. "At least the sound was muffled."

The nurse unwound the paper towels around my hand. Almost all the ice had melted, and the towels were soaked. She dropped them in the trash and examined my hand. My fingers were frostbite red, but the pain had eased, and there didn't seem to be any swelling. Slowly, I curled my fingers into a fist. It hurt and my joints were stiff from the cold, but my fingers bent without hindrance.

"No! No! Don't bend them. Let's get an X-ray first," she said. She stood and picked up her notes. "Let's go take the pictures. Then the doctor will be in."

She took me down the hall and took two quick X-rays of my hand while West waited in the exam room. When the nurse returned me to him and left us alone, I carefully looked over my hand. "They aren't broken," I said, wiggling my fingers again.

"What about your purple middle finger?" he asked.

I looked at it more closely. "It could be a busted blood vessel under the skin."

"I don't know. It looks broken to me," he said.

I shook my head. "It's not. I'm sure."

He raised an eyebrow. "Want to put a wager on it?"

I laughed. "Absolutely. What did you have in mind?"

He thought for a moment, and I was thankful for the excuse to stare at him.

"I've got it," he finally said. He gripped the front corners of the exam table on either side of my legs and leaned on his arms toward me. "If it's broken, you go out with me on Friday, and we do *anything* I want."

The temperature in the clinic jumped about a thousand degrees.

I swallowed. "Anything?"

He leaned closer. "Anything." His tone was dark and dangerous.

The butterflies in my stomach were about to rattle me off the table.

Suddenly, West burst out laughing. "I wish you could see your face right now."

I hid behind my hands.

He took my wrists and gently pulled them away. "I'm kidding, Lucy. I promise I won't go all *Fifty Shades* on you."

That only made me blush harder.

"Not yet, anyway," he added with a wink. Then he pointed at my face. "But if I want to eat cereal in my underwear and watch the latest Avengers movie on Netflix, you're not allowed to judge me."

I laughed. "OK. What if I win?"

He straightened and stuffed his hands into his pockets. "The same terms. On my dime."

"Really?" I asked.

He nodded. "Yep. No limits. No budget. We do anything you want."

I stuck out my good hand and he shook it. "West Adler, you have a deal."

———

Thirty minutes later, he pulled into the parking garage at the Summit Tower and parked a few cars down from my new

SUV. "That's mine," I said, pointing to it as we walked to the exit.

"I like it. Did they treat you well at CarMart?" he asked.

"They did. Thanks to you."

He shook his head. "They would have anyway. They're a good company."

"Still, I appreciate you letting me throw your name around."

"Anytime."

We walked into the downstairs lobby. "You really don't have to walk me back to the office. I'm fine."

He laughed and looked over at me as he pressed the up button for the elevator on the wall. "No, I need to see you safely back to work because if I've learned anything in the very short time I've known you, it's you're a liability."

I playfully shoved his shoulder with my left hand, and he reached out and grabbed it. He didn't immediately let go. *One Mississippi...two Mississippi...three Mississippi....*

"I saw you trip on the stairs, by the way," he said, watching the numbers above the doors light up as the elevator descended.

"What? When?"

"The day I dropped you off after you wrecked your car. You tripped walking up the front steps outside."

I opened my mouth to lie, but what was the point? "I didn't know you saw that."

He chuckled. "I know."

Eight Mississippi.

The doors slid open and two men in business suits walked off. West's hand was still wrapped around mine when we stepped inside. I feared I might drop dead from a heart arrhythmia by the time we reached the sixteenth floor. He looked over at me from where he was leaning against the glass wall and handrail. "I'm sorry you hurt your hand today, Lucy, but I'm glad I got to see you."

God, I hoped my hand wasn't sweating in his.

"And I'm glad it wasn't broken," he said, cracking a smile.

I lifted an eyebrow. "Are you?"

He nodded. "Absolutely. It takes all the pressure off me having to plan a perfect second date."

Yep. I'm going to die. Cause of death: heart explosion.

"It's going to be hard to top urgent care though, so good luck," he said, managing to keep a straight face.

I wished I could say something witty back, but my mind had turned to goo...pink, bubbly, glittery goo. When the elevator dinged at my floor, I actually forgot to get off. West had to tug me forward before my feet started moving. He looked toward Claire's desk. "Think you can handle it the rest of the way by yourself?"

"I think so." But dang it, I didn't want to. "Thanks again, for everything, West."

He squeezed my hand. "I'll play the hero anytime you need me."

We lingered there for a moment, neither of us wanting to move. Finally, he smiled and took a step back, dropping my hand but not my heart as he backed away. "I'll see you Friday?"

"If you don't do anything between now and then to make me forget I've forgiven you for not calling." My brain definitely worked better outside his cologne-filled bubble of personal space.

He laughed and bowed to me at the elevator. "I wouldn't dream of it."

The doors slid open again, and he stepped backward inside.

I waved with my good hand. "Bye."

"Bye, Lucy."

―――――

The parking lot at the Rollers' Sweatshop was packed when I pulled into the lot that evening. I ended up having to park across the street from our practice building. Zoey pulled in behind me, and we walked toward the building together. "What on earth is going on?" she asked, looking around at all the cars.

"I have no idea, but I have a bad feeling about it," I said.

She looked over at me. "I'm surprised you're skating tonight. How's your shoulder?"

"It still hurts like hell, but I wasn't about to skip out on practice. I'm going to tell Shamrocker I have to take it easy though if we do any contact," I said.

We walked through the front door and found the entire team putting on their skates. I gulped. Olivia was gearing up with Grace and Monica near the bathroom. Zoey and I hurried over and dropped our bags. "What's going on?" I asked my roommate.

"I'm not sure, but Styx said the whole team would be here tonight," she said.

"Probably because of the disaster at playoffs," Grace whispered.

I unzipped my bag. "This is bad."

"Why are you here?" Olivia asked. "Shouldn't you be on the injured list?"

My eyes widened. "Do we have an injured list? I feel like I should have a permanent spot reserved if we do."

She smiled. "Sorry I didn't respond to your messages earlier. It's been a crazy day. I didn't know if I was going to be able to make it."

"It was a weird day for me too," I said, pulling on my knee pads.

"Yeah. What happened? Your messages were very cryptic."

"I had a date."

"A date?" Grace asked.

"A date with who?" Zoey wanted to know.

I held my finger over my lips. "I don't want to say. Nothing may come of it, so let's not make a bigger deal out of it than it is."

"Make a big deal out of what?" Monica asked, scooting closer so she could hear.

"Lucy went on a date," Grace told her.

"Was it *him*?" Olivia asked.

I couldn't stop my lips from bending into a smile.

"Wait. Are you talking about the guy you were stalking at the bout?" Zoey asked.

"That's the one," Olivia answered, tying her skates. "You saw him today?"

"He took me to the emergency room," I said.

"The emergency room?" all four of them asked in unison.

"Well, urgent care." I held up my hand. My middle finger was taped to my ring finger. "I slammed my hand in my office door. Nothing's broken, but the doctor taped my fingers to keep me from moving the middle one. It's bruised pretty bad along the joint."

"Geez, Lucy," Olivia said, shaking her head. "You really should be permanently on the list."

I tightened a loose wheel on my skates. "I know."

"And a visit to urgent care isn't a date," she added.

"He called it a date, and he held my hand when he walked me back to the office," I told her.

Her head snapped back in surprise. "Really?"

"Wait. What kind of hand-holding?" Monica asked. "Pancaking or waffling?"

We all turned to her.

"What?" I asked.

"The kids in my class say this is pancaking." Monica clasped her hands together. "And this is waffling." She laced her fingers together. "Waffling is for dating."

"I guess we were pancaking," I answered.

Monica shook her head with mock sadness. "I'm sorry, Lucy. I just don't know how serious he is about it then."

We all laughed. "Do sixth graders hold the jury on the telltale signs of true love now?" Grace asked.

"They're probably a hell of a lot smarter about it than we are," Olivia said, strapping on her helmet.

"Truth," I agreed.

"Amen, sister," Zoey said.

Olivia stood. "So are you going to see him again?"

"Friday night."

This evoked collective "Ooos" from my friends.

"Where's he taking you?" Monica asked.

"Anywhere I want. He lost a bet, so I get to pick. And you guys will have to help me plan it because I have zero dating experience in this city."

Suddenly, all three coaches skated out from a group that was gathered at the cage, grinding to a stop in front of us. Midnight Maven was still sporting a busted lip from the bout. None of them were smiling.

"Fresh Meat!" Shamrocker screamed. "I need your attention! There's been a change of plans." She pointed toward the cage. "We have a guest coach this evening! Medusa!"

For the first time ever, there was no applause when Medusa rolled into view. I think we were all too stunned to clap, and certainly too worried to be excited. Her skates pounded against the floor as she skated over.

"Listen up, everyone." Medusa didn't even have to shout. It was so quiet in that crowded room, a mouse would've been heard taking a dump in the rafters. "I'm embarrassed," she said flatly, resting her hands on her hips. "I'm humiliated, actually. We were the fifth-ranked team in the world, and we were beaten by the thirty-second ranked team on our first day at the division play-offs." She pointed out at all of us. "And if you aren't as ashamed as I am, you don't belong here."

She crossed her arms and stared at the floor a moment. "So

here's what's going to happen. Since, obviously, we don't know how to play this game, we're going back to the basics. I'm demoting everyone in this room back to Fresh Meat."

The few jaws I could see in my peripheral vision dropped just a smidge. I wanted to turn around and survey the room, but I didn't dare.

"Shamrocker tells me this session of Derby 101 has four weeks left," Medusa continued. "Every person in this room is now required to attend all of them if you want to play for the Music City Rollers next season."

She crossed her arms and stared the whole room down. "Any questions?"

ELEVEN

I HAVE SOME BAD NEWS.

That's not the kind of text message a girl wants to get from her crush two days after a wonderful, albeit very weird, first date. My heart withered, and I would have slumped back in my office chair if my body would've allowed it. There had been no *taking it easy* as I'd planned for practice on Monday night. Medusa had punished the Rollers, and our Fresh Meat group certainly earned our title because of it.

You're really a woman? I texted back.

West: *Not the last time I checked.*

Me: *Then what's up?*

"I feel like it's something I should explain in person."

I looked up, and West was standing in my doorway holding a small bouquet of colorful daisies. Butterflies erupted in my stomach, and my face broke into a huge smile as he walked in the room. "How do you keep getting in here?" I got up and walked around my desk to meet him. "You're going to get our receptionist fired."

He handed me the flowers and pointed to his head. "It's the hair. Ladies can't say no to the hair."

"I have absolutely no doubt of that." I lifted the daisies to my nose. They smelled like feet. "Thanks for the flowers. They're beautiful."

"They're fake," he said with a chuckle. "I stopped at the Dollar Barn for paper towels this morning and saw them."

I laughed. "Excellent. Then I can't kill them." I leaned against my desk. "What's your bad news?"

He stuffed his fists into the pockets of his jeans, causing his shoulders to stretch the pale blue fabric of his polo shirt. "Friday isn't going to work for our second date."

I steeled my face, refusing to show my disappointment. I forced a small, pathetic laugh and waved him off with my hand. "It's OK. Not a big deal."

He took a step toward me and hooked his fingers around my hand. "I was hoping we could push Friday to date number three and have lunch today instead."

I swatted him across the head with the fake flowers. "That's a dirty thing to tell a girl, West Adler."

He laughed and moved even closer to me. The testosterone wafting off him was making my brain hazy. "But isn't this the phase of dating where we're supposed to be all mysterious and not say what we really mean?"

I pointed at him. "Don't you dare start that with me."

He pulled our hands up between us, then pressed his palm against mine and laced our fingers together. *Waffling! We have waffling!*

"Then how about I tell you that I simply couldn't wait till Friday to see you again?" He kissed my fingers. "Can I take you to lunch?"

"Lily?"

Crap.

West turned toward the door, and I looked around him after a quick survey of his backside, of course. Audrey walked into my office carrying a legal pad and a pen. "Am I interrupting something?" she asked, her eyes daring me to say that she was. A second later, Peter walked in behind her, seemingly flustered, like she'd pulled him away from something important—because she probably had.

I stood, and West took a step back. "Of course you're not interrupting. Audrey, this is my friend West Adler. West, this is my boss Audrey Scott and her assistant Peter Jansen."

They all shook hands.

Audrey cut her eyes with clear disapproval. "Yes, I remember you were here on Monday as well."

West nodded. "I was here on business Monday when I heard Miss Cooper scream out in pain."

On business?

Audrey's brain must have been riding the same train as mine. "You were here on business? What did you say your name was?"

He tapped his finger over the embroidered logo on his shirt. "West Adler."

Peter leaned forward and whispered something in Audrey's ear. I watched the light bulb flicker on behind my boss's glaring eyes. "Oh yes, Adler Construction. I didn't realize you weren't finished with the building."

"We are finished. I was doing a walkthrough to make sure we didn't miss any details," West lied. "That's when I heard the young lady scream, and I took her to the hospital."

"That's right," she said, turning her attention back to me. "Was anything broken?"

"No, ma'am." I'd already told her that, twice.

"Excellent. Well, thank you, Mr. Adler, for coming by to check on her, but we really do have a busy day ahead of us," Audrey said.

West touched the small of my back. "I actually came by today to take her to lunch."

Her laugh dripped with derision. "She doesn't go to lunch."

West crossed his spectacular arms. Even Audrey glanced down at them. "Is she not allowed to go to lunch? Because I'm pretty sure that's illegal," he said.

She checked her watch. "I didn't even realize it was so late. And yes, of course she's allowed to take a lunch break. I just meant, she usually eats in her office."

He frowned at me. "Well, we're going to have to change that." He smiled and motioned to the door. "Shall we?"

Before Audrey could think of a reason for me to stay, I scurried behind my desk and picked up my purse off the floor. "I'd love to." I grabbed my phone and dropped it in the bag. "Audrey, can we bring you something back?"

Audrey's wide eyes couldn't figure out where to stare. She looked at Peter for help, but he didn't offer any. "No—No, thank you," she stammered. "But I need to talk to you about the email you sent me this morning. I've got a call with Jake in about twenty minutes."

I joined West by the door. "We can talk about the video stats when I get back. Please schedule some time with Jake to record a couple of short teaser videos to post over the next week. Just short clips to remind people that he'll be streaming live from the party next Saturday. The clips don't have to be live though."

"I agree. I'll talk to him about it today." She looked down at the clipboard. "I'm thinking he should post them on Sunday and Thursday."

"That's a great plan. We can put them on all his social-media accounts and send it out to the fan club. All he has to do is record them."

"Will you be available for the recording session?" she asked.

I smiled. "Of course, just let me know when and where *after* I get back from lunch." Instinctively, I almost clamped my hand over my mouth and apologized, but I didn't. Behind Audrey's back, Peter was struggling to keep a straight face. West and I passed by them into the hall. "Can you pull the door closed on your way out?" I asked her, shocking no one more than myself.

I heard a tiny snort from Peter's direction.

"Um, sure," she said.

As we walked toward the front office, West was struggling to keep a straight face. I couldn't even look at him. We heard my office door shut behind us, and he lost it. I covered his mouth with my hand to stifle the laugh as we stumbled into the reception area.

"Oh man. That was so funny," he said.

"I've never talked to her like that. Maybe roll—" I stopped myself from saying "maybe roller derby is starting to toughen me up." I laughed to cover my blunder as the door to the hall closed behind us. "Did you see the look on her face?"

West nodded, still chuckling. "Priceless."

Claire looked up, confused.

"We're going to lunch," I told her. "Please send my calls to voicemail."

"OK. Have a nice time." She waved as we walked out the door, unable to mask the pleasant surprise in her voice.

My phone buzzed with a text message on our walk through the lobby. It was from Peter. *You just made my life —P.B.J.*

I snickered as West pressed the button to call the elevator. "I hope I didn't get you in trouble back there. Maybe I should have called first," he said.

I waved my hand. "Don't worry about Audrey. That was her resting bitch face. She's like that even on a good day, if she ever has any."

"How do you stand it?" he asked as the elevator doors opened and we stepped inside. He pressed the button for the lobby.

"I avoid her as much as possible. Her sister's pretty great though. Ava. I like her a lot," I said.

He shook his head. "I can't believe she calls you Lily. How long have you worked here?"

"A couple of months."

He turned to face me. "Why don't you say something to her? Correct her?"

I shrugged. "There's a certain window of time for making corrections like that, and that window closed a long time ago. I honestly worry she might fire me out of embarrassment."

"Let her fire you. You can come work for me. What is it you do again?"

"Online marketing."

He nodded. "Our company could definitely use some of that."

I raised an eyebrow. "Audrey was coming in to talk about the views and clicks on the new music video Jake Barrett released to promote his album that drops this week."

He touched his chest. "I could totally make a music video."

"Oh, really?" I crossed my arms.

He leaned toward me, tipping his chin slightly up and squinting with mock disgust. "Don't look at me like you're Audrey Scott. You don't know my life." With that, he popped his collar and put on his sunglasses. He began humming the melody to "Stayin' Alive" and disco dancing for all of downtown Nashville to see through the glass walls of the Summit Tower.

The elevator doors slid open. West froze, mid *Saturday Night Fever* stance, as the two women waiting to get on erupted in laughter. So did I. He pressed his lips together and slowly lowered his John Travolta disco finger.

"Don't stop dancing on our account," the older of the two women said as they walked inside. "I was just about to break out some dollar bills for you."

West's shoulders were shaking with silent laughter as he

pulled off his sunglasses and pinched the bridge of his nose. When he looked at me, happy tears sparkled in his eyes.

"That was impressive," I said as the elevator began its descent again.

He turned his palms up. "But how many views and clicks would it get?"

"Millions, no doubt."

Still laughing, he slipped his arm around my waist and pulled me against his side. My knees felt like jelly underneath me. When we reached the lobby, he wished the women a good day and led me toward the parking garage.

"So about this Jake Barrett party," he said as we walked to his truck.

I narrowed my eyes at him. "Is that where all this super-human charm is coming from lately? Are you trying to get into my good graces so I'll take you to the party at Jake's house?"

"What?" he asked, a slight pitch of offense in his deep voice. He pulled me closer, digging his fingers into my hip bone. "Absolutely not. I'm trying to get into your good graces so I can get *into your pants*, silly girl."

I laughed so loudly it echoed off the concrete walls of the parking garage. "Seriously?"

He shrugged. "Of course. I'm a dude." He looked at me and jerked his thumb over his shoulder toward the building. "Didn't we just agree to skip the mystery and say what we really mean?"

"Well...yeah, but...um..."

We reached his truck, and he put one hand on the passenger-side door handle and used his arm to maneuver me against the back door. Suddenly his face was inches from my own, and he was smiling as he stared at my lips. "I don't think I've seen you this flustered since the car accident. Are you nervous?"

I swallowed.

He leaned in and lowered his voice to a whisper. "Good."

Then, with a forceful jerk, he pulled the door open and laughed. "Relax, Lucy. I'm joking."

I took a deep breath and let it out in a shaky chuckle.

He smiled as I got inside, then leaned in my doorway. "Well, sort of." He winked at me and closed the door.

———

Lunch was ridiculously delicious. West took me to a new place that had recently opened in The Gulch, just a few blocks down from the skyscraper his company was building. Biscuit Love was aptly named with fluffy biscuits piled high with chicken and gravy (on mine) and shaved country ham, fried eggs, and gravy (on his).

We sat at a table near the window that overlooked the bustling sidewalk outside. "This may be the best breakfast I've ever had," I said, wiping a dribble of gravy from my chin.

"Wait, try this." West held up something that looked like a donut hole to my lips. It was oozing with smushed berries and cream sauce.

I bit into and had to will my eyes to not roll back in my head. "Oh my god." I chewed the bite slowly, savoring the flavors. Blueberry, lemon, cream cheese...

When I opened my eyes, West was biting his lower lip as he watched me. "You're beautiful, Lucy."

I licked my lips and laughed. "You know, I'm really liking this whole honesty thing. Everyone should date this way."

He leaned on his elbow. "I completely agree. I'm going to do this with all the women I'm seeing."

My mouth dropped open enough for him to notice.

"I'm kidding."

I reached over to his plate and picked up the rest of the donut hole. "You like teasing me," I said, popping the rest of it in my mouth.

He sat back in his chair. "You make it *so* easy. I've never seen anyone blush as quickly as you."

"Those things are delicious." I pointed to his empty bowl.

"Should I order some more?" he asked.

I shook my head and wiped my mouth with my napkin. "God, no. I'll be in a food coma by the time I get back to work. Thank you for lunch."

"Thank you for joining me." He pushed his plate away. "Tell me something I don't know about Lucy Cooper."

"You know a lot," I said with a laugh. "My address, my medical history..."

He pointed at me. "Your STD status."

I laughed. "And that. What else is there?"

"Do you have any pets? You already met mine," he said.

"Not since I was a kid, and never for any significant amount of time even then. My mother always loved the idea of having animals until we actually had them, so the dogs and the teacup pig never lasted very long around our house."

"You had a teacup pig?"

I nodded. "His name was Keith Richards."

West laughed. "You had a pig named Keith Richards?"

"He was born with a birth defect that made him walk a little sideways, so Mom started calling him Keith Richards." I thought for a second. "We also had a hedgehog named Donkey Kong for a little while."

"Did your Mom name him too?" he asked.

I shook my head. "My brother, but he's just like her. I told him we should name the hedgehog Sonic, obviously."

"Obviously," West agreed.

"So he named it Donkey Kong." I chuckled and chewed on the end of my straw. "I almost forgot about that."

"Do you have any more siblings?"

"Nope. Just me and Ethan. Oh, wait. I guess that's not exactly true anymore. I now have a stepbrother named Bryan who lives in St. Louis."

His head pulled back. "So your parents are divorced?"

My shoulders sagged. "No. My mom passed away last year."

He frowned, and it was almost as adorable as his smile. "I'm really sorry to hear that. Was she sick?"

"Lung cancer. By the time she was diagnosed, it had spread all over her body. There wasn't much they could do to save her."

West reached across the table and put his hand on mine. "I'm really sorry, Lucy."

"Thank you." The corners of my eyes were beginning to tingle. We needed to change the subject. Fast. "What about you? Any siblings?"

He withdrew his hand. I was determined to not read into it. "I have a brother," he said.

"Please tell me his name is East," I begged, clasping my hands beneath my chin.

He balled his napkin and threw it at me. "His name is Lucas."

"Is he in the construction business too?"

"No. We're not really close. He lives up near Bristol now and works for the city."

He was probably the mayor if the rumors were true about the Adlers.

"I went to school in Johnson City, then lived there for a couple of years before I moved back home."

"I know exactly where it is. You're a Buccaneer?" he asked.

I nodded. "It was the farthest place I could go away to school and still get in-state tuition."

He laughed. "That's always a good reason. I did the opposite. Went to school practically in my backyard at Belmont."

I already knew that.

"What did you study?" I asked, though I already knew that too.

"Business."

I raised my hand. "Marketing."

"You know, we'd make one hell of a corporate power couple," he said.

My eyebrow lifted. "Is that a proposition?"

His perfect lips spread into a smile. "It's certainly looking like it could be."

I leaned my elbows on the table. "OK. I have to ask. Why did you wait a month to ask me out? I really thought we had a connection the day we met." I held up my hands. "Then nothing for weeks."

He sat back in his chair. "Do you want the truth?"

I nodded, though I wasn't so sure about it.

"I was seeing someone when I met you."

My heart deflated with all the force of a punctured balloon.

Then he reached across the table and took my hand again. "I wanted to call you. I wanted to see you. But I needed to do it the right way."

Something tugged in my chest. It was my heart swelling again.

"Will you forgive me?" he asked.

I smiled. "I think I already did."

When we got back to my office, he pulled up to the curb instead of parking in the garage. "I have meetings this afternoon in Franklin, so I have to run. Sorry, I can't walk you up," he said.

"It's all right. I think I can find my way. Thanks again for lunch. It was great."

He pointed up at the building. "I hope your boss doesn't give you too hard of a time."

"She will, but you won't be the reason. And even if you were, it would be worth it."

His smile was intoxicating. "I should be done by four or so today," he said. "Do you have plans for dinner?"

No, but I did have practice. Mandatory practice. Practice I wasn't ready to tell him about.

"I don't, but I have other plans tonight I can't get out of," I said, hoping that would be explanation enough.

It wasn't.

"Another hot date lined up?"

I put my hand on the door handle. "Wouldn't you like to know?"

"I actually would." He stretched his arm along the back of our bench seat.

I hesitated. "I'll tell you someday, maybe."

He sighed. "We're still on for Friday though?"

"Absolutely."

"Any hints as to where we're going?"

"Nope. I'm keeping that a secret too." I opened my door.

"I thought we agreed to not play games," he said, cutting his eyes over at me.

I slid out of the truck and leaned back in from the curb. "No, West. *You* agreed. I never did."

He laughed. "That's how it's going to go down, huh? Me laying my heart out and you keeping secrets?"

"Only for a little while. I'll see you Friday, West."

———

"Guess what," I told Monica later that evening as our small group of friends pushed and shoved each other around one of the two tracks that were taped onto the floor of the practice arena. There were two tracks to accommodate all the skaters who'd taken Medusa's warning literally. That meant *everyone* had shown up for our defensive-blocking practice.

Monica pushed Zoey off the track. "What?"

"There was waffling today," I said.

She gave me a high five as Zoey scrambled to catch back up with us. "Congratulations, Lucy!"

"Zoey, you have to come back onto the track *behind* Monica!" Maven shouted at us.

"You saw him again?" Olivia, our mock jammer for the drill, asked as she tried to push between me and Grace.

I nodded. "He came by my office and took me to lunch."

"That's awesome," Grace said.

"Congrats," Zoey added, shaking my shoulder.

"Does the waffling constitute a relationship serious enough to tell your friends who this mystery man is?" Monica asked.

I bit my lower lip. On one hand, I *really* wanted to tell them. It had been such a long time since I'd had girlfriends to share boy news with and much longer since I'd had boy news worth sharing. But on the other, West was a team sponsor. What if Olivia was right, and word got around that we were dating? Would the girls think I was trying to whore my way onto the team? Would the coaches feel obligated to keep me even if I didn't deserve to be there? Nope. Couldn't do it. Not yet.

"Can't. Afraid I'll jinx it," I lied. Sort of.

Grace bumped me with her hip. I didn't wobble nearly as much as I expected. "How are we supposed to live vicariously through you if you never give up the details?"

I laughed. "So you're living vicariously through my love life now too?"

"Yeah. Not exactly. I'm just hoping someone can tell me there's still hope in the dating scene, in case I ever stop hating men," Grace said.

Zoey shoulder checked Monica. "How's the divorce coming, Grace?"

Grace's arm was anchored against mine. "It's coming, but not fast enough. We're currently fighting over the dog."

"The dog?" Olivia asked, her face squashed between Grace's arm and my shoulder as she tried to come through the wall we'd formed to block her.

Grace pressed into me. "Yeah. Our Golden Retriever, Bodhi. Technically, I gave him to Clayton as a birthday gift a few years ago, but he's *my* dog. Clay doesn't give a shit about him."

"Your husband's name is Clayton?" I asked, straining to keep contact with her.

"Yeah. Clayton Byron Maxfield the Third."

"He even sounds like an asshole," Olivia said.

Grace laughed. "Right?"

Olivia finally busted Grace and I apart. She patted my helmet. "You're the jammer."

I skated to the back of our little group, and she took my spot with Grace. I skated as fast as I could toward them to try and break through, like a vicious game of Red Rover on roller skates. I hit Grace's protruding backside and bounced back without breaking them apart.

She did stumble a bit though. "So is this thing with the mystery man getting pretty serious?"

"I wouldn't call it serious. Today was our first *real* date, I guess. I mean we can't really count him driving me to urgent care." I skated at them again and collided where their shoulders met and pushed against my toe stops to try and burst through.

"But you still like him?" Olivia's voice was strained and she pushed against Grace to hold me back.

I sighed and my face broke out in a gooey smile against Grace's arm.

She turned and pointed at me. "Enough said."

I took advantage of her movement and broke through the small space. "He wanted to go out again tonight."

Grace took my spot as jammer. Olivia and I braced for her impact. She busted us apart like a bowling ball, knocking the wind out of me. I held up my hand, panting. "I need a break. Go attack Zoey and Monica," I told Grace.

"Wimp," she teased as she caught up with our other friends.

Olivia and I skated easily. "Did you tell him you're doing this?" Olivia asked, motioning around the track.

I shook my head. "Not yet. The skills test is coming up soon. I'm going to try and keep it quiet till then. There's no point in making myself look even more stupid if I don't pass."

Olivia smiled over at me. "You'll get there, Lucy."

"You really think so?"

"I do." She looked down at her skates. "To be honest, I thought you would've already quit, but you didn't. I really think you can do it. I'm proud of you."

I gave her shoulder a playful shove, a move she usually used on me. "Look at you being all sentimental and shit."

She laughed. "Don't get used to it."

We skated for a half a lap in silence. "I'm really afraid I'm going to fail. I don't know how I'm ever going to get twenty-seven laps. My record is only twenty-four."

"You just need to skate more. We'll start going to the park and the skating rink on my days off. I'll help you."

"Olivia, all your days off are spent here."

"Yeah, I guess that's true." She looked around. "Maybe Zoey, Grace, or Monica can go with you."

I stopped skating. "That gives me an idea."

TWELVE

ON FRIDAY MORNING, I was drafting the email for Jake Barrett's fan club announcing his "Live from the Release Party" forthcoming video when Ava Scott walked into my office. She jingled the keys in her hand. "You ready?"

My mouth fell open as confusion swirled around in my brain. "Ready for what?"

She lifted an eyebrow. "To go to Jake's?" She sounded as perplexed as I felt.

"We're going to Jake's?"

"Audrey emailed me on Wednesday and said I was taking you to his house today to video something for the fan club," she said.

"At two o'clock today, right?"

"She told me ten."

I opened up my email inbox and went to the folder marked with Audrey's name. I quickly found the message and clicked it open. "Yes. Here it says, 'Will you be available for Ava to take you to Jake's house on Friday at two? Please advise.'"

Please advise. I chuckled. Thanks to Peter, I'd never again be able to read her emails without laughing.

Ava was looking at her phone when I glanced up. "My email says, 'Can you set up the interview for Jake on Friday at ten question mark.'" She groaned. "You know what happened? She keeps trying that speech-to-text thing on her phone. The line actually reads 'question mark.' Look." She walked over and showed me her phone.

I laughed. "Oh wow."

She sighed and tucked her phone back into her pocket. "I'll call Jake and see if we can reschedule it." She started to turn toward the hallway.

"Ava, wait. I can go." I looked up at the clock. It was half past nine. "It shouldn't take that long, right?"

She cupped her hands around her mouth and lowered her voice to a loud whisper. "I have no idea what we're doing, honestly. I'm just your driver."

I laughed. It was hard to believe she and Audrey were even related. "Let me finish up this email and we'll go."

"Great. I'm going to grab a drink from the break room," she said, and then she was gone.

I finished the copy for the email and sent it off to be proof-read and sent by Jake's fan club manager, then I shut down my computer and gathered up my things. As I started to get up, I froze. *Oh crap. I'm going to Jake Barrett's house. Right now.*

I plopped back down in my seat and attempted to check my hair in the reflection of my computer monitor.

"You look gorgeous, dah'ling," Ava said dramatically at my door once again.

I stood. "I get nervous around clients."

She waved her hand like it was no big deal. "Jake is the last client you ever need to worry about in this office."

Easy for her to say. She wore a black pencil skirt and a sleeveless ivory cowl-neck sweater. She looked like Nashville's modern-day tribute to Audrey Hepburn with her flawless makeup and her smooth dark hair up in a twist. *Wait.* "Ava and Audrey," I said, closing my door behind us as we walked out. "Are you two named after the actresses?"

She smiled and gave a slight nod. "Our mother was obsessed with the Golden Age of Hollywood. We have a brother named Cary and had a Himalayan cat named Clark Gable."

"That's hilarious. Did you call him Clark?"

She shook her head. "Nope." We paused at Claire's desk on our way out of the building. "Claire, I probably won't be back in today," Ava said. "But if Jim Beale or anyone else from Torrent calls, please have them call me on my cell phone."

Claire scribbled some notes on the pad of paper. "Do they have your cell number or should I give it out?"

"They should have it, but if they don't, give it to them," Ava said.

Claire looked at me. "Are you coming back today?"

I nodded. "Yes. I'll hopefully be back in a couple of hours."

"Do you have a lot of work to get done?" Ava asked, holding the door open for me as we exited the reception area.

"Unfortunately. Audrey has me rewriting all of our clients' marketing plans to include live video."

She pressed the button for the elevator. "She mentioned something about that. She wants to use it with everyone now?"

I nodded.

"Melvin Brooks? Does he even have a computer?"

"No, and he still uses a flip phone. I'm putting it on the plan just so I can turn it in and she can see how ridiculous it is."

She laughed as we got on the elevator. "You're a fast learner, Lucy."

Ava drove a sleek, expensive black sports car that I'd often seen parked in a reserved space in the garage. Inside it smelled like new leather and money. So I assumed the hassle of putting up with her sister had its perks. "Was your sister always so..." I struggled to find a word that fit Audrey that wouldn't risk me getting fired.

"Bitchy?" Ava asked with a laugh as she merged onto I-65 South.

I glanced out the window to hide a smile. "Well, I was going to say something else, but—"

"Why bother? Bitchy fits."

I laughed.

"And no, she wasn't always so difficult." She gripped the steering wheel with both hands and checked her blind spot to change lanes. "I think it's the pressure she puts on herself. She built the company out of nothing, you know?"

I shook my head. "All I really know about the company is what's on the website, and despite my pleas for more content, that's not much."

She smiled but didn't look at me. "There's a reason for that. Audrey has a past in this town that she'd like to keep buried as much as possible."

My mouth gaped a bit. "Do tell."

"Have you ever heard of the band Sugar Creek?" she asked.

I thought for a second. "It sounds familiar."

"Back in the nineties, they were a country duo formed by two Nashville newcomers, Jana Carter and..."

"Don't tell me, your sister?"

"Audrey Scott," she said.

I turned all the way toward her in my seat. "Audrey was in a band with Jana Carter? Well, shit. That explains a lot."

"What do you mean?" she asked.

"Every single time Jana does something online, Audrey bitches me out for us not doing it better. The whole live-video thing started with her." I gripped my forehead. "I can't even begin to believe Audrey was ever in a band."

"Siri, play 'Bleeding Heart' by Sugar Creek," Ava spoke to her phone. A familiar tune flooded through the speakers.

I laughed. "Shut up! I know this song!"

"They even won an ACM award for Best New Artist that year," she said.

She pointed at me. "If you ever dare tell a soul that I told you, I'll deny it."

"I'll never tell." We listened to the song for a moment in silence. "What happened to them?" I finally asked.

"Well, Audrey was always interested in the business side of things. She already had an MBA by then, so she was really good at it. Todd Calaway, Sugar Creek's manager *and* Jana's boyfriend at the time, didn't like that Audrey was doing a better job than he was. He encouraged Jana to go solo, and the rest is history."

"Wow," I said.

"I think it's what drives Audrey still. It's like she always has something to prove to the music business, that not only Jana made the right choice, but so did she."

"That makes sense." I'd felt that way about moving away from home the first time. Like I needed to be super successful to prove to everyone that I made the right decision. That I was truly destined for bigger things than Riverbend. And I'd accomplished it, for the most part. I'd graduated college and gotten a great job far away from home. Then Mom got sick, and even though I'd only returned to the small-town life to help take care of her, in a way, it still felt like defeat. When Dad's sudden remarriage gave me the excuse I needed to escape from Riverbend again, that same determination returned tenfold. It was what drove me at my job, and was probably what drove me at roller derby too.

"What happened with Jana and Todd Calaway?" I asked.

"They were together till she signed with Shoestring Records. Then she dumped him and got a new manager."

I cocked an eyebrow. "Kind of ironic given recent events in your love life."

She sighed. "It's more ironic than you think. Guess who Lawson signed with?"

I clapped my hand over my mouth. "No."

"Todd swooped in the moment news of our failed wedding hit TMZ."

"Wow," I said, shaking my head.

For the rest of the drive, Ava talked about the music business and the fiasco her personal life had stirred in it. She barely touched on the reasons she'd broken up with Lawson Young, and still, if I didn't feel bad for her already every time I heard "Bitch, Please" on the radio, I certainly did by the time we got off the interstate in Franklin.

"This is it," Ava announced a little while later when we pulled up to a tall iron gate.

She pressed a button that was clipped to her visor, and the gate slowly rolled to the side. I gulped. "Do you ever get nervous?" I asked her. "Around celebrities all the time?"

"Around Jake?" She laughed. "Hell no. The magic fades quickly after someone has thrown up on your shoes—more than once."

"Eww," I said.

She drove down the long cobblestone driveway. "I've known Jake since before he had a pot to pee in. I was working at a bar on Broadway during college, and he was a regular act there on Friday nights." She chuckled quietly. "We were kids then. Barely old enough to drink."

Ava put the car in park, in the dead center of the circular driveway, right in front of the steps to the front door. "Come on. It's time to ruin your fantasies about Nashville's elite."

———

Jake Barrett, number sixteen on *People Magazine's* current list of Most Beautiful People, opened his front door wearing gray sweat-pants that left not enough to the imagination, a Dallas Cowboys jersey older than me, and Adidas flip-flops over white tube socks. It was like Ava Scott had made me a promise about bursting my celebrity bubble, then shifted the universe to keep it.

"Ava," Jake said, stepping onto his welcome mat that read COME BACK WITH A WARRANT. He wrapped his arms around her, exposing a hole in the jersey's armpit big enough to fit my head.

"You smell." She pushed him back a step. "I told you to take a shower before we got here."

He strained his eyes, looking down at the spot on his wrist where a watch was not. "What time is it?"

"Ten forty-five," she said.

He groaned. "God, it's so early." He raked his fingers through his wild brown hair and finally noticed me standing on the step behind my boss. "Well, hello there. What's your name?" His eyes were bloodshot and heavy.

"Jake, this is Lucy from my office," Ava announced.

He flashed his superstar grin. "Hello, Lucy."

I gave a small wave.

"She's very unimpressed to meet you," Ava said, flashing a knowing smile at me over her shoulder. Then she pushed him aside and led the way into his foyer.

His house was beautiful. Chocolate wooden floors, high ceil-ings, and stone archways. But *wow*, he needed a housekeeper. Ava knelt down and picked up a lone pink sparkly stiletto off the floor and dangled it off her fingertip. "I don't even want to know," she said, tossing it against the wall by the door.

"You missed one hell of a party last night, Ava," he said, scratching his chest and yawning so wide I could count his fillings.

She pointed toward a hallway. "Please go take a shower and put on decent clothes."

Jake put his arm around her waist. "Wanna come wash my back?"

Her face soured. "Gross."

He laughed and kissed the side of her forehead. "Give me five minutes."

She held her nose. "Please, dear god, take ten."

"Make yourselves comfortable!" he called, walking toward the hallway.

"The camera and lighting guys will be here at eleven!" she yelled.

"Yes, ma'am!"

I looked at Ava when he was gone. "Camera and lights?"

She nodded. "For the video."

"Whose idea was that?" I asked.

"Audrey's."

I shook my head. "You can't advertise a live video with a full-production ad clip. It needs to be casual and definitely unedited."

She thought for a second. "You know, what? You're exactly right." She pulled her phone from her purse and tapped the screen. "I'm going to call Maurice and cancel."

"Will I get in trouble?" I asked.

"I'll take the blame if Audrey's mad. We'll add it to my list of transgressions." She laughed, then spoke into the phone. "Hey Mo, it's Ava..."

While she was on the phone, I helped myself to a tour of Jake's living room. There was a black baby-grand piano in the corner and overstuffed leather furniture centered around the largest flat screen TV I'd ever seen in my life. It was mounted on the stone fireplace, up above the mantle that held three CMA awards and, *holy shit*, a Grammy.

I walked into Jake's massive kitchen. I'd only ever seen

anything like it on the Food Network. The Food Network kitchens were much cleaner, however. Jake's marble countertops were covered with beer cans and half-eaten trays of stale-looking wings and wilted fruit. Beyond them, his refrigerator caught my eye. It was large and steel with a touch screen that covered one of its French doors. For a second, I wondered if it might actually be Optimus Prime's culinary sister. On the front was a magnet holding a picture. The magnet had a chicken on it, and the photo was of Jake kissing the cheek of another woman with graying brown hair.

"It's a chick magnet." Jake's voice behind me almost made me yelp.

I grabbed at my chest as I turned around. His hair was wet and standing up in a thousand directions. He was wearing nice designer jeans and a black T-shirt that was so tight it clung to all the reasons he was in *People Magazine*. "You startled me," I said, panting.

"And that's my mom," he said, pointing the photo.

How sweet, I thought. "Really?"

He laughed. "No. That's Loretta Lynn."

I looked at the photo again. It was Loretta Lynn.

"Where's Ava?" he asked, looking around the kitchen.

"I'm here." Ava walked into the room and dropped her purse on the lone clear spot on the counter—next to a full laundry basket and a half-eaten bowl of fruit salad crowned with a woman's pink bikini top. "The camera crew is canceled."

He held up his hands. "Then why did you wake me up?"

"Lucy's going to shoot it on her phone," Ava said.

My eyes widened. "I am?"

"Sure. Tell him what to do," she said, pointing at Jake.

He stretched his arms wide. "I'm all yours, Lucy. Direct me."

Oh boy.

I cleared my throat. "OK, well, where are you most comfortable in the house?"

Jake cocked an evil grin and winked at me.

"Oh my god," Ava said with a groan. "The bar. He's most comfortable at the bar out back by the pool."

I laughed. "All right. Outside is good." I looked at Jake. "We need to shoot two different videos to post on two different days, so can you grab another shirt?"

"Here." Ava reached into the laundry basket and tossed over a fleck of fabric I wasn't sure would even fit me. "You can wear this one."

He shook out the blue T-shirt. "This one has a logo on it." It was a Bud Light brand.

"Then here." Ava threw him another shirt, rolling her eyes. "And I swear, I'm sending Happy Maids over here as soon as they're available."

"Oh, I love this one," Jake said. The shirt he was holding up was red with white letters that read HUG DEALER. He grinned at me. "The ladies love it."

"I'll bet they do," I replied. "You ready?"

He gestured for me to go first. "Lead the way."

Ava huffed and grabbed his arm. "She doesn't know where she's going, you dumb idiot."

He laughed. "Oh yeah." He draped his arm over her shoulders. "It's a good thing I'm cute, right?"

"You're impossible," she said.

I followed them down a hallway to a door that led out to a huge open concrete patio. There was a large pool with a waterfall and built-in hot tub. Next to it, a gas fire pit was still burning, probably from the night before. Surrounding it were wooden chairs on one side and an arched stone wall covered in throw pillows on the other. To the left, in front of what appeared to be a raised stage, was the bar Ava had suggested. It was littered with half-empty liquor bottles, paper plates, and...a guy asleep on a barstool.

"Jake, who's that?" Ava asked, her hand on her hip.

He just shrugged and held his hands up.

Clearly frustrated, Ava looked around. "Lucy, why don't you shoot the first one at the fire pit, and I'll get rid of the drifter and clean up the bar for the second one."

"OK," I said.

Jake and I walked over the stone wall. He reached under the fire pit and the flames went out. "I'm going to hate to see that gas bill," he said.

I pointed to the edge of the wall. "Jake, why don't you sit here, so I can get the pool in the background."

He sat down among the mix of teal and yellow pillows. "Here?"

"Perfect," I said, pulling my phone out of my purse and navigating to the video camera. "Dang it. I wish I'd brought my tripod for this thing."

Jake perked up. "I have one. It's in my bedroom. Hey, Ava! Run to my room and grab the tripod for the phone. Lucy needs it for the video!"

Her eyes doubled. "I don't wanna."

He waved her off. "There's nobody in there. It's in the corner behind the recliner."

"Should I hose it down with disinfectant first?" she asked, her face sour as she walked back toward the door.

"Ha. Ha. Ha," he said flatly with a smirk. When she was gone, he looked at me. "She secretly loves me."

I nodded and turned my palms up. "Doesn't everybody?"

He pointed at me. "You and I are going to get along just fine, Lucy. How do you like working at Record Road?"

"Working for Ava's great," I said.

He flashed me another moneymaker grin. I was surprised there wasn't an award on his mantle for that too. "And Audrey?"

I didn't respond.

He held up two fingers to his temples like horns and hissed.

I burst out laughing.

"She's damn good at her job though," he said.

"Absolutely," I agreed.

He settled back against the pillows. "So about this video. What do you want me to say?"

I held up my phone to check the lighting. "It will be short. Maybe twenty seconds or so. Just be casual."

He put his feet up on the bench and laid down.

"Not that casual," I said with a laugh.

"You have to be very specific with him. Use small words," Ava said, walking over and handing me the tripod.

Jake sat back up and flipped up his middle finger toward her. She laughed and walked back to the bar.

"Just say, 'Hey this is Jake Barrett. I'm having a release party for my new album...what's it called?" I asked.

He scowled. "You don't know the name of my new album?"

I cringed. "I forgot."

"*The Gun Show,*" he said, flexing both of his biceps.

I burst out laughing. "Oh yes. How could that slip my mind?"

He kissed his right bicep. "I'll bet you'll never forget again."

"Feel free to push him in the pool!" Ava shouted.

Those two. They were fun.

"Just roll the camera. I've got this," Jake told me confidently.

"OK." I held up my cell phone and centered him in the middle of my screen. I clicked the record button and nodded slightly.

"Wait," he said, holding up a finger.

I stopped the video.

"Ava, when's the party?" he called out.

"Not this Saturday but the next at six. But don't say that in the video. Say 'this Saturday' instead. And you'll be recording at seven before you get drunk and act like a moron."

"Are you trying to confuse me? Am I supposed to say six or seven?"

"Seven," she and I answered together.

He nodded. "Got it."

I clicked record again.

He waved to the camera. "Hey, guys. Jake Barrett here, coming to you from my backyard. I wanted to let you know, I'm having a party here next Saturday...shit."

I stopped the video. "This Saturday," I corrected him.

"I know. Do it again."

I clicked record.

He started speaking. "Yo, this is—"

Ava cut him off. "You're not allowed to say yo, Jake. Try again."

I stopped and restarted the recording.

"Hey, guys. Jake Barrett here. I'm having a party this Saturday, and you're all invited to watch live. Tune it at seven p.m. to join me and my friends as we celebrate the drop of my newest album, *The Gun Show*"—he paused to flex—"in stores and available online everywhere this Friday." He pointed at my camera. "Saturday, right here at seven. I'll see you then." And he winked.

I was surprised, shocked actually. "That was really good."

He slowly dusted off his hands. "I'm a pro, honey."

"A pro would've nailed it on the first take!" Ava called. She'd successfully moved the mystery man asleep at the bar over to a lounge chair by the pool.

"You're so mean to me, Ava!" he cried dramatically, making his voice crack with emotion.

I laughed and played the video back on my phone. It was good. I got up and walked to the bar to show Ava for her approval. She bent over my shoulder and watched. "He cleans up pretty well, doesn't he?"

With a short sigh, I nodded. "Yeah."

As if on cue, even though there's no way he could've heard us, Jake Barrett stripped off his black T-shirt. The sky opened up, and heaven's glorious light shined down. I almost dropped my phone. "Holy smokes," I said under my breath.

She fanned my face. "Jake, put your clothes back on. You're going to give Lucy a stroke, and I really don't want to have to hire a new web person."

If my face wasn't already red, it was then. I wanted to crawl behind the bar.

Jake laughed and put on his red shirt. He pointed to the text across the front. "Does Lucy need a hug?"

I held my hand up to stop him as he walked toward me. "Lucy is just fine."

He hugged me anyway. *Oh my.*

"Come on, let's get this done. If he hugs you too long, you might catch the pink stiletto's cooties," Ava said, pulling him off me.

I shot the second video. His spiel was almost a carbon copy of the first, but we filmed it at the bar instead of the fire pit. And besides the new shirt, Jake also wore his signature brown leather cowboy hat that Ava had found discarded in the grass by the pool.

"Is that all you need?" Jake asked when I tapped the stop button on the video.

"I think so," I said.

Ava held out her hand. "May I?"

"Sure." I handed her the phone, and she played back the clip.

"What's the plan for Saturday with the video?" he asked me.

I looked at Ava. "Has Audrey given you any specifics?"

She crossed her legs. "She's been planning to have a full production team here for it, but I think I'm going to cancel them too." She held up my phone. "You're onto something, Lucy. This is good. Feels like a home movie. It needs to be like this at the party as well."

"I agree," I said. "I think that's why Jana Carter is having so much success with her videos. It's like she invites the fans into her home."

She flashed me a grin. "That's exactly the angle of reasoning I plan on using with my sister. I'll also nail down the specifics about what she wants to shoot."

Jake raised his hand. "I'd like to play a song. We're going to have all the equipment set up for that anyway."

I drummed my nails on the bar top. "Might be kind of hard with the acoustics. I'll test it out this week and see how the sound comes across on the video."

"Perfect," Ava said.

"Will I see you Saturday?" Jake asked me.

I nodded. "Yeah, I'll be here." I looked at Ava. "I was wondering...can I bring someone?"

She turned her eyes and cut her eyes at me. "Like a date?"

"Maybe."

Jake and Ava sang a melodic "Ooo" at the same time.

I hid my face behind my hand.

"Who is it?" Ava asked. "Anyone I've heard of?"

"Maybe," I said again.

She pointed at me. "It's Humphrey Bogart, isn't it?"

I'd almost forgotten about that, but of course, Ava of Golden Hollywood wouldn't. "Yes."

"You're dating him? The Adler guy?" she pressed.

"Adler," Jake said. "Do I know him? Sounds familiar."

"Adler Construction," she said.

He nodded. "Oh yeah. They're everywhere."

I held up my hands. "It's not that serious. We've only been out a couple of times, so please don't make a big deal out of it."

Jake hooked his arm around Ava's neck again. "What makes you think we'd make a big deal of it? We'll be on our very best behavior."

I didn't know Jake that well, but I was sure that didn't mean very much. I groaned and ran my fingers through my hair. "Oh god."

"Of course you can bring him," Ava said. "And Jake's hungover right now. He won't even remember this conversation by next Saturday."

Jake nodded. "That's true."

I pulled my phone back out. "Can I make one more request?"

"Go for it," he said.

"Can I fangirl and get a selfie to send to my dad?" *And everyone else I've ever known in my whole life.*

Jake smiled and took the phone from my hand. "Only if I get to take it."

He held the camera high in the air and aimed it out our faces. "Cheers!" he said, kissing me on the cheek as he snapped the photo.

THIRTEEN

AVA DROVE me back to the office, and I spent the next couple of hours rewriting the marketing plans for our entire client roster. When I was sure everyone was gone for the day, I called Ethan to check in while I finished trimming and editing the videos we'd shot at Jake's. When I finally left the office at five and fought my way through rush-hour traffic, I narrowly beat my date to my door.

I'd planned to shower, flat-iron my hair, and put on makeup, but I had barely enough time to even change my clothes. I quickly dressed in black yoga capris, a spaghetti-strap tank top, and an off-the-shoulder heather gray sweatshirt. I angled the neckline so it drooped off my right shoulder and fully covered my left because the bruising from my collision with Grace had faded to an ugly brownish green.

My doorbell rang at exactly six o'clock.

When I opened the door, I almost whimpered. West was wearing jeans and a navy T-shirt that looked like it had been tailored to mold to his body. Hell, he was loaded; maybe it had been. I was so distracted I forgot to say hello.

His eyes drifted from my face down to my sneakers and back up again. "I hope this means we're staying in to watch Netflix and eat cereal."

Smiling, I pulled the door open wide and stepped out of his way. "Sorry to disappoint, but we are going out. Come on in."

He paused to wipe his boots on the doormat, and I thought I might melt into a puddle right there in the foyer. "Nice place," he said, glancing around my apartment. He fingered the fake daisies I'd put in a vase on the table by the door. "Nice flowers."

"Thanks. Did you have any trouble finding it?"

He shook his head. "Nope. I've lived here all my life. Nashville's not that big."

I closed the door. "Speak for yourself. I can hardly get to work without getting lost."

"Or getting in an accident," he teased.

I groaned. "You're never going to let me live that down, are you?"

He laughed. "Absolutely not." His eyes popped open. "Wait, I have something for you." He shoved his hand into his back pocket. "Now, it's not a traditional third-date gift, but this might save your life someday."

I cocked an eyebrow in question. "OK."

He handed me a small can.

Turning it over in my palm, I read the label out loud. "Hornet and Wasp Killer." I held it up and laughed. "And travel size no less."

He nudged my arm with the back of his hand. "It'll fit right in your purse or your tidy little glove compartment."

I hugged it to my chest. "I'll cherish it always. Thank you."

He put his hand over his heart. "I'm a protector. What can I say?"

My purse was sitting on the table by the door. I made sure he was watching as I placed it inside. He winked and gave me a thumbs-up.

I nodded toward the hallway. "Can you give me five more minutes? I just want to pull my hair up."

"Why?" He reached out and twisted a strand around his finger. "I think it's beautiful."

I almost fell on the floor. "You do?"

"Absolutely."

I smiled. "OK, but I must warn you." I pointed toward my head. "There's a sixty percent chance of rain this evening, and that kind of humidity might turn me into Cousin It by the end of the night."

He squished his mouth over to one side as he considered it. "Maybe bring a ponytail holder just in case."

I tapped the side of my purse and looped it over my shoulder. "It's right next to my bee defense."

He opened my front door again. "Fantastic. Are you ready to go?"

"Yep," I said, walking outside.

"Will you tell me where we're going now?"

I smiled as I pulled the door closed behind me. "Nope." I looked down at his shoes. "You are wearing socks, right?"

His eyes widened. "Yes. Is that a clue?"

"Maybe."

"I'm intrigued. A date where socks are mandatory," he said, lost in thought as we walked down the stairs.

He opened my door when we reached the truck and held my elbow as I climbed inside. "You look really cute, by the way," he said as I buckled my seat belt.

I smiled, and he closed the door.

Watching him walk around the front of the truck, my heart raced with excitement and fear. There was little doubt West Adler truly liked me, but at the same time I couldn't help but feel like an unlikely contestant on *The Bachelor* wondering if I'd receive a rose at the end of the night or be sent home.

He got in and cranked the engine. "All right, Lucy Lou. Where are we headed?"

I plugged the address into Google Maps on my phone. "Drive to Brentwood."

"Yes, ma'am," he said, putting the truck into reverse. "How was your day?"

"It was busy. And definitely interesting."

He looked over at me. "Really? Why?"

"Stop driving a second and I'll show you," I said.

"Fascinating." He pulled over sideways into a row of empty parking spaces.

I found the selfie from earlier in my photo album. I clicked it open and passed him the phone.

He frowned. "Not sure how to take this. Another guy kissing you on the cheek?" He offered the phone back to me.

"No, really look at it. Do you know who he is?"

He focused on the screen again. After a second, he laughed. "Is that Jake Barrett?"

"Yep."

"Then I *really* don't know how I feel about him kissing you on the cheek." He smiled and handed me my phone again before putting the truck back in drive. "I can compete with a lot of dudes, but he's not one of them."

"He's really funny and super nice," I said.

West chuckled. "You're not making me feel better, Lucy."

"Would it make you feel better to know he said I can bring a date next Saturday?" I asked, my heart thumping in my chest.

He grinned over at me. "Only if you're talking about bringing me."

"You've made the short list of potential suitors. We'll see how tonight goes."

"That's good because tonight, I'm going to blow your mandatory socks off!"

I laughed. "You don't even know where we're going."

"Then I'll have to improvise."

Ten minutes later, he pulled into the parking lot of the Brentwood Skate Center. He looked up at the neon sign and laughed. "Are you kidding me? Roller skating?"

"What's wrong with roller skating?" I asked as he parked the truck.

"Nothing's wrong with it if you're twelve," he said.

We got out of the truck and met by the tailgate. "Are you too manly and mature to take me roller skating?" I asked.

He hooked his arm around my neck, pulled me close, and pressed a kiss against the side of my head. "I'll take you anywhere you want to go, my dear. I just assumed you'd pick someplace fancy, like a steakhouse or a wine bar."

I grinned up at him. "Then you don't know me very well."

He leaned his head against mine as we walked to the door. "And I can't wait to find out more."

We rented skates when we got inside. I could have brought mine, but I feared it might raise questions I wasn't yet ready to answer. As we laced up beside the rink, I realized we were the only childless adults in the building who didn't work there.

West pointed at me when his skates—size twelves, *yay!*—were on his feet. "If I my bust my ass, you're not allowed to laugh or tell anybody."

"I can't promise I won't laugh," I said, standing up beside him. The old wheels felt rickety underneath me. If my derby skates were Cadillacs, these were jalopies.

He stood and wobbled a little.

I offered him my hand. "Need some help?"

He playfully smacked my hand away. "I'm a grown man. I can do this by myself."

I laughed. "I can get you one of those walkers on wheels."

"You're not funny, Lucy."

I mimicked his move from the first day we met and held up my fingers millimeters apart. "I'm a little funny."

Without waiting for him, I rolled across the 1980s geometric printed carpet to the slick and shiny roller rink. It was crowded with preteens, little kids, and a few parents. Disco lights swirled around me and Bruno Mars crooned over the speakers. I looked back at West. He was slowly inching his way toward me.

Maybe this was a bad idea, I wondered. But then a little boy in plastic trainer skates rolled past West and slapped him a high five. The kid was barely taller than my date's knees, and West's face lit up like a Christmas tree.

"You know, I was pretty good at this when I was a kid," West said when he finally reached me. The song had changed to a Maroon 5 number.

"Maybe it's like riding a bike." I rolled backward to give him some room to step onto the rink.

West gripped the carpeted half wall that bordered the curve. "We could have gone anywhere in Nashville, Lucy."

I laughed. "Don't make me skate this room without you."

He reached for my hand and laced his fingers with mine as we rolled slowly around the wide turn. "What made you pick this?"

I shrugged. "Maybe it was the roller derby thing the other night. It looked like fun."

"Did you enjoy it?"

"I did," I said.

He smiled. "Maybe next season I can introduce you to a few of the players."

"That would be awesome." I wanted to tell him the truth. But I didn't. I would tell him eventually, but not until I knew how far this relationship was going to go. "West, how did you get into roller derby?"

"Some of the girls work out at my gym. They gave me tickets last year to a bout, and I've been hooked ever since. Adler Construction sponsors the team now."

I didn't dare tell him I already knew that. "Besides roller derby and the gym, what else do you do?"

He thought for a second. "I like going out downtown sometimes. And I've got season tickets to both the Predators and the Titans."

"So you're a sports guy."

He nodded. "Is that a bad thing?"

"No. But you know, I've never been to a professional game of any sport."

His fingers squeezed mine. "Well, we'll have to fix that this year."

My heart thudded in rhythm with Adam Levine's voice. A little girl, maybe nine or ten, skated between us, ducking under our hands. He laughed and pulled me closer to him to close the gap. "I must say, this was a pretty fun idea."

"Yeah?" I asked, looking up at him.

He nodded. "Yes. Even if we're the only grown-up couple in here."

"Want to see a trick?" I asked, releasing his hand.

"Of course."

I turned around and skated backward, carefully watching over my shoulder. It was a move we'd practiced on Wednesday night.

He clapped his hands. "Hey, you're pretty good!"

No sooner had the words left his lips than I lost my footing and fell flat on my backside with a hard thud. He burst out laughing and got himself stopped a few feet past me. I pushed myself up and caught up with him.

"That's what happens when you get cocky," I said.

He shrugged. "It's more than I can do."

We made a few more laps around the room. "Is this all you have planned?" he asked, then patted his flat stomach. "Because I'm going to need to be fed soon."

I pointed to the snack bar. "They have pizza and hot dogs."

He raised an eyebrow. "Do you want pizza or hot dogs?"

"It doesn't matter to me."

"I tell you what. We'll skate for as long as you want, but then I get to pick the place to take you for dinner. Deal?"

I smiled. "Deal. But I want to play skeeball too while we're here." I glanced at the arcade. "I'm going home with that stuffed Minion, if I have to spend every quarter in your bank account."

He laughed and took my hand again, this time pulling it up to his lips and kissing my knuckles. "Then I'll make sure you win two."

We left an hour and a half later with two yellow Minions—Kevin and Stuart—and West asked how I felt about Chinese food. We picked up a to-go order and got on the interstate toward downtown. "Where are we going?" I asked, admiring the sparkling Nashville skyline up in the distance.

"You got your surprise. Now it's my turn. I've got to earn the invite to that party, remember?" He winked across the cab at me.

He took the exit for Demonbreun Street and then turned down Twelfth Avenue. I recognized the new high-rise condos his company was building when he parked in a construction lot a few blocks up from Biscuit Love. "What are we doing here?" I asked, getting out of the truck.

He came around carrying my Sesame Chicken and his General Tso's. "You'll see. Come on."

Using a digital keypad, he let us into the building. The ground floor was unfinished and dusty with steel beams and unfinished drywall. He pressed the button for the elevator. "It works?" I asked.

"Yeah. Even though it doesn't look like it down here, the building is pretty close to being finished."

The elevator doors opened and we stepped inside. Plastic lined the floor and was covered in dirt. He pressed the button marked Roof. We finally reached the top and walked through a short vestibule to a glass door that led outside. On the roof was a pool without any water and one lone folding table and a few metal chairs. But the view. Holy cow, the view. We could see all the way to the river, past the glittery lights of the downtown bar scene.

"Come on," he said, taking my hand.

He deposited our food on the table, then led me over to the edge that was lined with a short concrete wall that came up to my chest. He stood close at my back, his warm breath tickling my ear, and a hand resting casually on my hip. His other hand pointed over my shoulder, drawing my attention to the Summit Tower off in the distance. "There's your office building. And there's the Schermerhorn Symphony Center, the new convention center, and the arena where the Predators play."

"And the Batman Building," I said, proudly pointing it out.

He laughed. "Yep." He turned the other way. "There's Music Row, and if you look really closely, you'll see the statue of the naked dancing people in the middle of all those spotlights."

"Naked dancing people?" I asked, straining my eyes to see in the dark.

"Yeah. Nashville's weird sometimes."

A chilly breeze blew over the rooftop, and West pulled me closer as I took in the panoramic view. Finally, I turned back to look at him. "Thank you for this. It's beautiful up here."

His smile was soft, and he tucked my still unfrizzy hair back behind my ear. "Beautiful," he whispered. Then he slipped his fingers under my chin and tilted my face up, slowly lowering his lips onto mine.

The kiss was gentle and soft until his tongue parted my lips. Then he drew my whole body against his solid form and raked his fingers back through my hair. Every sane and rational thought in my brain fizzled away as my fingertips traced the hard muscles across his shoulders, all the way up the back of his neck.

Then he broke away, resting his forehead against mine. "I've wanted to do that for a long time." His voice was low and husky.

I hadn't realized my eyes had closed until they reopened and I saw him smiling.

"Ready to eat? Our food's getting cold," he said.

"I don't even care," I answered and kissed him again.

———

It was close to midnight and raining when we arrived back in front of my apartment building. I turned to him in the cab when he shut off the engine. "You don't have to walk me up, West. There's no sense in both of us getting soaked."

"And miss the chance of kissing you goodbye at the door? Not a chance, girl." He pointed to the two Minions sitting between us. "But first, it's time for a custody battle. Which one are you taking?"

My mouth fell open. "I want both!"

"Well, you can't have both. You can keep one here, and the other you'll have visitation rights to at my house."

I crossed my arms. "I don't even know where you live."

"I live in Brentwood, not far from here. You can come visit him anytime you want."

"I want Stuart." I picked up the one-eyed Minion and hugged him to my chest. I patted Kevin's head. "But I love you too."

He laughed. "Now that that's settled. Are you ready?" He nodded toward my building.

"I'm ready."

We were both soaked and laughing by the time we reached the covered steps that led up to my floor. "Sixty percent chance of rain, my ass. It's like a monsoon out here," West said over the loud rain. He ran his fingers through his hair, sending water droplets flying in every direction.

His shirt was drenched and clinging to his chest. My eyes drifted down the distinct center line of his torso. He laughed softly, and I jerked my gaze up to meet his.

"Sorry," I said, covering my face with my hand.

He pulled my hand away. "Don't ever apologize for looking at me that way." He pushed my drenched hair back off my shoulders. A fat raindrop drizzled from my hairline, down the side of my face to my neck. His eyes trailed it until they fixed on my collarbone, his teeth gripping his lower lip. He inhaled a sudden shaky breath, then blew it out slowly before motioning up the stairs. "Shall we?"

My brain raced as he followed me to my front door. *Do I invite him in? Do I force him back out into the rain? Will he think I'm using the rain as an excuse if I—*

"Lucy, what happened to you?" His finger hooked into the back of my sweatshirt that was sagging with the weight of the rainwater.

I looked back at the bruising on my shoulder. "It's nothing. Old bruises. I fell a while ago."

He traced the outline of the massive bruise, sending a chill down my spine. "It looks really bad." He pulled the shirt down even lower.

I gathered the neckline of my sweatshirt up to my chin and turned around to face him. "West Adler, if I didn't know better, I would think you were trying to peek down my shirt."

His brow wrinkled with a scowl. "I worry about you."

"That's sweet." I released my grip on the collar, letting the wet fabric slide back down my skin. Again, West's eyes followed. This time, we were at my door. "Do you want to come in? Wait till the storm passes?"

His Adam's apple bobbed with a forced swallow, and his eyes were still fixed on my damp chest. "That's probably not a good idea. I think I need to say goodbye here and go stand in the cold rain for a while before driving home."

I laughed. "Fair enough. I appreciate your honorability."

He finally met my eyes. "It's all an act, I assure you. Because there is nothing honorable happening in my head right now."

Taking a small step toward him, I put my purse and Stuart down by the door, then looped my arms around his neck. "I'll take that as a compliment."

Enter, Evil Lucy.

He shook his head and slid his arms around my waist. "You have no idea how much of a compliment. I thought you were beautiful before, but now I want it to rain on every date we ever go on. Hell, I might drive you through the carwash with the windows rolled down just for the view."

My nails lightly scraped the back of his neck, triggering a shudder that rippled through him. He closed his eyes and took another forcefully slow, deep breath.

Yes, it was mean of me. I knew exactly what I was doing. He was fighting so hard to be a gentleman, and there I was tampering with the launch button. On purpose. But how could I not? It had been so long since any man had trembled at my touch—and never one this handsome. This tempting. This delicious.

He wedged his hand between us, his palm up and his eyes still closed. "Give me your keys. Quick."

Confused, I retrieved my keys from my purse, then placed them in his open palm. He immediately tossed them down the hallway back toward the stairs, and they clanged against the concrete floor. Before I could ask or figure out why, his mouth crashed onto mine and my back was against the door. His rock-hard body, every single inch of it, pressed into me.

Cool raindrops mixed on our lips as we kissed, then his fingers tangled in my wet hair and pulled my head back to expose my neck. A small moan escaped my throat as he kissed it, his lips tugging and nipping at the flesh that had so effortlessly captured his attention.

Then his hands slid forward and cradled my jaw as his lips came down hard and hot against mine again. His tongue fluttered against the tip of mine, a tantalizing move that spun my mind to very dark and dangerous places.

It was then that I found my hand on the doorknob, twisting and turning hopelessly against the secured lock. *The damn keys* was the only coherent thought in my brain.

West splayed his hands against my door and finally tore his mouth from mine, leaving my lips raw and bruised and desperately wanting more. "I...have...to go," he panted against my ear. "But good god, I don't want to."

I released the two fistfuls of his shirt that I hadn't realized I was gripping. "Please don't leave me." My voice was a breathy whisper.

He shook his head. "Don't say that, Lucy, or I won't."

I threaded my fingers up through his hair, drawing his face back closer to my own. "Don't go."

He kissed me again, his tongue gently tangling with mine as one arm snaked around my waist, plastering my hips against his body. Then he suddenly pulled away and walked down the hall. I heard the jingle of my keychain around the corner from the alcove that shrouded the door. My heart throbbed against my ribs.

When he returned, he handed me the keys and picked up

Stuart and my purse. My hand trembled as I tried to put the key into the lock, and West put his hand on mine to steady it.

When the door was open, I stepped inside, but West didn't follow.

I turned around, and he handed me my things, carefully eyeing the threshold like it was the Bridge of No Return. My shoulders slumped as I hugged Stuart to my chest.

"Come here," West said quietly.

I stepped forward, and he slipped a strong hand back behind my head.

"Soon," he said, studying my eyes. "Very soon."

Then he kissed me and walked away.

FOURTEEN

"HE'S TOO PERFECT," I told Olivia at practice the next day. We were warming up together on the track, letting the All-Stars and the Rising Rollers dart around us like obstacles.

She turned backward on her skates so she could face me. "I hate to say it, but I kind of agree with you. What guy gets that hot and heavy and then leaves?"

"My point exactly." I skated up beside her. "I mean, nobody's that noble."

"What do you think's wrong with him?"

I shrugged. "I really don't know, but I can't get the question out of my head."

"It could be nothing, Lucy. Perhaps the universe thinks it's time for you to have something great in your life." She sighed and shook her head. "After all you've been through, I'd say you deserve it."

"Thanks, but it's easier for me to believe he has a brain defect or that he's really a serial killer."

She laughed. "Maybe you need therapy. What happened after he left?"

"He went home, and we texted till three o'clock this morning. I heard you come in around one."

"What did you guys talk about all night?"

"Everything and absolutely nothing." I started to count on fingers. "His favorite movie is Legends of the Fall. He thinks Matchbox Twenty is the best band that's ever recorded music. And he likes to read, but only funny stuff like *Shit My Dad Says* and anything by Tucker Max—though he made me swear to never tell his mother."

"Classy," she said.

"And we talked a lot about that kiss." My legs quaked thinking of it. "At one point, I thought he might drive back over to our apartment and finish the job."

"It was that good?"

I held my hands up. "So good it makes me question his morality."

She burst out laughing.

"Hey, Lucy," someone said behind me. It was Full Metal Jackie. "How's your shoulder?"

I groaned. "Ugh. The bruises still haven't healed from last week, and I'm afraid almost all your arnica cream is gone. If you'll tell me where I can buy it, I'll get you a replacement."

She put her hand on her stomach. "I won't be needing it, remember."

I smiled. "Oh yeah."

When she was gone, I looked at Olivia. "He saw them last night. The bruises."

She playfully slapped my arm. "You didn't tell me you were getting naked in the breezeway!"

"Naked?" Zoey asked, joining us on the track. "Who was getting naked?"

Olivia pointed at me.

"I didn't get naked. It's a wide-neck shirt. It got wet and sagged off my shoulders."

"What did he say?" Olivia asked.

I clasped my hands together, smiling. "That he worries about me."

Olivia put her hands on her hips. "I say that all the time, and you usually hit me."

"It wasn't quite the same tone."

Shamrocker blew her whistle. "Fresh Meat bitches, huddle up!" She was talking to *all* of us, not just the actual Fresh Meat group which had continued to dwindle over the grueling weeks of training.

"Think they're done punishing us for the All-Stars being off their game?" I asked Olivia quietly as we skated over to join our group.

"Not hardly. All four weeks, you heard Medusa," she answered.

I looked around. "Where is she?"

Olivia shrugged.

"The actual newbies have 27 in 5s today," Shamrocker announced. "If you're a veteran, pick a newbie for whom you can count laps."

Groans and murmuring echoed around the room from the newbies. Me, mostly.

"We're going to use both tracks so we can get these done as quickly as possible. Styx will keep time on Track A." Shamrocker held up her stopwatch. "I'll keep time on Track B. If you're not counting, get your gear off and get lined up on the wall. That includes the newbies once you're finished with your time trials."

"Get our gear off?" I asked Olivia to make sure I'd heard her correctly.

She shrugged.

Olivia, Zoey, and I lined up beside each other with the first group of skaters on Track A. Olivia bumped her fist against mine. "You can do this, Lucy. Keep your knees bent, breathe, and keep pushing."

Kraken was going to count for me. She flashed me a thumbs-up from the sidelines. Olivia's words replayed in my head. *You can do this, Lucy.*

The whistle blasted.

Olivia lapped the rest of us by lap number four, but I ignored her and kept going. My ankles no longer burned since the blisters had hardened into callouses. And my lungs felt bigger, able to hold more power-boosting oxygen.

"Five!"

"Six!"

"Seven!" Kraken called. "Good job, Lucy!"

I pushed through the corners, keeping low when I entered and skating to the outside coming out of the turns.

"Eight!"

"Nine!"

"Ten!"

"Eleven!"

"Twelve!"

I passed Zoey. She was breathing heavy, but she was still moving.

"Thirteen!"

"Fourteen!"

Styx's arm shot into the air. "That's halfway!"

Whoa. Really?

"Fifteen!" Kraken yelled.

"Sixteen!"

"Seventeen!"

"Eighteen!"

A stitch pulled in my side. *Breathe in through your nose. Out through your mouth.*

"Nineteen!"

Olivia flew past me again.

"Twenty!"

"Twenty-One!"

"Twenty-Two!

"Twenty-Three!"

"Twenty-Four!"

Stars began twinkling in the corners of my vision, and sweat dripped off my jaw. The stitch in my side was no longer held at bay by breathing tricks. My side constricted in pain. I needed to think about anything else. Find a happy place.

West's mouth on mine at the door.

Olivia came around my left again, nudging my arm as she passed. I smiled and pushed to catch her. I pushed harder and harder, into the turn, then sailing out of it.

"Thirty seconds!" Styx shouted.

"Twenty-Five!"

"Twenty-Six!"

The whistle blasted again. Two turns away from hitting twenty-seven laps.

Olivia spun around on her wheels, popping up onto her toe stops in a perfect tomahawk stop. She pumped her fists in the air and skated back toward me. "You did it, Lucy!" she cheered, slamming into me. We both toppled backward, falling in a heap, laughing.

"I didn't do it," I said, panting as she rolled off me. "I was half a lap short."

She reached over and slapped my helmet. "Half a lap though!"

Zoey skated over, her chest heaving with ragged breaths. She clapped her hands. "Good job, Lucy."

"Thank you," I said.

"How many for you, Zo?" Olivia asked.

She put her hands on her hips. "Twenty-two. I'm getting there."

I clapped my hands. "That's excellent." And it was. She'd beaten more than all of us combined.

Kraken came over and slapped me a high five.

"Hey!" Styx yelled. "Get off my track!"

We looked over. Styx was grinning, and she gave me a covert thumbs-up.

Olivia got up and skated off the track; I crawled off, but I didn't care. *Twenty-six-and-a-half. I'll take it.*

Grace got twenty-nine laps. Monica got twenty-six like me. Olivia, The Prodigy? Thirty-one.

Medusa walked in as the last of the newbies finished. She was wearing sneakers, short shorts, and a sports bra. Her black-and-pink hair was pulled up into a tight knot on her head, and she carried a sweat towel and a water bottle in hand.

"This isn't good," Olivia said as we pushed our gym bags to the corner of the room with everyone else. "Styx says she's a personal trainer now and that she hates it when Medusa leads off-skates practice."

"Crap."

The torture began with sidestep jumping jacks and a hateful exercise called gate swings. Medusa rattled on about the importance of groin stretching and thigh strengthening until I wanted to throw my water bottle at her head. Then we did a series of yoga moves infused with cardio, body resistance, and self-loathing.

And that was just the warm-up.

Then we had to run—not just laps around the track or even the room. Oh no. We had to run laps that included the stairs on both the front and the back of the room. Up the stairs, across the bleachers, down the stairs, across the room, up the bleachers, and so on until hot, angry beads of sweat (and possibly blood) drizzled into my eyeballs obscuring the stairs beneath my tired feet. I tripped three times.

We finished the hour with burpees, wall sits, and a planking contest where the winner could sit out the rest of practice. Medusa won, of course, and *"lucky for us"* the workout continued!

When she blew the final whistle, I collapsed where I stood in a puddle of my own perspiration on the floor. I was so tired, I couldn't even whine. Poor Zoey was hacking up a lung, hunched over the trashcan, Olivia was spread eagle beside me, and I didn't even care where Grace and Monica had ended up.

"I see lights," Olivia said, panting. "I think it's death and the tunnel to the other side."

"I won't"—*hehn-hehn*—"argue"—*hehn*—"if you"—*hehn*—"want to go," I struggled to say.

Her hand flopped over onto mine. "You've been a good friend, Lucy. Don't ever forget me."

It was a solid three minutes before I had the ability to sit up. It would be another ten before I could walk to get my bag. Styx came over to talk to Olivia. Even she was red faced and sweaty.

"Is this what it's going to be like around here from now on?" I asked, pulling my shirt off over my head because the air conditioning on the wet fabric was giving me goose bumps.

Styx nodded. "Probably for a while." She reached over and slapped my leg. "This is good for you though. You were worried about passing your endurance test. Now you're sure to kill it at tryouts."

I jammed my finger into my chest. "If it doesn't kill me first." I looked at Olivia. "You ready to go home?"

They exchanged a quick glance. "I've got some errands to run after practice. I'll meet you at home," she said.

I raised an eyebrow. "You don't have a car here."

"I can give you a ride," Styx offered. "I have some *errands* to run myself."

My face broke into a knowing smile, but Olivia snapped her finger over her lips. "Not one word," she whispered.

I zipped my lips closed and pushed myself up. "Well, I'll see you later then."

When I got back to my apartment, I didn't bother to lug my bag inside. I grabbed my damp shirt and dirty pair of socks out of it and trudged up the stairs. A pair of legs were sticking out from my door. I smiled. "I told you to call first," I said as I approached.

When I rounded the alcove, I stumbled back. It wasn't Ethan. It was West—and his Minion. "Kevin missed you and Stuart," he said, waving its arm at me. "I told him we'd come visit."

I smiled, and his eyes fell to my bare stomach. I was still in my sports bra and Under Armor capris. "Sorry, I wasn't expecting company when I got here," I said.

"It sounded like you were expecting someone. Do you come home to find men at your door often?" he asked, standing up and brushing off his backside.

I laughed. "Yes. I thought you were my brother."

He took a step toward me, dangling the Minion by the hand at his side. "I'm definitely not your brother."

I looked up into his handsome face and noticed tan lines where his sunglasses usually rested. "No, you're certainly not." He bent to kiss me, but I stopped him with my hand on his firm chest. "West, I just came from the hardest workout of my life. I'm nasty."

His arms went around me anyway. "I don't care." And then we were kissing again in the breezeway.

I finally pulled back to catch my breath. "Let's go inside. All I can think about is what I must smell like. I need to take a shower."

He narrowed his eyes. "Is that an invitation?"

"No," I said firmly. "Come on."

We went into my apartment, and I put my keys on the hook by the door. "You can hang out in the living room or my room. I'll just be a few minutes."

"Your room?" he asked with a playful grin.

"Sure. But don't get any ideas," I said as he followed me into my bedroom. "You're no longer allowed to start stuff with me that you're too gentlemanly to finish."

He jabbed both thumbs at his chest. "I should win an award for the restraint I showed last night. You think it was hard for you? Ha!"

When I went into the bathroom, he was looking at the photos on my dresser. I peeked back through the door. "Make yourself comfortable."

"I'm going to snoop through your stuff. Cool?" he asked, holding up a framed picture.

"Whatever floats your boat, West Adler."

Before getting in the shower I sent a quick text to Olivia. *Don't bring Styx back here. I have company. ;-)*

She responded while I waited for the water to warm. *Don't worry. Styx is helping me with the new specials for the restaurant this month. What do you think about a parmesan chicken couscous dish called Becouscous I Said So???*

I laughed. *I think you're an idiot.*

Olivia: *Then I'll consider that a win.*

Despite my tired and aching muscles, I exhibited super-human speed in the shower, washing and deep conditioning my hair as well as shaving my legs in record time. I dressed quickly in my walk-in closet and dabbed on a tiny bit of makeup while I blow dried my hair.

When I walked back into my bedroom, West was lying on my bed with Kevin and Stuart propped against the pillows next to him. He looked at his watch. "That was impressive. Eleven minutes."

"You were timing me?" I asked.

He sat up on the edge of the bed. "Yep. You can tell a lot about a girl by how much time she spends in the bathroom."

"I'm sure that's true." I walked over and stopped at his knees. "What do you want to do?"

He rested his forehead against my stomach. "Such an unfair question."

I raked my nails through his hair. "OK, what *else* do you want to do?"

His eyes sparkled as he looked up at me. "I was hoping we could grab something to eat and maybe catch a movie. Have you ever been to Franklin?"

I shook my head. "I don't think so."

"You'd remember it if you had. I think you'll like it."

I looked down at my outfit. "Is this OK to wear?"

He smiled. "You look amazing."

I leaned down and kissed him.

He stopped just as his fingers tangled in my still-damp hair and drew in a labored breath. "I'm a strong and determined man, but this is pushing it."

I offered my hand. "Come on. Let's vacate the danger zone."

Downtown Franklin was a vibrant blend of the past and the present, small-town Americana meets modern affluence. Modern shops and restaurants with old soul vibes converged with historic buildings and war monuments. The idyllic heart of the city could have been ripped straight from a Dickens novel or a Norman Rockwell painting. As I stepped out of the truck, a horse-drawn carriage rolled by, and I briefly wished it was snowing.

West took my hand. "You hungry?"

"Starving."

"I know the perfect place."

We crossed the street and walked to a building marked "Gray's" with a massive, vintage neon sign. "It used to be a pharmacy," West said. "But they've rehabbed it into one of the best bars and restaurants in town."

I raised an eyebrow. "Did *you* rehab it?"

He laughed and put his hand on the small of my back as he steered me through the door. "I didn't build everything in the state of Tennessee."

"Just checking," I said, flashing a smile over my shoulder.

It was too bad he hadn't been the one to renovate the building. It would have gained him a few more cool points, not that he needed any. The dining room was informal and rustic, with antique mirrors of all shapes and sizes hanging on the unfinished walls. We were seated at a booth near the bar. "This place is really cool," I said, still looking around with wonder.

"There are two floors above this one." He pointed to the ornately tiled ceiling with his menu. "It's got a pretty cool bar with a stage for live music up top."

I smiled at him. "You were right. I like it here."

"Wait till you try the shrimp and grits."

West was right—the shrimp and grits was amazing—but I only knew because I tasted his. I had to order the Sweet Tea Chicken and Waffles as soon as I read the description. Whipped honey butter and bourbon maple syrup? Yes, please.

When I finally put my fork down, after licking every drop of buttery goodness from the tines, I pointed at my plate. "That may be the best meal I've ever had in my life."

He wiped his mouth with a napkin, then dropped it in his bowl. "Yeah?"

I reclined back in my chair to accommodate the food baby I'd grown since sitting down. "Absolutely. It was so good, I feel I have no other choice than to let you accompany me to Jake's party."

"Is that an official invitation?" he asked, leaning on his elbows.

"Yes. West Adler, will you be my date next weekend?"

He sucked a sharp breath through clenched teeth. "I don't know. I'll have to check my social calendar. It is pretty booked—"

I kicked the side of his boot under the table.

"Of course, I'll go." He rolled his eyes and tossed his hands up dramatically. "Gah! It took you long enough to ask me!"

I sat forward on the edge of my seat. "Then I guess that makes us even."

He clapped his hands slowly. "Well played."

The waiter brought our check, which he quickly snapped up.

"On that note. Do you still want to see a movie?" he asked, pulled a few crisp bills out of his wallet.

"Sure. I wonder if the new *Ghostbusters* is still playing. I love Melissa McCarthy."

"Me too, but it's not that kind of theater." He stood and offered me his hand.

I was confused. "How many kinds of movie theaters are there?"

West waved to the bartender as we walked out the door. "You'll see."

We walked a few blocks to the Franklin Theatre. I looked up at the marquee. "*The Sandlot?* We're seeing the little kids' baseball movie?"

Planting his feet on the sidewalk, he turned to me. "Lucy, it's the greatest movie of our generation."

I blinked. "Maybe *your* generation, but certainly not mine."

He gripped his chest as he stumbled to the back of the ticket line. "*You're killing me, Smalls!* How old are you, for real?"

I sighed. "I'm twenty-eight. Why? How old are you?"

He groaned. "Thirty-two."

My eyes narrowed. "No, you're not. You're thirty-three."

His mouth dropped open. "No. I'm thirty-two. But *you* cyber-stalked me!"

Shit.

"*The Music City Herald* misprinted my age in their article."

He threw his head back and laughed. Hard. "You're so busted."

"Of course I looked you up online. Some of us grew up in the

Information Age, you know? You probably grew up on encyclo-
pedias and phone books."

He leaned toward my face. "Hey, I had an AOL account."

I covered my mouth and snickered.

We moved forward a few feet in line. "So what's the greatest
movie of *your* generation, youngling?" Then he pointed at me.
"And if you dare say *The Notebook*, I may have to end this relationship right here."

I bit my lower lip as I considered it. "The first one that comes
to mind is *The Dark Knight*, because...Heath Ledger."

He nodded and rubbed his chin. "Yep. Yep. Good choice."

"But I think I'd have to go with *The Departed*."

His hands fell to his sides. "Oh man. I think I just fell in love
with you."

I laced my fingers together and hugged them to my chest.
"That scene where Leonardo DiCaprio kisses Vera Farmiga for
the first time in her kitchen up on the counter..." I let out a
singsong sigh.

West's head fell quizzically to the side and he squinted. "Not
exactly the reason I was thinking, but still a good movie."

It was our turn at the ticket window. "Are we really
doing this?"

"Have you even seen *The Sandlot*?" he asked.

I shook my head.

"Oh yes. We're doing this." West smiled at the clerk. "Two,
please."

———

On Sunday, I posted Jake's first video clip announcing Saturday's party to his Facebook page. Within an hour, it had over five
thousand views. By the time I reached the office Monday, the
number had jumped to fifty thousand. When Audrey came into

my office just after twelve, I was reading through the endless comments.

Immediately, "Bleeding Heart" by Sugar Creek played in my head, triggering an uncontrollable grin. I would never be able to look at my hardass boss the same way again.

"Good morning, Audrey."

"Did you see the video traffic?" She sat across from me and crossed her legs. "What can we do to get it to a hundred thousand?"

"Wait," I suggested. "I'm sure it will get there on its own. Or I can set up an ad campaign to get more traffic if you want to spend money."

"Yes, do that. When is the next video going live?"

"Thursday."

"Excellent. Push some campaign funds toward that one as well." She stood and knocked her knuckles against my desk. "I want to set some records with the video on Saturday."

"Yes, ma'am. There's also a scheduled reminder that will go out Saturday morning to everyone on his email list, and the social-media team has posts and tweets scheduled throughout the day as well."

"Very good," she said.

She turned to leave, but my hand shot forward. "Audrey?"

Her brow lifted.

"Jake had mentioned wanting to play a song for the live video on Saturday. I've been testing out the sound quality for an acoustic versus electric performance, and if he can play the song acoustically, it will sound a lot better on the live feed."

Her lips pressed together as she thought it over. "But there isn't an acoustic version of the title song."

I picked up his new CD that was laying on my desk. "No, but track number four is acoustic. I thought maybe he could play it instead."

She tapped a finger against her mouth. "But 'Never Be Mine' is a love song, not a party song."

I smiled. "It's a great love song. Something to think about."

She nodded. "I will. I'll talk to the label about it. Thank you, Lily."

Sigh.

When she was gone, my office phone beeped. Claire's voice came over the speaker. "Lucy, can you come to the front office, please?"

Odd. "Sure. Be there in just a second."

On my way to the front, I passed Peter's door and heard hushed voices through the crack. Suddenly someone shouted. "Lucy!" It was Ava.

I looked in Peter's office. "Hey, guys."

Ava quietly clapped her hands. "Good job on the video. Jake called a few minutes ago. Even he's impressed."

"We all are," Peter added.

My body felt like it might float off the floor. "Thank you."

When I reached the front office, a familiar scent greeted my nose, but I couldn't place it. "Hey, Claire. What's up?"

She pushed a white plastic bag toward me. "Get this out of my office before I gain five pounds just from the smell."

"What?" I pulled the bag open and peered inside. It was a food container from Gray's on Main in Franklin. I popped the lid open. Sweet Tea Chicken and Waffles. There was a card tucked in the corner of the bag.

I'll be thinking of you licking your fork. Have a great day, Lucy. –West

———

I feel like celebrating, I texted West on Friday morning.

Between Jake's two promo videos that week, he'd gotten a

half a million views. Audrey was practically dancing through the hallways, and I was the glorious heroine. She still didn't know my name, but she was singing Lily's praises nonetheless.

I'm guessing the video yesterday went well? West texted back.

Me: *Very well. My hard work last night paid off. 341K views. 12K reactions. 1,712 comments. 2,113 shares. Move over, Jake Barrett. I'm the superstar at the office today.*

West: *I'm proud of you, babe. Celebrations are already in order. I've made plans for us tonight if you're free.*

Me: *I'm all yours.*

West. :) *I love it when you say that.*

We hadn't seen each other except for a quick lunch on Tuesday. I'd worked late every night that I didn't have practice, and the night before, I hadn't gotten home until after ten. I was exhausted, but god, I missed him.

Me: *What did you have in mind?*

West: *6PM tonight. 321 Honey Oak Trail, Brentwood.*

My teeth sank into my lower lip. That street had the ring of a residential address. *Is this a fancy place? Should I dress up?*

West: *Definitely not fancy, but bring Stuart. Kevin's lonely.*

I squealed and stamped my feet with excitement under my desk.

"Mr. Adler strikes again, I see." Ava walked into my office with a knowing smile.

I put my phone down. "Do you have some sort of radar that detects when I'm about to make a total idiot out of myself in my office so you can come watch?"

She laughed and sat down across from me. "I wish. If I had that kind of technology, I'd use it to avoid my sister. What's he done to put that smile on your face this time? More Bogart?"

"I'm going to his house for the first time ever tonight."

"Ooo, exciting stuff. Will you be staying the night?" she said, just above a whisper.

I held my hands up. "I don't know. We haven't yet...you know."

Her smiley eyes danced with excitement for me. "I want all the details on Monday."

"Won't you be at the party tomorrow?"

"Of course. He's coming with you, right?"

"He is."

"I can't wait to meet him." She glanced at her watch. "Since you're working tomorrow, you should wrap things up early and get out of here by noon."

I straightened in my seat. "Are you serious?"

"Absolutely. I'll tell Audrey myself."

I clapped my hands together. "Thank you, Ava."

"Don't mention it. I'm supposed to tell you that Jake's going to do one song for the video tomorrow. We were thinking we could start the video inside the house before he walks out to greet the guests. We'll show the cake and maybe ask a few of his friends to jump in on the video—"

"His friends?" I asked.

"Yeah. Lincoln Hunt, Marty Atkins, and Clint Jones will all be there, I'm sure." Something snagged her attention. "I think Trip Wiley might be coming as well."

I straightened in my chair. "Trip Wiley? *The* Trip Wiley?"

"Yep. The actor. They're pretty good friends, and Jake mentioned something about him being here on location."

I gripped my temples and laughed. "How is this my life?"

"Welcome to Nashville, sweetheart. After he introduces a few of his guests, then he'll go straight to the stage and play a condensed version of the album's second single. It's not even out yet."

"Which song?" I asked.

"An acoustic love song called 'Never Be Mine.' Audrey thinks it will be a great way to tease the audience with it before it hits the radio, and the sound quality will be better for the video."

I couldn't believe what I was hearing. That had been *my* idea. Not Audrey's. I flopped back against the seat. "Wow."

She smiled and nodded. "It's brilliant, right? As difficult as she can be, Audrey does have some of the best ideas in the business."

My teeth clenched. "Yep. That's a brilliant idea."

"You OK?"

I sighed and pinched the bridge of my nose. "Sure. I'm fine. It's going to be dark Saturday night, so I'm assuming this time we will have lights and audio."

She nodded. "Of course."

"Is there some kind of script Audrey wants to follow?" I asked.

"I think she's going to let Jake wing it."

My eyes doubled. "Is that a good idea?"

She smiled. "Have you ever seen Jake perform live?"

"No."

She stood and leaned one hand on my desk. "You're going to see why he won Entertainer of the Year last year."

I knew that was meant to impress or excite me, but the warning bells clanging in my mind made it hard to feel anything other than terror. Uncensored. Unscripted. And broadcast live to hundreds of thousands of people. I let out a shaky breath.

"Don't worry. He can handle it." She pointed at me from my door. "I'll see you tomorrow, Lucy. Don't work too late."

When she was gone, I drafted the copy for the social-media posts including the links to buy Jake's new album online. All I would have to do at the party is log in, press record, and pray for the whole thing not to blow up in my face.

At noon, I tiptoed down the hallway and out the front door without being noticed. The last thing I wanted was for Audrey to spot me and make me stay. I also wasn't sure I'd be able to hold my tongue if she stopped me. Jake performing the acoustic song had been *my* idea. Not hers. But to confront her would only put a damper on my otherwise wonderful day. I don't think I exhaled until I reached the parking garage undetected.

It was nice not having to navigate the treacherous interstate during rush hour, and I made it home in record time. Olivia was there, dressed for work with her hair in a tight bun on her head. She split a glance between me and the clock on the oven when I walked into the kitchen.

"Is everything OK?" she asked.

"Yeah. My boss let me leave early."

"That's nice."

"Guess what."

"What?"

I gripped her arm. "I'm going to West's house tonight."

"Congratulations." She held up a finger. "Hold on a sec." She walked to her bedroom, then returned a moment later and handed me a business card. "She does the best Brazilian wax job in Nashville. Just off Church Street in Brentwood too."

I looked at the car. "Oh no. I'm not getting waxed."

She shrugged. "Suit yourself, but he would love it."

I put my hand on my hip. "How would you know what *he* would love?"

She leaned in like she was going to tell me a secret. "Because he and I do the same job."

"Olivia!"

She winked. "Or hopefully he does, for your sake."

The heat that filled my face actually burned. "You're... That's..." I covered my face with my hands. "Oh my god."

She was laughing at me. "Are you going to make it to practice tomorrow?"

I fanned my face with a piece of junk mail off the counter.

"Yes. I'll put my bag and a change of clothes in the back of the car just in case I don't come home tonight."

"I may not come home either. Styx lives just a few blocks from the restaurant."

"How's that going?" I asked.

She grinned. "Good. We have to be really careful though. She lives in the same building as Medusa. It's like we're sneaking around on our parents."

"Would it be so bad if you got caught?" I asked.

"With the warpath Medusa has been on lately?"

"Good point."

"Besides, have you told anybody you're dating a sponsor?"

My nose scrunched up.

"So you understand."

"Not much longer though, right? We can both come out of the closet after the skills test and it's only three weeks away."

"That's right." She sighed. "I can't wait." She looked at her phone. "I've got to run. I've got a mandatory staff meeting soon. Let me know how it goes tonight."

"I will."

"Good luck," she said with a grin.

"Thanks. I need it."

———

I wasn't sure what I was expecting when I pulled into West's driveway, but what I found surprised the hell out of me. It was an old log cabin. In *Brentwood*, of all places. It wasn't very big, two stories with dormer windows poking out of the roof. And it had a front porch as wide as the house lined with a handrail made of gnarly mountain laurel. A stone chimney stretched high above the rooftop, puffing out gray smoke that seemed to mingle with the clouds.

The driveway wound around the side of the house and down a hill. Wait, the house was three stories counting the basement and two-car garage underneath. I parked in front of one of the stall doors and slid out of my SUV.

In the quiet of the woods, an animal scampered through the leaves and suddenly all I could think about was my dad. He'd love this place.

Before starting up the rock steps to the front path, I smoothed the skirt of the short ivory dress I'd settled on for the evening. It was light and airy with loose long sleeves that were slit open from the shoulder to the elbow showing just a glimpse of skin underneath. My hair was down and curled in loose waves, and while I did *not* get a bikini wax, I did take the time to shave my legs all the way up.

The front path was long up to the porch, giving my nerves ample time to ramp into overdrive by the time I rang the doorbell. And then the door was open, and West was standing there, holding two glasses of red wine. He was barefoot, wearing loose blue jeans and a plain white undershirt.

"Wow," he said, his eyes running down the length of my dress. "You look...*wow*. Come in." He stepped aside, handing me a wine glass as I entered the house. "Congratulations on a very successful week."

"Thank you." I smiled and sipped the wine as he closed the door behind me.

The interior had been recently remodeled, no surprise there. It was still rugged and manly with oversized furniture facing a burning fire on the rock hearth. Tall windows looked out over the woods and a large fenced-in backyard.

I inhaled oregano, garlic, sausage maybe. "Something smells amazing."

"I made dinner. Or I tried to, anyway." He pointed at his T-shirt. "I'm afraid I lost my favorite button up in the process."

"Oh no. What happened?"

"I didn't realize marinara sauce could blow up." He made an explosion motion with his free hand. "Sauce everywhere."

"Remind me, and I'll clean up your shirt before I leave."

He hooked his arm around my waist, a mischievous smile on his chiseled face. "Who says I'm going to let you go?"

He bent to kiss me, and just as our lips connected, a violent rumble like thunder with claws clattered across the hardwood floor. Before either of us could react, two heavy paws slammed against my lower back. As I fell forward into West, wine splashed everywhere.

"Cash, down!" West boomed, reaching behind me.

West released me to wrangle the dog out the front door. When he'd tumbled the deadbolt, he turned back toward me. The front of his jeans and his shirt were covered in bright pink splotches. "I'm *so* sorry," he said, coming back to my side. "I put him in his bedroom, but he's figured out how to open the door."

"A dog that can open doors?" I asked, rubbing my sore hip.

"Yeah. I'm going to have to switch to doorknobs rather than the handles you push down. Are you OK?" He swore when he looked down at my dress. "Oh, Lucy. That damn dog."

Wine drizzled down my chest. "I'll live, but I do need to wash it before the stain sets."

He took my empty glass and put it down on the counter in the kitchen. "Come on." He took my hand. "I'll find you something to wear."

Past the kitchen was the master bedroom. It was big, almost the size of the living room. Another fireplace burned in the corner with a large television mounted above it. Two double doors led out to a small deck.

Walking toward the bathroom, West pulled off his shirt, and I no longer cared about the craftsmanship of the cabin. His broad shoulders formed a solid capstone to the perfect V-shape of his torso. They bulged and relaxed as he pulled the shirt free from his arms and tossed it into a hamper sitting against the wall. I spun around before he caught me staring again, my pulse throbbing in my ears. I heard the fly on his jeans unzip, and I leaned against the footboard of the bed.

A moment later, his footfalls reentered the bedroom. When I turned, he was dressed in a new pair of jeans and a fitted red T-shirt with a busy black print on the front. He pointed at it with both fingers. "Now if I spill anything, no one can tell."

"Good plan," I said, still unable to peel myself away from the support of the wooden frame.

"You all right?"

"Yes." *Nope.*

He walked to the dresser and pulled open the second drawer. "I'm afraid the only stuff I have that will remotely fit you is pajama pants and T-shirts." He pulled out one of each and closed the drawer with his elbow. "I hope they're OK."

I accepted them with a forced smile. "Thank you."

"I'll let you change." He took a few steps toward the door.

"West?"

He stopped.

I gathered all my hair over one shoulder and turned my back to him. "Can you help with the buttons?"

Full disclosure: this was a *line*. This was a deplorable line of damsel-in-distress bullshit. I'd put the dress on by myself, and I could certainly get out of it by myself. It wasn't that complicated. But why the hell would I? I considered myself a respectable, young—dare I say, *lady*—but only so far. I'd had all the virtue and honorability I could stand.

He stepped to my back, and his fingers freed the pearl nub held by a delicately crocheted loop at the base of my neck. Then he freed the second. And, slowly, the last. His hands lingered there for a moment, just between my shoulder blades, before tracing the rim of the fabric up to my shoulders. Was he trembling? I sure as hell was.

A chill rippled through me as he pushed the neckline down to my arms.

Then he paused.

"I had a plan." His voice cracked with tension. "I had a whole romantic plan for tonight. Wine. Dinner by candlelight. I even bought strawberries."

I turned around to face him, holding the front of the dress up over my chest. "Do you want to wait?"

He pulled my hand away, letting the spoiled fabric drop to my ankles. His eyes fell with it. "God, Lucy. What do you think?"

FIFTEEN

I SHOULD HAVE GONE for the Brazilian wax job.

West's eyes, his hands—his *mouth*—had been everywhere. And it was good. Damn good. Slow and intentional, desperate but restrained. Had I any inclination to leave the bed at all, I would've called Olivia at work to tell her about it. But neither of us moved, not until long after the sun had dipped behind the oak trees that surrounded the house.

Dinner was ruined. The pasta had clumped together into one big ball of sticky carbs. The sauce had gone dry and had burned to the bottom of the pan. And the breadsticks were still frozen in the freezer. West ordered pizza, then rewarded Cash with the leftovers for helping him get laid.

He put on a movie in the living room, but we made love on the couch instead. A couple of times, West's attention snagged on the bruises dotting my hip bones, but I distracted him with other body parts to keep him from asking questions.

It went on like this all night. Intermittent bouts of sleepy sex so effortless and surreal I had trouble distinguishing if I was awake or lost in a sensational dream.

He was inside me when the sun came up.

Then we dozed until the alarm on my phone sounded at eight. His arm tightened around me. "No," he whispered, his breath warm and hot against the back of my shoulder.

My brain was saying the same thing. Not to mention my legs. I wasn't sure I'd be able to walk, let alone skate. I wanted to stay in bed, but my alarm was chirping otherwise through my cell-phone speakers. Still, I snuggled back against him and laced my fingers with his. "Last night was amazing."

"Amazing doesn't do last night justice."

I wiggled against him. "Wanna do it again before I leave?"

He laughed softly in my ear. "Want to? Yes. Able to? Not if you held a gun to my head." His hand squeezed mine. "Why do you have to go?"

"I have a workout group that meets on Saturdays. You know that."

"Are you kidding? I won't have to go to the gym for a week after last night."

My eyelids were feeling heavy again, so I pushed myself up, letting the sheet gather around my waist. "I made a commitment to be there. I have to go."

His fingertips trailed up and down my spine. "What time's the party tonight?"

"I'm supposed to be there by seven." I looked back at him. "Did I tell you Trip Wiley might be there?"

He was smiling with his eyes still closed as he held up two fingers. "At least twice."

I couldn't help but touch his bicep as he curled his arm back around his pillow. "Can I use your shower?"

"If I say no, will you stay in bed with me?"

I didn't answer.

He opened one eye to look at me. "Of course."

I bent and kissed the side of his face. He groaned when I moved to get up.

As I feared, I had gummy legs walking to the bathroom. I turned on the shower, and as I waited for the water to warm, I surveyed the damage in the mirror. My lips were red and raw. My hair was standing on end. And there was a suspicious mark on the back of my bad shoulder that could have been part of the fading bruise or could have been a hickey.

"Hey, babe. Do you know what I did with my purse?" I called back to the bedroom as I stepped into the massive glass shower.

"Not sure, but I'll look for it."

I watched through the open bathroom door to try and catch a glimpse of him naked. Then there it was. Six foot something of solid *man*. He returned a moment later with my bag narrowly hiding his better parts. "Do you need it in there?"

"There are two travel bottles of shampoo and conditioner in there. Can you hand them to me?"

He put the bag on the counter and rifled through it. "I think someone was planning to seduce me and stay the night," he teased.

"I'm not sorry."

"Better not be." Suddenly, he laughed. "What the hell were you planning to happen last night?"

I wiped my eyes. "What?"

"You've got bandages, moleskin, latex gloves." He held up a strip of black fabric. "Are these fishnet stockings?"

Whoops.

He was grinning when he pulled the shower door open and handed me my bottles. "Is there something you're not telling me?"

Oh, West. You have no idea.

Rather than lying, I poured the shampoo on my head and lathered it into my hair.

His laughter slowly fizzled until he was studying me like a

predator about to devour its prey. "You know what you asked me earlier?" He stepped into the shower and pulled the door closed behind him.

"Yes."

He pulled my slick, wet body against his and proved he wasn't as spent as he thought he was.

I was late to practice. Very late.

And when I got there, I had to change in the bathroom from West's pajamas to my workout clothes. When I was finally geared up and warmed up, the team was working on whips. I recognized the move from watching the veterans practice. Out on the track, Olivia skated up behind Grace, grabbed her arm, and Grace slung her forward. Olivia sailed around the track.

"Where've you been?"

Medusa skated up behind me, the heat of her glare almost palpable.

"Overslept."

She studied my face like she was debating whether to tell me to get to work or to get out. "What the hell are you waiting for? Get out there."

She didn't have to tell me twice. I sprinted on my skates to catch up with my friends—and to get away from Medusa. "Come on, Lucy!" Grace yelled, holding her hand out.

I skated toward her, grabbed her hand, and she twisted her whole body to whip me forward. I'm sure I was flailing around the track like a cartoon character trying to maintain my balance. Despite the weakness in my thighs and lack of sleep, I miraculously didn't wipe out. I slowed when I reached Olivia.

She pulled out her mouthguard and hooked it on her collar.

"Nice of you to join us today, Miss Cooper. You look like you had fun last night."

I put my hands on my cheeks. "Is it that obvious?"

"To me?" she asked. "Yep."

I gripped her wrist guard. "It was spectacular."

Her eyebrow had a skeptical arch. "Spectacular?"

"Olivia, it was so good, I sneezed in the car on the way here and it hurt my vagina."

She burst out laughing. "Had you regained your virginity?"

If it were medically possible, it had been long enough to regrow a hymen. My last relationship had been with Ryan Dixon, the guy whose heart I'd broken when I left Charleston to move back home and help take care of Mom.

"Thankfully, no," I said.

"You're seeing him again tonight for the party, right?"

I smiled. "And with any luck, I won't be sleeping at home after."

She bumped me with her hip, and somehow I didn't fall. "Well, I won't wait up."

"Are we here to work or are we here to chat?" Medusa barked at us.

Olivia elbowed me. "Come on. Let's do some hip whips."

We took turns grabbing each other's waists and hurling ourselves forward. A move not made for someone with an over-worked groin region. Maintaining my center of gravity was exceptionally difficult.

Grace and Monica were doing leg whips across the track. I pointed at them as Grace did a karate-like side kick and Monica grabbed her skate. "Don't even expect me to do that."

"It was that good, huh?"

I grabbed her waist and pulled to propel myself forward. "Yes, but I wouldn't be able to do that anyway."

"Stop, stop!" Medusa was yelling at us again. She skated over and pushed me out of the way. "You're not pulling enough, newbie. Olivia is sturdy on her wheels, really grab and put your weight into it."

She grabbed Olivia's waist and pulled herself around much faster than I had. She spun backward on her skates. "Now you."

I grabbed. I pulled. I moved a few feet. Nothing impressive enough for Medusa.

She tapped Olivia on the shoulder. "Go skate with Styx." Then she shouted over her head. "Styx, work with The Prodigy!"

So Olivia's name had traveled. I wondered if they all called me Trip Hazard behind my back.

"Who are you again?" Medusa asked.

"Lucy."

"Yeah. That strikes fear into the hearts of bitches everywhere," she said with a smirk. "Get behind me. Grab my hips and go."

I skated up and grabbed her, but she immediately slapped my hands and plowed to a stop. "You've got fingers and palms, not just fingertips and nails. Really grab my hip bones, Lucy. Again."

She started moving, and I followed behind. I grabbed two handfuls of her taut waist that time.

"Good! Pull!"

I yanked so hard, she wavered a little.

"Excellent. Next time you pull, skate out of it. You're not getting a free ride here. Maximize your speed by sprinting out of the whip. Again!"

We continued this a few times around the track. Then she whipped off me. She did a lot of yelling about bending my knees and settling into my hips. My oh-so-painful hips.

"Now, arms!" she instructed. "Right hand to right hand, and grab my forearm with your left. Bend your knees and skate out of it."

I charged her, grabbed onto her hand, and flew forward,

sprinting on my skates. I'd never moved so fast outside a car or a roller coaster in all my life. I had to sidestep around Zoey to not plow into her.

"Again!" Medusa called as I came back around.

After three laps, I was panting and pouring sweat. I held my hands up in a "t" shape. "I need a break. Water!"

She looked at the clock. "It's been nine minutes."

I bent at the waist and grabbed my knees, breathing so hard that my mouthguard flopped out onto the concrete. Then her skates were in front of me. Black, with white skull laces. I straightened and wiped sweat from my eyes.

She was pissed. "Next time, don't show up late and half asleep, still wearing your boyfriend's clothes."

I swallowed and nodded my head.

She blew her whistle and skated back to the track.

———

It was four o'clock when I woke up in my bed to a text message from West. *Pick you up at 6?*

I'd been asleep for three hours.

Thanks to Medusa, I hardly had the strength in my arms to text him back. *6 is perfect.*

After practice, I'd come straight home, skipping lunch with the girls for the first time since we began the tradition. *Everyone* knew why. And if they didn't before, they knew it when Olivia serenaded me with "Like a Virgin" and the rest of the team joined in.

I spent the next hour in the bathtub like I'd done in the early days of derby. The water was as hot as I could stand it and mixed with Epsom salt and eucalyptus. Hopefully, in that water, I'd reclaim my A-game. A lot was riding on Jake Barrett's party. Half the music industry would be there. West Adler would be there.

Audrey would be there. Never mind the hundreds of thousands of fans who'd potentially tune in online.

Being sore and lethargic was *not* an option.

After the bath, a Red Bull, and a double-dose of ibuprofen, I felt more like myself. I dressed in a new outfit, specifically purchased for the occasion: a slinky black shirt and dark skinny jeans that—*holy crap!*—were already tighter in my thighs.

My doorbell rang at exactly six o'clock. Punctual, that man.

I opened the door, and his cologne and pheromones flooded my apartment.

The first thought in my head: *He's seen me naked. Very naked.* Flashes from the night warmed the room's temperature by a few degrees. I resisted the urge to fan my face.

"Hi," he said, all smiles and sex appeal.

"Hi." I stepped back. "Come in."

He crossed the door and stopped in front of me, gently holding my waist as he leaned down for a spearminty kiss. "I missed you today," he said against my mouth.

My lips were still tender. "I missed you too."

"How was your workout?" he asked as he followed me to the living room.

"Exhausting. I came home and slept for three hours."

"I went back to bed after you left. Then I got up around one, played fetch with Cash for about ten minutes, and went back to bed till I texted you." He leaned in my doorway as I went to grab my boots. "And I cleaned up the disaster in the kitchen, finally. I'm still sorry I ruined dinner."

I laughed and sat down on my bed to pull my boots on. "I'm not. You were otherwise occupied, and it was perfectly fine with me."

It was kind of dark in my room, but I was pretty sure he was blushing a tad.

"I'm not going to lie. I think that was the best night of my life."

I stood and walked over to him. My boots brought me a little closer to his eye level. I slid my hands along the sides of his belt. "Mine too. Although, I have been walking a little funny all day."

He ducked his head. Yes, he was definitely blushing. He finally met my eyes again. "We have to go, or we won't leave this room."

"Yes, we do. My boss will kill me if I'm late." I started to move past him, but then I paused.

"What is it?"

"I do have a question before we go. It's a little awkward to ask."

He crossed his arms. "I'm intrigued."

"How should I introduce you tonight?" I gulped, the noise detonating in my ears. "I mean, it's only been a couple of weeks, but..."

His mouth bent into a slow, unreadable smile. He leaned in, his cheek brushing mine. "Nothing about last night was casual, so I'm going to be pretty pissed if you say I'm just your friend." Then he pulled back to look at me, grinning. "Especially to Trip Wiley."

Like a tightly compressed coil finally being released, I exhaled a breath I didn't realize I'd been holding. "Trip Wiley's already taken."

"Lucky for me," he teased.

He seriously studied my face for a second. "No games, right?"

"Right."

He offered me his hand. "Are you ready?"

———

A valet met us in the driveway when we pulled up in front of Jake's house. He was holding a clipboard. "Name, please?"

I leaned across the cab. "Lucy Cooper with Record Road Nashville."

He scanned the paper with his pen. "Welcome. May I take your key, sir?"

West put his truck in park and slid out of the cab. "Take it easy on her," he said and flashed a wink back at me. "She just got a new bumper."

I laughed and rolled my eyes.

A second valet opened my door and offered me a hand down onto the driveway. Music floated over the house from around back by the pool. "The front door is open, ma'am. An attendant inside will check you through."

I blinked. *Check us through?* Was this the same house where I'd seen a bikini top in a day-old fruit-salad bowl just a few days before? "Thank you."

He gave a polite nod, and I joined West on the front step.

"Fancy digs," he said, checking out the front wall of the house. He was surely noting things like angles and lines, roof pitch and brick choice. "And no, before you ask, I didn't build it."

The front door opened before we reached it, and a woman in a black fitted business suit greeted us. "Hi! Come on in!"

I looked around in awe. *Definitely* not the same house. Parts of the house were blocked off with fancy velvet ropes, including the living room, the stairs leading up, and, of course, the master bedroom. And every speck of it was gleaming. Ava must have hired the cleaning company, and they must have had superpowers.

"Can I get your name?" The perky woman had a pointed southern pang.

"Lucy Cooper. Record Road Nashville."

She walked around behind a small black writing desk. "There you are. Would you care to check anything? A coat or your purse?"

I pressed my purse to my side. "I'll need it, but thank you."

"The party is just down the hall, out on the patio by the pool."

She walked with us part of the way. "They will be recording a live video that will go out to Mr. Barrett's fan base at seven o'clock."

I'd only met Jake once, but it was still funny to hear him referred to as Mr. Barrett.

"If you have any questions, my name is Lorainne. I'll be here all night."

"Thank you for your help, Lorainne," I said.

"Enjoy the party!" she called after us.

As we passed by the kitchen, West pointed out a wall blocking a hallway built from cases of craft beer. "This is going to be fun."

"There's a full bar outside too, and a small concert stage," I told him.

He tugged on my hand to stop me. "Thanks for bringing me, Lucy."

"Hold your gratitude until later. My boss is here. And you know"—I widened my eyes—"every party has a pooper."

"*We* are going to have a great time," he said and kissed my forehead.

I'd been impressed my first visit to Jake's house, but he had outdone himself for the party. Or whoever planned it had outdone themselves, at least. The pool was illuminated in hues of purple and blue as floating white lights twinkled on the surface of the water. New cushy and colorful furniture dotted the patio and surrounded the blazing fire pit which was stocked with what appeared to be a s'mores bar. Overhead, a canopy of globe string lights glimmered against the fading sunset and recorded country music twanged from the sound system. The stage was fenced with tiki lamps, their flames dancing against the darkness.

Partygoers were scattered around the backyard oasis, some dancing, all drinking. I scanned their faces and saw a few that looked familiar, but none I could place.

"Is that Reba McEntire?" West whispered in my ear.

My eyes searched for red hair.

"Over by the cake," he added.

The five-tier cake, decorated with flames and music notes, had its own table between the bar and a treble clef ice sculpture rising out of a beer trough big enough to water a herd of cattle. The woman in question? Not Reba McEntire. Most likely.

"Lucy!"

An arm waving from the bar caught my attention. It was Ava. I tugged on West's hand. "Come on. You need to meet the other half of Record Road."

Ava could have just come from a New York runway in her sleek black slip dress that was split down the front halfway to her bellybutton. Her dark hair was pinned lazily on top of her head with gentle tendrils falling around her face. She greeted me with a kiss on the cheek. "It's so good to see you, Lucy," she said over the music.

I squeezed her arm. "You look beautiful."

Ava did a slight curtsy. "Thank you."

"Ava, this is West Adler," I said, turning to him.

They shook hands. "It's nice to finally put a face with your name, Mr. Adler. I've been hearing about you a lot lately."

My heart was squealing inside, but West gave my hip bone a reassuring squeeze. "That's good to hear. Thanks for letting me come."

"Any friend of Lucy's is always welcome with me. Have you met Jake yet?"

He shook his head.

"We haven't even seen him," I told her.

She rolled her eyes. "Maybe he can't find his way around the house now that it's so clean."

I laughed and gestured around the patio. "I really can't believe this is the same place we were at a few days ago."

"I know, right?" She scanned the crowd, pausing a couple of

times to return the waves of partygoers. "I don't see him anywhere."

I checked my watch. "We should find him and get ready to start shooting. We're supposed to go live in twenty minutes."

"Yes, we should. He's probably in the house." She took a step toward the door.

I hesitated, looking at my gorgeous date.

"Go on," he said. "When you come back, I'll have us a couple of cold drinks ready."

I hated to leave him. "You sure?"

He squeezed my hand. "Positive. I'll either be by the bar or tearing up that s'mores station when you get back."

I leaned in and kissed his lips like it was the most natural thing in the world to do. He was smiling when I pulled back. "I'll hurry," I said.

"Break a leg!" he called as I walked back to the house with Ava.

She looped her arm through mine. "Gee whiz, you weren't kidding about that one. He's impressive. What's wrong with him?"

I laughed. "I've been asking myself that same question for months."

———

Ava knocked on the door to the master bedroom.

"Come in!" Jake yelled from the other side.

She twisted the knob and pushed the heavy carved wooden door open. Jake was standing in front of the full-length mirror, buttoning a black rhinestone shirt next to a leggy blonde in stiletto heels.

Ava's head tilted. "What are you doing?"

"Getting ready." He nodded to the blonde. "This is my stylist, Zusanna."

Zusanna's lipstick was smudged, and her skirt was rumpled like it had recently been pushed up to her waist. She waved. I waved back. Ava did not.

Ava walked over to his closet and threw open the door. "You need to wear the gray shirt. The one from the album cover with the rolled sleeves."

He followed her and pulled her out of his closet. "I'm not wearing the gray shirt."

Ava put her hands on her hips. "You know better than I do now?"

He tugged on the hem of his black shirt. "I like this one."

"The album is called *The Gun Show*," she reminded him. "And since when do you miss an opportunity to showcase your biceps?"

"Since the girl at Neiman Marcus said this shirt makes me look like a young Merle Haggard."

She flicked a rhinestone button. "Merle Haggard wouldn't have been caught dead in this monstrosity. And honestly, I'm surprised you bought it. It looks like you stole it from a closet at Graceland."

Grinning, he leaned toward her. "They don't call him *The King* for nothing."

"Whatever," she said, rolling her eyes. "Are you ready to do this?"

He flipped his collar up. "I was born ready, baby."

Scowling, she folded his collar back down. "Let's not make it worse, Elvis." She lowered her voice. "Can you please ask your stylist to wait for you at the party? We don't do girlfriends in front of the fans, remember?"

Jake grinned as Ava scraped a smudge of something shiny off his collar with her fingernail. "She's not my girlfriend."

She glared at him.

"Zusanna," he said, his voice smooth and seductive. "Would you mind waiting for me at the bar by the pool? My fans await."

Ava smirked so hard her head jerked back.

"Yes, darling," Zusanna cooed. She edged between Ava and Jake, pressing her body against his as she kissed him long and hard on the mouth.

Some stylist.

Then Zusanna turned on her heel and swished her hips so wide I watched to see if she'd smack into the doorframe on her way out. She didn't, sadly.

When she was gone, Ava's face soured. "Really?"

Jake snickered. "She's hot."

"I'm going to tell your mother," Ava said.

He pointed at her face. "You'd better not."

She grabbed his finger.

The click of my smartphone snapping into the grips on the tripod seemed to snap them both out of a private moment. Ava straightened and stepped back away from him. "Are we ready to work?"

As if on cue, there was a knock on the open door. We all looked over as Audrey walked inside, followed closely by two men dressed in black shirts and cargo pants carrying audio and lighting equipment. Then a third man entered with a video camera.

"Good evening, everyone," she said.

"What's with the camera?" Ava asked, beating me to the question.

"They're going to do the shoot tonight," Audrey asked, her tone implying we were stupid for wondering.

I slipped my hand up. "I thought we were keeping the video casual."

"We are," Ava said. "We discussed this, Audrey."

"But the lighting and the audio will be better through the live-streaming mobile studio that these guys can use," Audrey said.

Ava crossed her arms. "The whole reason we changed the song and stage setup was so Jake could do the acoustic number for the sake of the video."

Audrey gestured to the video team. "And now they can do even that better. The whole world is going to be listening the first time he plays that song. We want it to be the best quality possible."

The whole world? Really? I was trying hard not to roll my eyes. To be honest, I was happy for the video team to take over the job. It'd be, sure as hell, less stress on me.

"No," Jake said, surprising us all. "I want her"—he pointed at me—"to shoot it on her phone the way she did the other videos."

"You do?" Audrey and I asked at the exact same time, both with equal amounts of surprise.

He nodded and plopped a brand-new black cowboy hat down onto his head, instead of his favorite old brown one. "Yes. She did a great job with the other videos, and I want her on this one too."

My heart swelled. I was pretty sure Jake had forgotten my name, and Audrey wouldn't have known it anyway, but he was singing my praises. Me.

Audrey blinked. "Well, OK, then."

"This wireless mic will hook up to her phone if you want to use it," one of the guys in black offered.

I nodded. "That'd be great."

He held out his hand. "I just need to install a quick app and connect it via Bluetooth."

I gave him the phone. "Excellent."

There were five minutes to spare to shoot a test video with the new microphone that was pinned to Jake's shirt. It sounded great. "I want to shoot the video myself, selfie-style, till I go up on stage. Is that OK with you?" Jake asked.

My head snapped back. "Sure. Whatever you want."

He winked at me. "I like your attitude."

"The music has been silenced out by the pool, but it will start playing *The Gun Show* when you walk out there," Audrey said. "We'll keep it low so it won't interfere with the video. Gus will be watching live on his phone here and using the radio to signal the guys in the sound booth if there are any issues."

Jake gave her a thumbs-up. "Hey, Ava. On second thought, will you bring that gray shirt in case I get hot?"

Ava's eyes narrowed to skeptical slits. "OK?" Her response sounded more like a question than an answer.

"Let's do this," he said.

My pulse echoed in my ears as he took the phone from me.

"You guys might want to move," he suggested.

"You're going to start shooting in here?" Audrey asked, clearly horrified.

He looked at his watch. "It's seven o'clock. I don't see why not."

We all scurried to the side of the room to stay out of his way. The production guys aimed their white lights at him. "Is this OK?" one of them asked.

"Perfect," Jake said. "In three...two...one. Action!"

SIXTEEN

"HEY, guys! It's Jake here. How y'all doin' tonight?" Jake's smile was wild as he looked into the video camera. "I'm actually coming to you live from my bedroom right now in Nashville, Tennessee!"

Ava was gripping my wrist so hard I feared she might draw blood.

On my other side, Audrey nudged my arm with her elbow. She had the video streaming on her phone with the sound muted.

"Tonight, we're about to throw down and celebrate my new album, *The Gun Show*. It hit stores yesterday and is already sitting at the top of the country music charts. So tonight is for you guys! The best fans in the world. And for my momma, Eileen Barrett. She's supposed to be tuning in from Phoenix tonight." He waved at the camera. "Hi, Mom!"

There were already over sixty-two thousand viewers.

I gulped.

"So welcome to my home. Please drop in the comments and let me know where you're watching live this evening," he said.

The comment section was already going crazy, but then the locations started coming in.

Watching live in Seattle, Washington!

It's 9:03 in the morning here in Canberra, Australia!

We love you in London, Jake!

"I love you, too, London!" Jake said, winking at the camera.

"Holy shit," Ava whispered beside me.

There were already over three hundred comments and a thousand stars.

Jake walked toward the bedroom door. "Are you guys ready to get this party started? I sure am. I think we've got quite the crowd waiting for us out in my backyard."

Jake's performance was impressive. There was nothing else in the world between him and the fans in that video. It was captivating to watch on Audrey's small screen. We followed him at a distance as he walked through the living room. "You guys want a mini tour of my house?" he asked.

Of course they did. All ninety thousand of them.

"There's my piano. I actually bought it at an estate sale from the legendary Erving Clyne. I can't play it for shit, but someday I'm gonna learn just to honor his memory."

Ava leaned into me. "Can he say shit on a live internet video?"

I shrugged. "He just did."

"Over here are my awards." He crossed the living room to the mantle and began pointing at the statues. "Here are my ACMs, these three are CMAs, and this is my Grammy." He held up a bronze star that was mounted on a black onyx pedestal. "And this one's my absolute favorite, my Fan's Choice Award." He flipped the camera back around to his face. "Every day I look at this star, baffled that you all thought I was worthy enough to have my name etched on it. Thank you, guys." He winked again.

Oh, he's good, I thought, smiling to myself.

The video had soared to over 150,000 live viewers.

Jake walked back to the kitchen and dining area and panned the camera around. "Believe it or not, this room does function as a kitchen on a normal day in the Barrett house." He turned the camera toward all the beer stacked on the counters and the floors, then lowered his voice like he was telling them a secret. "I think someone's planning on doing some partying tonight."

When he reached the end of the hallway, he turned his back to the door and aimed the camera at his face. Ava and I were watching on her smartphone.

Jake flashed the fans his million-dollar smile. "Are you guys ready to go and hang with some of my friends?"

Comments were scrolling so fast through the video sidebar that my eyes couldn't keep up.

The door swung open behind him, probably cued by someone with a radio, and the crowd erupted in cheers and applause on the patio. Confetti rained down. Music blared. A spray of colorful fireworks exploded somewhere on the far side of the expansive lawn.

Jake's eyes sparkled in the video, glistening with genuine tears of joyous surprise. And in that second, I became a fan of the man himself, not just of his music or his exceptionally gorgeous face. And I was sure, I wasn't alone. Certainly, everyone who was watching fell a little harder in love with him that night. All 212,000 of them.

"You guys want to meet some of my friends?" he asked the camera, stepping out onto the patio. He looked around the crowd. "We've got almost a quarter of a million people watching live right now, so don't do anything stupid!"

Everyone laughed.

"There's Stone Anderson over there manning the beer cooler as usual." Stone, the current reigning bad boy of country music, raised a beer bottle in salute. "And next to him, Lincoln Hunt. Wave hello, Lincoln!" Jake yelled. Lincoln Hunt was said to be the best steel guitar player in history. It was rumored his hands were insured for a million dollars each. He was waving both of them in the air.

"Jake!" a booming voice shouted.

We all turned.

Holy shit.

The crowd had parted like the Red Sea for Trip Wiley. *The* Trip Wiley.

"Trip!" Jake looked back over his shoulder and thrust the phone into my hands. Startled, I nearly dropped it before making sure the camera was facing the right direction.

And my jitters were justified. Sure, Jake Barrett had made *People's* Most Beautiful People list, but the same publication had named Trip Wiley Sexiest Man Alive two years in a row. And gawking at him in the flesh, the title was deserved.

Trip Wiley was heart stopping.

The two heartthrobs embraced, and I was pretty sure I felt the entire internet swoon at my fingertips. Trip clapped Jake on the back, then they both turned, arm in arm, to face me—I mean, the camera.

Jake pointed at Trip. "This guy needs no introduction, right? But just in case...Trip Wiley, ladies and gentlemen."

Everyone on the patio cheered. Trip waved to them and the fans watching live online. "This is an excellent party, my friend. Congratulations on the new album."

"Thank you. Thank you." Jake jerked his head in the direction of the stage. "I'm thinking about playing a new number. You want to hear?"

"Absolutely!" Trip answered.

"Let's do this!" Jake beckoned me, the camera, to follow as he walked through the crowd toward the stage. He paused several times along the way for high fives and to point out various superstars to those watching live at home. We also took a detour by the cake and the ice sculpture. I made sure to get the new album's cover front and center in the video footage.

I had a front-row view when Jake climbed the stage and picked up his guitar. An arm brushed mine, and I gulped when I realized Trip Wiley was standing right next to me. He smelled like soap and sugar, clean and delicious. *Oh my god.*

The live viewer number broke a quarter-million just as Jake strummed the guitar strings and began to sing. His voice was low and melodic, seductive and smooth.

I knew this day would always come.
I never thought I'd feel this numb.
You walked away.
I let you go.
And never once, did I let you know
But here we are.
So close. So very far.
And I told myself I'd be fine.
But now, darling, I know...
You'll never be mine.

A penny could have fallen onto the concrete and the noise would have shattered the silence on the patio. It was just Jake and his guitar, his eyes firmly fixed on me...*no, dumbass,* on the camera. Wait. No. Not the camera. I glanced over my shoulder, careful to not wobble the video.

Ava was standing just behind me.

Oh boy.

Jake continued the song. I wondered if anyone else noticed. I wondered if Audrey noticed. I found her in the crowd. Thankfully, her eyes were glued to her phone. But was there something going on with Ava and Jake? Surely not. The blonde. The stray stiletto. The bikini top. No, there couldn't be.

And there'd better *not* be. I shuddered thinking of what Audrey would do.

An arm slid around my waist. West had found his way to me through the crowd. He winked but didn't speak.

The song finished with Jake holding out the last note. *"You'll never be miiiiiiiine."*

Jake walked to the edge of the stage in front of me, held his guitar by its neck, and bowed for his audience. The ones present and the 278,113 watching live online.

As he straightened, the flame from the nearest tiki lamp licked Jake's arm, and suddenly his entire left side burst into flames. Screams pierced the night air as Jake flailed wildly on the stage. West charged up the stairs, quickly tackling the singer to the ground and suffocating the flames beneath his body weight. I was frozen where I stood, filming the whole ordeal with my cursed smartphone.

One of the sound guys rushed over with a large bottle of water, pouring it over the two men rolling on the stage. Ava pushed past me and ran up the steps, followed closely by Audrey and a few others. After a second, they moved aside as West offered Jake a hand up.

"I'm OK! I'm OK!" Jake was shouting as West hauled him to his feet.

Jake hugged West, then pulled back to shake his hand. Jake's shirt was scorched and exposing red flesh underneath. They were talking too quietly for me to hear, but West's face was flushed and his eyes were wide with panic and adrenaline. Jake clapped him on the back. "My hero!" he announced. "West Adler, everyone!"

Ava grabbed Jake by his ridiculous collar.

He nodded and I read his lips as he promised her he was OK. Then he grabbed the microphone and laughed. "I think I'm going to need a new shirt!"

Ava ran her hands down her face as she walked across the stage toward me. She pointed at the ground and Trip Wiley bent to pick something up. He handed her Jake's gray shirt.

Jake looked at the guys in the sound booth. "I think this calls for some new music."

His new title song, "The Gun Show," played over the speakers again as Jake stripped off his charred shirt and slipped his hulking arms into the gray one. Patches of skin were bright red on his chiseled chest and side, but they appeared to be only minor burns.

He was lucky.

Or was he?

There were almost three hundred thousand people watching online.

When Jake finished buttoning his shirt, he took back the microphone Ava was holding for him. Then he walked toward me on the stage. "I hope you guys enjoyed *The Gun Show* tonight. Don't forget to pick up the new album now wherever music is sold. Goodnight!"

"Well, that was one hell of a show," West said, carrying two beers over to where I stood by the pool looking at the video in my hands.

Ava was punching Jake in the arm as they walked over behind him.

"You really saved my ass up there, West," Jake said, catching Ava's fist in his hand when she moved to strike him again.

"I'm glad he had the reflexes to react," I said. "The rest of us were too stunned to move."

Jake clinked his beer bottle with West's. "I owe you one, brother."

"Don't mention it, man." West took a long drink, his weary eyes fixed on the stars above us.

"Jake, how about a picture with the big hero?" a man called to us. It was the event photographer.

"Absolutely!" Jake hooked his arm around West's neck for the shot. They smiled as the camera flashed. "I want a group picture too," Jake said, pulling Ava under his other arm. West was kissing the side of my head when the camera flashed again.

Jake thanked the photographer, then leaned over my shoulder. "How'd the video come out?"

"Very dramatic." I looked down at the button on the screen. *Do you want to post your video?*

Ava was looking too, and she answered out loud. "No! Not without talking to Audrey first."

Just as I glanced up at her, Jake reached over me and clicked the button to upload. "Absolutely, we do!"

I fumbled the phone.

It fell straight into the pool.

Shit.

The four of us stood there, motionless, and watched it sink to the bottom of the blue water.

"Oops," Jake said.

West looked at me. "Want me to go in after it?"

I blew out a sigh that puffed out my cheeks. "Why bother?"

Jake's big hand squeezed my shoulder. "I'll buy you a new one."

"You bet your ass you will," Ava snapped. She looked around and leaned toward him. "Did you plan that shit, Jake Barrett?"

West and I both turned to look at him. I'd been wondering the same thing.

Jake held his hands up. "Me? Why would I do such a thing?"

She glared at him.

He grinned. Then he pointed to the phone resting on the bottom of the pool. "Think the video still uploaded?"

"I don't know," I said.

West put his beer down and pulled out his phone. After a few taps on the screen, he turned it around to show us. "It's up there."

Jake howled. "Holy hell! Over a million views already! Are you serious?"

I gripped my temples. "Where's Audrey?"

Ava rubbed her forehead. "Probably in the house washing down Xanax with moonshine."

Jake draped his arm around her neck. "What are you so worried about? This is a marketing dream. There's no such thing as bad press, Ava."

She closed her eyes. "You'd better pray you're right."

"You two were rock stars tonight. I really appreciate everything," Jake said to me and West. "Mi casa, su casa. You can have the guest house tonight if you want to party and crash here."

West and I exchanged an awkward glance. "Thanks," he said.

Jake nodded toward the house and looked at Ava. "We'd better go find your sister and make sure she hasn't had an aneurysm."

Ava smiled, sort of. "Have fun, guys."

When they were gone, West laughed and wrapped his arms around me. "What a night!"

"Do you want to stay here?" I asked.

He shook his head. "Hell no."

"Thank God," I said, resting my face against his chest. "I want to get out of here as soon as possible."

Relief washed over his face. "Say no more. What do you want to do about your phone?"

I shrugged and looked down in the pool. "Leave it, I guess. It's trashed now anyway, right?"

He nodded. "Afraid so."

"I don't even care. My brain is so fried right now. I can't believe all that just happened," I said.

West pulled me against him and kissed the side of my head. "Nothing's ever boring with you, Lucille. Finish your beer. Let's go home."

———

Sunday morning I awoke to something hot, wet, and rough sliding across my face. My eyes fluttered open just as Cash licked my face again. I scrambled back in the bed, slamming ass-first into West. He groaned and rolled over toward me.

Cash jumped onto the bed.

"Down, boy!" West yelled, snapping his fingers at the dog.

Cash plopped down next to me, panting in my face.

I laughed as he rolled over for me to scratch his belly. I did.

West sighed. "He's impossible. I need to put him in obedience training."

Cash's back leg jerked rhythmically when my nails found a sensitive spot beneath his ribs. "What happened to your other dog? Puck, wasn't it?"

West curled into my back. "Puck's not mine. She belongs to my ex."

I was sorry I'd asked.

West pushed up onto his elbow and reached over me, gently pushing the dog sideways. "Get down, Cash," he ordered firmly.

Cash just looked at him, frozen with his paws still in the air.

West laughed and dropped his forehead against my shoulder in defeat. "I give up."

I ran my fingers through his hair. "What do you want to do today?"

He kissed my collarbone. "This," he said, sliding over on top of me. "Are you going to run off like you did yesterday?"

I raked my fingers down his strong back. "Nope. I don't have to be anywhere till work tomorrow."

Using his knee, he moved my legs apart and then settled between them. "Does that mean you're sleeping over again?"

"I have to go home and change and get my stuff for work at some point." He was trailing kisses up the side of my neck. "And I guess I need to see about getting my phone replaced."

"Do you have insurance on it?" he asked between nibbles.

"Yeah, thankfully."

"They'll send you a new one. You just fill out the paperwork online," he said.

"You've done this before?"

He nodded. "Went through thirteen phones last year."

"Thirteen?"

He pulled back and looked at me. "You trash cars. I trash phones. Don't judge me."

Laughing, I drew his head back into the bend of my neck and squirmed beneath him. "No judgment here. I need to get on it though. I have a feeling this is going to be a crazy week at work."

"Because of last night?" he asked in my ear.

"Yes," I said. "Last night was either a PR sensation or a disaster. Good or bad, it's viral now and that means a lot of work for me. I hope I don't wind up fired over it."

"Why would you be fired?" His fingers tangled with mine under the pillow behind my head.

"Because my boss is crazy," I said. "She'll be looking for a head to roll if this goes south."

His teeth scraped against my neck. "What about her sister? She seems pretty cool. Definitely seems to like you."

"Yeah, but she may be on the shit list, too, after last night." I remembered Jake's song. "Did you get the impression that something might be going on with her and Jake?"

"Isn't there?"

I shook my head. "There's not supposed to be. We've got

pretty strict rules spelled out in our employee handbook thanks to Ava's last interoffice romance."

"Oh yeah?"

"That song 'Bitch, Please' by Lawson Young was written about her," I said.

He cringed. "Oh, that's bad." He looked up again, this time with disappointment etched across his face. "That's a bummer. I liked that song, but she's really nice."

"I know. So you see, there will be drama at work this week."

"I don't envy you."

"You don't ever have drama at your job sites?"

He pressed his elbow into the mattress and rested his head in his hand. "I work with a bunch of dudes, mostly, so we don't deal with a whole lot of romantic affairs gone south."

"Must be nice."

He returned to nuzzling my neck. "No. You know what's nice? This. This is very nice."

I hooked my leg around his under the covers and pressed my hips against him. "Yes, and all the drama can wait till tomorrow because I have no phone to hear about it."

SEVENTEEN

THE DRAMA CAME ON MONDAY, starting with me being fifteen minutes late to work. I'd slept over at West's again, against my better judgment, and had slept through the alarm he set on his phone. I'd been forced to sneak into my apartment to not wake Olivia, then rushed back out the door only to get nailed by rush hour traffic.

Thankfully, Ava caught me by the arms and dragged me into her office as soon as I walked into the hallway at work. "You did it, Lucy. You did it!"

My eyes widened. "I did what? I haven't been online because I don't have a phone."

That wasn't exactly true. West had checked the video while we ate dinner the night before because Jake tagged him in it and some of the pictures on social media. The video had been seen over two million times then.

"Sorry about that." Jake's voice startled me. I hadn't noticed him sprawled across the sofa in Ava's office. "I'll write you a check to get a new one."

"It was a hundred-dollar deductible to replace it. The insurance company is delivering a new one today," I said.

"Ava, give her a hundred bucks," Jake said.

Ava's face was dancing. "I'll give her anything she wants! The video has gone majorly viral. Like worldwide on all social media channels."

"How many views?" I asked.

Jake held his phone up over his head. "A little over seven million."

My mouth gaped. "In two days?"

"In two days!" Ava said with a squeal. "Jake tagged a bunch of people in it and they started sharing it with their followers. Then Trip Wiley tweeted it out and posted it on Facebook, and it's gone crazy ever since. The *Tonight Show* is calling, James Corden, *Good Morning America*. You name it! Jake's flying to New York this afternoon!"

She was talking so fast I could hardly keep up.

Jake swung his legs off the armrest and sat up. "Best of all, my new album is sitting at the top of the charts." He pointed at me. "All thanks to you, little lady."

Heat rushed to my cheeks.

"All thanks to *me*, you mean." Audrey's voice splintered the joy in the room. We all turned toward her as she swept into the office. "This was my idea, after all. Or did we forget that?"

I swallowed, tears prickling the corners of my eyes.

Ava took a step toward her sister. "Audrey, let's not forget who was the one to—"

Audrey's hand shot up to silence her. "I'm not discounting Lily's contribution to our endeavor here. I'm just asking for a bit of a reality check before we all get a little too carried away with the accolades."

Something snapped inside my head, and two versions of my own voice spoke to me like warring angels sitting on my shoulders. "*Hold your tongue, Lucy. It isn't fair, but you don't want to say or do anything that might jeopardize your career. It's not worth it.*"

My other voice sounded a whole lot like Stone Cold Kelly teaching me to execute my first hit in roller derby. "*Dig up some anger, channel its energy, and destroy.*"

"Carried away with the accolades?" I asked. "Audrey, Jana Carter gave you the idea. You couldn't be outdone by her, so you pushed the idea on me, and I busted my ass to make it happen. For a month, I've sweated over this project, lost sleep over it. Then you came in and tried to screw it up—*twice!* And let's face it, that video wouldn't have gotten half the attention had Jake not set himself on fire. So excuse me while I appropriate the accolades in this room."

They were all staring at me. Speechless.

But not for long. Audrey's face twisted up as quickly as it had gone slack. "Lily, I don't think you—"

"My name is not Lily. My name is Lucy!"

The blood drained from Audrey's face. She licked her lips and straightened her suit jacket before turning on her heel and stalking out of the office. I didn't exhale until she was gone. Then I heaved in a painfully deep breath.

Ava's jaw was still dropped. "Oh my gosh."

I covered my mouth with both hands. "What have I done?"

Jake was snickering. "I'm so turned on right now."

I turned to Ava. "What do I do?"

She shook her head. "I have no idea. This is uncharted territory." Her movements were rigid as she crossed the room. "Let me talk to her."

Frozen, I watched her leave.

Jake slowly peeled himself off the couch. He came over, put his arm around my shoulders, and gave them a reassuring jostle. "Chin up, buttercup. We all lose our shit from time to time."

I gripped my temples. "But she's my boss. And I don't lose my shit on anybody."

He laughed. "Well, maybe it was time." He bent at the knees to bring his mouth level with my ear. "And between you and me, she's had that one coming for a few years now."

"Whether she's had it coming or not won't matter when I'm unemployed and can't pay my rent."

"You've got skills, Miss Lucy." He squeezed my shoulder. "If you get canned, you can come work for me."

———

I didn't get canned, at least not yet. Audrey didn't speak to me again. Ava came by twice to check on me, but apparently, Audrey wasn't talking to her either. Then Ava left to fly to New York with Jake, and I sulked alone in my office the rest of the day. I couldn't even call Olivia, Ethan, or West for support because all my contact's phone numbers were probably still at the bottom of the pool at Jake's house.

Thankfully, I was busy managing the cyber traffic swarming our office. Jake's numbers climbed another million views just during the work day, and since Friday, he'd gained almost a million new followers on all his social-media accounts. I was glad for the work too. The success of the video might be the only thing to save my job.

My new phone arrived just in time for me to leave. I realized as I locked up my office, it was the first time I'd been out since I holed myself up that day. My neglected stomach churned out a painful growl. As I trudged down the hallway, I didn't even care that everyone was staring from their offices or that I was leaving fifteen minutes early. Audrey's door was closed. Thank God for small blessings.

I hooked my purse over my shoulder when I reached the receptionist's desk. "A package came for me?" I asked Claire.

She handed me a brown cardboard box.

"Thank you," I said.

Her gaze held mine for a moment, and crinkles appeared around her eyes as she grimaced. "Did you really tell off Audrey this morning?" she whispered.

I sighed and nodded my head.

The corners of her mouth tipped up in a slight smile and she tapped her palms together in a silent round of applause. I wished it made me feel better. It didn't.

I held up the box as a wave. "See you tomorrow, if she doesn't fire me before then."

"Good luck, Lucy."

On my way to the Sweatshop for Monday night practice, I stopped and forced a greasy cheeseburger down my throat. The last thing I needed to crown my spectacularly awful day would be blacking out on the derby track. The sandwich settled like a brick in my stomach.

I was late to practice thanks to traffic and the extra ten minutes I sat in the car feeling sorry for myself. When I lugged my bag inside, most everyone was already warming up on the track. Several heads whipped toward me when I dropped my bag onto the ground, and a few skaters began to point and whisper. "I know, I know. Late again. Sue me," I muttered, ripping my bag open and yanking out my skates.

I'd pulled on my knee pads and was unlacing my right skate when Olivia skidded to a stop in front of me. She ripped out her mouthpiece. "Oh my god, Lucy! I was beginning to think you were dead!"

"Not that lucky." I grunted as I shoved my foot into the boot.

"I've been calling you for two days!"

I rolled my eyes up to look at her. "My phone fell in Jake

Barrett's pool Saturday night. I got a replacement today, but I haven't had time to set it up. I left you a note by the coffee pot."

"I didn't see it. I went to Bongo Java this morning." She dropped onto her knee pads. "I've been so worried."

"You should have called my office."

"I did, but the receptionist said your phone was set to Do Not Disturb."

That was true. It had been in case Audrey felt like yelling some more.

"Sorry. It's been a really crappy day." I tied my skate.

"Are you OK? Is it West?" she asked.

I stomped my right wheels on the ground to force my right foot into its boot. "No. West is about the only thing going right in my life right now." I tied and double-knotted the laces.

She put her hands on both sides of her helmet. "Oh, Lucy. We've got to talk."

My face snapped up. "Why? What else is wrong?"

A whistle blasted out on the track. Olivia looked back over her shoulder, then shot a pained glance at me.

"Prodigy, get your ass out here!" Medusa shouted.

Olivia winced. "We'll talk when we get a break." She stood up on her skates but hesitated before heading back to the track.

I flapped my elbow pads up in the air in frustration as she skated away. "What the hell's going on?"

Nobody answered.

With a huff, I finally stood up on my skates and caught up with my teammates. "Get warmed up," Styx said as I slowed with a T-stop near the group.

Alone, I began skating laps around the track, trying to eavesdrop on the whispers that hissed around me. They were talking about me. I knew it.

Shamrocker's chipper singsong voice came out loud and clear. "Fresh Meat, listen up! You're rounding out your final days before your skills test. So the next few practices are going to revisit all the basics. We're going to focus on the most challenging parts—"

"Except tonight!" Medusa's voice drowned out Shamrocker. A hush fell over the group. Clearly surprised, Shamrocker rolled back a few inches. "Tonight, we've got some other lessons to learn on this track. I don't feel like some of you are bringing your A-game to these practices. And I sure as hell don't feel like some of you know the meaning of being part of a team."

She was staring at me. "Geez, I was late twice. I get it. But I'm here," I grumbled under my breath. I should've gone home and put the day to rest with a bottle of wine and a bubble bath.

"Tonight we're going to work on pack drills together, and we're going to be doing a lot of hits. Big, hard, lay-a-bitch-out kind of hits!" Medusa yelled.

I expected everyone to cheer like they usually did. They didn't. This was not a good sign.

"Everybody find a group. Four blockers one jammer!" Medusa pointed at me. "Lucy Cooper, you're with me!"

Shit.

Styx grabbed Medusa by the arm and said something, but I couldn't hear what it was.

Medusa jerked her arm free. "I suggest if you want to protect her, you get your ass out there and teach her how to block."

OK. Excellent. I won't have to worry about getting fired or paying my bills. Medusa is going to kill me. Awesome.

Olivia skated quickly to catch up with me. "Lucy, maybe you should go home."

"What the hell is going on?" I asked, tossing my arms up.

Medusa blew her whistle again, and the team scattered and regrouped in practice packs of five. Styx raced to my side and grabbed me by the front of my shirt. "Brace yourself, Lucy."

I swore.

Shamrocker joined us.

So did Maven.

Medusa skated onto the track behind us.

"What did I do?" I asked, panic rising in my voice.

Maven shoved my helmet. "The video. Now get in your stance and keep your head down!"

I stopped skating. "The video?"

Shamrocker pulled me forward into the center of the group. Medusa was coming right at us. Nope. Medusa was coming right at *me*. Styx sidestepped and hit Medusa square in the shoulder, pushing her to the outside.

Per the rules, Medusa reentered the track behind Styx and charged us again. This time, Maven hip checked her into the center of the ring, then pulled me to the middle of the pack again. It was then I realized the severity of my situation. Maven didn't have a caring or protective bone in her body, at least not inside the track. And especially not against Medusa.

A few of the other packs had skated off the track to watch.

I was in trouble.

Serious trouble.

Medusa got a running start, her skates slamming against the concrete as she came at us full speed. Shamrocker cut sideways and rammed her shoulder into Medusa's side. I stayed between Maven and Styx, but looked back and caught a glimpse of the team captain's red-hot face. Her eyes were on fire and burning into me.

Medusa jerked back to her left, hopped on her left skate to spin backward behind Shamrocker. Styx moved to fill the hole, but not fast enough. Medusa exploded through the small space between me and Styx, sending me stumbling forward. She jumped as I fell, and one bizarre last thought flashed through my brain as her skate came right at my face.

Huh. Medusa's wheels are Atomic Turquoise.

The concrete was cool against my skin when I opened my eyes, sort of. My right widened only a sliver. Haloed heads with shadowy faces hovered over me against the backdrop of the ceiling halogens. I briefly wondered if I was dead.

Terror ripped through me. And pain.

So much pain.

My arms flailed, and someone pinned me down.

Nope. Definitely not dead.

"It's OK, Lucy!"

My breath was rapid. I could see my mouthpiece rising and falling on my chest.

"She's awake!"

A light flashed in my eyes. "Lucy, can you hear me?"

I nodded. I think.

"Somebody get some ice!"

A head moved, blocking the light. Doc Carnage was over me. I knew her face from practice, but I don't think we'd ever spoken. This was a hell of a way to meet. She held up two fingers. "Can you see me OK? How many fingers am I holding up?"

"Two."

"Do you know what day it is?"

"Monday." I tried to sit up, but someone held down. It was Grace. Olivia was there too. Her helmet was off and her eyes were red like she'd been crying.

"Lucy, do you know what happened?" Doc Carnage asked.

"Me—Medusa." My chin was quivering.

Someone swore. There was yelling on the other side of the room. A few of the girls looked over, but they wouldn't let me move. The gym door slammed hard against its metal frame.

"Did somebody call an ambulance?" the doctor asked.

I reached for her. "No. No ambulance."

She looked down at me. "You need a head CT, Lucy. You lost consciousness."

"I'm OK," I insisted.

"Team rules, kid." It was Shamrocker.

"I'll drive her," Olivia said. "Don't call an ambulance."

"Is that all right, Doc?" someone asked.

Doc Carnage nodded. "That's fine. As long as she goes."

Grace helped me sit up. Pain splintered through my skull. I winced.

Zoey was beside my legs. She caught my mouthpiece before it hit the dirty floor.

"Glad you were wearing a helmet," Doc Carnage said as she unbuckled my chin strap. "That was a hard fall." She carefully pulled off the helmet, then checked my scalp for lumps and blood.

"Medusa's gone," Styx said, appearing next to Olivia. "Maven's taking her home."

"Good!" Kraken barked.

Several others voiced their agreement.

"What did I do?" I asked, rubbing the back of my battered skull.

Styx knelt beside me. "West Adler. You did West Adler."

Maybe it was the brain bruise because the information took a second to compute. "Oh geez. West used to date Medusa?"

Styx nodded. "Just a couple of weeks ago."

The room began to spin again. I dropped my head between my knees to try and hold onto consciousness. "I didn't know," I said, panting into the cavern formed by my legs.

A hand rested on my back. "We know. Olivia said you didn't tell West you were playing," Styx said.

"He didn't tell you he was dating Medusa?" someone asked.

"Why would he?" Olivia was quick to jump to my defense. "He wasn't aware Lucy knew Medusa."

I straightened, and my head throbbed again. "He has no idea."

"Well, thanks to Jake Barrett making national news, everybody knows now," Styx said.

"Medusa lost it when she saw the pictures," Shamrocker added.

"That's no excuse for what she did! Lucy ought to press charges!" Olivia shouted. She dropped beside me. "I tried to call and warn you, but you didn't have your damn phone!"

I reached for her hand and squeezed. "It's not your fault." I looked around. "And I'm not pressing charges. It's roller derby." I found Monica in the crowd. "It's not a matter of *if* you get hurt, but how bad and when, right?"

A few of the girls laughed.

Doc Carnage examined my eye. "It's time for you to go to the ER, Miss Jokes. Let me know what they say."

"Thanks, Doc," I said.

Olivia and Styx helped me out of the room to a chorus of well-wishes from my teammates. If I could still call them that. I'd potentially lost my job, all my newfound friends, and quite possibly my brand-new boyfriend, all in the span of a day. That was some kind of destruction record, even for me.

I leaned back in the passenger's seat and rested the ice against my face. My head was throbbing against my skull.

Olivia got in and started the engine. "Are you all right, Lucy?"

"Head hurts," I said, pulling my knees up to my chest.

"I'm sorry. I'll be quiet."

"No. Tell me what happened."

The turn signal on her car sounded firecracker loud in my aching head. "After work Sunday night, I went to Styx's apartment. Medusa was there. She stormed out when I came in, obviously pissed about something. I was afraid it was because I was there."

"So you and Styx were outed too?"

"Everybody's so worked up about you, nobody cares about me and Styx."

I tried to smile but couldn't. "You're welcome."

"Ha, ha." She turned left at the red light onto Wedgewood Avenue. "You and West were tagged in pictures and the video from Jake Barrett's party. It's been all over the news."

"I know. Up until now, that was a good thing," I said.

"Medusa, and everyone else, assumed you knew that she and West had just broken up. She went ballistic."

Part of me couldn't blame her.

"But I didn't know."

"That's what I told them. Medusa wouldn't hear it though."

"I wonder if West knows," I said, watching the buildings zoom by out the passenger-side window. "I don't even have a way to call him."

"You can use my phone," she offered.

I sighed. "I don't even know *your* phone number, much less his."

"Want me to see if Styx has a way to get in touch with him?"

"No. I'll figure it out when we get home."

"That's probably for the best. She's pretty pissed off at him too," she said.

"Why?"

She shrugged. "He broke up with Medusa right after her mom died. That's a pretty shitty thing to do."

I couldn't really argue.

"Styx said things were already falling apart with them before Medusa went to New York, but the timing sucked. He flew up there for the funeral and then broke it off with her about a week after she got back." She was quiet for a second. "I guess that explains why he went MIA on you for a while."

I closed my eyes. "What a mess."

They took us straight back to a triage room, one of the few

benefits of having a potential brain bleed, but then we waited for almost an hour to get the results of the CT scan. That was generally a good sign. Had they suspected anything serious, they would've started drilling holes in my head.

The female doctor who had ordered the head CT scan finally walked into my room. "Good news, roller girl," she said, looking up from the clipboard in her hand.

I pushed myself up in the bed a little. "I like the sound of that."

"You have a concussion, but your scan was normal. There's no further brain injury."

I relaxed. "That is good news."

She scribbled something on my chart. "You need to take it easy for a few days, but you can go home. No driving till the dizziness and headache pass. You can treat it with acetaminophen or ibuprofen. Keep ice on that eye, and get lots of rest, physically and mentally."

I groaned. "Not much chance of that."

"Take tomorrow off, at least." She pointed at me. "And no skating for a while."

"How long?" Olivia asked. "She's got tryouts in two weeks."

The doctor hugged the clipboard. "Once the headache is gone, you can do light aerobic exercise. If symptoms don't return, then you can skate *without* contact. If you still have no symptoms, check in with your regular doctor first, but you should be OK to return to full play in two weeks."

"Thank you, Doctor," I said, replacing the ice pack on my eye.

"I'll have the nurse come discharge you." She turned and left.

"That's good news. You should be back in time for the skills test," Olivia said.

I almost laughed. "I'm not taking the skills test."

"Why not?" she asked.

I held up a hand. "Because it's Medusa's team. There's no coming back from what happened tonight."

Olivia stood. "So you're just going to quit? And let her win?"

"There are no winners in this, Olivia."

She huffed and walked to the doorway. "Whatever."

Ten minutes later, a nurse wheeled us out to the waiting room, and what I saw made my breath hitch in my chest. Grace, Monica, Zoey, and Styx all stood from their chairs. "You guys," I said with a whimper.

They all came over and sandwiched me in a group hug. It hurt, but I didn't care.

"How are you feeling?" Zoey asked.

Monica knelt down beside me. "What did the doctor say?"

"Just a concussion. I'll be fine."

Grace handed me a small bouquet of gas station flowers. "Can we do anything for you?"

"I just want to sleep."

"I've got your car," Styx said. "I'll follow you guys to your apartment with it, then Grace is going to drive me home."

"Thank you."

Styx squeezed my hand. "Don't mention it. We're family."

It seemed like an eternity until I was finally tucked into my bed. "Can I do anything else for you?" Olivia asked as she pulled up the comforter to my chin.

My eyes were closed, so I pointed blindly across the room. "That box you brought in with my stuff. It's my new cell phone. Can you set it up for me?"

"Of course. Do you need it?" she asked, her voice growing faint as she walked to the living room.

"I need to tell my boss I won't be in tomorrow. That is, if I still have a job there."

Her footfalls returned. "Why wouldn't you have a job?"

I sighed. "It's a long story, and my head hurts too bad to tell it."

"Is your boss in your contacts?" she asked.

"Yeah, and hopefully my contacts will download from the cloud."

"I'll take care of it. Don't worry. Do you want me to contact West?"

"No. I'll call him tomorrow. I can't deal with it now."

Her fingers raked the hair off my forehead. "OK. Get some rest, Lucy. I'll be here when you wake up."

EIGHTEEN

"LUCY?"

It was Olivia.

I pried open my good eye to look at her. She crossed my bedroom and sat down beside me. Her hair was pulled up in a bun, and she was wearing her work clothes. Light was shining through my bedroom window.

"What time is it?" I asked with a yawn.

"Almost ten in the morning. I've got to go to work soon, but I wanted to check to see if you needed anything before I left. Or I can call in sick and stay home."

I rubbed my sore face. "Oh, I need to call my boss."

"I took care of it," she said. "I programmed your new phone last night and called and left a message on Audrey Scott's voicemail."

I vaguely remembered us already having this conversation.

"How's your head?" she asked.

"Sore."

"Want me to stay? I can."

"No, I'll be fine. Thank you though."

She pointed to the nightstand. "I put painkillers and water by your bed. And some crackers in case you woke up hungry."

I smiled. "Thank you."

"West came by last night, but I didn't want to wake you."

"He did?"

"Yeah. He blew up your phone all night when I finally got it to turn on. Then he showed up here around ten. Someone from the team told him what happened."

"What did he say?" I asked.

"He's really upset. He says he hasn't talked to Medusa in about a month and didn't have a clue about any of this." She picked up my phone off the nightstand and handed it to me. "Call him. He's really worried."

I sighed. I was worried too. Never had I intended for any of this to happen, and there was no way I could see to set it right.

"And call me if you need anything."

"I will. Thanks for everything," I said.

She smiled back when she reached my door. "What are best friends for?" Then she was gone.

There were four text messages and two voicemails from West.

I opened my text messages.

Checking to see if you got your new phone.

Guess not. Call me when you get it.

I'm really worried. Are you OK?

Next, I listened to the voicemails he'd left.

"*Hey, Lucy. I just heard what happened at practice. God, I hope you're OK. Call me back as soon as you can.*"

"*Hey, it's West. I'm coming over, just so I know you're all right. I'll understand if you don't want to see me, but I promise, I had no idea about any of this. I'd never do anything to hurt you. Be there soon.*"

A final text message from him had come that morning. All it said was, *Lucy.*

Nothing in me wanted to call. What was I supposed to say? *'Hey, West. Remember that beautiful, sexy, badass Wonder Woman you were screwing before me? She kicked my ass because I'm pretty sure she wants you back.'* No. I'd call him later, I decided, and rolled over and hugged my pillow.

Beside me, Stuart, my bright yellow stuffed Minion, was staring at me from the other side of the bed with his lone, big round eye. He was judging me.

With a painful groan, I reached back to the nightstand for my phone and dialed West's number before I could talk myself out of it again.

He picked up on the first ring. "Hello?"

"Hey."

It sounded like he had the wind knocked out of him. "Hey. God, Lucy. Are you OK?"

"My face hurts and I have a concussion, but I'll be fine."

"Lucy, I'm so sorry. I had no idea about any of this. Please, you have to believe me."

"Shh. Headache, remember?"

"Sorry." His voice was just above a whisper. "What can I do? Can I come over?"

I closed my eyes. "No. Please don't. I just need to rest. And *not* think. Doctor's orders."

He was quiet for a beat. "I understand. I'll do anything you need."

I smiled and a tear trickled from my swollen eye. "I know. I'll call you later."

"OK. Bye."

"Goodbye, West."

Before putting the phone down, I dialed one more number. My dad's.

"Yello?"

"Dad?" My voice cracked.

"Hey, Lulabean. Are you OK, honey?"

Emotion punctured my chest like a wooden stake. "No."

"Lucy, what's wrong?" he asked.

"Can I come home?" Tears streamed down my face, and I tried to steady my quivering chin.

"Of course you can come home. What's the matter?"

I sniffed. "I've had a really bad week."

"I assumed you were having a really wonderful week. We saw you on the news at Jake Barrett's party. I was excited to hear about it."

"Everything's kinda gone to shit since then."

Dad chuckled. He always thought it was funny when I swore. If he only knew. "I'm sorry, honey. Need me to come get you?"

"No, but I want to come home. The doctor says I can't drive today, but maybe tomorrow. I've got some personal time I can take at work."

"The doctor?" Alarm flooded his deep voice. "What happened?"

"I have a concussion. I'll be OK. I just can't drive." The call waiting beeped on my phone. I looked at the screen. *Incoming call. Audrey Scott.* "Dad, my boss is calling. I'll let you know when I'm on my way."

"All right, Lulabean. I'll keep my phone on me if you need anything at all."

"Thanks, Dad. I love you."

"I love you too."

I answered Audrey's call. "Hello?"

"Hi, it's Audrey. I got a voicemail from your roommate saying you were in the hospital. I thought I'd call and make sure everything was OK."

"I'll be fine. Had an accident yesterday and hit my head. I have a concussion, but it's nothing too serious."

"Mercy," she said. "Is there anything we can do?"

"Actually, yes. I may need to take tomorrow off too if I can't shake this headache. I can work from home so we don't fall behind." *If I still have a job, that is,* I thought.

"That won't be necessary."

Oh, here we go. You're fired, Lily.

"Take as much time as you need. You've earned it with all the extra hours you've put in lately and with the huge success of Jake's video. We owe it to you." She paused. "I owe it to you."

Maybe the concussion was more severe than I thought. Surely, I couldn't have heard her right.

"We'll see you in a few days," she said. "We can get caught up then."

"Um...thanks, Audrey."

"Thank *you.*"

The line went dead in my hand. I stared at the phone for a second, then turned the ringer to silent and rolled over, hugging my pillow.

The pain in my head had waned to a dull ache by the afternoon, and around two, a knock at the front door coaxed me out of bed. I shuffled out to the living room in my pajamas and paused to check my hair in the hallway mirror. It was probably West at the door. I looked through the peephole.

Dad.

He'd come straight from work. His mail carrier shirt was still clean, telling me he'd left before starting his daily route. The buttons down the front were straining more since the last time I saw him, thanks to all the casseroles, no doubt.

I pulled the door open, and he gasped when his eyes fell on me. "Oh, Lucy." He rushed inside and gripped my chin to examine my battered face. "Who did this to you? What's his name? I swear to God I'll—"

I put up my hands. "Calm down, killer. It was a girl named Medusa."

His head snapped back. "What?"

I sighed and leaned against the open door. "You came all the way from Riverbend?"

"Of course I did. It sounded like you might be in trouble. Looks like I was right."

I put my arms around his neck and crumpled against his shoulder as all the emotions swirling within me rushed out like water through a broken river dam.

He rubbed my back. "What happened?" After a moment of snotty sobbing, he reached back and closed the door. Then he took my hand and led me to the living room.

I sank onto a couch cushion and plucked a tissue from the box on the coffee table. I wiped my eyes and blew my nose with a loud honk. Dad was smiling gently when I looked at him again. "Sorry," I said. "I have a head injury. I think it's messing with my emotions."

"Why do you have a head injury?" He leaned forward, balancing his elbows on his knees.

"I started playing roller derby a couple of months ago." I watched as his face shifted from worried to perplexed.

"Roller derby?"

I nodded.

"On roller skates?"

"Yep."

He stroked his goatee. "Huh. Well, that explains the head, I guess."

"Sort of. The team captain knocked me out yesterday when she found out I was dating her ex," I said.

His brow rumpled even more. "Your brother said you weren't seeing anyone."

"I am now." *Or I was, at least.* "It's really new. Anyway, I didn't know he used to date her. Then she saw us together in those pictures from Jake Barrett's party." I pointed at my swollen eye. "She expressed her frustration at practice yesterday."

"And you had it checked out by a doctor?"

"Yeah. I'll be OK."

He leaned his elbow on the back of the couch and cradled his head in his palm. "Why didn't you tell me?"

My nose scrunched up. "I didn't tell anybody. I didn't know if I'd actually make the team. It's really hard. And I knew you'd worry."

He gestured to my face. "And I'd obviously be right to worry. You look like you've been in a car accident."

I thought for a second. "I actually *was* in a car accident. Did I tell you about that?"

His mouth dropped open. "What?"

"Oops."

With a heavy sigh, my father ran his hand down his face. "Lucy, what's happened to us?"

My head was starting to throb again. "I don't know, Dad."

"Sure you do." He put his hand on mine. "Talk to me. I can't fix it if I don't know what's broken."

For a moment, I stared at the couch cushion. A squiggly thread was poking out of the seam. I pulled it, and the fabric splayed open leaving a gaping hole to the fluffy stuffing inside. I frowned.

"Lucy?"

I sighed. "Do you really have to ask?"

"Yes, I really do."

I sank back into the cushions and hugged a pillow to my chest. "Four months, Dad."

His eyes crinkled. "I'm afraid I'm going to need a little more information."

"Mom was only gone for four months, and suddenly, you were over it and on to another family that I don't even know how to be a part of."

"Lucy, you haven't even tried to be part of it."

I tossed my hands up. "I don't want to. I'm not ready, and I don't understand how you are."

Dad's gaze fell to the carpet.

"I miss Mom, and we can't even talk about her anymore."

When Dad looked up, his eyes were glassy. "I miss her too, Lucy. Every single day. You don't move on from what your mother and I had. She was mine, and now she's gone. And it's hard for me to talk about her because I miss her so much." He took a deep breath. "Katherine makes that easier for me. How hard is that to understand?"

It wasn't hard to understand in my head, but wrapping my heart around it was a completely different challenge altogether. I truly didn't want him to be lonely or sad, but I couldn't make myself sound like it or make my heart feel happy about it. That was exactly why I'd kept my mouth shut and stayed out of Riverbend.

"You just went looking for her, for *anybody*, so soon. It was a little hard to not take personally," I admitted.

He was quiet for a moment. "It was personal. Lucy, you don't belong in Riverbend. You've never wanted to live there. And you would've stayed for me. I thought maybe if you weren't so worried about me being lonely, you'd get back to the life you were pulled away from when your mom got sick."

I couldn't believe what I was hearing. Surely, hallucinations from the concussion.

"Don't get me wrong, I'm also no good without a wife. As much as I don't like to admit it, I need somebody around." He cleared his throat. "But I didn't start dating again because I wanted to replace my family and get rid of you and Ethan. I did it partly so you kids wouldn't feel so obligated."

I heaved in a deep breath. "Wow. I did *not* expect that."

"You didn't ask."

I laid my head on his shoulder. "I'm sorry, Dad."

He patted my knee. "It's OK, honey. None of this has been easy."

"Do you really love Katherine?"

"I do."

I sighed. "She's so different from Mom."

"She is. That's part of what I like about her." He put his arm around me. "With Katherine, I don't have to be so alone, but because they're so different, she never feels like a replacement for your mom."

A strange mix of sadness and relief washed over me. I hugged him again, this time snuggling my face against the curved slope of his neck, that spot beneath a man's chin that seems solely carved as a space for the tearful cheeks of weary daughters.

"I love you, Dad."

He pressed a kiss to my forehead. "I love you too, Lulabean."

———

Dad stayed for dinner, then drove back to Riverbend alone. I promised to come for the weekend as long as the coaches didn't mind me skipping a practice I couldn't participate in. I stayed in bed again all day on Wednesday and woke up early enough to watch Jake Barrett on *Good Morning America*. Then I drove myself to the Sweatshop that night to watch practice.

Grace, Monica, and Zoey all skated over and met me at the door. Olivia had to work.

"How are you feeling?" Zoey asked, enveloping me in a hug.

I smiled. "Better. The headache is gone, and since the swelling is down, I can see properly out of my eye again." I was searching the room.

"Medusa isn't here," Grace said as if reading my mind. "She's been unofficially suspended."

"Really?" I asked.

Monica nodded. "They've called an emergency team meeting here tomorrow night. They're holding a vote that could kick Medusa off the team."

My head snapped back. "Are you kidding?"

"Nope," Zoey said. "Maven told me it's the first time in the team's history they've done anything like it."

"They can do that? Kick her out?" I asked.

"It's in the Code of Conduct. You can't intentionally hurt your teammates," Grace answered.

"Are you guys going to the meeting?" I asked, looking around at them.

They shook their heads.

"It's only open to team members. We were hoping Olivia might be able to eavesdrop through Styx during the meeting," Zoey said.

"She's at the restaurant tonight, but I'll ask her." My eyes fell to the concrete floor. "I can't imagine the Rollers without Medusa."

They all agreed. Then Shamrocker blew her whistle. I waved as they skated back to the group.

My phone buzzed in my hand. It was a text message from West. *How are you feeling?*

Me: *Better. Thank you. Sorry I've been quiet the past couple of days. Been a lot to process with a head injury.*

West: *It's OK. Can I come over?*

Me: *I'm not at home. At practice now.*

West: *Practice??????*

Me: *Calm down. I'm just watching. And Medusa's not here.*

West: *I hear she might be off the team.*

Me: *Yeah. I don't know.*

It bothered me that he knew. Was he still talking to her? My brain tinged at the thought, and I pressed my eyes closed. The phone buzzed again.

West: *I miss you.*

Me: *I miss you too. Will you be home tonight? Maybe I can stop by later.*

West: *Absolutely.*

"Lucy, hey." I looked up as Styx plowed to a stop in front of the bleachers. "How are you?"

"Better. Thanks again for your help the other night," I said.

She waved her hand. "Don't worry about it."

I smiled.

She leaned a knee pad on the bottom bench. "Olivia said you're thinking about not taking the skills test."

I looked away.

"It'd be a real shame if you don't. You've come a long way to give it up now over something as stupid as this."

I shrugged. "I don't even know if I'll be cleared to skate by then."

She put her hands on her hips. "I know where you live now, and I'll personally come kick your ass if you don't show up and the doctor's say it's OK."

The corners of my mouth twitched up.

"What are you doing here if you can't skate?"

"Maven said even if we get injured, we're expected to be here, remember?" I asked.

She grinned and crossed her arms. "It doesn't sound like someone's completely given up roller derby then."

I didn't answer. "Are you guys really voting to kick Medusa out over what happened?"

Her eyes fell to the floor. "The team has rules. She broke them."

My heart twisted. "Will you let us know what happens?"

"Of course." She jerked her head toward the door. "You don't have to stick around. We're just recapping everything from now until the test."

"I was thinking about taking Saturday off. Would that be OK?" I asked.

"Sure. Take as much time as you need. Considering all that's happened, I think we can cut you a little slack."

My heart deflated.

She pointed at me. "Just be there on the twenty-second."

I nodded. "I'll try."

I stayed for the first half of practice, then decided to leave early since I had the coach's blessing. When I reached the Old Hickory Boulevard exit off I-65, I could circle around the on-ramp and head home to Brentioch, or I could turn right and go to West's house.

I turned right.

West's cabin was lit up against the mountainside when I pulled into the driveway. Cash bounded through the grass to meet me when I stepped out of my SUV. He crashed into my chest with his muddy front paws, knocking me back against the driver-side door.

"Cash, down!" West shouted behind me.

I pushed the dog off, then leaned down to scratch his head.

West came around the back of my car, and I straightened, turning toward him. He froze and stumbled back a step when his eyes fell on my face. "Oh, Lucy."

Cash nudged my leg with his nose.

In a few long steps, West closed the distance between us and pushed my hair back off my face to inspect the damage. He cringed. "Looks like it hurts."

"It does."

"I'm so sorry this happened." He kissed my forehead, then wrapped his strong arms around me. He'd showered recently and smelled like soap and fresh cologne. It was intoxicating.

Pulling away, he took my hand and led me up the steps to the walkway. Cash was right on my heels as we walked to the front door.

"You stay," West told him, blocking the entrance with his leg when we went inside.

I caught the door before he closed it. "Can't he come in?"

The dog's tail wagged.

West smiled. "If that's what you want."

Cash trotted proudly into the living room.

"I made dinner if you're hungry," he said.

I walked to the sofa and sat down in the center. Cash jumped up next to me and plopped his head in my lap. "I ate before practice. Thank you."

West was looking in the refrigerator. "I have wine."

"I'm good."

"Cheesecake?"

"West, come sit down."

He closed the refrigerator door, then stared at it a second before finally turning around and walking over. Instead of sitting, he stood in front of me. "Why do I feel like you're about to break up with me?"

I sighed and didn't answer. I didn't have to.

His gaze fell to the floor. He put his hands on his hips. "Because of Medusa?"

I reached for him, and he took my hand. I pulled him down next to me. "Because of me. I've got a lot of things to figure out."

His arm stretched along the back of the sofa behind me. "Why can't we figure those things out together?"

I stopped petting the dog, and he immediately wiggled his snout under my arm. I snapped my fingers in the direction of the floor. "Cash, get down." He whimpered, but slid off the sofa and collapsed by my feet. I turned toward West. "I like you so much."

He tucked my hair behind my ear. "I like you too. This is good. *Really* good."

I nodded. "It is. You're right. But for the first time in forever, I'm doing something just for me. And now it's all screwed up."

"And it's my fault."

"It's not your fault, but this does complicate the hell out of it."

"Aside from this shit with Medusa, how does me being with you complicate it?" He touched his chest. "Not to sound full of it or anything, but I'd like to think being with me could only be a good thing for you in derby."

I turned up my palm. "That's exactly what I'm talking about. Two months ago, I sucked at roller skating. I'm still not that great, but I've busted my ass to get ready for the skills test. Now I'm afraid they'll judge me differently because of all the shit with Medusa and because of you."

He rubbed his forehead and stared out the window. "So that's it? I'm out so you can do this alone?"

I reached over and tangled my fingers with his. Maybe waffling would say what my words were obviously failing to. "I want you, West. But one way or another, I need to finish this *for me.*"

I think he stopped listening after "I want you" because his hand slipped behind my head and pulled my lips to meet his.

And the kiss was perfect. Long. Slow. Deep and desperate. His teeth tugged at my lower lip, and his tongue slid, warm and heavy, against mine reminding me of all the things he'd done to my body on that very couch just a few days before.

Panting, I pulled away while I still could.

"Stay," he whispered, his wet lips against my forehead.

My fingers curled into his shirt. "I want to, but I won't." I cut my eyes up at him. "I waited for you for a while. It's your turn now."

He traced his thumb across my lips. "You're worth waiting for, Lucy Lou."

I smiled and breathed him in one more time. "I certainly hope you mean that."

NINETEEN

THURSDAY MORNING, I returned to work and slipped into my office undetected before even Claire arrived to man the reception desk. Laying on my leather chair was a white envelope with "Lucy" scrawled in messy handwriting across the front.

I slid my finger under the flap. The card inside had a picture of a donkey on the front and the words "You Kick" printed above it. I laughed and flipped it open.

Lucy,
You kick ass. Seriously. Thanks for helping make my launch such a success.
Sorry about your phone.
Jake.

There was a five-hundred-dollar gift card inside.

His stats had continued to soar in my absence. The video

views had climbed to over ten million, the new single was still at the top of all the US charts, and the album was on a trajectory to be the biggest-selling country album of the year.

I propped the card up on my desk and tucked the gift card in my purse.

"You're lucky it wasn't a basket of fruit a week for a year. I talked him out of that one," Ava said.

I looked up as she walked into my office.

She gasped and covered her mouth when she saw my black eye.

"It looks worse than it feels," I said.

"What happened to you?"

I sat back in my chair. "I'm playing roller derby."

She turned her ear toward me like she wasn't sure she'd heard me correctly. "Roller derby?"

"Yep." I pointed at my eye. "I took a pretty nasty hit Monday night and caught a set of wheels to my face."

"Yikes. Do you wear a helmet, I hope?"

"Yeah. It probably saved my life," I said.

"I'm glad you're OK. All I heard was you called out sick."

My office phone beeped. "Lucy?"

It was the first time I could recall ever hearing my name correctly off the lips of Audrey Scott. Ava and I locked eyes. "Yes?" I asked.

"Can I see you in my office for a moment, please?"

I stood. "Sure. I'll be right down."

Ava met me on the other side of the desk. "Be strong. You'll be fine," she said as we turned toward the door.

My nerves were screaming otherwise.

Audrey's door was open when we reached it, and Peter was sitting across from her desk. Thank God.

"Good luck," Ava whispered before cutting across the hall.

I knocked on the door. "Audrey?"

Audrey and Peter looked up and both did a double take when they saw my face. "Oh...hi, Lucy," Audrey stammered. "Peter, would excuse us? And close the door on your way out."

Peter stood and walked toward me with a small grin as he lowered his voice to a whisper. "Show no fear. She feeds off it." He gently nudged me through her door, then closed it behind me.

Uh-oh. I closed the door gently, then crossed the room and took a seat in one of the armchairs across from her.

"How are you feeling?" she asked.

"Better after a couple of days of rest."

"I'm glad." It was obvious she wanted to ask about my face. I could tell by her perplexed expression of worry, a look I was quickly becoming accustomed to. But she didn't ask. Instead. she leaned over a stack of papers on her desk. "I've been going through your weekly reports since you've been gone."

To find a reason to fire me, no doubt.

She slipped her glasses back on and picked up the top sheet on the stack. "Since you started here five months ago, across the board our clients have seen a fourteen-percent increase in social-media followers, a four percent-increase in email campaign opens, twenty-two percent in clicks, and a mind-boggling thirty-one-percent increase in post engagement."

"Yes, ma'am. Something like that," I said staring past her head out the window at the Batman Building in the distance.

"I haven't seen growth like this since the initial social-media boom of the early 2000s." She crossed her arms. "To what do you attribute your success?"

I put my hands in my lap and stared at the floor a moment. "I'm good at my job," I finally said. "I work really hard to find out what's working in our market and in other markets, then I test it out and monitor success."

"Is that what you did here?" she asked, handing me a sheet of paper with a printed version of Jake Barrett's ticket sales ad with the Atomic Turquoise truck.

"Yes. We started with four different versions of the ad. I monitored which one was selling the most tickets, then pulled the budgets from the other three and fed them into this one. We can also retarget to the people who clicked on the ad, but didn't complete their purchase."

She was quiet for a beat. Then she took off her glasses and laid them by her keyboard. "I hired you to post on social media and draft emails." She lifted the stack. "This work is so far above and beyond your job description that I'm not even sure how we ever managed without you."

Please advise? She couldn't have said anything to shock me any more.

Audrey let the stack drop with a heavy thud. "And I owe you an apology, Lucy. The success of Jake's video is to no one else's credit but yours. I was wrong to try and take that away from you, and I'm sorry."

When I smiled, tears spilled down my cheeks. I laughed and wiped them away. "I thought you were going to fire me."

She folded her hands on top of the papers. "Quite the opposite, actually. I was thinking of giving you a raise and an intern."

"Really?"

"Really. I can only imagine what other ideas you could come with if you have someone running all these detailed reports."

I wanted to leap across the desk and hug her. I didn't, however.

"Thank you, Audrey."

"No, Lucy. Thank you."

———

After work, I drove to the Sweatshop. The parking lot was full, so I parked across the street and pulled my jacket tight around me as I crossed the gravel lot. For the first time that fall, it was cold enough to see my breath.

The door's hinges creaked when I pulled it open, and almost every face in the room whipped toward me. There were more members of the Music City Rollers present than I'd ever seen at one time before. And they all looked so different than when they were ready for a game or practice. A lot of them were dressed for their day jobs. Maven was in khakis and a purple polo shirt bearing Hope Haven's logo. Styx was wearing old cargo pants and a T-shirt covered in paint. Doc Carnage was in hospital scrubs. Shamrocker looked exactly the same.

Medusa wasn't there.

The Duchess was standing in front of the group. My entrance had obviously interrupted her. "This meeting is for official team members only," she said.

I waved. "I know. I won't stay. I'd just like to say something, if I can."

"This isn't a court of law," Maven snapped.

I looked at The Duchess. "Please?"

Her head bowed slightly. "Make it quick."

My stomach churned as I walked over beside her. "Hi, everyone. Some of you may not know me, but my name is Lucy Cooper. I'm the Fresh Meat recruit who had the incident on Monday with Medusa." I swallowed, and it echoed in my ears. "I heard there's a vote tonight that will decide her future with the team." I took a deep breath. "I'd like to ask you all to vote to let her stay."

Whispers fluttered through the crowd.

I held up one finger. "One bout. That was all it took for this sport to become the thing I wanted more than anything else in this world. From that first night I knew I wanted to be part of this family, and now I feel like it's about to be torn apart because of me."

The Duchess shook her head. "It's not because of you. It's because there was a violation of our Code of Conduct."

"Yes, Medusa intentionally came after me with more force than necessary because she was angry over a misunderstanding. But will my future bout opponents come at me with any less intensity than what she did? Her hit would have been legal had I not fallen forward."

I looked around at all the faces in the crowd. "Medusa is one of the very best skaters in the world. Please don't let a few laps skated in anger and an accident-prone newbie terminate that. This is one of the best experiences of my life, and I don't ever want to regret putting on my first pair of skates."

Silence.

I offered a weak smile to The Duchess. Then I turned toward the exit. As I neared the door, the applause began. Slowly at first, then everyone joined in. The Music City Rollers were clapping and cheering—for me. I looked back and waved, then smiled as I walked out of the room.

———

Olivia texted later that night with the official report from Styx. The Rollers voted for Medusa to stay, but she lost her position as team captain. A new captain would be voted in at the next team meeting in November.

After work Friday, I left Nashville and headed west on I-40 to Riverbend. It was the first time I'd made the trip since Dad's backyard wedding to Katherine at the end of summer. I parked next to her car in the driveway.

At the front door, my hand automatically reached for the

doorknob, then froze midair. This wasn't my house anymore. I pressed the doorbell instead.

Ethan opened it. "What are you doing, weirdo?"

I smiled.

"Geez! Your face!" he shouted, taking my overnight bag from me. "Dad said you had a shiner, but holy hell, that's terrible!"

I followed him into the quiet house. "Where is everyone?"

"Out back. Dad's grilling burgers and there's a fire for s'mores after dinner."

I was only half listening. My brain was trying to process my old but very new surroundings. The living room was definitely taupe. And the couch was now chocolate instead of lavender. New sensible tan curtains hung in the place of Mom's butterfly drapes, and our old coffee table with cigarette burns and baby-teeth marks had been replaced with a brown leather ottoman. It was all very modern and tasteful and clean. Very domestic. Very plain.

Very different from the cheerful whimsy that had colored my childhood.

My bottom lip trembled.

Ethan's arm curled around me, pulling my head against his bony shoulder. "She's really gone," I choked out between my noisy whimpers that echoed around the stale living room.

He reached for a framed photo on the end table by Dad's recliner. "Not completely."

Me and Mom just a few days before she went to the doctor.

It was a particularly hideous picture of me. No makeup. A zit the size of Mount St. Helens on my chin. Wearing a sweatshirt with horizontal stripes. But in it, my mother's bright smile was fixed securely in place. Something she never lost over the excruciating seventy-eight days that followed.

The best and worst seventy-eight days of my life.

"There are pictures of her all over the house," Ethan said. "Katherine insisted. Said it would be good for you and me."

I sniffed and returned the photo to its place on the table. Then I tugged on my little brother's shirt. "Come on. I'm hungry."

When we stepped onto the screened-in porch, I paused for a moment to admire the view. Golden rays glistened off the water as the sun sank behind the evergreens across the wide waters of the Tennessee River.

"Is your sister here?" I heard Katherine ask below.

I stepped into view at the top of the stairs and waved. "Right here!"

Dad waved a spatula from his post at the smoky gas grill. "Come on! I've got a burger with your name on it!"

Katherine rose from her lawn chair to greet me. Golden-gray hair framed her face, and she wore black pleated pants and a cowl-neck sweater. Her lipstick was a deep raspberry maroon, and her knockoff designer sunglasses had tortoiseshell frames.

She *didn't* remind me of Mom.

I hugged her. "Hi, Katherine."

"We've missed you, Lucy." Her second squeeze to punctuate the hug made me believe her. "Your dad's heart has had a hole only you can fill. Did you have a good drive in?"

I nodded. "No rain. Little traffic. No complaints here."

She smiled. "Well, complaints wouldn't do you any good anyway. What did you think about the changes in the house? I hope they weren't too jarring for you."

"It's very different," was the nicest response I could muster.

She looked at my dad. "It was very necessary since *someone* quit smoking."

I blinked. "Dad, you quit smoking?"

"Two months now," he said. "Didn't want to say anything in case I couldn't do it."

That, I understood.

His spatula dripped grease on my shoulder when he pulled me into a hug. "Welcome home, Lulabean. Do you want cheese on your burger?"

After dinner, I walked down to the dock, which jutted out like a splinter into the vast river. It was lit with tiki torches, the same kind that had set Jake Barrett on fire the weekend before. I wished it was warmer so I could kick off my shoes and dip my toes in the water.

Up the river to my right, moonlight flickered off the choppy water as far as I could see into the night. To my left, the river seemed to end where the city lights danced beyond the trees at the water's edge. But I knew that's not all there was. That old river curved around the bend, meandering its way in horseshoe hook turns through the vast unknown. It kept on flowing.

So would I.

Laughter floated down the river bank behind me.

So would *we*.

———

"Hey!" Ethan called from the living room. "Does anyone know someone who drives a black truck?"

I jumped up from my seat, bumping the table and causing Dad to dribble black coffee down his white T-shirt. He swore. "Sorry, Dad!" I ran to the living room's front window and pulled back the brown curtains.

A black truck was coming down the driveway toward the house. I gripped Ethan's arm and squealed with excitement.

"What? Who is it?" he asked.

It wasn't until the truck parked behind Katherine's car that I realized it was too small to be West's. The driver-side door opened, and a woman slid out of the cab.

My mouth fell open.

Ethan's eyes strained. "Who is that?"

"Medusa."

Dad yanked the curtains the rest of the way back. "The same Medusa who hit you?" I hadn't even realized he'd gotten up from the table.

My head fell to the side. "Yeah."

He looked down at me. "Want me to handle this?"

I put my hand on his chest. "I doubt she drove all this way to finish the job. I'm going to go see what she wants."

I walked to the front door. She was halfway up the front steps when I pulled it open. She froze and gave a small wave.

I stepped out the door and pulled it closed behind me. "Hi."

"Hi." Her black-and-pink hair was tied in a knot beneath a blue trucker's hat with a beer logo on the front. She shoved her hands into the pockets of her blue jeans. "Can we talk?"

Perplexed, I nodded my head and started down the steps. "Come on. It's a nice day. Let's go around back."

We walked in silence around the back of the house. I waited for her to speak.

"I heard what you did at the meeting." She looked at the ground as she walked. "I came to say thank you, and I came to apologize."

"You came all the way to Riverbend?"

She sighed and nodded. "I came all the way to Riverbend. Styx told me you were here. She got the address from your roommate."

Leave it to Olivia to not give a girl a heads-up.

There were a few chairs left out from the bonfire the night before. I gestured to them, and we walked over and sat down.

"I'm sorry for what I did to you, Lucy. I recognized you at practice from the last bout. West was sitting with you in the crowd for part of it. But I didn't connect the two until your faces kept popping up together online. I assumed he'd cheated on me with you and that you knew it. I was wrong."

"I didn't know he had dated you. And we just started seeing each other. He never cheated, at least not with me."

Medusa shook her head. "West isn't a cheater. I think he was going to break up with me after the last bout. Things had been off for a while, and he called the next day and said he wanted to *talk*." She used air quotes. "But then I got the call about my mom, so he didn't." She stared at the ground. "He's a good guy. He'll be good to you."

My mouth squished to one side. "I broke it off with him."

"You did?"

"Yeah." I pointed between us. "All this happened, *and* I don't want anyone to think he's giving me any kind of leverage to get on the team."

She nodded. "Makes sense. I really hope you'll forgive me, Lucy."

"I already have." I kicked my heels against the dead grass. "I get it. Acting a little nuts when your life is upside down. My mom died last year."

She looked down. "Styx just told me you sent the gift basket. I felt even more like shit when I found out."

"Yeah. I've been kicking myself since the hospital for not signing my name on that card."

She laughed. "Is that why you joined the Rollers? You were feeling nuts?"

I shrugged. "Maybe, but I think it was more to find out what I'm made of."

She smiled. "As so eloquently stated on our flyer."

"Yeah."

We were quiet for a little while, then she stared out at the river. "I feel nuts. And who knows? Maybe I am." She hugged her arms against the chill in the air. "Does it get easier?"

Good question. "Not really, but the pain evolves. It changes into something a little more manageable. I'm sorry about your mom."

"Thanks." She looked over at me. "Styx said you're thinking about not taking the skills test."

My nose scrunched and I didn't respond.

"Look at me."

My eyes met hers.

"Let's forget all the Medusa/Lucy drama for a minute. I'm speaking as a coach right now and your former"—she rolled her eyes—"team captain. You've got what it takes to make the team. I've watched you come a long way in the past few weeks. You're good enough to pass."

"There's no way I'll be judged fairly after everything. You know that," I said.

"What if I get a retired skater to come judge you?" she asked.

I shrugged. "Maybe. I still can't hit twenty-seven laps in five minutes though."

"Wanna hear a secret?" she asked.

I looked at her.

"I couldn't pass my 27 in 5s at first either, and when I started skating, it was only 25 in 5s."

"Seriously?" I asked.

"Yep. In fact, I was so bad when I started Fresh Meat my teammates nicknamed me Butterskates."

My eyes bulged. "You? Really?"

She laughed. "Yes, really. Keep at it. You *will* get better."

I raised an eyebrow. "By Saturday?"

"You're so close. All you need to do is skate all week, every day, and build your endurance." She straightened and looked around. "You brought your skates, right?"

I nodded.

She looked all around us. "So did I. Is there any place that's paved in this podunk town?"

I thought for a second. "The park, back toward downtown."

"There's a downtown?"

I laughed.

She stood. "Come on. We'll do this together."

TWENTY

ON FRIDAY, I followed up with a general practitioner who was accepting new patients in an office near my apartment. She asked a million questions about the headaches, my memory, and any symptoms after exercise. When she was satisfied, she finally cleared me for skating.

After skating the park with Medusa, I skated every day that week, and by Saturday I felt ready—or as ready as possible, anyway.

When we were all geared up in the practice room, Grace pulled our little group into a huddle. We linked our arms around each other's shoulders and put our helmets together.

"Girls," she began, "we've worked hard to get here. Zoey has literally fought her way back from death. Monica has balanced back to school and our grueling schedule. Lucy didn't die. And Olivia, well...screw you, Olivia." We all burst out laughing. "No matter what happens today, I'm so glad we did this together. I love you, guys."

"We love you too, Grace!" Monica said, kissing Grace's cheek.

"Ready to do this?" Olivia asked, putting her hand inside the circle.

We piled our hands on top of hers.

"On the count of three, we yell Fresh Meat," Zoey said. "One! Two! Three!"

"Fresh Meat!"

Shamrocker skated over. "Huddle up, Fresh Meat Bitches! Let's get this party started!"

Everyone gathered around her. The group had whittled down to just thirteen remaining newbies. Across the room, the judges were seated in folding chairs. The Duchess was there. So was Full Metal Jackie, Kraken, Doc Carnage, Medusa...she caught my eye and pointed to Stone Cold Kelly. Medusa mouthed the words, "She's got you."

I smiled and gave her a thumbs-up.

They were all holding clipboards and pens and chatting among themselves.

"This is how it's going to go down. Your skills test is divided into three parts. Basic skating skills and contact skating skills. The first test will begin with the dreaded 27 in 5s. Might as well get it over with, right?"

There was collective grumbling from our group.

"Part one will also include falling, stopping, and maneuvering. If you pass part one, then you move on to part two. Contact and game play. You'll be judged on play-specific skills like whips, blocking, and hits.

"If you pass part two, you can take the written rules test. You need eighty percent or better to pass. After that, you'll officially be a Music City Roller. Any questions?"

No one responded.

"OK. Then let's get started. We'll begin with pace line drills to get warmed up. Line up on the track!"

I was pretty sure I passed the line drills with fives across the board. I didn't fall once or trip anyone, even when weaving in and out of the line. Next was the dreaded 27 in 5. My heart was pounding like a sledgehammer in my chest as I skated up to the starting line. Olivia, Grace, Monica, and Zoey all lined up alongside me.

Olivia squeezed my shoulder. "You've got this."

I nodded, but my palms were sweating inside my wrist guards.

Medusa was standing next to Kelly on the sidelines. She waved to get my attention. "Remember what I told you. Breathe and focus on pacing yourself. Five-and-a-half laps per minute. That's all you need."

"Thanks." I forced a terrified smile.

Shamrocker blew the starting whistle.

Olivia immediately took the lead, of course. Grace fell in behind her. Then me, Monica, and Zoey. I kept my eyes fixed on Grace's back. Medusa had also said to try and keep pace with whoever was in front of me. We entered the first turn. *Push, stretch, step. Push, stretch, step.*

We skated out of it to the outside center line, then back into the other turn. *Push, stretch, step. Push, stretch, step.*

"One!" Kelly shouted.

By the fifth lap, Grace was pulling away from me. I pushed harder.

"Six!"

"Seven!"

"Eight!"

"Nine!"

"Ten!"

Medusa held up two fingers when I came back around again. That was two minutes. I pushed harder and extended my strides.

"Eleven!"

"Twelve!"

"Thirteen!"

"Fourteen!"

"Fifteen!"

"Sixteen!"

Medusa was holding up three fingers.

My cheeks puffed out and sweat slid down my face. As I passed Zoey, she cheered, "Good job, Lucy!"

I kept my head down, my eyes fixed on Grace.

"Seventeen!"

"Eighteen!"

"Nineteen!"

"Twenty!"

"Twenty-one!"

"Final minute warning!" Shamrocker shouted.

I did the math in my head. There wouldn't be enough time.

"Twenty-two!"

"Twenty-three!"

"Twenty-four!"

"Thirty seconds!"

Olivia who'd already finished twenty-seven laps skated alongside me. "We'll finish together. Push!"

"Twenty-five!"

"Twenty-six!"

The whistle blasted...but not before my skates crossed over the starting line again.

———

I was panting.

I almost threw up.

But I passed.

Olivia grabbed my hand and raised it into the air. Zoey

caught up with us first and wrapped her bony arms around both of us. Medusa came next. Then Grace and Monica.

We all passed except for Zoey, but that was expected. We knew she'd get it the next time.

Olivia grabbed my helmet. "I'm so proud of you."

I laughed. "I'm kinda proud of me too!"

She laughed and pulled me into a hug.

Medusa slapped me on the back. "I hate to be a ball buster here, but you've still got a full day's worth of testing to do."

She was right, but the endurance test was the one I was most worried about. Once it was behind me, I had the confidence to pass the other skills with relative ease. By the end of the final test on skates, we were all red faced, heaving, and dripping with sweat, but the four of us made it.

Shamrocker passed out the written tests and pencils to all who were still standing, figuratively. I was laying on the floor, flat on my aching back, by the track. "Fill out the top with your actual name, your derby name, and your derby number. When you finish, take off your gear and go wait on the bleachers."

I rolled to my side and looked at Olivia. "We have to have decided on our derby name?"

She was reading over the test. "Looks like it. Good luck."

The test was harder than I expected with questions about penalties, scoring, and official reviews. Was the lead jammer whistle one long blast or two? I wasn't even sure what a "Game Structure Penalty" was. We had studied throughout our training, but staring at those questions, I wished we'd studied more. The paper was trembling in my hand when I turned it in.

Olivia was already taking off her skates when I got to where our bags were shoved against the wall. She looked up. "That was freaking hard."

My eyes doubled. "I know. I'm not sure I got eighty percent."

She pulled off a knee pad and made a sour face. "Me either."

I nibbled a fingernail while we waited in the bleachers. Zoey was sitting beside me, as anxious as the rest of us to see our results.

Finally, Shamrocker walked up in front of us with her clipboard. "If I call your name, come up and get your test along with your new skater packet. If I don't call your name, we all sincerely hope we'll see you at the next round of Fresh Meat in the spring."

Olivia reached over and gripped my hand.

Shamrocker held up the first test. "With a written test score of ninety-eight percent, Dr. Hooker, number $100."

We all erupted in cheers and stomping against the bleachers as Monica walked down to get her test. All the judges and coaches shook her hand.

"With a score of ninety-four, number 5, 5 Scar Jeneral!"

"With a score of ninety-two, number 6-ft-2, Britches Get Stitches!"

Olivia cupped her hands around her mouth and screamed. Grace did a pageant wave as she descended the benches.

"With a score of eighty-eight, number 212, Rocksee Rolls!"

"With a score of eighty-six, number 220v, Electra Cal!"

I'd chewed a bloody hole inside my cheek.

"Also with a score of eighty-six, number 34DD, Goldie Knocks!" Goldie Knocks's aptly chosen derby number was nearly bouncing out of her tank top as she walked to get her test. I was jealous.

"With a score of eighty-four, number 12Gauge, Slugs Bunny!"

"With a score of eighty-two, number LoL, Lights Out Lucy!"

I slowly rose from my seat, my cheeks hot as the sun, as the room erupted in thunderous applause. Olivia jumped up and hugged me.

"I knew you could do it!" she cheered with tears in her eyes.

I kissed her cheek. "Couldn't have done it without you."

My thighs burned as I walked down the bleachers, and when I stepped off the bottom one, I tripped and stumbled forward. Shamrocker caught me, laughing hysterically.

"Oh my god. That was perfect," she said, steadying me.

The red in my face deepened.

She handed me my test. "Congratulations, Lucy."

"Thank you."

Medusa jogged over and grabbed me around the middle, hoisting me off my feet in a huge hug. The crowd cheered louder. When she returned my feet to the floor, her arm stayed slung around my neck. "I'm proud of you, Trip Hazard."

I glared at her. "That's not my name."

She laughed and nodded her head. "Lights Out Lucy, is it?"

I smiled.

She winked. "I like it. It's perfect, really."

"And finally, with a passing score of eighty, number..." Shamrocker paused for dramatic effect. "Bloody 4, Union Jackhammer!"

The room cheered, but my heart fell through the floor. Olivia didn't pass. Most jaws were dropped, including Grace and Monica's. Styx was staring up at the ceiling. Medusa crossed her arms.

Olivia was staring straight ahead.

I wanted to scream.

"Remember, if you didn't make it this time around, the next Fresh Meat session starts in March! If you passed, you're officially a member of the Rollers' training team, the Rising Rollers, and you're invited to skate in The Monster's Brawl next Saturday. Check the message board for more information!" Shamrocker shouted.

I looked up at Medusa. "Olivia's the best skater we have. If she doesn't deserve to be here, none of us do."

"Not my call, kid," she said.

Olivia walked down the bleachers and stopped in front of

Shamrocker. The coach handed her her test and gave her a hug. I stomped over and ripped the papers out of Olivia's hand. "It can't be that bad. Surely, only a question or two short!"

"Lucy, stop," Olivia said.

But it was too late.

The test was blank.

I blinked. "You didn't even take it?"

Shamrocker rocked awkwardly from her heels to her toes. "I'm going to leave you two alone to discuss this. Congratulations again, Lucy."

When she was gone, I held up the papers in the air. "What the hell, Olivia?"

She smiled and pulled me in for another hug. "I told you. I'm just here for moral support."

I smacked her across the head with the test.

She laughed. "My place is at the restaurant. I love my job, and this sport takes a lot of time away from it."

"I'm going to do my best to convince her otherwise," Styx said, stopping at my side.

I looked at her. "Did you know about this?"

Styx nodded. "She told me a few days ago. Swore me to secrecy."

I pointed at Olivia. "You suck."

"I know." She slung her arm around my neck. "You can berate me over a round of beers. It's time to celebrate."

TWENTY-ONE

THE MONSTER'S BRAWL, Saints vs. Sinners was scheduled to start at six o'clock on Saturday night. I was on the Sinners' roster and was expected to dress accordingly minus the jersey which would be provided upon arrival. The Brawl was open to the public, and according to the Rollers' online message board, the party was almost sold out. Costumes were *not* optional.

Even though Olivia wasn't skating, she took the night off to accompany me to the bout. She even dressed in a full vampiress costume, complete with a cape, a wig, and bloody fangs. Styx came over to get ready with us, and when she walked into my bathroom, I drew back with a gasp. Her face was painted with professional precision to match the skull tattoo on her leg.

"You scared me to death!" I laughed and gripped my chest. "You look terrifying."

Olivia kissed her square on her black lips. "I think she looks hot."

Styx held up the box in her hand. "Do you want me to paint your face?"

My eyes widened as I finished sweeping my hair up into a ponytail. "And cover up my badass bruises?"

Styx grinned and dangled the box off her fingertip. "Or make them even *more* badass."

When Styx was finished, I looked like someone had bashed my face in—again. The actual bruise was brushed with crimson, deep purple, and black and extended all the way back to my hairline and up to my eyebrow. She'd applied latex cuts to my forehead and nose and blended them in with my skin before covering them with fake blood. The corner of my mouth was painted to look like it was ripped open, and she covered my whole face with a thin black dust.

I looked awful.

And awesome.

I admired her work in the mirror. "This is amazing. Is this what you do at your work?"

"Sometimes," she said. "What are you going to wear tonight?"

"Didn't the message board say we'd get jerseys to wear?"

She nodded. "Yes, but it's tradition to at least wear crazy tights."

"I have fishnets," I said.

Olivia pointed at me. "Hang on." She returned a moment later with a brown paper gift bag.

"What is this?" I asked as she handed it to me.

"A little good-luck present."

I looked inside and pulled out the wad of fleshy red material. "What the hell?" I grabbed the waist, letting the legs dangle. The material was thin and shredded.

Olivia tugged on it. "It's Fresh Meat pants!"

Styx made a gagging noise. "They're disgusting!"

I laughed. "You're so weird."

Olivia pulled Styx toward my bedroom door. "Put them on. You're gonna be late."

The parking lot was full at the Rollers' Sweatshop. Styx drove us around back and parked in a small lot I didn't even know existed. We lugged our gear through a back door. The inside of the Sweatshop looked completely different. A disco ball dangled from the ceiling, the bleachers were pulled out all around the room, and a skate-rental table was set up in the cage. A sign hung above it that read "Sober skaters only. Don't make us call off your jam!"

Beyond the cage was a guy dressed as a hot dog selling hot dogs next to a full bar with a beer keg and a huge cauldron marked "Bitches' Brew."

Olivia grabbed my arm. "I'm going to get a drink. Have fun tonight."

I slung my heavy bag around to my back and pulled her into a tight hug. "I wish you were skating with me."

"Part of me does too." She looked at me with fake blood dripping from her fangs. "Hit some bitches for both of us, OK?"

"I will."

Styx led the way through the costumed crowd. I lost count of how many witches there were. Vampires were plentiful as well. There was a person in a full T-Rex suit and someone dressed as a gorilla on skates. The entire Justice League was accounted for, including three beautifully sculpted men wearing nothing but speedos and body paint as The Flash, Batman, and Green Lantern.

The Music City Jeerleaders were dressed as themselves.

Zoey was at the scoreboard table in a bright yellow dress with her cute pixie hair dyed blue. She was Joy, the incurably optimistic character from Disney's movie *Inside Out*. She caught my eye, smiling brightly, and held up two thumbs.

On the track, a few skaters were warming up. Judging by the halos and angel wings, they were from the Saints team.

"Come on," Styx said. "The Sinners are over here."

We started across the room.

"Lucy!" a booming voice called.

My head swiveled in the direction of my name, and a waving, bloody machete caught my eye. Jason, from *Friday the 13th*, was motioning me over. Because of the hockey mask, I had no idea who it was, but I did recognize the woman in the slutty Freddy Krueger dress with the long razor claws beside him.

Ava.

I laughed and ran over to hug her. "Oh my god, what are you doing here?"

"I looked up the website." She smiled. "I can't believe I didn't get a personal invitation."

"I never thought you'd come!"

She waved her claws around the room. "What's not to love? This is awesome."

I looked up at the man beside her. "Is this who I think it is?"

Jake lifted the mask just enough for me to see his face. "Shh. Don't tell anybody."

I covered my mouth and giggled. "Thanks, you guys."

"Good luck out there," he said.

Ava grabbed my arm. "And be careful!"

"I will!" I waved and ran back to my teammates.

"Do you have your jersey?" someone asked, grabbing me by the arm.

I realized when my eyes focused on her that we hadn't met before, but she was wearing skates and a bedazzled tank top that said Music City Sinners on the front. "No, not yet," I answered.

"What's your name?" she asked.

"Lucy."

Styx grabbed my shoulder. "Your name is Lights Out Lucy."

I laughed. "Oh yeah."

The woman turned, and I saw the name across her back. *Susan.* The only skater on our team—or on any team that I'd seen

—who didn't have an outlandish derby name. I liked her already. "Here you go," she said, handing me a shirt. "Hurry and change. Leave your stuff in the bathroom."

I scurried across the room to the bathroom. It was packed with Saints and Sinners alike. I found a semi-open spot in the corner and took care with my face paint as I stripped off my shirt and put on the black jersey. Then I dropped to the floor and put on my gear.

"Good luck tonight, newbie," Kraken said before she skated out door. She was on the Saints' team. "You're going to need it," she added with a wink.

I was one of the last skaters to leave the bathroom. When I did, a hand grabbed my arm. "There you are!"

I looked over. "Dad!" Katherine was standing beside him. She was wearing a black dress and a Cruella de Vil wig. Dad was wearing a white shirt with black spots painted on it. "You guys look great!"

He put his arms around me. "Look at you! Are you supposed to be yourself?"

I stuck my tongue out at him. "Very funny." I skated past Dad to Katherine and gave her a hug. "Thanks for coming. This means a lot to me."

"We wouldn't miss it," she said with a smile. I believed her.

"Have you seen your brother?" Dad asked.

I shook my head. "He's here?"

"He rode in with us," Katherine said.

"I'd look for the booze or pretty girls if I were you." I jerked my thumb over my shoulder. "I've got to get with my team. I'll see you after?"

"Yes." Dad grabbed my hand when I turned to skate away. "Hold on a second. Let me see that jersey."

My stomach tightened.

"Lights Out Lucy," he read aloud.

I turned with a sheepish grin. "Do you like it?"

He belted out a hearty, jolly laugh. "I love it. Come here." He hugged me one more time. "Be safe out there."

"I will." I kissed his cheek before skating away.

Styx was waving her arms near the corner of the room. All the girls in black, including me, skated over and gathered around her. "All right, everybody listen up," Styx said. "The Duchess is coaching for the Saints, so we have the coach from the Rising Rollers, Haley 'Hale Damage' Jones."

Haley Jones. Olivia's friend from college.

I looked around for my roommate but didn't see her anywhere.

Haley was short and trim with bleached platinum hair with bright purple streaks. She wasn't wearing a costume, just a Sinners jersey like the rest of us. "Girls, tonight's about having fun and breaking in the newbies. We're only playing fifteen-minute jam sessions with a fifteen-minute break in between. After the bout is over, you'll sign your jersey with the silver paint pens. We'll auction them off during the after-party which is held here." She pointed her finger around at all of us. "No booze till after the bout!"

"Boo!" someone said behind me. I turned to see Medusa. She was wearing a Sinners jersey as well. She lowered her voice so only I could hear. "Think they put us on the same team to keep us from knocking each other out again?"

"Each other?" I asked, securing my helmet strap. "Pretty sure I owe you one."

She bumped me with her hip. "I'm glad we're on the same side."

"Me too. It might keep me alive."

Grace and Monica were on the Saints' team.

"Like I said, tonight's about the newbies, so you'll all be on the track first. Any volunteers for starting jammer?" Haley asked.

Medusa grabbed my arm and thrust it into the air before I could snatch it away from her.

Haley pointed at me. "You. What's your name?"

"Lights Out Lucy," Medusa answered before I could refuse.

She threw the helmet panty with the bright teal star at me. "Lucy, you're jamming."

I glared at Medusa. She winked.

"So my other newbies will be starting blockers for her." She looked down at the sheet in her hand. "That will be 5 Scar Jeneral and Goldie Knocks. Susan, you jump in there with them. And Medusa will be pivot." Haley tossed the striped helmet panty to Medusa. "Any questions?"

"I can pass the star to the pivot, right?" I asked.

Haley nodded. "Yes."

"Good." I slammed the star panty into Medusa's chest.

She laughed and shoved my hand away. "Oh no. You don't get off that easily."

The announcer was Daddy Ho'maker, the same guy from the last season bout. This time, instead of wearing a tuxedo, he wore a Mad Hatter's costume and top hat. "Happy Halloween, derby fans! Let's make some noise for our Music City Rollers!"

"Go! Go! Go!" Haley shouted, pointing at the track.

I fell in line behind Medusa as we skated out to the oval. The Saints' team was in front of us, and they skated to the sidelines. Styx looked over her shoulder. "Pack it up, girls!"

Everyone huddled close to her. I followed along as we crouched in a group.

"Skating tonight for the Music City Sinners, number 1111 Riveter Styx!" Daddy Ho'maker bellowed.

Styx popped up and waved.

"Number 13EE, Susan!"

Everyone cheered.

"Number 5FT3, Lady Fury!"

The room went crazy.

He went through several more skaters. "Number 10, Medusa!"

Everyone was on their feet and screaming. One young girl on the sidelines was actually crying with hysterics. Medusa popped up and waved both arms.

"And introducing your newest Music City Rollers in their very first bout, number 5, 5 Scar Jeneral!" Beth waved. "Number 34DD, Goldie Knocks!" Goldie stood and jiggled her boobs. The crowd went nuts. I'm pretty sure I heard Ethan's heart explode. "And number LoL, Lights Out Lucy!"

I popped up and waved to the crowd.

We skated off the track and stood on the sidelines as the Saints were introduced. We slapped high fives with them as they skated by. After the playing of the national anthem, Medusa slapped me on the back. "You ready to do this?"

I gulped. "Nope."

She laughed and pulled me up off the bench. With the star panty stretched tight across my helmet, I skated out to the track. "Just remember. Keep an eye on Coach Hale Damage. If you make lead jammer, she'll tell you when to call off the jam. Do you remember how to do that?"

Using both hands, I karate-chopped my hips.

"Good." She struck my helmet. "If you get jammed in, hand me the panty. You can't throw it at me."

"OK."

"Breathe, Lucy."

I sucked in a deep breath, held it for a count of three, and blew it out slowly.

Monica lined up with the blockers, and Grace skated over behind the jammer line with me. She was wearing a star panty as well. She slapped me a high five. "Yes! I'm so glad we're doing this together!" she cheered.

"Me too! Are you ready?" I asked.

"So ready!" She gripped my wrist guard. "Guess what?"

"What?"

"My divorce went through today!"

I threw my arms around her. "You're finally a free woman!"

She hugged me back. "Yes!"

"I'm so happy for you, Grace."

"Hey, jammers!" It took a second to realize Medusa was screaming at us. "No hugging the enemy!"

Laughing, I popped my mouth guard into place and looked around the crowded room.

I wonder if West is here.

Right in front of the line, Medusa locked arms with Susan and 5 Scar Jeneral. "Get ready, Lucy!" she screamed.

The referee's whistle blasted. I took off from the starting line. My teammates swung sideways and knocked Grace out of bounds. My wheels smacked the floor as I fought my way around Monica and Judge Dreidel. I pushed through them, and Midnight Maven, dressed like a freaking angel, swooped over and slammed into me. I fell hard on my knees just inside the boundary, but I popped back up and ducked to the side as Medusa cut right and hip checked Maven. I squeezed through the tiny opening. Electra Cal rammed me with her shoulder, but I planted my feet and hit back like Kelly had shown me.

The crowd was screaming and stomping the bleachers. The noise was intoxicating. My skates slammed forward into the clear, and there were two sharp whistle blasts. The referee was pointing at me. *Lead jammer! Holy shit, I'm lead jammer!*

A powerful blow came from my back right followed by a long whistle. I stumbled but didn't lose footing. I kept skating forward as Maven passed by me outside the track on her way to the penalty box. Grace was caught behind a wall named Medusa and Susan. I rounded the back turn and came up on the pack again, slamming chest first into the crack between Monica and Electra Cal. I made it through them and pushed forward.

Someone was screaming.

"Lucy!"

That's me.

Coach Hale Damage was striking her hips.

Shit!

I mimicked her motions and the referee's whistle blasted four rapid chirps.

Laughing, Medusa skated over and hooked me around the neck with her powerful arm. My mouthpiece popped out onto the floor. The rest of the skaters on the track swarmed me in one giant group hug.

Daddy Ho'maker's voice boomed. "And the first two points of the night are for the Music City Sinners by a brand-new jammer, Lights Out Lucy!"

———

The Sinners beat the Saints 98 to 72. It was a great bout. I jammed on and off the whole night and actually lived to celebrate it. When the final whistle sounded and we skated off the track, the first person waiting for me was Ethan. "Who would've guessed my sister's a badass?" he asked, lifting my skates off the floor as he hugged me.

When he set me down, I rolled back to look at him. My brother was wearing referee stripes. I pulled at the sleeve. "What's this?"

"It's a costume, but I think it's a good look for me. I've gotten three phone numbers since I got here. They're offering referee training in January. I'm thinking about trying it out."

"Here?" I asked.

"You still gonna let me crash on your couch?"

I hugged him again. "Anytime you want."

"I'm going to get a beer. You want one?" he asked.

"Maybe later. First, I need water," I said.

Kraken smacked my helmet as she skated by. "Good game, Lucy!"

"Good game, indeed," Styx agreed as I approached the bench. "Did you have fun?"

I smiled so wide it hurt my face. "So much fun."

She winked and tossed me a paint pen. "Good. Don't forget to sign your jersey and take it to the auction table."

Not even caring I was just in my sports bra and meat pants, I stripped off my black shirt at the bench and signed the back with the silver paint. *Lights Out Lucy, #LoL*

It felt good. Damn good.

"I'll pay five million dollars for that jersey," a man said behind me.

I froze, and a smile crept across my face.

When I turned, West was smiling too. He was holding the head of his gorilla costume under his fuzzy black arm. His blond hair was matted on his head, and his face was red and dripping sweat. On his feet were a pair of rented roller skates.

"Nice skating, Lucille."

"You're here," I said, my heart pounding harder than it had on the track.

That earth-shattering smile melted my heart as he slowly rolled toward me. "You didn't think I'd miss your first bout, did you?"

"You knew I made the team?"

He glanced back toward my teammates. "Let's just say a mutual friend tipped me off."

I caught Medusa's eye, but her gaze quickly darted away.

West shrugged his hairy shoulders and put the gorilla head

down on the floor. "Looks like you're all out of excuses now for why we can't be together."

"Looks like I am."

He turned up his giant padded palms. "Geez, Lucy. Are you going to kiss me or what?"

Hell yeah, I was going to kiss him.

Laughing, I skated right into his arms, taking care to not knock him off-balance. Then we kissed, and it was perfect, despite the pungent stench of sweat between us and his gorilla hair tickling my armpits. Bells chimed, and angels sang—literally. A few of the Saints, still donning their halos and wings, belted the chorus to "Hells Bells" behind us. West laughed against my mouth.

He pulled back and rested his clammy forehead against mine. "So is this the part where we live happily ever after?"

I smiled and reached back for his hand. "We'll start that business tomorrow." Waffling his gorilla fingers with mine, I pulled him toward the center of the room. "Tonight, we skate."

And he wobbled a bit as we rolled onto the track.

GET THE EPILOGUE

Want to read the epilogue for Lights Out Lucy and find out what happens at the Monster's Brawl afterparty?

GET THE EPILOGUE
at www.musiccityrollers.com

THANK YOU FOR READING!

Please consider leaving a review on your favorite retailer! Reviews help indie authors like me find new readers and get advertising. If you enjoyed this book, please tell your friends!

The next book is coming soon!

Be the first to know about its release:

www.musiccityrollers.com

JOIN
HYDERNATION

OFFICIAL FAN CLUB

★ Want leaked chapters of new books?
★ Want the first look at what's coming soon?
★ Want to win some awesome swag and prizes?

Join HYDERNATION, the official fan club of Elicia Hyder, for all that and more!

Join on Facebook
Join on EliciaHyder.com

The Soul Summoner Series

#1 Amazon Bestseller

ORDER IT NOW

Book 1 - **The Soul Summoner**
Book 2 - **The Siren**
Book 3 - **The Angel of Death**
Book 4 - **The Taken**
Book 5 - **The Sacrifice**

ABOUT THE AUTHOR

Bestselling author Elicia Hyder played women's flat track roller derby with the Nashville Rollergirls under the skater name "eL's Bells." After a black eye, a broken finger, a severely pulled groin, and two knee injuries, Elicia hung up her skates to focus on a safer hobby—writing.

She has fictionalized her experience in her latest novel, Lights Out Lucy: Roller Derby 101. More novels are to come in the Music City Rollers series.

Elicia still lives in Music City with her superhero husband, five (loud) children, and two co-dependent dogs.

www.eliciahyder.com
elicia@eliciahyder.com